The Phantastical Tale of Aster and his Red Gem

Hardcover: 979-8-9865352-2-7

Paperback: 979-8-9865352-0-3

Ebook: 979-8-9865352-1-0

Edited by Ari Augustine/Maria Tureaud
Cover art by Michael Rogers
Map by Soraya Corcoran

Writeous Ink
Salt Lake City, UT

To Mrs. Tierney.

Blame her. She encouraged it.

1.

OF ELEMENTS & ALOOFNESS

There were no stains upon the land, for the land was what it was in all times and all seasons. Perfectly attuned to exist in a sense of harmony that could be nothing but designed. Mortals, on the other hand, were walking stains. Stained inside, staining outside.

Like Aster, for example. The moment he reached an important, life-altering conclusion he had existed in tangible form for just over a couple of decades, if one measured time in such a fashion, and most mortal beings did. The impetus for his decision was the cascading, haunting repetition of the waves continuously brushing the cliffs that dropped their foundations far into the water.

It was the edge of the world as Aster knew it, the crust of a land called Thuidium. He stood, wincing at a sound that most would have considered musical; people who knew their grief began and ended somewhere far from the unceasing swoosh of waves climbing onto rocks.

The tune rising up from below was but a noxious clamoring of remorse that yanked at Aster's attention. Knowing she stood at the very same precipice before casting herself off was a thought that stung, like salt to the eyes.

Oren joined his son in silent reverie, one that didn't last long. He intruded upon the melody of the sea. "That was a fine breakfast you prepared. Never had eggs like that. Nice of you to still stop by and make your old man a meal."

"It's not a chore." Food had never been a chore. Consuming, it, crafting it, and serving it were akin to putting a painting on display.

"No, but when you spend a lot of your day cooking at the Den it just makes it that much more special when you take time to do the same for your father."

"Consider yourself my..." And Aster paused to consider what specific label he would ascribe to Oren. "...assayer. That way it won't seem like a free ride."

"Assayer, huh?" Oren let the word hang in the moment.

The only interruption on this thought was the incessant tune of water colliding with rocks. Aster put his attention on the sun, letting his eyes reach up towards that magnificently luminous disc in the sky, a stunning brilliance he'd always believed to be powered by the souls of the enlightened. If the tales were true, that is.

"Is she up there?" Aster shaded his eyes against the glare.

Oren turned not from the ocean. "I'm sure she is. She was probably one of the most enlightened people that I knew."

"Even after what she did?" There was a prayer in his tone—not a curse—and pleading in his eyes.

Oren's eyes, the color of deep waters, went soft and crinkled at the corners. "Even after all that, I don't doubt both Life and Death saw the brightness of her soul, how full of enlightenment."

A flutter of a smile passed across Aster's lips. Not that he sustained the expression, but there needed to be at least an attempt to let his father know he accepted the words of consolation.

The feeble attempt at a smile didn't pass muster with Oren. "You're better served not standing there listening to this tune all day." The waves pushed against the land. The land stood resilient. "I've done all I can to try and cure this sadness of yours. Teaching you magic helped for a while. Remember the first spell you learned?" Oren asked in a voice that almost reached out of the past searching for ears that were much younger, less knowing.

The question failed to lure Aster's attention away from the ocean's perpetual give and take which, from atop the rocky pillars, looked like a gentle sway.

Aster sighted inaudibly, hoping to signal his disinterest in whatever point to which Oren was leading. The spray of the tide, and the crunch of sand and pebbles underfoot filled the wordless moment with sounds of a meaningless nature.

"You really tried to sing that spell," Oren mused with the laughter in his voice.

"Didn't cut it, did it?" Aster turned slightly giving himself over to the reminiscence. Now that the moment was far in the past it was funny to think about, how flat and toneless his first attempt at a spell had been.

"You thought magic was just for mommies and daddies." The chuckle came out of Oren like a refreshing breeze.

Aster relaxed his cheeks and let a genuine smile trace across his lips. "A kid never sees the world how it really is. I don't know if every kid dreams of one day having sway over the elements." Aster looked into Oren's face excavating past the tender blue eyes, beyond the deep lines possessing his father's forehead and the corners of his father's mouth. "If only everyone had parents who bothered to teach them that magic was within reach with just a bit of effort and study."

"You may have had a slight advantage with me being magically adept and all, but you put in the work to learn the words and tune your voice. It's time you did something with all those lessons. Take your magical education to a new level."

Aster waited for the definitive point that would be revealed after all the polished history and charming preparations had been cleared away.

"Give yourself a goal," Oren concluded.

Goal.

The word struck a chord, mightier than the churning of the sea. For a moment, goal had more texture and bulk than that one haunting word: mother.

"I believe...you're right." Aster peered into his father's eyes as his mind clung and clawed to the word *goal*. "I need to do something. Make something."

Oren returned Aster's smile, one that hung loosely upon his face.

"That's what I need, isn't it?" The question poured out like it was asked by a six-year-old who had just found his way back home, barely beating the setting sun.

"You'll know best what you need, Aster." Oren's smile tightened. "But if you still fancy your old man as wise, I would say it's the right direction."

Wise is how he fancied the old man. There were moments when he looked upon his father and, try as he might, he couldn't help but revert to that little boy who saw all the answers tucked away in a maze of lines; not deep lines, but enough of a crease around those eyes and that mouth to showcase the abundance of days through which Oren had passed.

The wide array of possibilities threatened Aster's enthusiasm, as did the sound of the ocean nuzzling against the fathomless pillars atop which they stood. "Truly, old man. Let's hear your suggestion."

At which point Oren directed them back towards the small cabin, a dwelling which some would call humble if they were genuine. Maybe even quaint, had they been of a more condescending nature.

The porch welcomed views of the sandy yard and beyond, to where the land ended in sheer cliffs. Inside, the smell of breakfast still clung to the air. The woven upholstery of Oren's simple armchair, in shades of olives and branches, tickled Aster's fingers as it always had. The other piece of furniture, a couch, sat adjacent the chair. Had the room ever changed? Had the table been any longer or shorter? The very grain of each plank and beam were familiar friends, names written in letters that only Aster knew. All told, the cabin looked fixed in time, a memory that could be recalled without subjectivity, cool and as soothing as aloe upon a burn.

"I've been absent-mindedly whittling these," Oren explained as he tossed a small satchel to Aster. "Maybe not as absent-mindedly as I thought," came an amendment from Oren, as he sat in his chair.

"You were fated to create…" Aster, sitting on the floor with his back against the couch, reached in and retrieved a small, wooden disk the face of which was engraved with a textured graphic. "Tokens?" It was the only word that found to be fitting of the little pieces of circular wood.

"S'pose you could call them that," Oren said. "Fated? I guess. If you believe in such things."

Aster ran his finger over the disk in his hand, brushing away the notion of some predetermined outcome. The natural texture of the wood still held sway, but had been carved away until aught but what looked like a mountain remained. The others were fashioned similarly: a flame on one, swirling clouds on another, and the last image looked like enlarged drops of water.

"So what's your game?"

"I think it would make this goal of yours a bit less daunting if you, pardon the jest, had one element of decided for you."

"Element. Good one, Dad." Aster considered the token a little longer before he dropped the wooden disks back into the bag.

"You've been brought up in the Magic of Life, the songs that allow us as mortal beings to have some control over the world around us. Use it. Get lost in the everyday application of your education and see how far you can take it. The potential for magic is in everyone so you never know what some unsuspecting individual will create. Invent, discover something great it before another country boy does." He sat back and waited.

And wait he must for this proposal, this plot, did not feel comfortable at first mention. Sure, Oren's idea was sound, echoing reason and logic. But did Aster really feel inclined to take flight from his native pain and grief, strike out on a pursuit that would leave the familiar, no matter how unpleasant? Weighing the actually unpleasant against the potentially worse. Or better? That is what Oren tried to offer, was it not? Relief from the presage of those cliffs and the mournful surf.

That's when the smile cracked, a slow unhinging of lips that had been sealed tightly together by the consternation of debating options and philosophies. A sense of resolve stole over Aster the same way a warm air stirs the sap.

"Go into the kitchen," Oren said when he returned the smile breaking upon Aster's face. "Don't look this way until I tell you to."

The game played out. Aster heard Oren shuffle the small disks around, wood scraping against wood, then summoned Aster. They sat there in a neat little row, face-down. "Pick a couple."

"Why two?" They taunted Aster with innumerable potential, the likes of which was almost too frightening to bear. The selection of these tokens awoke a sense of finality.

"One seems a bit too narrow a scope. Three seems too broad," Oren explained. He leaned forward on his little throne; it had always been his throne. As far back as Aster could recall Oren had occupied that very same chair.

He probably noticed the trepidation worming across Aster's face. "This isn't a threat or a consequence. Think of the two disks you select as your inspiration."

The first disk felt smooth but solid. Aster gripped it between his fingers, studying the emblem upon its face without revealing it. Oren blithely gazed on, not begging to see which token had been selected. It was as if he let Aster discover and process every step in his own way, at his own pace. The pieces were his to squeeze together; the picture was his to create.

All this talk of potential greatness was a concept that sounded enticing at first mention, but was not free from the density of responsibility. And work. The work that would proceed that shining moment. This wasn't such a terrible activity. It was merely wood after all. Possibilities were a beautiful thing. That thought alone ignited curiosity. Relief, like invisible hands, untied all the muscles that had been knotted up by every question. From jaw to shoulders, even down to the toes that now wiggled free of doubt. Nothing had quite crystallized yet, but at least there was a sense of heading.

"One more," came the urging from Oren.

A deep breath. A finger that bobbed as it hovered over the three remaining tokens. First, it circled very first one. Then it loomed above the last one. Would he be better served selecting the two that had been placed next to one another? Their un-characterized backs laid there with a rampant, almost mocking, stoicism. Oren continued in his patience—he had an admirable store of it—and leaned toward Aster, moving him to decide.

His finger landed on a token. He slid it closer and lifted it to inspect its character and absorb the impact the little image would have. Small as the carving may have been, light though the wood felt, these were more than tokens and emblems, ideas and notions. The concepts reached down and struck roots beyond the withering touch of distraction and criticism.

Aster cleared away the remaining tokens, slipping them back into their little abode of the leather pouch. He set his two chosen ones down and flipped them.

Mountain.

Flame.

"Earth," Oren noted. His body relaxed back into his seat he gave his own hands a quick glance. "And fire. That's a tricky mix."

"A little bit." The mystery of this coupling roiled behind Aster's eyes. He knew the potential of each element on its own—the power and passion of fire, the consistency and weight of earth—but together? How would they harmonize?

A quite passed across Oren's face and he smiled, an inspiring gesture, held a world of confidence. "It will be interesting to see what you're going to create with those two."

Creation. A ponderous word Aster tried to balance behind his glassy stare which he held on his way out of the cabin. He even missed the sudden incline of the path and nearly planted his face into the dirt; he quickly looked back to see Oren standing motionless on the porch, watching. Aster tucked the thought away until he was back on level ground. The dirt path rolled on towards Lamiston.

The town was a collection of structures of the residential and commercial variety, looped together by a wall more decorative than defensive. Buildings mingled in a miniature maze, with a handful hugging what was affectionately referred to as the town square, though there was nothing square about it: an empty space more circular, to match the rotund layout of the hamlet.

Aster ducked into the Hart's Den, the primer watering hole in little Lamiston. The only watering hole, in fact. No human settlement could qualify as civilized without the presence of such a place. The Hart's Den, where the sociable of Lamiston congealed to revel in the mundane, speaking of the trivial as if it were fantastical.

The flow of conversation swirled about the tables and chairs undulating in its usual rhythm. All the sounds muffled into a sort of fog as Aster entered the kitchen, third in line of places where he invested most of his time; home and Oren's took the top two spots, respectively. Back here though there was that same sense of sanctuary, as if the world had been crumpled up and stuffed into a compost pile.

The fires burned, filling the kitchen with their ferocity. Not intense enough to forge a new sword, but just enough to toast some bread. Melting the cheese intense. The air tingled with aromas that practically tasted, as if the air could be chewed on. Was there a need to actually eat when the scents were so bold?

Hardly.

Aster danced about mixing this, slicing that; he flayed. He seared. Each time he sent a plate out, the sounds that snuck back into this little oasis were merrier and merrier. The cheers rang in deep bellows and high, clear pitches. Yet, they didn't stick as much as they used to. They evaporated, no longer caramelizing.

For a moment, the dance stopped and the kitchen waited in silence; waited on more orders for culinary delights, to be summoned from pot and pan. The heat from the stove fires drove sweat from every pore. Aster swiped a cloth rag across this forehead and sipped water from a clay cup.

Lately, delving into the culinary arts didn't take Aster far enough away from the memory of her death, from the bemoaning tide. Her ghost followed him down his escape route, into the kitchen, molding and souring the fragrance of ingredients fresh from the earth.

It was time to put on a brave face—the face of one steeped in a passion for food—and step away from the stove to see what the crowd thought of their meals. Not that everyone in the Den came to eat, but a good deal ordered fodder with their libations.

The kitchen door swung open and Aster took a gander at the crowd. A hail of cheers greeted him as he surveyed the mass of patrons. The closest table with nearly empty plates had resounding praise to heap upon the cook.

"Practically melted in me mouth," said the stodgy fellow who ran the local stables as he foraged crumbs of bread from his beard.

His mate offered similar praise. The tenderness of ripe meat, the crunch of sweet vegetables. The words infused themselves into Aster's mind. He let them; didn't question their authenticity.

Aster drifted to a final table where on plate in particular looked to be bearing a fair share of food yet to be touched. "I just wanted to see how you're enjoying the meal?"

"You know I'm a fan, Aster," the local surgeon began. "Your creations delight. I was just wondering, is there any way to spruce up the flavor a bit?"

"Uh, what do you mean Serenoa?" Aster crossed his arms over his chest as he braced for a bit of criticism. His eyes darted down towards her plate and quickly scanned her food. It had a generous amount missing so it must not have been that bad. All the elements were there: meat a tad rare, vegetables glistened with trace amounts of fat, salt sparkled like stars. What was the matter here?

"It doesn't taste bad," she hastily added. "Sometimes, I just have a yearning for something to surprise my mouth. Maybe give my tongue a kick."

With a solemn apology, Aster vacated the tavern floor and retreated back to his kitchen. Yes, it was his. Not Twiggy's, who owned the whole establishment. Before Aster stepped into this kitchen, it sat cold and dusty. Aster fed it life, filled with warmth and the delightful aromas that still hung in the air even when the cooking stopped for the night.

Then why did the last review sting so much?

Aster leaned into the counter and scanned his dried herbs. He marveled at all he had collected. Still, they weren't enough for absolute praise?

2.

OF COMPLEX MAGIC & WATER

'A kick'. The phrase echoed in Aster's mind. He wanted to reach in, yank it out, and stomp it into powder. Maybe he could sprinkle that on a dish.

The realization snapped Aster to attention. Kick. Fire. Earth. He fled the kitchen. Cut through the mash of calls and laughter and made a clean escape from the Den. The cool night air breezed by him whipping up this idea into a stiff peak.

The night could not pass quick enough. What hours remained until the break of day would be filled with the gathering of books of lore and learning from off a shelf. Aster hauled them out into the open and combed their combined knowledge, looking for the key words. They vaulted off the page, words like "heat", "furnace", "soil", and "structure". Such words, simple in and of themselves, sent Aster soaring and chased away all thoughts of sleep. He weighed the new information against spells he had already learned, considering how best to leverage each in this pursuit.

All the cogitation and research—searching within himself and without—was the goal Oren mentioned, the usefulness that would lead his mind away from those haunted cliffs.

Lamiston's round town square vibrated with the calls and chatter of bartering. Priula guarded her bushels of leafy green vegetables more fiercely than a mother-hawk kept an eye on the nest, all while squeezing every possible mint from Vetch, who seemed to think she was being entirely too protective. Aster breezed past the exchange. In his stride, he gave the briefest of glances to Durian and his woven stuff, blankets and shirts of captivating make. Aster smiled at the homely man. No time for shopping. A more pressing matter awaited.

"That's a giddy stride you have," he called as Aster approached.

"How was the harvest?" Aster gently secured his hand around moist burlap cloth as he greeted his father.

Oren stood by his skins of water, weighed down by whatever contingent of mussels he managed to scrape off the rocks that morning. "Cut the small talk. You aren't here to check on my stock. What's going on with you?"

Now that his father had given him approval to dispense with the mundane pleasantries—harvests, the weather...all so functional—Aster had to keep from flexing his excited muscles; he didn't want to crush the prize before it had been declared.

The time to declare was now. Aster unrolled his fingers. Upon his palm, atop the moisten burlap, sat two conical shapes in blend shades of orange, red, and brown all swirling together.

Oren slowly reached out and plucked one from Aster's hand. He held it up by a small, green stem and examined the offering . "They fruit or something?"

"Truly," Aster said, assuring himself as much as Oren. "When I've perfected them and figure out how to actually give them seeds," Aster finished rather lamely as he bit at his thumbnail.

Oren gave the tender fruit a gentle pinch. "And this is where you arrived with fire and earth?" He squinted, eyeing the creation as his lips shifted this way and that.

The skepticism Oren draped upon the little fruit squelched Aster's pride, which had been stirring just out of sight, in anticipation should the amazement come gushing forth, but when there was no wonderment forthcoming, the corners of his mouth folded in quickly.

A chuckle escaped Oren, gruff sounds that shook the air between the two men. "I should not be surprised that your mind went right to food." He clasped a firm, fatherly hand upon Aster's shoulder. "Glad to see you applying all that magical instruction to something you love. Now, tell me what I'm in for." Oren dangled the novel bit of fruit before his eyes.

The words were a crank spurring Aster's mind into a passionate whirl. "The other night I served up what I thought was a perfect dish. The meat had cooked for hours, seasoned with fresh herbs and plenty of butter. Flawless, right? And the person goes: would be nice if it was flavored with a kick." There was no need to fill in the rest of the events: Aster reeling from the comment followed by the searing mental illumination. Oren understood.

He chuckled again as he wrapped an arm around Aster's shoulders, drawing them closer together. "Let's have it, Aster. There's no idea or thought of yours that will ever sound ridiculous to me."

Oren's voice was enough to shoo away the insecurities buzzing about this creation, vultures waiting for a peck at the vulnerable idea. "Try it, Dad."

Oren withdrew and put the fruit to his nose, inhaling deeply to pry from it a hint at what awaited his taste buds. No such luck, so he dared a bite. The skin broke under his breaching teeth. He chewed and for a moment it looked as though he were consuming another failed attempt.

This was the fifth incarnation, but the first Aster had ever shared with another soul. It obviously wasn't a scolding mess—unlike that first round, the memory of which still bit Aster's tongue—but perhaps this round had come out too bland, lacking enough of fire's influence? From the smooth expression on Oren's face, as he finished the one bite he had taken, it wasn't too far-fetched a conclusion. Then came the sign, one that eased Aster's mind: Oren's mouth elongated into an exaggerated O-shape.

He didn't expel it from his mouth, a promising turn for this iteration of the fruit. After some rapid breathing to usher in cooler air, Oren said, "I think I get what you mean about heat. Well done kiddo."

"That good?" Aster sniffed at his own sample before biting.

In that bite was his answer: yes, that good. The oily juice leaked and rolled back toward his throat, the impact of which released a swell of heat. Not without a chorus of flavor. First a precursor playing at the taste buds like tendrils of smoke escaping a campfire, quickly chased by a phantom sweetness, the subdued sweetness of an apple or a peach.

Aster alternated between smiling and wafting out the burn. "That's not bad," he wheezed. "Pretty obvious that fire is present." And then the idea burst upon his mind: "I think that's what I'll call it. Fire fruit."

"Aptly named. Not that there's so much heat. Flavor comes through. Since they don't have seeds are you just going to churn out these Fire Fruits individually on request?"

"No," Aster replied. Preposterous idea, trying to create one fruit at a time. Did Oren believe that this was for amusement? Bringing an entirely new variety of edible plant into the world just for the sake of doing it? His brow furrowed, as if weighing the various possible ways to respond. His heart was in this and he wanted—no, needed—Oren to understand this went beyond amusement. "This isn't a trick, Dad."

"Then what is it?"

The market bustled around them, but in that moment the streaks of people crissing and crossing faded; the sounds of their chatting dulled. All that was left was the sound of the ocean nudging up against rocky cliffs.

"It's a creation," Aster said, a breathy as a gently tide brushing into the shore.

The wry smile Oren displayed meant he seemed to discern what his son thought, felt, even though but three words had been spoken. He bowed his head for a moment. He may have been worried about his son's state, silently taking inventory of all the times he could have done better by the boy; a father alone bears a world unto himself.

The market played on. The buyers bought. The sellers sold. The town was alive and Aster wished to feel that way, more intimately. It was then that a word popped into Aster's mind, a word he had heard spoken by someone. Maybe he read it while studying some other matter? "Martese," Aster declared.

Which declaration pulled Oren right out of whatever thought on which he'd been stewing. "Say again?"

"That's what it's called, right, when you bond with a particular element?"

Oren offered a tentative nod.

"I've researched until I've gone cross-eyed. Paper cuts from all the pages I've turned. I've ached from all the experimenting. The way I see it, if I can bond with earth then I'll be in the right state to make this plant fruitful. The rite of the Martese is what makes that happen." Aster's eyes fixed on his father, as if waiting for approval. "And like all the other times, you'll be there to help guide me through it?"

Oren's lips tightened as he led Aster away from the square and towards the Hart's Den. A low swell of voices rolled through the great room as they entered. Lamps flickered here and there. Wooden chairs grumbled against the wooden floor.

"Whatcha serving up today, mate?" Came a random call as Aster and Oren maneuvered through the tavern.

"Not a thing, Clay. I'm just a regular patron at the moment."

Glasses raised in honor of empty plates as Aster and Oren skirted all the noise to hold congress in a booth as far away as possible from the main body of the tavern.

"A unique bit of magic, the Martese." Oren mused before he gulped down the beverage served him. He sighed, releasing the pungent tang of fermentation all over the enclosed seating. "Haven't a clue what the words are, what implements are needed. Are you sure you need to go through it? There are other ways, other spells—"

"Ones that give life?" Aster cut in abruptly. "I'm sure this is the best way forward, Dad."

From Aster's experience, the Martese was a ritual much discussed but hardly invoked. Not among the average practitioner. Oren's reaction was evidence that Aster needed to find out more, to experience this rare magic.

All around them the noises of the tavern mounted into a jovial cacophony. Aster leaned in toward the table. "Who else do you have in your inventory of powerful friends and associates?"

Oren knocked his small glass receptacle against the table, hammering out his hesitation. "Since you're so fixated—"

"Dad, you always told me that the best, truest form of validation is accomplishment. Your words."

"I believe that is what I tried to teach you."

"You regret hammering that lesson into my head?"

Oren scratched his chin. "Not so much as regret it, no. I just wonder if it was the only lesson I should have taught you."

The chatter washed over them, words that had been mashed together into indecipherable tunes, enjoined by hundreds of other tiny noises.

Oren's eyes bore down, shifting like he searched for a specific word on a cluttered page. His lips went narrow, hanging in a slight frown as he assessed what he saw. Aster lowered his cup of water and waited for some pronouncement of wisdom. Instead, Oren patted Aster's hand. "I just hope I didn't mess you up."

"No, Dad. You didn't."

The gap in their conversation was flooded with more dun. "I'm just glad you're still around helping me. I'm not too old to still have it, so is there anyone else you know who is familiar with the rite of the Martese? Someone you trust?"

Oren's focus retreated into his small cup. His eyes dulled as his glance swam in the empty receptacle, no longer reading or searching. One hand slipped away from the earthen mug. Since there wasn't more drink in which to hide: "There is. Well, there was. This person I knew years ago."

"Oh? Let's hear it."

The request, applied with as causal a tone as possible must have rocked Oren for his brow tightened and lips faded. "There's another way. Find some patience, boy."

Boy? The label stung. It was a smack on the head without the touch. It was a leather belt released and folded. Even though Aster was in his second decade of living, it still stung more than both.

Oren's mouth opened and then closed. "Look Aster, let me think more on this, and consider other practitioners I'd be more comfortable with. " He made to pat Aster's hand, but knocked his little cup against the table one more time before abandoning the booth and their conversation.

Aster would try to heed Oren's council and wait for the right mentor. That didn't mean that he had to be unproductive. This was an opportune time to dig that well, a task that had been on his list of intentions for some time. Wait. Patience. Cumbersome words.

Pixee had to notice his meandering gait as they walked the mile or so past the wall of Lamiston proper. He stood at the bottom of the small hill that rolled up to his own front door. She stood there with her head barely meeting at the height of Aster's shoulder. Though, to be fair, Aster was a bit taller than the average fella.

"Why did you dye it that color?" she asked, extracting the very thought from Aster's mind.

The red door seemed like a good idea at the time, when he and Oren had built the place. It now looked obnoxious, like some sort of unearned luxury. A bit ostentatious from their current vantage point. Aster shrugged back at Pixee.

His house wasn't large. Nor was it a hovel. It sat on a plot of uncultivated land. Short, coarse turf to the front and wild grasses and shrubs at the back. He had managed to clear away enough vegetation behind the house, giving him a band of just dirt right outside the back door.

"Why am I looking at your patch of dirt, then?" She crossed her arms over her chest and stared up at Aster with the seriousness that never seemed to leave her face.

"I wanted to check and see if there was a water source," he said explaining the purpose of her presence.

Under a waning afternoon, Aster knelt against the dry dirt. There would be plenty of sunlight left even as summer petered out and autumn crept into the world.

She joined him. "And you don't know how to do this?"

"Not something I ever learned."

Most spells, from what Aster understood of magic, were simple enough to learn; if a person knew the right arrangement of words to chant, they could connect their intention to the energy that flowed through all the elements, derived from the essence of the Universe itself. Or so the tales told.

The tales technically mentioned "singing" to the energy of each element, but that wasn't a specific talent held by every human. Not in a meaningful way. Sure, every human voice could squawk out sounds. To make them harmonious, efficacious, with feeling and appeal? Therein lay the distinction. Fortunately, the spells worked even if they were merely chanted.

Aster reminisced about the struggle to match his voice with the elements, knowing how to chant to the rhythm of the energy. Undulating like the earth. Slowly rolling like a river. Booming like a gale. The power of spells came in the arrangement of words and the tone in which they were chanted. It was all sounds.

Pixee, though, seemed aloof from the entire process as she traced a finger around in the dirt. No words. Not a single syllable chanted.

"If only all magic were so easy."

She looked at him. "Cute," was all she said, without offering an actual response. Aster caught the half-hidden smile that snuck up across her lips as she returned to the task.

Her hands worked mechanically at first, moving in a way like someone repairing a wheel, or framing a house; it looked less like magic and more like an excavation, until Pixee's posture took on a different bend.

She seemed to have reached the element. No sound was let loose, not even the sight of arrival. A fog of Pixee-shape, Pixee-shade, slipped and dripped off her fingers. Ethereal it looked, twisted like roots of existence, without bounds, that wanted for more than water and soil. There seemed to be no defining the colors that swirled and swam off Pixee's skin.

Aster watched this form of magic, this indigenous magic. It was all so perplexing, for it contradicted everything Aster had ever been taught about using magic. It made depth a part of the equation.

"I really should learn some—"

Pixee held up a finger, commanding Aster to resume his silence as she scoured the ground following the fog that had sluiced from her being. She smiled at Aster. "Here."

"You Primul and your easy magic," he sighed. She didn't need to be told. Obviously, and maybe she was constantly, reminded by mortals of how easily her race of people—the first species of sentient life in creation—connected with the elements.

"You act like the mortal way of magic is so burdensome. You know, you really should be happy to have learned anything about manipulating the elements at all."

Her candor snapped back tauter than a palm across the face. "Get digging before I forget where that spot was," she said.

3.

OF QUESTIONING DIRT

He pointed at the spot she had revealed and absently drew a square in the dirt. Primul. The concept hung there, for examination.

With all that crowded Aster's brain these days, he couldn't help but glom onto Pixee's state of being. Not because it made her different in his eyes, but because she was a being of legend. Except she actually existed, imbued with the same energy that flowed through the elements themselves, as if her race had been lifted right out of the vat of the Universe itself. It was the source of their intimate connection to the elements.

Aster leaned in, eyes narrowed, lips tightly drawn until he caught sight of her gaze fixed on him. He jolted upright.

"Stop it," she said. "You're weird."

Aster distributed his attention more evenly across his surroundings. That didn't release that one thought from his mind. The goal that would save his greater goal from dying. He sucked in some breath and held it like a prisoner. "So, um…"

She rolled her eyes at him.

"Being Primul and all you have a special connection to the elements. I thought…" He released a sigh, the restless bout of breath, "You probably could perform something like the rite of the Martese for me?" The proposal had been proposed but Aster maintained a rigid posture, wrenched tightly by the mere prospect of accomplishment.

"You would think that. Can't blame you, but it's the wrong assumption." Pixee shrugged and she just stared in return with her unflinching eyes, and her unsmiling mouth.

Aster formed a silent plea with his pitched eyebrows.

"I can feel how much you want to me to be able to match you with an element, but it's not simple. That bit of magic actually requires some learning, not just intuition. It's not sensing the presence of an element, but entering the very essence of an element and goes beyond bending an element to my will." Her eyes glazed over and for a few heartbeats she seemed to have gone somewhere, a thought that took her away from Aster's inquires. "It's magic beyond my capability. Let me put it in terms you can visualize. I can get some vegetables together and even find some chicken. Doesn't mean I know how to make it all taste good. Right?" She shrugged at him. "Better to be blunt, get that false notion all the way out of your mind so you can move on."

"Thanks," Aster replied ensuring that the one syllable he'd uttered was as flat and monotone as over-boiled cabbage. He looked away from her. Looked anywhere she wasn't as he slumped his shoulders, fighting to accept these unfavorable circumstances.

In the quiet that ensued, the world had somehow shrank and expanded all at once. Is that the way it goes when hope is smothered into submission? All the magical power he had learned to wield suddenly amounted to little more than a child's wooden play-sword. Here Aster was, with his dull toy-weapon trying to cut his way through a thicket. A haunted thicket he'd never leave.

He must have accidentally mumbled some of those thoughts aloud, because Pixee placed a well-meaning hand on his. "That's a pot of ashes, if you think your life begins and ends with all these projects you have in your head."

"Yeah, well—" but whatever there was to counter Pixee's point died before it met the open air.

"There's a lot more to living. Much more. There's being in love. There's loving. There's discovery."

"Truly. There's all the pain. Loss. A lot of death and can't forget the stagnation," Aster added.

She smacked his cheek. He looked at her, more surprised than angered.

"There's twice as many journey's as destinations, Aster. Learn to stop looking back and start enjoying the process. And not every process requires some novel feat of magic either." She retreated back to her haunches and waited for Aster to acknowledge her sagacity.

He stared at her. "Well and good."

"Smart," she said with a tussle of Aster's hair.

"Surely, wise Primul."

"It's not even that," she said. "It's not because I'm Primul that I knew or didn't know this or that. I figured out what's what because I'm paying attention to what's happening around me. To what I'm doing." She rocked forward a bit. "That's what I told Allium multiple times when she was a lass. She finally got it after a few rounds."

Allium. The name strummed some beautiful chords in Aster. At the mere mention of it, the memory of her face would resurface as if from the deep. Not that it happened often. Oren was overly-cautious about bringing up the subject of Aster's mother, a caution forged from his own grief and used as a defense for his son, because there was no denying it: that name led to an assault of memories harsh and unrelenting. But Pixee, she still uttered the name without apology.

The emotions crept up from inside Aster. It was time to get a move on, so Aster—ignoring Pixee's use of his mother's name—placed his hands within the etched square and began to utter the words, since he actually needed them:

Mine voice has been found
Tasting bones in the ground
Spade to strike the depths
Untether the flesh

The very dirt within the square drawn by Aster was now tethered to his intention and obliged that will; it shifted as every tiny seam, hardly to be seen at first, unknit. How far down this unknitting took place was Aster's focus as he closed his eyes, bent his mind on that small patch of earth, and sliced through the dirt with his words, shoving his imagining deeper and deeper as if he spoke with a shovel and tore a path to the water below.

A small cone grew within the parameters set-down by Aster. It rose as dark, dewy soil spewed forth. The crawling, creeping things that made their home far from the sun's reach scurried and wriggled away from the tumult: worms, beetles, and the like. It wasn't long until the earth flowed as if it were liquid.

With each repetition of the words Aster hoped that his animus would make contact with the hidden water supply. "Depths" his voice called out and then it stopped as his words were shoved back into his throat, stuck like pieces of food too large to swallow or even spit back out.

Pixee looked on, her right eyebrow pitching at Aster's stall. "You alright?"

Aster cleared his throat. "Guess I reached the water."

Aster plunged his arm down into the cylindrical vacancy until his shoulder pressed the cone of displaced dirt into a more flattened shape. Down his hand went through the cool emptiness. Nope, no water, just more dirt.

He shook his head at Pixee as he drew back, flinging and swiping away bits of soil from his arm, a perplexed stare fixed on the magically dug hole.

There was a moment of investigation into the sudden halt of magical-digging, including such tactics as staring quiet fixedly, tilting one way then the other, and finally sitting back and scratching the back of the neck.

"It should have kept going," he explained, more to himself than to Pixee.

She crawled over and examined the depths. Her right eye pinched closed while her left swiveled. "How far down did it stop? If you felt an end then for sure something got in the way."

Aster joined her, blocking out whatever light had been falling down into the hole. "Are you sure this was the right spot?"

"I know the feel of water." Neither smile nor wink creased her face. Smooth as polished marble was her expression.

"Then you're saying my spell was the problem?" He ventured back into the hole with his already soiled arm.

There was a bottom. Moist was the proper description for how it felt as his fingers groped around with the aid of his eyes. His fingers danced with an impeding clod for a brief moment before he drew back towards the surface with the offending clump. Aster gave the mass a proper squeeze hoping he'd see it crumble, a suitable consequence for slowing his progress. His exertion was met with resistance. Lots of it.

"It's hard," he explained. "Like a rock."

"No, that's not right," Pixee replied. She stared over Aster's shoulder at this suspicious chunk of dirt. "Your earth spell would have pulled even a rock out of the way."

The mystery deepened and neither Pixee nor Aster dared look away, like some imaginary fear scattered their reason. There was nothing for it though. It sat without effect in Aster's palm, all dirty and dark, robed soil. He pried at the layer of caked-on dirt, plucking the drier bits first.

"Enough with the manual labor." Pixee grabbed the bundle from Aster's hand and set it down. She focused on the little lump as her fingers deftly twittered about pulling at a thread only she could see. She worked her native magic until a tiny translucent sliver drooped from the side of the bundle of soil.

The glistening strand became some sort of netting, shimmering like the purest silver, which she tossed aside where it sat upon the ground like morning dew. The dirt flaked away, drier than soil that had been sunning for days, crumbling almost like sand to reveal the oddest possible explanation.

"A gem," Aster noted.

Pixee withheld her agreement. "No, that too would have bent to the will of your words."

Aster dusted away the remaining dross. Absent the earthen cloak, the rock—for lack of a nicer label—boasted a red hue. Not like blood, no. That was too dark with lingering hints of purple. The only apt comparison would have been the petal of a rose. Not just any rose either. It was akin to the sort of rose that was un-assailed by the world around it. No polluting twinges of orange, blue, or green. Just red in its purest form. The first red thing in creation.

"Well, look at that." Aster lauded the discovery as he held it aloft, ensuring the sun blessed each facet with ample light. It practically ate up the rays and spat them back out with a lustrous sheen untouched by the world; literally and figuratively. "What do you suppose it is, if not a gem?"

Pixee hadn't produced an answer, which was troubling in a benign sort of way. Even though it wasn't morphing and attacking or poisoning as he handled it, Aster still wanted to know. Just for the sake of knowing.

He lowered it and set it back upon the ground as he gave Pixee a quizzical look, waiting for her to say something fraught with wisdom.

In her Primul way, Pixee picked at the stone with a glance, drilling into the hue, forcing her will to discover the very nature of that which she looked upon. Her focused stare left her eyes to glaze and sparkle, somewhat.

The investigation took on a new dimension as Pixee's skin once again oozed a shadowy form. The wisps of Pixee caressed at the rock, searching for familiarity.

A spark, poignant and almost blue, reached Aster's sight. Pixee flinched and the other-worldly effect was gone. She was whole and present.

Aster bore down upon her with wide eyes and a gaping mouth. "Well?"

"It's more than gem." Pixee sucked at the finger which had endured the jolt. "Some sort of power lingers in its makeup, whatever that may be because it's not simply elemental."

They both peered down at the red rock. Rock because neither had the language with which to properly label this enigma. "You know," she assessed. "I hate to bring it up—"

"Then don't."

"—but there's one guy."

Aster's chin fell, as if the very suggestion rested with the same volume and pressure as the entire ocean itself. Granted, that particular feeling would have more of a crushing effect, but really to go there and talk *him* was tantamount.

Pixee's honey-colored eyes just oozed pragmatics. She could be wrong, once in a while. She wasn't perfect. She wasn't gifted with omniscience.

She stared back as though she were.

4.

INTERLUDE: AN EXCHANGE BETWEEN LIFE & DEATH

There's a common misconception about Life and Death. Life's recollections of the past aren't pristine, and Death? Well, Death doesn't know what's coming, and despite such awkward misgivings they both saw the present more clearly than any mortal being, which was a good thing. Since every few generations, there would be that person who rose up thinking themselves above Life and Death, as if those immortal deity-like beings were slave-masters and not merely the arbiters of the natural cycle of mortal existence. There had not been too many mortals, in all the history of existence, with enough moxie to actually take-on the eternal order.

Life and Death lingered beside the deepest chasm in their realm, their keen glances slicing through the surroundings when a red twinkle—far away from where the great Creators loiter—caught Death's eye.

"You did remember, didn't you?" Death said, even though the answer is going to be obvious; this is Life after all.

"Not that I recall." Life made an attempt at recalling. Not an earnest attempt.

Death sighed, as is so often the case. "Shall we order the Stewards to collect it?"

Stewards. The only avenue through which Life and Death would reach out from their own layer and touch the mortal one.

As was so often the case with Life: "No." Life paused before carrying on with the thought, to make sure it checked out. "No, I don't think we really need to. What will the mortals learn if we send out the Stewards every time something potentially dangerous comes up?"

Death, sighed. Again.

"I never grow weary of that sound," Life joked. "If this episode gets too carried away I will make sure to send out those Stewards myself."

Death considered the anemic commitment. "Have you ever paid attention long enough to realize when that happens?"

It was Life's turn to sigh.

5.
OF WHEELING
& DEALING

The archway into Lamiston proper, the one gaping towards the coast, stood in a perpetual yawn, of the welcoming sort; not the yawn of fatigue or boredom. Many times had Aster passed under that configuration of whitewashed masonry, so practical in design. Today's venture was of a specific nature. That certain specificity was nestled in Aster's pouch, fastened to a tightly woven strap draped neatly across his torso.

It bounced dutifully against his hip as he marched his way across the round town square. Aster maneuvered between an assortment of structures until his path ended at the door of a windowless façade. Above the door swung that familiar sign of letters seared into wood, and stained in a slightly ruddy shade: Curios by Rustle.

Not that the man ever made a Death-tilled thing in his life, except a hand-crafted was a mess.

The door swung back with nary a sound. The open floor was filled with a contingent of cabinets, all standing upon clawed feet wrought of iron, most of which were open, displaying aged tomes that existed since the page was invented with words that no one probably knew how to speak. Then there were those in this maze of curiosity that were shuttered with panes of glass. The shelves in these cabinets bore an assortment of objects: the horns of beasts long dead; rocks so colorful that those colors hadn't even been named yet, or blades of the most sterling steel with handles ornately carved out of bones.

"By Life's left eye, it's Aster." Rustle stood by a counter, his sandy blonde hair brushed away from his forehead exposing his brown eyes. The grin he wore ensured most of his teeth were displayed. That had been Rustle's way as long as Aster had known the man. He smiled through the worst, laughed at most danger even while pissing himself, and he always found the most dangerous danger. He beamed at Aster with arms crossed over his chest while his fists inflated the size of each bicep.

At the salutation Aster mustered half a grin, a morose attempt really; a gesture curdled by a history Aster loathed to recall. Rustle's face was ever an aching reminder of loss.

Still, despite all his foibles, he managed to keep this little shop afloat, and in a simple town like Lamiston. One had to wonder what he did—or didn't do—to keep it thriving, and so far away from the bulk of Thuidium's more populated locales. There were plenty of bustling settlements in which to do business along the River Crest, that strip of dark, deep water that cut a meridian line across the face of Thuidium.

In the end, the world didn't run on shiny pieces of mint alone. There was more to barter with than precious metal. All around Aster was the currency of the magical, for elevated minds that saw beyond the temporal. Rustle knew, more than most, how to deal in ideas as much as precious objects.

Aster responded to the greeting by letting his pouch slip from off his shoulder and setting it on the counter. He draped an arm over it. "I stumbled across something the other day while digging for a well. Pixee said it's singular."

"That right? Pixee said that?" Rustle blithely peered at Aster.

"She did and seeing as I trust her a good deal more than you—"

"Come with it Aster, when are you going to give up your hostility towards me?"

No fluttering smile or parade of failed jokes could erase the dubious feeling that scratched at Aster when he saw Rustle. Every strike to gain favor with Aster only broadened the gap. "Look, let's just do this bit of business. There's no reason for us to try and be friends."

Rustle sank away from Aster's bundle with a resigned shrug. "I didn't have anything to do with what happened. You know that right?"

Aster peeled back the flap to his pouch in silence. That was not to be spoken of. Ever. Rustle was well aware of how Aster felt about the whole situation with Rose. With an expression like tempered iron, Aster cleared his throat and threw their conversation into the theme of business as he rolled the red gem—after due consideration, the designation of *rock* had been completely abandoned for the more alluring nomenclature—out on to the counter. At the sight of the revealed treasure, a gleam of intrigue glittered in Rustle's eyes. The unmistakable sheen of conspiracy.

"To me, it looks like a gem. Pixee wouldn't call it that. What say you?"

Rustle pored over its facets, his gaze latching onto this new curio. He licked his thumb and plied the saliva-stricken digit across the different angles, rubbing matter-of-factly.

"Earth magic didn't move the thing at all."

"Well, isn't that a revelation," Rustle almost whispered.

"It's that curious, is it?"

"It's something, alright."

There may have been hints of ideas trickling out of Rustle. "Just tell me what we're dealing with here. I don't have time for your dramatics."

Aster scooped the red gem—yes, that title sounded more accurate with each application—away from Rustle's pawing fingers.

"Fine. Fine." Rustle looked at Aster with an unwavering gaze. Finally, down to business.

"I don't have an exact name for what this is, but it isn't a diamond or a precious stone of any sort. There's something organic deep inside." He eyed the stone a bit warily. "Did a Primul not even guess its exact nature?"

Aster shrugged as he reflected on the moment they discovered what lay hidden beneath the muck and grime. There wasn't much said about what it was. Pixee had merely surmised what it was not. She didn't intimate that it had any specific history. That look on her face though, there was suspicion in her expression as she handled it, somewhere between curiosity and fear. No, not fear. Aster had no idea what a scared Pixee looked like. Curiosity and awe. Yes, just a quick flash of awe, as if she had been introduced to some form of greatness. Then she suggested bringing the gem here.

It was a pain to admit Rustle's acumen for the novel, the unwonted, but the man knew his stuff. He had seen a thing or two. Felt a thing or two. He could spot the authentically unique and having his confirmation lent a sense of relief.

More than relief, the confirmation stirred Aster's ambitions. "So you're saying it is valuable?"

Rustle's gaze narrowed and for a moment he didn't say a word, didn't flinch. Then his face relaxed as a grin sprouted. "You schemer, you." He paused with his attention now alighting upon the gem. "Right off-hand, I'd say there's some value to it."

"I need a more concrete assessment, Rustle."

Rustle leaned closer. "Why don't you let me know what you need and I'll let you know if your gem is worth the trouble."

"I'm not looking for just a satchel full of mint. I need someone who can appreciate the potential of this item. You get what I mean?"

Rustle smirked. "No idea, man."

"You find me someone who is practiced in the rite of the Martese. Is that plain enough for you?"

Rustle nodded as if the word had swept away all frivolity. "Savvy. I think this red gem of yours might actually be worth the trouble."

"Then you might know some people?"

"I maybe know some people."

Back to the waiting game; Aster's least favorite. It was such a waste of life, being stationary instead of being the one who initiated an objective and moved it all forward towards accomplishment.

That was the way of it, sometimes. Not that Aster couldn't find preoccupations to fill the drooping lulls between pivotal moments. This just meant more time in the kitchen of the Den. More time to ponder the application of the fire fruit. Oh, how it would flare up the meat. It would brighten the vegetables. It wasn't too soon to test it out. A slight fear glazed the excitement and wonder brought about by this new amazing fruit.

There in the kitchen, slicing slow-roasted beef, it still felt like there was nothing to be done. There was a well to finish, land to cultivate, cheese to set. The daily grind blurred into shades and shadows as the fire fruit came into sharp and distinct focus.

Then the day arrived when Rustle announced he had found a potential buyer. The news lit up Aster's mood. Could it have been the same person Oren had mentioned, the one with the know-how to guide Aster through the Martese?

In that buoyant disposition, Aster set aside his carving knife, rid his hands of grease, and brushed his dark, wavy hair back behind his ears. He grabbed his leather pouch—never far from his person when it bore the red gem—and vacated the kitchen.

The meeting which Rustle had set up was to take place at the Hart's Den. Fitting and, thankfully, public enough.

The room was in its usual loud, dim way. The all-too familiar crowd of bodies were seated and standing haphazardly about the place. As Aster's glance dug through the dimness he spotted a solitary figure seated in a booth away from the bulk of the patrons. There was a maleness to the shape of this person, shoulders broad and padded, perhaps with years of work. The head upon the taut upright neck, was nearly bald; fuzzy like a peach. This could not be the figure of an accomplished, sage practitioner. No, this person had the bearing of a solider. Misgivings stirred through Aster's limbs, but despite them he couldn't help but investigate.

Repeating *red gem* to himself, the identifying phrase which Rustle prescribed, he slipped past some tables. Using the softest step of which he was capable, Aster came upon the waiting individual from behind hoping to catch a glimpse of the one physical description mentioned by Rustle: a missing left thumb.

The approach was not soft enough apparently for the potential buyer was out of his seat, squaring off against Aster before he even had his foot fully planted. The movement was so sudden that even some neighboring patrons stopped their conversations.

Aster smiled them away and then insisted his thudding heart resume a more peaceful cadence. "Red gem. Red gem." Aster spat out while presenting his empty palms to the stranger. The small blade secured in the stranger's left hand was a feat unto itself considering there wasn't a thumb to help in the task. "So you're Sedge."

"Yes." He lowered his weapon, albeit slowly. "Habit, when someone tries to sneak up on me. You're Aster then?" Sedge resumed his seat as if he hadn't just brandished a blade. "Right, now that we've established this meeting is the handiwork of Rustle, let's get down to it."

This was going to be one of those types of deals, of the sort that included the shady characters with whom Aster always suspected Rustle of being in league. He moved past Sedge, ever so carefully, and seated himself in the booth across the table. The initial contact had been dodgy, but the longer Aster examined Sedge, the more incongruent his actions seemed, especially with those green eyes, a soft shade like the color moss.

Aster pulled himself out of his scrutiny and, instead, looked at the table. He started picking at a sliver of wood. "I guess my attempt to establish your identity before sitting down wasn't as smooth as I had hoped. It's not easy spying out a missing digit from across the room."

Sedge held up his left hand and gave the ball of his hand a wiggle. The short nub, where a thumb was usually stationed, moved. "Truly, I see what you mean."

"So….spent most of your life in combat situations?" Not that Aster cared, personally, about this person's life-story. It was an assessment and since the chap had no forthcoming response—his glance darting about the room, a relentless grip on that dagger, and an ear cocked towards the door—Aster wanted to vacate the meeting as quickly as possible. Surely this man, so diligently trained in fighting and so clearly on edge, was not the right person with whom to be dealing.

"I have," Sedge finally offered.

Aster held the strap to his pouch a little more tightly.

The mint chimed as it spilled from the little satchel that Sedge had tossed out onto the table. Aster peered at the last minute grace to save the bartering. The pile of metallic coins lacked a certain substance. One shouldn't turn one's nose up at any amount of mint no matter the size of the pile, so in a display of politeness Aster toyed with the cool, silvery coins, counting them. At least feigning to.

"Nice. I'm not really looking for currency. Well, not metallic currency." He let the coins drip from his fingers.

"Rustle told me something about your desperation for magical knowledge." Sedge gave a quick glance to the rest of the room.

That sentence, and especially the word *desperation*, came careening into Aster's ears with its boldness and Sedge was sure to see the reaction all over his face.

Desperate? Was that how Rustle viewed Aster's conditions? This tenuous grasp on the concept of discretion explained a lot of Rustle's troubled experiences.

"Um, truly. He said he knew someone who could get me exactly what I wanted for this stone." Aster drew out the gem, just for a moment; for effect.

Its facets drank in the light of fire more than it drank in the light of the sun. The orange flames brought out a sultry red hue in the stone, a shade so seductive that Sedge couldn't hide his hungry glance. That was all Aster needed to see: he wanted this gem as much as Aster wanted to be rid of it. The reason why was the only unrevealed bit.

Aster broke the spell as he slipped the gem away, veiling its beauty from sight. "I hope you can appreciate that I would be able to get exactly what I want for this." He patted the pouch. "You're probably not the only person-of-interest Rustle knows."

"Oh, I know the kind of people Rustle would send you to." Sedge smiled a greasy, knowing smile. "You'd get more than you wanted."

Aster's satisfaction slunk away. "How do you mean?"

6.

OF INTERRUPTIONS
& A SHIFT
TO PLAN B

Sedge went silent at the sound of shuffling chairs. Nearby patrons nearby vacated their table with an abundance of chatter and cheering. Sedge made ready to continue his monologue. He leaned in and licked his lips. He paused as if to feel the room. Maybe appraising the background noise with a sharp ear.

For Aster the background noise faded to a low drone, like bees dancing about a field of wildflowers, in anticipation of what Sedge had to say, just a merry sound of no consequence. What aching observation was Sedge about to spill out over the table between them? This person was a stranger, whose words could have all been as concrete as smoke, but he sold his opinion better than Rustle sold curious objects: "Thanatist," Sedge whispered.

It was as if his disclosure had punch, like steam escaping a lidded pot. Aster sat back and stared at Sedge. The word had been spoken among the practitioners of magic, but always in a whisper as if it were contaminated and anyone saying it too readily, too loudly, with even a hint of neutrality would somehow be implicated, cursed. It was one of those early lessons from Oren: be free as you want with elemental magic, the Magic of Life, but don't attempt learning to mess around with souls, a practice he named Thanatos. "The soul is the most essential part of your existence," he'd say in his wise, fatherly way. "It's between you, Life, and Death. You don't want some human with all their biases, and passions interfering in that sacred relationship."

"You're sure about that?" Aster tried to stifle the memory of Oren's cautionary teachings. "Everyone claims to know some twisted mind who dabbles in that stuff," he said with a dismissive laugh.

"Are you so desperate that you would want to find out?"

Another heavy question for Aster. Yet…

It was more than "yes" or "no". The desire for this goal outpaced so many other considerations. The longer he sought to achieve a certain outcome, the muddier the ethical path became, cumbersome and long compared to other options, like those carved out by one as loathsome and questionable as a Thanatist.

Sedge waited for a reply to a question that was apparently not rhetorical, as Aster had at first thought. Aster opened his mouth to respond when more shuffling of tables and chairs interceded on the conversation. Closer this time. More insistent.

Sedge was greeted with a rather deliberately aimed fist across his face. Was anyone seeing this? The room was filled with the usual frivolity; nary a break in the tune of socializing to indicate that anyone cared about a small tussle breaking out.

Two men positioned themselves in the booth quickly after checking Sedge's face. A rather burly figure with a smooth head and face blocked Aster in while a shorter bearded man, donning a smile, sat down next to Sedge.

The two knaves were dressed for long travel more than battle, but there were still weapons, mostly of the compact variety, about their persons. That was enough observation for Aster, about whom they appeared unconcerned as their focus rested entirely on Sedge.

"You found me, Gules. Terrific," Sedge said with a face stripped of expression. "Was this assignment of your choosing or did my father mandate you and Ocher find me?"

Father? The story unfolding perplexed and concerned Aster. Family dramas had a curious flavor to them. There was no telling when the fascination would veer into the realm of danger.

"Oh, good Sedge, it was more than a pleasure to find our warlord's little princeling and make sure he was returned safe and sound. Your father worries about his number one commander." Gules caressed Sedge's cheek with the flat side of a small blade. "Especially when he takes off. In the night. Without orders."

Sedge's family drama took that wild turn into danger and though there were questions aplenty about why he had come here to buy this gem, there was no reason to stick around and ask them.

Aster tapped the Ocher character on his bulky shoulder. "Excuse me. I'm just going to slip on past you and let you handle your business with Sedge."

Ocher sat, like a boulder, glaring at Aster, arresting any intentions to slip, slide, or otherwise vacate the booth.

"And who is your friend here?" Gules kept the dagger close to Sedge's throat letting the metal pinch but not bite.

"Nope," Aster replied, "not a friend. Just a case of mistaken identity."

It was natural that Aster would clutch at the strap of his pouch. Not the smartest move; the interrogator lashed out a hand and swiped the strap. It broke free of Aster's grip and the pouch flew out of his possession.

"Let's see what sort of business these two had together, shall we, Ocher?"

Ocher's laugh rumbled out of him as he loomed over Aster. "Let's."

Gules' eyes widened as the muscles along his forearm flexed, capturing the one item of interest residing in the pouch. The only item to be found therein, really. If Aster hadn't hung his aspirations on the gem, that knowing look across the table would have had no effect. How nice it would have been to be insulated from all the anxiety that Gules' discovery incited.

At least he handled the gem with a certain amount of care. "Is this what you came all the way out here for, Sedge?"

Sedge leaned into the tip of the dagger. It entered his skin just so, drawing forth a crimson thread. "Exactly."

And the booth erupted into commotion.

The red gem slipped from Gules' hand as he wrestled with Sedge's attack. The table had been shifted by the movement, pinning Ocher to his side of the booth which meant Aster was also stuck, and now the rest of the tavern ladled their attention onto the sudden flurry of limbs and bodies. Aster had a hope that some of them would notice the outsiders and jump in to break up the kerfuffle and free their favorite chef. A few furtive glances were cast towards the booth but no one was dispatched to interrupt. Go figure. Next time, pick the seat facing the crowd.

Sedge shoved Gules out of the booth. Ocher rose from where he sat and lunged for Sedge's ankle.

The red gem was there, sitting alone drinking in the stray flicks of fire light. Before helping Sedge—at the moment it was merely a consideration, a fleeting notion—recovering the gem was the priority. No need attending to someone else's safety before securing one's own future.

Out of the gawking crowd, Rustle emerged. His wide eyes seemed to shout *how in all of Life's bright eye did you bungle this?* Either way, the peaceful transaction was mutilated. The fight carried on, with Sedge kicking away Ocher's grasp as Gules grappled to pin Sedge's torso against the floor.

The situation presented a clear exit. The door was right there, beckoning for Aster to slip away from the conflict, which belonged wholly to this stranger with whom no bond nor oath had been made.

Aster shuffled around the tangled bodies and nearly achieved a proper eschewal, but not before a hand dragged him into the fray.

The floor boards heaved under the impact of Aster's body. The force of Ocher's grip brought Aster closer to being pummeled. Sedge had found his way out of Gules' hold and began to administer a fury of punches down upon the knave.

Why he was on the floor? And why was Ocher engaging with someone who had no connection to Sedge's dereliction of duty? These were questions that needed to be saved when the threat of physical harm was not so near.

The man was beastly. Ocher brought not only height to the battle, but a breadth that Aster did not possess. He loomed again, shading out what little light the lamps and hearth provided. Aster clung to his pouch, to where the red gem had been safely replaced, as Ocher loomed harder, menacing with that bald head of his.

There was a metallic ring and the knave collapsed onto his side. Instead of Ocher's bulk, Rustle stood beside Twiggy, who clutched his improvisational weapon: a familiar frying pan.

Twiggy stood assessing the remnants of the altercation: two unconscious bodies and blood staining the unstained floor. His quizzical gaze darted from the mess to Aster. The face could only communicate so much and the whole situation was beyond silent expressions.

"Quite my fault," Rustle offered. "Nothing to do with your cook, here." From a pocket Rustle produced some mint while offering the tavern owner a crooked smile. "Also, feel free to take some of the better weapons from these fellas, to help with the costs," he added.

Twiggy accepted the amends, and before appraising the proffered weaponry: "Aster, mate?"

"I uh…" Explaining the situation was trickier than expected. It needed more time. Instead, Aster offered a shrug. "Just need a couple days away from the Den, is all. I'll be back in after I clear up some… personal matters."

Twiggy, not wholly convinced that the situation was completely resolved gave Aster another questioning glance. Aster responded with an assuring nod. The tavern keeper took the reply in stride, returning to the bowls of the bar with not a little skepticism carved onto his features.

"I set you up for success and you just can't ease into it, can you?" Rustle said as the chatter and socializing resumed all about them .

Aster glanced down at Sedge sprawled out upon the floor, free of his attacker, but bleeding nicely, wetting the dry wood. "This is your idea of an ideal set up? Did you even bother to check this Sedge-character out?"

Rustle hoisted the character from off the ground. "Truly, I did my research which is why I offered the gem to Sedge in the first place. Good thing I showed up, too. You know, Aster, sometimes you just need to be like water. Be. Like. Water."

Aster looked Rustle dead in the eyes. Didn't just look; he stabbed with his unflinching gaze. The muscles in his jaw knotted and rolled like there was snake slithering along his jawline, preparing for the most scathing reply.

The air outside the tavern was sweet; sweeter now than it had been. Avoiding death and harm heightens the senses, washes the world, and leaves it refreshed.

"I made it perfectly clear what I wanted and you sent me this." Aster waved Sedge's floppy arm about.

Rustle gave Sedge's limp body a heft. "You should seriously consider giving him a chance. He's good guy. You're writing him off because you only see a warrior. You have not idea what else he's capable of, what he has to offer."

"No, Rustle. He's given no indication that he knows a lick of magic. Throwing hands and swinging blades but not a single spell. He can't give me what I'm looking for."

The ensuing pause was the proper time to give Sedge another consideration. It was a brief one, lasting no longer than the time it took

Aster to scan the man with narrowed eyes, down and then up again. The assessment remained as it was.

"You assured me. Worth the trouble. Your exact words."

For a moment they carried on in as much silence as possible. There was still the labored breathing and grunting of Rustle as he tried to haul Sedge's solid body along. It was almost a pathetic attempt since Rustle was quite a bit leaner and shy of being as tall as Sedge.

"Here," Aster offered the pouch to Rustle. "Let's trade. I can at least bear him to your place for you."

With a decided sigh, Rustle switched burdens with Aster. "Actually, my place is just a bed in the back of my shop. Since you have an entire house, to yourself—"

"You think you're clever, huh?" It was Aster's turn to hoist. He gripped his hand tight to Sedge's obliques, slightly yielding with and underlying firmness. "I'd like to know, what did this man offer you to broker this deal?"

"Besides a whole lot of mint?"

"Yes," Aster said, "besides the mint?"

"Connections. I've got a business to look out for. He knows practitioners from some of the busier settlements out there in the world."

"Figures."

"What figures?"

"I ask for a specific price but you make this about yourself. Your selfishness is actually astounding. I didn't think it possible but here I am. Astounded." Aster hoped the jab stung as much as he intended.

Rustle toyed with the satchel's strap. Something in the sag of his lips told Aster it stung, just the way he had hoped.

"This isn't manipulation," Rustle said, his tone decidedly defeated. "It's just being practical. Come with it Aster. Just a little bit of ethical help is all I'm asking."

Sedge's body, sagging against Aster's own frame, was substantial; he stirred and his eyelids fought to open as a groan dropped from between his barely parted lips. Sedge made an attempt to stand on his own, which pulled his face into a wince.

Rustle had a point. It wouldn't be ethical to leave this wounded man to heal in a place that wasn't a home, regardless of how much of a stranger he was. Aster considered depositing Sedge at the doorstep of the local surgeon, a healer of repute. Wouldn't that be one of the first places his foes would check?

"Fine." Aster leaned towards Rustle, being careful not to let the weight of Sedge take them both down, and grabbed his satchel back.

"If you're this resistant to selling the gem to Sedge then maybe…" Rustle's voice faltered. His eyes roved away from making contact with Aster, as if the next sentence were being forced. "…I may have another individual who can give you exactly what you want."

Aster pinched his lips tightly to restrain the smile that threatened to grow at the sound of Rustle's offer. A simple, partial nod was all that Aster offered in reply before bearing his burden away from Lamiston proper.

There was surely a spell to ease the heft of an unconscious body. But Death's Lips if he knew the words for it. Aster filed away the fear of reprisal from Gules and Ocher, and the mystery of Sedge's home life. It all meant nothing, because it wasn't going to help with the attainment of the fire fruit.

If those goons did come knocking, there were ways to handle their aggression. There was plenty of time to think of those ways as Aster hauled Sedge back to his home.

7.
OF FATHERS, MOTHERS, & OF SURPRISES

The well never did happen. The beginnings of it sat there, just beyond the back wall of the house, like some mouth waiting for a meal.

The arrival of the red gem, and all that it promised, relegated the well back to the status of a side-project to finish if the inclination ever arrived. It was tough to throw away time that could be measured out and boiled into accomplishments.

During the first day or two of Sedge's stay, there had been every opportunity to complete the well since the wounds still held sway over this stranger's body. No matter how long Aster stared at the unfinished task, keeping his back to the front door for too long felt like a mistake.

Now that Sedge was pretty much healed, or at least to the point of being able to leave Aster's bedroom, the fear of goons dispatched by a warlord only intensified. The door could only stand so valiantly against an attack. It was a house, not a fortress.

"Waiting on someone?" Sedge held a hand to his bandaged side as he watched Aster from the bedroom doorway.

Aster stirred but didn't divest his attention from the front door. He shook his head as he kept watch upon the entrance with beleaguered eyes waiting for it to betray him.

"If no one has shown up looking for me by now, I'm sure you're in the clear." Sedge cut across Aster and sat himself down on the couch. "And by the time their search resumes, I'll be long gone."

The assurances Sedge dished out held little value because he was foreign. His words, spoken in the most familiar language were, therefore, foreign as well.

"Have you even slept since you brought me here?"

Aster gave Sedge a brief moment of acknowledgment, just long enough to adequately display the dark circles holding up under his eyes and the generally disheveled appearance.

Sedge turned towards Aster. "I can take watch while you get some sleep?"

The offer placated nothing. Aster stood and presented his full back to Sedge. "You're feeling better? Able to walk about?"

"Uh, truly. I can be out of your hair tomorrow. If you would like?"

It was the first sentence Sedge uttered to which Aster gave full credence. It rang with sweet relief, magically unwinding the tension lacing up and down his back. "Good."

He heard Sedge rise from the couch. "I'm going to get a little more rest then, to make sure I have the stamina to get as far from here as possible." He made a slow retreat back to the bedroom. There was the briefest of glances from his moss-colored eyes, gratitude perhaps.

Aster was not swayed by this stranger's placating words, sweet as they sounded. Nor by the pitiful state of the man's health. He may have said he was ready to strike out but he still moved with a weariness. "Sorry if Rustle misled you. He should have better explained the situation. You weren't a good buyer from the beginning."

Sedge's face wasn't crestfallen as much as it was bunched up. His lips turned down as he cocked his head to one side. "You never did hear me out, so I'm not sure how you can make that claim."

"Fine. Let's have it out then. Do you know how to perform the Martese? Because I'll trade the red gem for nothing less." Aster waited, drummed his fingers against his own bicep as his eyes plied Sedge for a response.

Sedge tapped a finger against the door frame. "Then you're right. You need some shady Thanatist to help you with whatever you're aiming for."

Aster turned his back on the front door for the first time in the four days as he maneuvered towards the kitchen. "It's a means to an end and that's as much as I need to share with you. Besides, Sedge," Aster paused and glanced back towards the bedroom. "I've seen the danger that follows you, so you haven't the right to make judgments about who is safe to deal with and who isn't."

Sedge dropped his chin to his chest while the baritone chuckle dribbled from between his lips. "I see. My brawls and daggers are more dangerous than someone who knows how to invade your mind? To toy with souls?" He snickered. "I don't know Aster, sounds like a deluded perception of danger."

"I'd rather go off what I've seen with my own eyes and have experienced for myself, not the dire warnings of some rogue." Even though this rouge echoed the same dire warnings as his own father, a realization Aster neatly tucked away.

In the face of Sedge's glare, Aster stuck out his chin, clenched his jaw and waited, stifling the sliver of doubt that lingered in the back of his mind.

"If you really are keen to find out how wrong you are about Thanatists, then that's your prerogative." Sedge scanned Aster, an unexpected depth in his eyes as he turned his bottom lip slightly out. He left it at that. "I'll trouble you for one more night's rest then be on my way." Sedge retreated into the bedroom and closed the door.

Aster stood between the dining area and the main room, alone for a moment before giving himself over the couch again to resume his faithful watch on the front door. Keeping guard did not seem as urgent now that Sedge had finally deemed himself healed enough to leave. That was when the bedroom door drew Aster's attention.

What he pictured taking place on the other side made him just a bit uneasy: a man occupying the most personal space in his life; a stranger, all wound up in the bedding; the same bedding that caressed Aster's most intimate parts.

The knob on the front door turned.

Aster snapped into action at the sound. He drew a small blade from under the couch cushion. The door began to open as Aster ducked behind the back of the couch. Only one pair of feet tramped their way into his home.

One person would be easy enough to take. The steps were too light to wake Sedge. Aster gripped the hilt of a boning knife securely as was possible, with his sweaty palm. The steps crept out in a calm rhythm, like someone who was completely sure they belonged there.

And he did.

"Expecting company?" Oren stood with hands on hips and his brow scrunched.

Aster lowered his weapon and tried to smile, but his racing heart and haphazard breaths stifled his relief. "In a way, yes."

Oren approached and put a hand on Aster's shoulder. He read his son's face. Those eyes felt like they were always peeling Aster apart. "Why? What's wrong?"

Aster pulled away and moved to replace the knife under the cushion. "That buyer Rustle lined up? It did not go well."

They both sank down on the couch. "Let's hear it."

"Turns out he is the son of warlord and his father doesn't take too kindly to desertion."

"Not many warlords would, I'd imagine. Fathers aren't too fond of it either, kiddo."

That label—kiddo—sounded eight sizes too small. It was a hat that barely sat atop the crown of Aster's head, so precarious and useless. Every conversation with Oren included at least one use of the word. Three times if the exchange was particularly involved. It sprang up like: surprise! Small hat for Aster.

The paternal endearment, overstated as it might have been for a man being two decades lived, wrapped Aster in a sense of warmth. "I didn't want to get caught up in his family skirmish but he was wounded so—"

"Wounded?"

"Some of his father's henchmen caught up with him while we were talking about a possible deal for that red gem."

Oren latched onto the word wounded. "You're well? No harm? No bruises?"

"No, Dad. I'm fine. I'm also experienced at life and accomplished in a litany of spells."

"Which one did you use to get away from the villains?" He gave Aster a playful punch on the knee.

"Actually, Twiggy knocked them out. With cookware." It had been a shame to admit, but there was nothing for it except to be honest.

"Good for Twiggy, stepping in to help." Oren laughed, a tune of pure contentment. The sound banished all the worry that had been staining their conversation.

Aster's life included a smattering of moments like this. Even after all the nastiness of—

He shuttered his own laughter and the thoughts that tried to emerge. He quickly looked away from Oren's smiling face. The front door was still ajar, admitting a slice of afternoon light. How deceptively warm it looked brightly peeking in with silvery rays without depositing any heat.

"I'm glad you made it out of that situation intact," Oren said into Aster's preoccupation. "Speaking of, I'm still trying to find someone who can help you with the Martese. Pixee is asking around as well. Hopefully we'll have someone soon. Don't want you to lose focus on your goal."

"Not going to have to worry about that, Dad. I'm going to make this happen. There's no question." He wasn't sure, but Aster thought he spied a shadow pass across his father's face, a cloud barring the sunshine for a brief moment. "What's that look for?"

Oren flinched and offered a tentative smile. "I'm just reminded of someone I knew, long before you came around, who was a lot like that when it came to stuff he wanted."

"You say it like it's a bad thing to go after the things you want. You were the one who taught me how important accomplishing a goal is. Want to shut out the bad thoughts? Stay busy, as you always said." The statement had flown so fast from Aster's mouth that Oren quailed a little bit.

Memory of the ocean rolled into Aster's thoughts. There it was, hundreds of feet below, arguing with the dark, ragged cliffs from which she had cast herself. The undulating song played out: *swoosh, woosh*. The foam attempting to climb as high as possible. Over it all, her voice carried because her voice had always been strong and certain, as if she knew everything there was to know, before it was known.

Aster almost said the word, the one he never remembered saying. Maybe he uttered a version of it when he was a small child, but if he had said that word then the use was far beyond the capacity of his adult mind to recall. He looked at Oren silently asking him to remind Aster the last time he said it.

"And I meant it," Oren said.

His voice chased away the cursed recollections. Aster unconsciously flexed whatever muscles he could. "I'm not a delicate child," Aster replied. "I know what I'm doing."

Oren smiled, to himself, as if he reached back into his mind and found some pleasant memory of a time untouched by woe. "No, you're not but that is the way of a father. You'll always be a concern for me, even if I don't have to worry about you like I used to."

It was a cozy thought. Aster let it flow through his whole being.

"And as such, I'm going to go check on your curious guest."

Aster sprang to his feet and attempted to get around his father in objection to this continuation of overly paternal concern. Yes, it was mostly endearing but there were times when it was a comfortable blanket turned wet, sopping, and too heavy.

"Just let me be fatherly, Aster." He gently ushered his adult son out of the way and stepped towards the bedroom. "I'm just going to have a look at the lad. It would ease my mind."

Oren stood with his head injected into the room and remained frozen for too long. Aster joined him at the door, trying to glance over his father, who was just tall enough to block any view of the bed. Oren looked back at Aster before glancing into the room again. Then back at Aster, his face etched with uncertainty. He swung the door forward, none too carefully and stepped out of the way. The bed was peacefully unoccupied, the sheets twisted into misshapen swirls. The window, installed in the wall to the right of the bed, was perched open, admitting a temperate breeze. In the midst of the serene setting instead of a experiencing relief at this unexpected vacancy, panic rushed in to overtake all his senses. He shoved past Oren and hurried to his chest of drawers.

Oren watched his son shuffle through clothes. "Don't tell me—"

Aster paid his father no mind. He knew it. Oren knew it.

Oren joined Aster in the combing of personal items. "Now, I don't say this to bring blame to you," he dropped handfuls of clothing. "But what made you stash such a precious stone among your clothing with a stranger nearby?"

Aster pushed aside the wild hair against his forehead as he tossed clothes here and there. "I thought keeping it in the pouch would be obvious. I didn't know he was conscious when I hid the thing."

Aster dropped his clothes and sank onto the bed. "That Ever Life-Loving…"

8.

OF DANGER
& CHUCKLES

Each step farther into the curio shop was made laborious by the news Aster bore. Rustle stopped his general busyness and dispensed a smile when he spotted Aster entering the shop.

His smile would not be met in kind. Even on the occasions that warranted such expressions, Aster was frugal with his smiles when it came to trading them with Rustle. Something about how flippantly he employed them. Putting one on to shoo away sad events, vexing problems, or in the midst of pensive moments always came across in poor taste.

Rustle slid the book out of which he had been reading aside before bracing the flat side of his forearms flat against the counter. "I told you I'd let you know when I had the meeting set up. The guy is very much interested. I can vouch for the depth of his magical knowledge too, so you'll get exactly what you want. He's shrewd. I've done deals with him before and let's just say he knows what he wants." The snort-laugh belied a sense of seriousness tucked away in Rustle's words.

"Oh." The right buyer, paying the right price and it was all about to fall apart. Sure, Oren and Pixee were putting in effort to make sure Aster could see his vision fulfilled but Rustle had someone all lined up now. With his aspirations so close to being met, disappointment in the turn of events was an understatement.

"So, if you're not here to barter that gem away then what brings you by? Sedge all healed up and out of your hair?"

"He is out of my hair."

Rustle resumed interest in the volume he had been combing through, eyes tracing back and forth across lines of script as if Aster wasn't standing right there. "I bet you're relieved, even if his presence didn't put you out too much." Then he just stopped, as if the words in the book had disappeared. His attention lingered on Aster then floated off as his eyes took on the sparkle of what could have been. "It's kind of a bummer that the deal with him didn't go so well. He really was interested in that gem."

Were his words a hint? Rustle couldn't have known, could he? With a shrug, the curio dealer once again bent over the book opened before him. It didn't matter if he knew about the missing gem or not. This was Rustle. Whatever the consequences were to be, let him deal with them. He was about due for some challenging times, wipe the smile off his face for a while.

"Funny you should say that."

Rustle's hands disengaged from the page as he folded his them atop one another. His narrowed glance rested on Aster. "Funny, how?"

"Probably more ironic than funny. You mentioned how much Sedge really wanted that gem. So much, in fact, that he stole it when he left."

For once, Rustle's smile fell; slipped away from his usually smug face like someone had peeled it right off. Had he finally caught on to when a smile was appropriate? It didn't matter. Rustle didn't matter so much. Not anymore. "Let your new buyer know that there won't be a deal after all."

Rustle's excessive consternation made it seem like his eyelids had been pushed back into his skull.

"I'm not going to turn this into a told-you-so moment," Aster began. "This is a huge let-down for me. You tell me I'm about to have what I want, that I'm so close to everything I have been cooking towards. I could taste it too." Aster allowed himself a moment of personal disclosure to Rustle. "It's beyond disappointing, but this is where we are right now. Sedge stole it and I'm back to step one—"

The shifting and riffling distracted Aster from finishing his thought. Rustle shuffled through items on shelves, hurriedly shoving possessions into a rucksack. He disappeared behind a tattered curtain that must have separated his sleeping quarters from the rest of the shop, reappearing with bundles of clothing in his arms. His face wore the stern focus of someone completely dedicated to finishing a task. That task was packing in the least organized manner.

"Your disappointment is going to reach a whole new level, so you better start packing too." Sweat percolated along his hairline and above his upper lip. He licked away whatever drops his tongue could reach. "Pack and leave Lamiston. Leave the peninsula. Actually..." he jammed a handful of clothes into his bag. "Leave and find the most remote corner of Thuidium and start your new life. Make it as far from here as a horse will carry you. Don't leave word. Don't tell anyone."

Aster made to reply, to seek out reason amidst all the mad drivel Rustle peddled. "Maybe if you stopped and took a breath we could figure..."

The curio dealer would not be gain-said. "Nope. Just get on your way. For once, trust me and when you're alive and thriving in five years, in whatever nook you've settled, you'll thank me."

His voice rattled with a staunch unease, basting the situation in surrealism as every other concern and question, even the red gem, was brushed over with Rustle's dire forecasts. "Look Rustle, it's no big deal," Aster pressed on through the confusion that started to trail up his own skin, like the erotic touch of a stranger.

All at once, Rustle calmed as if Aster stood beneath the eye of a storm. He let his belongings sink to the floor in a heap. Even though his movements stilled, Rustle's eyes still looked harried.

"You wanted someone magically adept to buy this gem and… AND…you didn't secure the Death-tilled goods. You've no one to blame but yourself for the consequences that are about to follow and if I get dragged into the chasm that will surely open up, I'll make sure I push you in first."

The threat struck like a physical blow. The concern bubbling up inside Aster knitted his brow into a bundle of creases. "Who in the ever Life-loving did you find to buy this thing?"

Standing almost righteously behind his counter, Rustle grinned. His knuckles whitened as he grasped at the counter like it was the edge of a cliff. "A strangely powerful and uncommonly narcissistic kind of person. The sort you wanted to sell to."

Aster didn't recall listing off any of those qualities, except for the *strangely powerful* part. The rest gave him pause though.

The ensuing silence, of viscous magnitude, blanketed the shop. Rustle's words were a sort of sludge clinging to Aster without hope of being wiped off, so they sat in it. Until the silence was cracked by footsteps.

Rustle's eyes fixed on Aster. He stopped breathing.

The steps grew closer. They were the sure steps of someone who knew they belonged in any place, at any time. Aster was surprised to find tension gripping him, up and down. He licked his lips.

"Curious and delightful."

The confident voice reverberated into Aster's ear, dark but melodious. It was the voice of someone with whom a person could sit at tea and philosophize. Yet, there was some undertone to the words that made Aster wary.

An alien hand gave itself roost upon Aster's shoulder. The fingers were smooth, the nails glossy and opaque, not long but not trimmed.

"How about you introduce us, Rustle?"

Aster slipped out from under the stranger's touch and met the instrument that piped out that voice. He was tall—not as tall as Aster—with a square jaw and a slightly lithe frame, from what Aster what could be discern beneath the clothes. It was the sort of body expected of one who spent more time canvassing the hills and mountains than studying books of lore and magic. His dark hair looked molded out of wax, with its sense of flow while giving-off the impression that it was unable to simply fall out of place. His lips called to Aster's mind the inside of a perfectly medium-rare stake. When he smiled a set of white teeth, as if they had been carved from pearls, showed forth. Even his breath smelled as if mint leaves grew upon his tongue.

The way the curio dealer ticked nervously at this man's mere presence spoke of a history that went beyond merely trading objects for mint.

"Uh, yes. Right." Rustle shook off some of his apprehensions, while others clung to him as he left the safety of his counter. "Aster, this is Oleander."

"Mister Oleander."

"Mr. Oleander," Rustle said, cowed like a cur. "He has expressed interest in your rare and curious gem." Rustle affected a grin, a flaccid gesture, while avoiding eye contact with anyone else in the room.

"Aster," Mr. Oleander injected into Rustle's feeble attempt at pleasantries. "Not to cut-off what sounded like a robust conversation, but I'd like to talk gems."

His face, though youthful in shape, had a wiser bearing deeper than the genial features would suggest. The smooth, defined features wrapped around a skull full of unfathomable knowledge, the sort of knowledge that would be dangerous for most mortals, Aster had to guess, since the man knew magic as uncommon as the rite of the Martese. Any response to such a clever and self-determined individual required due consideration, as would any obligations made to him. No haphazard replies or blithe promises.

Aster carefully navigated what to say, but any way he diced it, the truth felt like betrayal. Rustle gave Aster nothing on which to go.

"Let's talk gems." Aster stuck out his chin and locked eyes with Mr. Oleander, eyes that seemed to have neither shade nor color to them, dark disks set upon little puddles of white. "It's been stolen." Aster stood, holding eye contact, waiting for a reaction.

Not a single line or crease marred Mr. Oleander's face. His lips were poised in the politest smile; nothing too showy, his perfectly aligned teeth tucked away. "I'm going to need you to remedy that. You see, a blood moon approaches, the first to be seen in decades and the last that will grace Thuidium for some time as far as I can tell. I can't let the opportunity pass, so I'll need that gem back before it rises." He patted Rustle's shoulder, turning the friendly touch into a menacing massage. "If there is no gem, there will be no Rustle," he looked Aster in the eyes. "No Aster." He shook Rustle by the shoulder, "And there won't be anyone to bail you out this time, friend."

Mr. Oleander glazed the shop's atmosphere with his noisome chuckle while he stalked amongst the displays mildly checking out the oddments like he was a predator assessing some potential prey.

All of Mr. Oleander's preaching, his voice rife with ambition, had stoked Aster's mind until but one word flooded his conscious thought: accomplishments. The trees had parted and there was the path, stretching out as plain as blood in water.

Mr. Oleander made his way to the exit. The steps of someone unbothered by the thoughts of those who stood by and watched.

Aster peered at Rustle, whose almost imperceptible shake of his head was like a tiny plea to not complicate the existing arrangement. What did Rustle know of desire? The true kind that ached in the soul, beyond the reach of mint and the opinion of others? He didn't know what it felt like to host a desire so fervently that you'd brave fire or stare down the wide open jaws of a ravenous beast.

Aster clenched his fists tightly, grinding his nails into his palms, just to make sure the shaking wouldn't be visible when he finally confessed to this stranger, this Mr. Oleander, his own ambition—the one rooted in the deep places of his psyche. Mr. Oleander needed to know he wasn't the only one with grand designs.

That ravenous beast whom Aster stared down was Mr. Oleander and he was hungry for the gem. The tremors stopped. The nerves settled and a smoothness took hold of Aster's body. "I can get that gem back," he nearly shouted.

Mr. Oleander slowed down but didn't stop.

"You'll need to perform the rite of the Martese for me first." Aster thought he had finished talking. "So how about you come back and we finalize this deal."

Mr. Oleander examined Aster through over the cases. He returned to where Aster stood and noticed the slight trembling. "So you're making demands of me?"

He was in it now, both feet; full immersion. Mr. Oleander's gaze was a hefty thing, as if there was literal mass to it and that mass pressed itself so insistently, two leaded beams stabbing back until blinking promised nothing but pain.

Aster set his posture, aligned his chin with the floor. "I'm just telling you what tool I need to be able to take care of this. From what Rustle has told me, you know how to perform this rite. Give me this and I'll give you the gem that you crave so much."

What Mr. Oleander thought wasn't evident. He stood there with the same stoic stare he'd worn since Aster uttered his—not exactly a demand, was it?—request.

Then a smile cracked open upon Mr. Oleander's face. His marble-like features broke and rippled. He glanced past Aster and nodded at Rustle. "This guy." He clapped Aster upon the shoulder. "I do admire the moxie."

This was probably the right time to relax the tough exterior and join Mr. Oleander in a smiling. Rustle wasn't grinning. He hadn't even pretended to relax. Must have been something in the deep history he shared with Mr. Oleander that kept him donning his usual grin.

Mr. Oleander stepped closer putting hands on both of Aster's shoulders. "I see the ambition in you. That request..." he made air quotes with the word, as if he knew Aster's thought. "It's clear you know what you want and you're prepared to do whatever it takes to get there. We're alike in that regard, and that's why I'm going to do this thing for you." Mr. Oleander winked at him.

He stepped away and surveyed Aster one last time, as if determining how capable he was. A decision had been reached. "Ever hear of the ripened moon?"

Aster's entire store of lore and learning passed in a mental flurry, yet not a single note existed in his memory about various moons.

There was the pearly orb that adorned each night. There were times it shown with an opulent sheen—known as the abundant stage—followed by a cycle of evenings that left it less bright until it looked like a dull rock—the new stage—which was to say: "No, can't say that I have."

"Thought not." Mr. Oleander sighed as a patient teacher would. "A quick lesson in the lunar." He leaned against the counter and sank into the opportunity to instruct Aster. "With the advent of the ever-so-rare blood moon, the new stage will not take place. The abundant moon will dull into a yellow color like a ripe banana. Thus the ripened moon."

Rustle exhaled deeply making room to inhale what came next.

"Delivering my gem before the ripened moon sets is an appropriate deadline, yes?"

If he didn't look so menacing in the eyes it would have been easy to scoff at his claim to the red gem, made so airily. Aster played along by offering a simple nod.

"If the stone isn't in my hand by the deadline, there will be consequences." Mr. Oleander continued in a placid stare. "Life-ending consequences. Downright soul crushing. Right, Rustle?"

Rustle said nothing. He looked like a possum, trying with every muscle to evade detection by a predator.

Mr. Oleander's tone, all silky and fit to be tied into a noose and strangle a person, was all the verification Aster needed that Mr. Oleander offered more than idle threats.

"In two days' time," Mr. Oleander called out as he breezed towards the door. "I expect to see you at my villa. Rustle knows the way."

The entire store—every shelf, every curio, even the very floorboards—almost seemed to unwind in the silence that Mr. Oleander left in his wake. The peace was short-lived as Rustle disrupted the stillness with his fervent packing.

"Stupid," he repeated with every article he crammed into his sack. "Not only did you not listen to me and leave, you got yourself even more entangled with that man."

"Why is that such a big deal? I get what I want. He gets his gem. It's like the theft never happened."

Rustle stilled his hurried movements to take mild pity upon Aster. "He's not a man, not anymore, and that is what you're failing to realize," he said in a frenzied crescendo.

Aster shrugged at the demonstratively exaggerated reply.

"He's a Thanatist. He isn't a dabbler either. His whole existence is this magic. He's deep in it," Rustle whispered, as if Mr. Oleander were still somewhere nearby. "Be cautious of someone who takes pleasure in toying with souls."

"You're the one who arranged for me to meet him. You. You picked him. Maybe you should have warned me before you told him about the gem?"

Rustle slouched against the counter pinching at the bridge of his nose. "Silly me for getting exactly what you wanted, like you kept saying to me, and for thinking you'd keep the gem secure. This could have been much simpler…and safer, I might add…had you just given him the gem." Then, only to himself but loud enough to be heard: "Stupid Thanatists and their unnatural views." Rustle's mumbling ended and the room settled back into a sluggish silence.

There was nothing for it though. The terms had been set. Events were in motion. The reverie melted away, crystallizing into actual plans.

"If we need to…" Aster swallowed hard to taste the idea that skirted on the edge of vocalization, just to make sure it was proper to even speak.

Rustle stopped flitting about and waited for Aster to vomit whatever the suggestion was.

"How about we just ask Rose to find the thief?" The words belied the complexity of the suggestion, logistically and philosophically. The chance that Rustle would see past those complexities and endorse the proposal was slim. He didn't crack a smile: not an encouraging sign.

Rustle closed the space between himself and Aster until the tiny red lines in his eyes were as apparent as the River Crest. He unleashed a wicked sneer. "Even if I could get you to her you wouldn't find the same women you were in love with so just let that fairy-tale go."

Yes, it had been something like a fairy-tale. If only the memory of what she and Aster had started could be evergreen instead of distant, and historical.

It wasn't so, because there was no hiding from the turn of events that had soured the beauty of what they shared, like a slab of meat sat under the sun far too long. There's no point in getting closer to check because it's obvious that the meat has turned, with the gray and green sheen glittering back. Yet, every now and then the temptation to confirm is just too great; there's no way to avoid taking a whiff.

Days spent with Rose, now long past, had been laid down in fluffy tones, days they'd spent talking or just basking in silence as the warm world existed around them. Yet, all that could be recalled of them were smudges forever running away.

Her lips had always been inviting, even in the morning as she cleared the sleep away from her eyes; her thighs were soft; her voice melodic as it described what she saw in a unique way. Every piece of her was like some note in a song that left him speechless, for there was no desire to interrupt her melody. Yet it all suddenly ended, like a hand cleanly severed from the body. Just rawness and pain left behind.

Rustle stepped back as he blinked away the last few words he spoke to Aster. His movements took on a slow, pensive quality as the suggestion of seeking out Rose dissipated.

Aster cut into the silence: "How long will it take to get to Mr. Oleander's villa?"

Rustle sighed. "About a day."

"I will be back first thing tomorrow for directions," Aster said. He then maneuvered towards the door, but before leaving he turned and asked Rustle: "And that ripened moon rises when?"

Rustle's sight was glued to the door, perhaps lost to the doom closing in. "Something you should probably have asked Oleander."

9.

OF MAGIC ELEMENTAL & SOULFUL

The adventure had begun and Aster met it upon a rented mule as he wore an encompassing grin. Had he informed Oren about this agreement with Mr. Oleander? Not a word, no. Was that exactly unethical? Probably not. Oren didn't need to be privy to Aster's every decision and course of action, so Aster carried on without another thought to the opinions of his father.

Astride his little nag, Lamiston shrank to a speck. Down the gentle slope that connected the peninsula to the rest of Thuidium he guided the ass. For many hours his route put Aster parallel to the coast, just a glance away, which rightly looked as if a great weaver had tired and abandoned their loom, for the world looked more like a tapestry than some forged disk. Through wild grasslands Aster traversed until he veered more inland, leaving behind Thuidium's rugged crust. Untamed grasslands rolled out before Aster.

When the sun abandoned the sky, its aureate train slipping slowly towards the Mountains of Lune far away, Aster neared his destination. He urged his steed up a hill. A plateau greeted them as the first phase of night reached up from the west, a deep cobalt canopy chasing away what was left of the sun's shrinking influence. Soon the moon would be resurrected where the sun had just buried itself. Before the land fell completely under the silky sway of night, Aster spotted the villa. It stood there gleaming with white walls and slate-tiled roof.

A slender ribbon of naked dirt, slicing through the turf, led to a front door that was, interestingly, dyed red. Aster paused, staring as he mulled over what it could mean. The silver-cast knocker interrupted the moment. A bear's head intricately wrought in fine details: fur, muzzle, and most notably vicious teeth. A ring drooped from the corners of its maw. Knocking felt like taunting the bear. A silly thought, most certainly. That scowl was doing its job guarding against timid visitors, though. He had been summoned here, and had every right to pass through that door. Aster raised a fist and rapped his knuckles against the cherry-red wood. He waited a brief moment and when he raised his fist to knock again, the door swung back.

"Well met." Mr. Oleander stepped back and gestured Aster in, promptly shutting the door after he was inside. "I admit," he said leading the way down a hall, "I had some doubts about your willingness to follow through." He faced Aster, grinning with full gusto. "Wasn't sure if Rustle had scared you enough into coming."

Eerie was the sound of Mr. Oleander's humor. "No." For some reason the word just flopped out as the most important word in that moment. It was his sword and shield. Was Mr. Oleander foe, though? "That wasn't necessary. I was on board when you agreed to perform the rite of the Martese for me. No need to put fear in me." Aster stood there in the middle of that hall looking up and down. "Interesting sketches."

Perfectly square frames lined the wall, filled with images drawn in what appeared to be charcoal. Their various shades of darkness, along with use of negative space, added depth to subjects as varied as words themselves. Some even appeared beyond description.

Mr. Oleander dispensed casual glances to a sketch or two. "Feats of magic, don't you know. Not simple ones either, so I began to commemorate each accomplishment."

Aster passed from one image to the next, daring to take in just a visual nibble of each graphic. Even in their flat state the drawings had a volume to them. They reached out in silence, daring any observer to peel over their details and assign an interpretation.

The final composition in this march of madness focused on a figure expertly drawn with realistic proportions and curves, holding a rose, rendered in painstaking detail. Yet, there was no face; a curious choice, in the same way that one would be curious about an angry wound. Aster leaned in to be sure of what he saw. From every stroke, each line, leaked a mood that could only be described as defiant loss.

Aster recoiled and glanced at Mr. Oleander who shrugged. There was more to this last drawing.

A sense of life had been tethered to the page swelling behind the inanimate lines. A faint voice seeped out from between the charcoal and paper. Maybe it belonged to the figure? Or was that sound a trick of the background, erratic scribbles that looked like the etchings of a spoiled child in the midst of a tantrum?

"You dabble in the magical arts," Mr. Oleander said, "but are you privy to the way it all works?" Even though Aster began to marshal his response, Mr. Oleander delivered his point without space for conversation. "You sing to the elements and they obey, etcetera, right? Anyone who knows how to throw dirt without a spade gets that. It's truly disconcerting and, honestly, a bit offensive that people don't care about the histories or the reasons behind the power. Knowing these the details makes me what one would call prodigious."

His voice rang with a certainty that felt inflated, too big for any room or roof to hold. He told the world that he had invented the world. Every natural law was his concept.

His gaze fixated on the image. "They just want the results. That is what binds all the other practitioners to their elementary level of magic. I grew and increased in knowledge, elevating my power. Not for the sake of power itself, mind you. You recognized this. It's why you knew you needed my help."

Aster politely nodded. Hopefully a bed awaited somewhere around the corner where the hallway ended. The day had been a long one of being jostled by an ungraceful beast. The aches began to settle into his back, his hips, and across his shoulder. Aster longed to put his body down and let sleep do its reparative magic. Let the education begin on the marrow.

Mr. Oleander remained unrelenting in his elucidation. "It's called the Magic of Life because Life loves a new arrangement of the elements. Life was the first to create. Took the raw elements, arranged and fabricated." It was then that Mr. Oleander peeled his glance away from the sketch and gave Aster all his attention. "Do you think Life lost all potential? Created all that there ever will be? Ever could be?"

"Ah, well—" What was there to say to such a leaden question, heavier than most metals and stone? Mr. Oleander was not being rhetorical, staring at Aster. "I'm sure there are always new creations to be thought up."

"That's right, Aster. Don't forget it. You can't shackle the urge to create. Artists. Inventors. They will have their way."

That statement struck more like a threat than mere philosophy. Aster cleared his throat. "Learn something new every day. I take it you have thoughts on the Magic of Death, then?"

Mr. Oleander's reply held a note of surprise. "Not so dense, are you?"

Was that the impression he had given Mr. Oleander? Of an ignorant rural peasant? Or maybe Mr. Oleander just thought of Aster as a child play-acting as a capable practitioner? Either way, the revelation was a touch insulting.

Mr. Oleander offered a consolatory smile to Aster as they finally turned a corner and met a door immediately to their right. "Magic of Death. Well, yes. Two sides of a coin and all that." Mr. Oleander gave Aster's shoulder an exuberant pat. "The fatigue is pretty blatant in your face, so here is your room for the night. First thing tomorrow morning, my little protégé, we'll marry you to an element."

The offer of a full night's rest was more promising than the Martese at the moment. Mr. Oleander pushed the door back, revealing a room that was furnished with naught but a bed.

And more sketches.

Aster sat himself down upon the edge of the bed, not relinquishing the drawings from his attention.

"They make you uneasy," observed Mr. Oleander.

"Not in any serious way, no," Aster said with a shrug.

Not altogether honest; there were moments wherein it made more sense to clutch the truth tightly, protecting it from exposure. Not that this situation warranted dishonesty, but to admit that the drawings reminded Aster of the end, of danger, and of pain was an admission that Mr. Oleander—let alone many people with whom he was far more intimate—didn't deserve.

Mr. Oleander stared at Aster in ponderous silence. It was a stare that felt like working in a kitchen without a single chimney or opening to release the oppressive heat of relentless fires. Aster stirred on the mattress hoping to break away from Mr. Oleander's accusing glance.

"No offense to you and your practices," Aster finally put out. "The drawings just make this form of magic seem much more dangerous."

Mr. Oleander kept a placid expression. "No. Not really," was his deadpan reply.

Aster looked past Mr. Oleander and timidly glanced at one of the illustrations. The shapes were lost to the world of light; perhaps that was the spell? A human head in silhouette as if it were one with the space that surrounded it. This subject, this personage, shielded itself against an immaterial force with hands pressed to its eyes, where sockets would be, hoping not to fall into some nightmare.

Aster tried all at once to understand and ignore the essence of what he saw. Minute objects, animals or worse, clawed and climbed out, squeezing between fingers. Drawn as small as they were, the skill of the artist was such that their gaping jaws and awkward teeth were not hidden from detection.

Mr. Oleander stepped back. "Death isn't inherently destructive, just as Life isn't always creative. Think about it: has dying presented a the path to an end?"

Deciphering between rhetorical questions and queries that were wanting of a reply proved to be a challenge. The line between the two didn't exist, as if Mr. Oleander decided which way the question was to go only after he posed it. A second or two passed, with Mr. Oleander taking in the drawings.

Aster ventured on with a thought: "Then why do all your pictures look that way?"

"That way." Mr. Oleander clucked. "Can't be all flowers, birds, and deer." He pointed to the drawing of the imprint of a human mind on the brink of madness. "It is kind of nice to see a person who can protect against an invading nightmare."

Like everyone else, Aster had heard wild tales about Thanatists, practitioners who were portrayed as draped in the skin of the dead, sleeping with the dead, toying with the remains of the dead.

Mr. Oleander could have hardly been confused for such a character, at first glance. His appearance was all too lively. Still, there was something about the tinkle in his voice when he spoke of the Magic of Death, the thing commonly referred to as Thanatos, verifying the gossip about him. Aster's grasp on his "live and let live" philosophy started to slip like fingers trying to hold to a chicken cooked in lard.

The drawing looked as though it would start howling and wailing at any moment. Despite the decrepit depictions, the horrendous intimacy of the details, those images were just slightly wondrous. The power the represented? The creativity in the use of magic?

"You need some sort of song to make all this...to happen?"

"Those silly songs and chants make magic seem all amusing and whimsical, don't they?" Mr. Oleander said. "Let's just say that the Magic of Death is more mature."

Aster scanned the rest of the images. There was one that griped Aster's attention. Where all the others sketches were merely black, white, and gray, dollops of red punctuated this drawing, like drops of blood frozen in an instant.

It looked quite like a mushroom with a cap that had a vaguely familiar shape; it was there on the tip of Aster's tongue. He knew what it was but seeing it stacked upon the spine of a fungus like that caused him to doubt. It's not that, is it? After more scrutiny, there was no denying that the mushroom's cap had a slightly toothy shape to it, dotted with those points of blood-red.

"Ah, Death Tooth mushroom has caught your eye, has it?" Mr. Oleander walked up to the drawing, blocking the view of it.

"That is the difference between the Magic of Life and the practice of Thanatos. This one little mushroom. The difference between your average practitioner and a Thanatist is the will to devour this ghastly fungus." He turned and stared. Not at Aster, but through him, back to some other time and place. "Many lose their sanity after ingesting the Death Tooth, but those of us with strong wills ascend in consciousness. We gain sight beyond the elemental and see the essence of living beings. It's why we have the capacity for this soul-magic."

Aster leaned over a bit, getting another glimpse of the apparently powerful fungus.

"I rarely get to tell this story." Mr. Oleander planted himself next to Aster and they sat there, about six inches apart, both upright gazing at the rendered Death Tooth. "It's lost to all but the hardiest scavengers of lore. Like most miracles in our world, it begins with the Truce. You remember that, don't you?"

Aster nodded, his eyes glued to the sketch, not sure whether to be in awe of Mr. Oleander's knowledge or afraid of how much he had dared to discover.

"In the midst of the great Truce between Life and Death, before the two Powers sealed their agreement by mingling their blood, a bit of blood escaped Death's wounded hand and settled on an unsuspecting fungus. How this escaped notice is anyone's guess, but the blood was stuck and the fungus now harbored a bit of Death itself. Its spores carried that gift to future generations. It's rare, but an intrepid soul will find one." He nudged Aster with an elbow in a jovial way before taking leave without so much as a good night.

The atmosphere in the room went catatonic. The deviant pictures hung upon the wall daring Aster to be bold enough to sleep the night in their presence.

10.

INTERLUDE: A DISCOURSE ON NAMES BY LIFE & DEATH

Their realm was filled with the hints and shapes of nature, not nature itself. The elements were for mortals. Life and Death languished in the iridescence, which constituted their layer, as if the whole thing had been peeled right off an opal.

"Why is that, I wonder?" Life wondered out loud. "It made no sense why we are consigned to this shell of a world while the mortals enjoy the splendor of our creation."

Death happened to be near, hearing the loud wondering. "My creation."

Something of a flinch passed across Life's features. What it said was beyond even the recognition of Death.

"I created the elements, lest you forget." Death saw the flaccid expression on Life's face. "Which clearly you have. You just happened to toy around with them."

Life cogitated on that statement and found naught to argue with. "Truly. I suppose that was how it all went."

"You ask why entirely too often. More than is good for you." For Death was not one to question why, but to simply be and do.

Life chuckled. "I doubt that there is much that is genuinely bad for an immortal being, cut right from the cloth of the Universe itself." Life reached out, grazing the shimmering atmosphere. "Such a vast, incomprehensible concept is the Universe."

"Yet here we are," Death commented. "Defined. Intended."

Life stopped grinning. "I know. It's what the mortals would call insane."

Death saw the puzzling on Life's face, as if another question stewed just below the surface of that face. Poor vapid being couldn't quite put it into words.

"I've always longed for the mortals to call me something other than Life, though."

Random, but a thought that they had in common. "Yes. Bless their myopic hearts, those mortals with their uncouth titles and names. Death," the word had to be practically spat and tasted something wicked on its way out.

"Such an infertile name they gave you. I always found your original name far more musical." Life looked Death in the face. "Imfa has more gusto behind it."

Death smiled. "The name of a creator."

"Wonder why they call you Death, though?"

That blasted question again: why? Who cares? Life, that's who. Cares and queries about the reason. Always been like that, since the elements came into being. Since the first souls were fashioned.

Death fought back a sigh. "Why do they call you Life?"

The volleyed question put Life to task, the search for an answer radiating and polluting the iridescent surroundings with waves of confusion.

"Point is," Death said, patting Life on the knee, "doesn't matter. You'll always be Elu. I'll always be Imfa. To them in their layer, they name us by how they see us. You're apparently an artist."

"And you?"

Death took a moment to sit with the distinction, which had been laid out. "I guess I'm the destination."

There wasn't another word spoken between the two for a while. The silence embraced the immortals in coziness. Then Life shifted and parted lips, marshaling another string of words. Death braced for more questions.

"Must be why they speak of elemental manipulation as if it is mine." Life beamed a little with the statement.

"Magic." Another word via the mortals that Death choked up.

"And." Life continued, beaming still, "why you get the mysterious branch of magic."

Death had naught else to say on the topic. "That blood is still on the loose. Have you sought the Stewards to secure it?"

Life pondered. "Don't recall. What I do know is that the layers are balanced. Souls come and they go. We've nothing to fear from that blood floating about. They wouldn't know what to do with it anyways."

"You say that but they figured out elemental manipulation." Death grimaced, "And some have even dared to manipulate souls themselves. You fail to give mortals the credit they are due. The Universe did design them, after all."

"You're the consummate worrier, Death." With a wink, Life trailed away to some other corner of the layer.

Death remained, cursing mortals for that title.

11.

OF RITES &

REJECTIONS

Aster sat up in the loaned bed and slowly woke from what seemed like sufficient rest. He'd know better after he shook away the fatigue, a process that lost all smoothness under the impertinent gaze of four decrepit images. A decade of abiding with them wouldn't have eased their presence. Every sketched eye—full of machinations against the very essence of humanity—leered back, dredging up the memories of her face while she stood over a young Aster, her own eyes full of the same mischief as these drawings.

The realization pitched Aster from the bed, and he hurried away from the room and the depictions of confusing bouts of magic. Hurried right into Mr. Oleander who stood in the hall poised to knock.

"Ready to get going? Good." Mr. Oleander turned away from Aster. "I like ambition in the morning. In fact..." He peeped back around the corner. "It's the best way to break fast."

There was gurgling from Aster's stomach was a plea that Mr. Oleander was joking and not being literal.

Alas, the direction Mr. Oleander took was not towards a kitchen or anything resembling one. It wasn't even towards a smoke house, or storage of fodder. He had been literal.

What a nuisance this endeavor proved to be.

They cut a quick trail around the villa and made for a little pond a dozen or so yards away, like a lone bead of glass among the grass. Or maybe it had been dropped from some other time and place. It looked peculiar, so far from any other water source. Why, Mr. Oleander could have created this pond himself. The way he admired his reflection in the water, it was quite possibly the truest explanation.

Mr. Oleander tasted the atmosphere. He unwound from around his shin and ankle the straps that bound the hard-leather soles to his narrow feet. He inhaled the earth and flicked a naked toe into the water. "Good enough. Nature is ready. Are you?"

Trick question? Ominous declaration? The sun shed light abroad like a fried yolk cracked open. How could one not be ready under the obscene amount of sunshine, coupled with that timid brush of air passing by every now and then.

"The sooner we get this done, the sooner I can get on."

"Aster, this isn't a one-night lay with a quick climax and you're on your way." His hands were heavy, heavier than they looked, as they each massaged a shoulder. "How are you at flirting? At wooing?"

"I, uh…wooing?"

"I thought so." He slipped off his outer shirt—linen from the look of its texture—exposing a fitted crossover jacket made of a light material, dyed to match the cobalt of a summer night sky. The absence of sleeves revealed arms of tightly woven muscle.

"No, I do just fine."

"You know enough to get them to your hovel, undressed, and spread for you, perhaps, but do you know enough to get them to call out your name?" Mr. Oleander drew in closer, dropped his voice. "Do you know how to make a woman's eyes roll back until all you see are the whites of her eyes as she pleads the name of Life?"

Aster leaned away from the assault of questions, that stirred up the list of recent trysts and how they had played out. Not very deep, just sex. Direct and, perhaps, a bit self-serving.

"Yes," Mr. Oleander surmised, as if Aster's thoughts had spilled out onto the grass. "You're beginning to recognize that you never knew the difference." He gathered Aster with an arm ushering him closer to the pond. "But that's well, friend. You can't get anywhere unless you know how to recognize the ineffective from the effective. So..." The water was painted with a glossy version of the sky. "If you don't mind me keeping with the sexual metaphor, I'm going to teach you a way to do more than copulate, shall we say, with the elements." He seemed pleased at his wit. "We'll send you into the very essence of a particular element. When it's right, an intimacy forms to the point of complete and total cooperation by that element." He nearly leered at the sky. "A submission, really."

"Uh, truly," Aster said with a single nod. The information made sense. It was all that he wanted and expected out of this rite. "What should I do first?" Aster couldn't see any artifacts to grab or a scroll to unroll. There was just an abundance of unmolested nature. It was a good start: all the elements present for testing.

"I have a pretty good idea of where you'll end up but to be sure I want to run you through the whole gamut." He paused and studied Aster for a moment.

This was going to feel like learning about magic all over again: wonder and dread exchanging secrets as they coated the situation, with nary a line to tell where one began and the other ended. Their invasion was allowed as a party of two.

"Air first," Mr. Oleander decided. The ritual had begun. And it began with air?

"To become bonded with an element through the Martese, you're going to have to find the element with which you can be uninhibited with. The one that doesn't scare you, but inspires your imagination."

The tone in which Mr. Oleander instructed complicated the elements. Dallying in spells had made air—and the others—seem rather like tools as opposed to entities carrying out favors. It was the first time that the dominance of air became noticeable. Defining an element that was so eminent became impossible. There was no encapsulating it in regards to its presence nor by its absence, because it was never absent, unless you resided in a layer where the elements were not.

Mr. Oleander clapped Aster on the back, causing him to start. "Who in their right mind would be scared of air?"

He stopped, dropped his hand, his dark eyes—with flecks of gold, making them look like the night sky—went fixed. They didn't widen. They didn't narrow; they just looked. His lips were drawn as the skin around his face and eyes sat undisturbed, smoothed like his face had been carved from granite. "You don't know the full power of the elements if you aren't scared of them right now."

"What if none of them scare me?" Aster's mouth began to draw up into a bit of a smirk.

"You aren't fit for this then, Aster." His pointed tone drove away any additional arguments or attempts at levity.

"Fair," Aster whispered back.

Mr. Oleander smiled solemnly. "Aster, trust me on this. Take it one moment at a time. You're going to be intimidated by the power of these elements. One of them will draw out your curiosity more than the rest, like a new lover. You'll fear that one special element like you fear disappointing a woman, or not seeing the sun rise. Take your pick of imagery."

The sudden solitude dawned on Aster, far from help should he care to call for any. Something about Mr. Oleander's focus made the realization less concerning. Mr. Oleander nodded. Aster replied in kind.

Mr. Oleander's voice distilled softly like an invocation, his voice a spell unto itself:

> *Unknit the streams and fields.*
> *One familiar world.*
> *Into a whisper*
> *Particulars cast.*
> *Steel your lungs against*
> *Pow'r of tongues now and past.*
> *Steel your crown against*
> *The shape of thoughts vast,*
> *That friends you may make*
> *Of element queer.*

He concluded the spell and stopped breathing until his face—no, his whole head—was sucked away. The rest of Mr. Oleander's body followed, then the grass before the very sky itself had been siphoned into some pocket of space and time away from the measurement of Aster's eyes and feet.

Blankness: out of all the words ever conceived since language began, it's the only one in the moment that exists, that can sum this new state.

It is not being. It is not a moment. There's no way to form such words, let alone the idea of them.

These lungs have capacity for naught but breathing. In and out.

Each exhalation rips away, like prisoners bounding towards freedom. They tear, those little puffs of bandits, gushing an indistinct babble of relief. Their babbling carries on, down a road that isn't there, because of blankness.

What is a road, after all?

The word won't come out. Just more escapees. Even attempting to evict it—ruh, ruh, roa—doesn't work. It won't come to fruition. R—rrrr. Nope.

"No words," comes a whisper out of the blankness, not the sort of whisper that's meant to dampen its voice. This whisper, a melodious baritone pitch, is growing; it slithers into awareness—slipping in easier than mussel slips out of a shell—which, such a thing sounds nicer than it is: seductive, affirming.

"Wherein the peak of time, I find a new friend. Care to play?"

Play? Play how? What in Death's Realm are you talking about?

It slides in noticeable, but non-intrusive. It's hinting at touch, but much more than that, miles and miles towering above the idea of touch and what that entails. All the connotations, the implications, and the applications crushing down on each shoulder. And this voice, in all its silken delivery, spreads across the atmosphere so there is no way to tell from whence it reaches, or how to avoid its weight: "You play with me. Are you not friend?"

Friend. What a wheezy puff of an attempt, stillborn speech.

"Let's see what you have to play with." Blankness glides away like some loosely tied robe. Falling off, falling for eternity.

How do you mean play? What's going on?

Ethereal, as intangible as time—but less so because time can be felt—this molesting whisper gropes its way deeper than any dream, wider than any wish, filling all of perception until not even breath has room. The escapees hush their cheers. Their sudden absence stokes panic. They tremble and cry until they die. Is this what death—?

No room left to ask questions. The whisper eats it all, gorging itself on the mere hope of room…

Aster gasped and groped for as much air as he could while he shoved Mr. Oleander out of his face. "What the…" he heaved. "What in all of Life's light was that?"

Mr. Oleander sat back on his haunches. "Air is not your element."

The grass was prickly. Aster rippled some from the soil just to be sure it was there. The sun bristled in the sky. Colors shoved their way back into his life: green, blue, yellow, and all the shade in between. Aster repeated words to himself, just to make sure he remembered them all and knew wherein to place them. Mr. Oleander stood back with a studious glance fixed on Aster, his dark eyes made darker against the sunshine.

"That was like a bad trip in the middle of a bad dream." The effect of which settled only slowly. It took a few breaths for Aster to regain a sense or normalcy and for his heart to ease its hurried beat.

Mr. Oleander studied Aster for a moment longer, roving over him with pursed lips and a furrowed brow.

After a moment of deliberation, he squatted back down. "We can call it if you want."

And with that one question their interaction melted from strictly transactional into a form that was a bit more personal.

"No," Aster cleared his throat to purge the tremble out of his voice. He stood, dusted away the bits of grass clinging to his pants, and looked Mr. Oleander in the eye. "Let's get on to the next one. Probably gets easier. Right?"

Mr. Oleander took a few steps away from where Aster now stood, and cleared his throat:

Bound into shape

Is your current state.

Eroded be time.

Dissolved be all garb.

Naked bosom leached

Until distillate

Most dear condensates,

Affect most fair

Found dry of tear by

Element most clear.

The words flowed from Mr. Oleander in a fluid pace. They were moving but not going anywhere.

It feels right, too. Not exactly knowing what it is. In this place, there's no room to think about, or imagine, the *it*. There's just the feel, the rightness...and a smile.

A smile that flows out reaching into little corners, where it pools until little ponds of chipper sentiment form. They spill out of place cascading into what is limpid.

That's all. Unformed, uninformed; no stage nor setting. There's just this notion of shape and space.

Crystalline drops of laughter tinkle into the limpid space. Ripples racing to tell the rest of the place—for place it surely is—of the contributions. Sound contributions too, genuine in form.

The smile persists.

Until it doesn't.

When it fails and the laughter stills, as if all existence has been gutted of mirth, the shapes calm into placidity, a blanket that stirs not.

Not until the shape of a hand peruses with such tenderness, as another smile bubbles up, and that smile grows into a cheek that's cupped by this mysterious hand, and an ear springs forth which the lithe fingers toy with. It's all tactile.

There's no face to receive, just a touch, a caress, born from nothing but a reaction. Alien hand belonging to no arm, just attending a body, isn't the sort of lover any sane person would welcome. Time to let go of this smile because it's corrupt.

The smile is dismissed and, unlike the laughter, splashes and spouts all over, a sputtering and tinkling all the way. Anything to disrupt this malaise of tenderness. It runs, a current of feeling that needs to be sluiced away. Quick swipes to shove it down to join the larger body again.

The once still and a pleasant environment, roils: tempest-tossed and cool.

Coolness creeps into cold, a slap to the senses. Nerves cower and then die, refusing to feel out what's happening. Every last sensation is swallowed, one meter at a time, until the very idea of feeling is choked.

Aches are obsolete. Pain so far in the past, it becomes myth. What's a response anyways? With anger drowned, along with hope and fear, nothing is left. Drowned, choked out of existence…

A gush of water had been forced out of his mouth unbeknown to Aster, who coughed it up, right down the front of his shirt. Choked coughing and strands of spit followed out over Aster's lips. After a time, when the panic had subsided and the coughs were just deeps breaths, Aster sat trying to wring-out his saturated garb.

"Water isn't it either." Mr. Oleander pushed off Aster's chest on his way back to standing. "You know, you may not last through the final two."

Aster sat, arms wrapped about his knees, as the water-soaked clothes latched to his skin. "There's going to be one of these that doesn't try to kill me, no?"

Mr. Oleander shrugged.

"Meaning?" Aster's eyes paused any and all blinking as his brows scrunched.

"Meaning, it's not a sure thing that you end up with a happy little Martese." Aster's expression sagged and melted as his lips turned down and his shoulders slumped. "Most of the time there's going to be one element that you bond with, but there are times, Aster, when it isn't going to happen. Fair warning."

After a final sputtering cough Aster rose and let the sun caress him wantonly. "Earth next?"

Mr. Oleander grinned:

> *Delivered away from voice and from heart.*
> *Nary a song nor kiss or story*
> *That you may digest the fact that bones are hard.*
> *For, veins of answers are bled in the dark,*
> *In the element that vomits pretend.*

Then began a pulsing and throbbing, like the beating of a mammoth heart, rubbing over every particle of Aster's existence.

Not the throbbing of some pregnant storm or the stirring cadence of a legion of soldiers marching in one rhythm. The homeopathic, soothing tempo of a mother's heartbeat shakes existence, like one big child needing to be put to sleep. The pulsing rattles every pebble, every grain of sand. There's something ever-so familiar about this sensation, like a symbol that is known collectively even if there isn't a personal memory of ever having experienced it.

Yet, all at once the beating stops and a stillness resumes, like the stillness of mountains looking down upon a valley; an examining stillness, keen with patience stacking into a compost heap of disappointment and wasted expectations. There remains only room for the culmination of intensity, as if a long-awaited climax is scaling ragged cliffs.

There's not even room for that maternal smile. Some sort of judgment is made and the smile crumbles into tolerance; tolerance decomposes into decision. The mother sighs; enough is enough for there is only time for the steady. The consistent. The substantial. The hills roll and the soil parts like a mouth ready to make a pronouncement.

Into a pit that is a void, blanker than blank could have ever been…

"That trip was a lot quicker than the others," Mr. Oleander said with a half-hearted chuckle as he patted Aster on the back.

The dirt was thick under Aster's nails, as if he had clawed his way out of the ground. He sat there examining the dark strips before staring at the scores, like defensive wounds, in the turf around where he sat. Aster pinched his eyes shut against the residual ache in his head, clenching his teeth until the throbbing let him be. "Not Earth, for sure. Fire it is."

"Let's not get ahead of ourselves." Mr. Oleander pulled out a slip of parchment. "Still need to meet the element. You don't see a woman across the square and assume she'll hitch herself to you. Right?"

"Oh, no. Nope, definitely not the way it works."

"No," Mr. Oleander confirmed.

Aster rose and waited. "I'm ready. Show me fire."

"This is fire," Mr. Oleander waved the folded parchment at Aster. "And you won't be meeting it—"

Mr. Oleander's words pushed and pulled levers inside Aster. There was a sense of falling, like all the parts that were supposed to stay above his waist plummeted to his feet while the muscles in his face didn't know whether to twitch, twist, or sag. At the same time, the heat in his body surged.

"—yet," Mr. Oleander concluded.

12.

OF SALTY MEMORIES

The ride back to Lamiston was a blur. Aster rushed as quickly as was reasonable for the lumbering ass upon which he sat. The beast was promptly returned to the stables and Aster put his long legs to task, for there was much to be done in preparation for the pending journey. It was all so burdensome. Not the logistics or planning; that would be the easy part.

Mr. Oleander dangling the final piece that would help Aster solve the fire fruit puzzle—making it a prolific plant—was the rudest machination with which anyone had ever hit Aster. It made sense from Mr. Oleander's point of view, securing the investment first; the thought that didn't ease the sting or quell the fire within, the one that seem to be propelling every stride Aster took.

He almost gained the western archway, when a familiar voice caused a hitch in his step. Aster turned on his heel at the sound of Pixee's voice.

"What is it?" He called back.

Her short legs sped her across the square. She stopped and looked as if she had a thought poised on her lips, but whatever she had intended to say was left unsaid and replaced with a scrutinizing glance at Aster's sweat speckled, grime-streaked face.

"You're up to something."

Aster's eyes darted around the square in search of a distraction, any clue with which to take this conversation in some other direction; away from the truth. "Not up to anything. I mean, I've got stuff to take care." He bit into his bottom lip, shoved his hands deep into his pockets, maybe deeper than they had capacity for. "Been taking care of stuff," he said in a lethargic tone.

Pixee fixed him with a potent stare. "The sort of stuff that keeps you away from the Den for days?"

Aster slowly restarted his stride, so as not to appear like a startled rabbit. "First of all, I let Twiggy know I was going to need some time away. I've just been seeing a guy about some magical training, is all."

She matched his steps. "Not Oren?"

"No, not Oren. There are other people who know stuff."

They passed under the archway and continued down the dirt lane. Aster tempered his pace into a gait that was more mild, more of a stroll than a trot.

"Are you going to make me keep tugging out little bits of information or will you just say it?"

Pixee had been a friend in the truest sense of the word for years and years. She even lent a hand with some magical education, but this inquiry—more like inquisition—rattled some nerves.

"What does it even matter?" Aster quickened his pace.

Pixee hurried alongside Aster. "See, the fact that you're hesitant to share what you've been up to tells me that you feel some kind of guilt or shame about it. What's her name?" She quieted for a moment, just enough to crunch out a few dozen more steps. "Or his name?" She chuckled in self-satisfaction.

Aster stopped. "I don't feel any guilt. I'm just…it feels like you're checking on me and I don't need it. I've got shit to take care of." He fumbled with the next thought. Quite reactionary, but it was what followed and Aster didn't fight too hard to stop it. "You're not my mother."

The words flew out like they had been launched by a catapult. Pixee's face remained stationary which was more dubious than a cascade of tears or a knot of lines. Any hint as to what she thought about the verbal retaliation would have been better than her impassive reprisal, but Aster didn't bother waiting to find out what brewed behind her eyes. He sighed and struck off once again.

Before he made it too far, she called after him. He slowed but didn't stop. Let her make up the distance.

She was right there, alongside his strident gait. "I'm not here to be your mother. I did tell her I would always help look after you, so if it seems like I'm checking on you, it's because I am."

He peered down at her. The unabashed admission nearly arrested Aster's stride. He bumbled his step, but salvaged his momentum and carried on.

"It's the sort of relationship she and I had," Pixee said, as if his mother had been around this whole time and they had recently sat down for a plate and a cup.

"I have a father for that," he said with some effort.

"Yes. You do, but…" she shrugged a bit. "A little help along the way wouldn't hurt. Not that a former Steward wasn't be capable of raising a child."

Pixee eased up and glanced at Aster, as though he should have known.

"I have to go." Aster left Pixee in his dusty wake.

He hadn't known, though. That slice of trivia, a silenced life experience kept from his very own son, was too cumbersome a deception. It made walking laborious scraping against the packed dirt was enough. There was no room to remember how to torque a muscle when the preponderance of being...being deceived shrouded every thought and function; a brain cornered.

Aster's lips, slightly ajar, sagged as the drying corners begged for a swipe of a moistened tongue. There was an attempt to summon some saliva from a throat that felt like it was filled with sand. Every attempt to clear the feeling ended in wordless grunts. Better grunts than truths that would spill too much honestly in front of Pixee. No, these feelings were best suited for one person and the longer this revelation rattled around the more stodgy the sense of offense became calcifying his plodding steps into a determined stride. This wasn't right—it's what a stranger didn't know—especially when all they had was each other. The splinter needed removing before it festered into resentment. Or worse.

Aster trotted down the hill and across the sand. Oren was there on the porch, whittling away at some driftwood. No real surprise there. What would his hands work out of that supposedly lost piece?

The knife caught Aster's eye, flecked with slivers and dirt.

"Doing well, Aster?" Oren set aside his project.

Aster wretched his focus away from the knife and hoisted it upon Oren. "You spend your whole life with a person—" Those weren't exactly the words he wanted to say.

The words he wanted to use—words with serrated edges—he swallowed hard, almost chocking them back up, as his cheeks bloomed warm and crimson. That was when the pools of saline budded in the corners of his eyes.

Every blink was an attempt to dam the tears in. "Emulating them as much as possible because you admire him—"

Oren lowered his piece of driftwood and raised himself from his chair to a height greater than Aster remembered. And his eyes. Once cool as a mountain lake, they now looked dark like the churning sea encased behind glass, so tight was the focus in his glance. The deep, fatherly lines of his face were smoothed out into a visage that was glossy and unfamiliar with all of its sternness. He was over there, like he just walked out of some story of legend, with his hand curled around his knife with an unsettling amount of comfort. The thought clapped: did Aster really know this man? His eyes told him no, he hardly knew who this person was, the man beneath those eyes.

"What are you saying?"

Under the commanding stare of his father Aster took a half–step back, his chest no longer puffed-up with a sense of righteous indignation. "Why didn't you ever tell me you had been part of the Order of the Stewards? How…"

Oren's glance veered away. There, at the crest of the hill that was the road stood Pixee. "Oh, I see," he muttered.

He approached, lending the full weight of his focus to Aster, his eyes were little puddles fit to be drowned in. "The most important part of my life wasn't being ordained into the Order. It wasn't being the portal for Life and Death into this layer. You—" he gripped the top of Aster's arm. "You are the most important part of my life."

"And mom?"

"She was." Oren's hands slipped from Aster and hung feebly at his side. "You're here."

"You always do that," Aster's voice rumbled out.

"Do what?"

"You always talk about mom like she never existed." Aster stepped away from Oren, meant to walk to some other spot then stopped. "I lost her too."

Oren's mouth fumbled with the sound of words, contorting around what he had intended to say, but nothing came out. Instead he walked away, taking himself closer to the cliffs. There was a crooked border where the sand turned to packed dirt, which turned to rock; the rock jutted out pointing at the sea and its matchless volume.

As Oren reached that line where the sand failed, a tremor shook the inner most mind of Aster. A memory whispering with the punch of a winter wind came in pieces, miscellaneous details like her breath piping in an even tempo; even above the sigh of the ocean it could be heard. She wore a simple white dress—probably of a light material, he couldn't recall that detail—with sleeves that flared like a bell. Those sleeves flowed gaily; just another stroll under the sun's peerless presence. Then came the last glimpse of her eyes as she gazed over her shoulder with certainty—eyes the color of grass that has not tasted rain in weeks—before she disappeared over the cliff.

A tremor crept stole through Aster. It intensified. Maybe no breathing would halt the process of recall. Beads of sweat grazed down his back and no amount of shifting could wipe them away. The memory deserved no attribution; rather, it needed to be pushed out of reach from whatever mechanism picked up memories and brought them forward. This memory was venom, pervasive and potent—smelling of the sea—spreading faster with every attempt to ignore it, clawing its way from every direction, out to every appendage. They tingled with it, but what was to be done with this feeling, both paralyzing and goading?

Oren drew closer to that spot casting his glance off into blue vastness of sea and sky. He peered back at Aster. His lips moved, but the sound failed, conquered by the swoosh of the ocean and that rumbling deep inside Aster's psyche. Oren resumed studying the sea. He made a slight step. A step too far.

The tremulous memory spurred Aster away from the little cabin, racing to meet Oren, who had inched closer to the edge. Aster dropped his shoulder and wrapped his arms around his father, tackling him from the side. They landed on the ground, away from the cliff.

"You don't get to do that to me," Aster sobbed. There was more to say, but words felt like useless sounds with no room to carry any amount of water.

Oren stilled his rapid breathing as he recovered from the impact. The corners of his mouth fell. "I'm sorry, son. I didn't realize how deep your wound was. I just...I also come here when I'm lost or confused." Oren slipped a hand around to the back of Aster's neck and drew his son close. Their foreheads touched. "I wasn't going to do anything. Not to you. I would never do that to you."

A shaking started in Aster's chest as sobs yearned for release. "Why did she?"

Oren's face blurred. Aster pinched his eyes closed as the tears scurried down his cheeks.

The cabin looked just as it had all through Aster's life: two pieces of furniture in the main area, pointed towards a fireplace, and a table stood near the little kitchen with a bedroom off to the side. It was like walking into a hug.

Oren handed Aster a cup filled with hot tea, it smelled of mint and some other scent Aster couldn't place. He inhaled the aroma wafting from the water as Oren sank into that old armchair, probably as old as he; it welcomed his body perfectly as Oren relaxed into the grooves carved out by years of sitting. The fire, fed by driftwood, peeled away the feeling of loneliness that had invaded Aster outside.

"It's always going to feel like she did it to you," Oren softly offered.

Aster lowered his cup and nodded. He knew that. Still, he didn't want that statement to touch his ears. "I feel like we haven't talked about mom in years."

"I didn't think it was right to bring up your mother's death. It seemed that the less you thought about it, the better. And I knew that's what you would remember first and last when you tried to think of her."

Aster sipped his tea. "I have other memories."

Oren waited, a patient stare reaching out. Aster only had eyes for his tea as he dove for one of those memories, any memory of his mother that didn't involve her death. Or even magic. He took another sip.

Oren looked back at the flames. "I know my approach was all wrong." His glance hopped back to Aster.

Aster just shrugged. "I don't know what to do with that, Dad. You sort of trained me to get to work when I had flashbacks of her, to what she did. Now, when I'm faced with the image of her standing at those cliffs or the memory of her putting me in that hole in the ground, I fall apart because I—" He quickly let the still-hot tea race down his throat.

Oren patted Aster's knee. "I know. It's my fault that you can't deal with those memories. By Life's eye, your first thought when I approached those cliffs was that I'd cast myself over?" He chuckled, but it was a grim sound as his eyes glistened. "I've certainly failed you. When you feel confused or angry about it, you can blame me. You should." He stared back into fire.

As the light outside waned, the flames increased in luminescence. They almost hurt to look at as night came on. It felt like the right time to finally say it all, let the thoughts and feelings effuse into the open. Maybe they were both ready to handle a conversation about how Allium died? There was only one way to test that idea.

"I keep seeing her smiling down," Aster said over the crackle and pop of the fire, as it ate away at the wood. "I'm looking up and she is smiling down like she would when she was just tucking me into bed." Aster wiped his nose with the back of his hand. "She acted like I'd come back out. I laid there in that hole and let her bury me, like this was all just another nap."

Oren looked sidelong at Aster, without any utterances. His unflinching eyes plied Aster with soft pity as the recollection seeped out.

It was the first time those words had ever left his mouth. For, since the memory was formed and sealed, it had remained unspoken. If that thought was never wrapped in words then it would always be elusive and maybe, just maybe, it could be denied.

Aster had given it birth. He looked to Oren, hoping for confirmation or refutation. Oren offered neither, just letting Aster live and feel the moment.

Aster continued: "I don't understand. Did she simply go mad? This is where you come in, Dad. This is where you finally help me make sense of it."

He shrugged in reply. "It's like that with magic—"

"No," Aster burst out. He launched from his seat and strode around the room like a gale unleashed upon an unsuspecting valley. "You don't get to use magic as an excuse for her." He paused in front of Oren, anger singeing the tips of his ears while the wetness of loss dangled at the tip of his nose. Aster dropped to his knees. "Just, please, Dad, help me try to comprehend."

Oren leaned out of his little pocket, kissed Aster upon the crown of his head. "You want to know why so badly. I see it. I hear it." He held Aster close to his chest. Oren pulled away slightly, just enough to look Aster in the face. "Trust me, there's no greater pain than not being able to protect you. I failed you the day she tried her crazy magical experiment. I failed you when she cast herself off that cliff. I'm failing you now."

He smelled comfortable, like he bathed in autumn. His words were a soothing ointment, easing the anger and drying the wetness. No substantive explanation why had been offered, but this man, this father, had said all he could and with a voice so strong yet vulnerable. No son could ask more of his father.

Aster resumed his seat on the couch. He sat rigid, posture perfectly upright in a place he had grown up. He was supposed to be able to slouch, sink into the cushions, and feel like part of the surroundings. He looked at Oren, trying to excavate every last secret— all the unknowns that were apparently burrowed beneath this crinkled, banal façade—with just a look. There had to be more than his father let on. But this emotional work, this purging of long-hidden sadness, was tiring. Digging for absolute understanding only compounded that fatigue.

"So now what?" Aster let a sigh escape as he gave up and dropped back against the couch.

Maybe his father would see the exhaustion and confess every event and thought that hadn't been yet shared with Aster. Instead, Oren stared down between his feet, lightly fidgeting with his fingers.

He leaned forward and examined Aster for a moment. "We'll handle the storms together. We'll try to forgive one another as much as we can, and…" his voice trailed off as he sat back. "And you fill your life with as much success as you can."

Aster nodded. The longer he thought about that last idea, he nodded more as if the notion of success propelled his head forward and back. "Truly," he finally said as he rose to his feet. "That fire fruit isn't going to create itself."

13.

OF DISAPPOINTMENT & COMPANIONSHIP

"I'm sorry I still haven't been able to find someone who can perform that Martese for you." Oren hoisted himself out of the embrace of his arm chair, the only throne that had ever mattered to either man. "There aren't a lot of local options. With magic like this, I'm not surprised. Powerful stuff. What's that look?"

The answer must have been scribbled across Aster's face.

"The Martese isn't some party trick to make life more convenient. We're talking elemental magic raised to new spheres of power," Oren explained in a sternness that reverberated in Aster's skull.

It was always there, sometimes tucked deep in Aster's heart and other times it floated on the surface, the desire to need his father or at least to make him feel needed. There were times, especially as Aster matured, that it took more effort. Now was one of those moments wherein Aster needed to summon the effort, a spell in and of itself, to make sure Oren felt needed even if he wasn't, in all honesty, genuinely needed.

Aster's eyes betrayed him, swiveling from one corner of the room to another. His glance touched upon Pixee as she poked her head around the front door, slightly ajar. "Safe to enter?"

Oren waved her in.

"What are we talking about?" She walked in, paused next to Oren.

"Martese and from the look on Aster's face, he seems to have found someone to help him with this bit of complex magic."

A gleeful grin was writ upon her face as she waited for the confession she had been unable to pry from him earlier.

The might of their combined gazes—two people of such import—bore insistently enough that it was only a matter of moments before the truth would surge forward. Why shouldn't they know? It was his life, after all. He was a grown man who knew what he was getting himself into. It was a means to an end, not an end itself. This wasn't him dipping into Thanatos, or even condoning it.

Oren crossed his arms over his chest in anticipation, while Aster hemmed and hawed. Then there was Pixee, standing hands resting on her hips. In a way, it was like they already knew the name Aster was about to speak.

"Aster," Oren coaxed, cutting through the silence, "who?"

And Pixee, with her knowing glance, like the little sister who couldn't wait to tattle on her brother. Whether they guessed the name he was soon to utter, they still had to wait for him to confirm their suspicions. Or fears by the stern looks cast his way.

"Mr. Oleander agreed to perform the rite for me." There, everyone knew. It felt like he had confessed a dirty secret like sodomizing a goat. "We made a trade—"

"Oh, Aster." Pixee's grin slipped away and she shook her head.

Oren just stared his fatherly stare as he dropped his arms to his sides.

Simple responses. By Life's left eye, those small, subtle gestures were potent though, delivering a vice-grip of disappointment that needed no fanfare or pomp. This must be what it's like to be strangled by a snake: silent, efficient, inevitable.

"Dad," Aster finally said, "it's fine. I'll be fine."

Oren sank back into his chair as he bestowed upon Aster another helping of uninterrupted staring. He released his son from what Aster assumed to be glaring disappointment, and watched the fire.

"If you knew Oleander the way Oren does, then you'd understand. If you knew the power and color of Thanatos like I do, you'd understand." Pixee said before she abandoned the conversation for a spot on the floor, her back against the couch, and chin on her knees.

The fire may have burned on, supplied with plenty of fuel, but the room was untouched by it. Sure, the light dispersed with an expected reliability, painting every object and person in a balance of an orange glow and shadows, but the attending heat was eaten up by the dire riddles. Aster sat at the edge of the couch and produced a serious look of such austerity that his face felt cramped. Oren had to know that Aster wasn't taking this lightly.

"Dad," Aster said.

Oren may have been a bit disappointed at his son's choice, maybe even scared, but he managed to heed Aster's words, even if just slightly.

"This business will end neatly. I'll be able to see my goal to its conclusion, and the world will be made a little more interesting for it. I just—"

Their glances met. Oren stared out from pockets of aged skin, crisp as parchment.

"—I want you to know that I'll come out of this as whole and complete as I am now."

Oren nodded. "Whatever price you paid, I hope it was worth it."

"Dad, he didn't ask for my soul or anything."

At the utterance of the word soul the room—even the very fire—collapsed into a silence so complete it felt like nothing existed.

Oren pointed a stiff finger in Aster's direction. "Careful how flippant you are about that topic."

Aster sighed. "I just need to get the gem back for him, is all." Aster stood. "I'm going to take Rustle and make that happen." He ventured away from the couch.

Something of a groan left Oren's lips. "And Pixee."

"Huh?"

"Pixee, would you please?"

She stood and paused by Oren's chair, watching Aster. "I can manage that favor." She patted his shoulder.

The eastern archway's shadow stretched confidently as the sun rose, as if it climbed right out of the water, an illuminate spirit ready to treat the world to hours of benevolent grace. It was the perfect moment to start an adventure. Beginnings rife with potential that looked satisfying, as satisfying as watching a plate stacked with piping hot meats and glistening sauces parade from kitchen to table.

"Is he always late?" Pixee scanned the lane for any movement. She sighed. "He's already marring this endeavor's efficiency."

The morning was quiet, and Rustle was not to be seen.

"I don't know," Aster mused. "He could be securing the steeds."

"I'd buy that excuse had we not already taken care of all those details." She fumed; it wasn't written all over her face, but the subtle twitches at the corners of her lips and edges of her limbs gave away her annoyance.

The fuming lasted for a brief moment before they spied Rustle turning a corner and meandering towards the archway. Though he was a small figure steadily growing taller, his smile was perceptible even from a distance. "And a fine morning to you fine adventurers," he said in salutation.

"A morning that is wasting away."

"At long last, I have the pleasure of finally meeting *the* Pixee." Rustle beamed, sticking out a hand. "I've heard the name so many times I feel like we've already met."

Aster made ready to formally introduce the two but was cut short by Pixee's intrusion: "No time for dawdling."

Rustle quickly withdrew his proffered handshake. Didn't seem any point to open the spigot of his usual charm. "Horses?"

Aster nodded out the archway. They passed under the amicable structure and veered toward the local stables along the northern arc of the wall. A mare for Aster and one for Rustle, while Pixee would not be beholden to some rented creature. She traveled with her own mount, a stallion of singularity, black like a slice of night on legs.

Rustle whistled long and slow, his eyes wide. "That's a pretty impressive animal."

Pixee sat astride the horse. Apparently, a saddle was not required and, by the look of the beast, would not have been tolerated. "Well observed."

With everyone set on their respective mounts, Rustle and Pixee looked to Aster in anticipation of his direction. Rustle cleared his throat as Pixee flapped her lips.

"You really have absolutely no idea, Rustle?" Aster wasn't convinced.

Rustle shrugged, his face donning a vapid gaze as if he didn't know why he was included with this cadre of adventurers.

"No clue at all where to find Sedge?"

Rustle looked about, aimless, then shrugged in reply.

"So we're starting with no leads. Fantastic way to begin the hunt." Pixee deplored.

"Putting it like that does make this endeavor sound pretty tedious." Rustle grinned as he fidgeted with the reins.

"I did put it like that," Pixee retorted.

"I believe..." Aster said with in a slow, measured pace. "Our best course is to seek out Rose. I know she'll be able to locate him."

He spoke more to himself, for he looked to neither of his companions when he finished voicing his thought.

Rustle chuckled. "Meaning you hope she'll know." He leaned towards Pixee. "Can't fault the guy for seeking out a former lover."

Rustle snickered at his jest. Pixee stayed aloof.

Aster wore the irritation all over his face, what with his lips drawn all tight. Seeking out Rose may have been no more than a gut-feeling, but it was too profound to deny. The suggestion had nothing to do with the romantic history between he and Rose, a story concluded long enough in the past that surely she wouldn't think of him that way any longer. Surely?

Aster shushed the warring voices in his head: the excited yippy one that yammered on about *"but what if?"* Then there was that other dour voice grumbling on about insecurities and building up false hopes.

That neither Rustle nor Pixee offered any productive ideas grated on Aster, who was ever aware of the timetable set forth by Mr. Oleander. Yes, he and Aster had bonded—somewhat—during the Martese, but that bond didn't negate Mr. Oleander's demand to have the gem back by the ripened moon. The conclusion of the Martese awaited. That was all that mattered.

It was understandable that Pixee didn't lend any specific strategy to this search, but Rustle should have wanted to locate Sedge as expeditiously as Aster. His lack of participation peeved Aster, who stared at his compatriots.

"Unless someone has a better way of locating Sedge, I'd love to hear it." Aster crossed his arms over his chest. "Have another contact, Rustle, that can direct us to wherever Sedge is hiding? I suppose we could go check the holdout of every warlord. Though, I'm not entirely sure how many there are. Rustle?"

Rustle shook his head just so, his lips drooping as Aster fired off all of these contentions.

"Oh, I know. We'll just take a couple weeks wandering around looking for signs of Gules and Ocher's whereabouts. They're probably looking for Sedge too. Or, they were. Of course," Aster feigned to scan the land roundabout as if he would spot an anomaly on the horizon. "If Sedge has returned home then they won't be out and about. I bet we'd find them just in time for the deadline to pass."

Pixee smirked at Rustle as she patted her horse's neck, mocking his silent pleas for support against Aster's rhetorical onslaught.

"Pixee, you must have some store of magic, a spell you can whip out, to help us locate Sedge? No?"

Pixee stopped her smirk and stared at Aster. "I'd have to check…"

"Since I'm the only one with a concrete suggestion…"

The others sat frozen by the decisive confidence bubbling out of Aster, as he urged his horse onward.

He stopped to survey the land, because he didn't want to let this gust of surety pass without letting it carry him to new heights. How, though? How did one ride a breeze? His mind wheeled, clouds riding the wind, with plans and leads.

"She always had the inclination of healing," Rustle explained into the ensuing silence.

Pixee seemed only mildly interested in what he said, with her paltry nods and anemic eye contact. Rustle was not deterred.

"Right, Aster?"

"True," Aster looked among the open glades that lay ahead. "A healer. Though, quite intuitive. More like a—" His lips drew farther apart preparing for the word as his eyes followed suit and went a little wider.

"A what?" Pixee positioned her steed next to Aster's.

"—a witch." The declaration shut Rustle up and, from the look on her face, gave Pixee a renewed confidence in Aster's plan.

"You really think she's one?" Rustle asked.

"It was there the whole time. It makes sense, because of how she practiced magic." It was rarely a song with here. There was always a mixture of some kind; bones or blood.

The giddy thrill of discovery was pulling his cheeks into a ever-widening grin. Yes, this was the path forward. The horse must have sensed it too, for she stamped and shifted. When Aster looked at his companions there was nothing of realization or anticipation on their faces.

Just an expectant glare from Pixee while Rustle looked at his hands, picking at his nails, as if Aster hadn't just laid out some insightful plan.

"You still have to find her still," Pixee said.

"Truly," Rustle said, "and if you find her and she can't or won't help, what then? We've landed at a dead end with even less time to chase a more substantial lead."

A valid concern; reasonable, with merit. He was right, there was only a finite amount of time to complete this hunt—Aster's hunt, not Pixee's or Rustle's. Well, maybe a little bit of Rustle's. The time to debate the best way forward was past.

"Cannaville," Aster declared to an audience that sported little comprehension. "A witch haven since the Conflict of Magics."

Still, no sense of understanding lighted in Rustle's eyes and, surprisingly, neither in Pixee's.

"It's history. Oren talked about it. The conflict between the Stewards and that coven. No?"

Pixee shook her head.

"Let's get a move on. I'll fill you in on the story while we ride. We should reach it before the sun sets."

It was a jostling ride across fields of waving grass and brittle turf. The Mountains of Lune loomed ever on the edge of sight as they rode away from the peninsula, putting the coast at their backs. As hard as they rode, they did not reach Cannaville that day. Aster would have pressed his horse on through the night, but Pixee urged otherwise, having seen the weariness in the steed as clearly as the pale moon above.

As daylight broke upon the land, the group resumed their travels, now following along the River Crest: a deep and wide ribbon of dark blue waters, with traces of green. After some time, signs appeared that they had reached one of the first settlements established along the great, bisecting river. Only hints of it now remained, for the locale appeared deserted with its rotted buildings while vegetation reclaimed what used to be well-trod paths.

"...and so after the coven was subdued by the Stewards, the dust settled and no one felt safe here, apparently." Aster dismounted at the edge of Cannaville. "From what I've learned out of tales and accounts, at least."

Even the bones of the place—decrepit structures that had survived time and circumstances—indicated that it hadn't been as orderly as Lamiston: no wall, no square, not even a pattern to how the still-standing structures had been arranged.

Aster led his companions past these relics. Everyone walked on their own feet with their horses treading close at hand. Save for the distant whisper of the river as it found its way to the sea, there was a pervading quiet that made them move especially slow. The absence of noise was thick about them. No birds or insects dared interrupt.

"Must have been quite the conflict to scare everyone away from such a prime location." Rustle's voice soft as an evening breeze.

Aster nodded in reply. He didn't know all the details of how the two factions fought or what display of power they used against one another. There wasn't a need to know, just like Aster didn't need to know the exact details of how his father and mother went about conceiving him; he just knew of the event, the generalities, and the result. He was here, alive just like the buildings were here. They were filled with history, but no future. That was enough for Aster.

Pixee veered away from the path. She spoke into her horse's ear, which stayed and stomped at some short grass. The other two mares naturally followed the dark steed. Aster let the reins go, trusting their mounts to the leadership of Pixee's horse.

"Does that black beauty have a name?" Rustle ventured as he directed himself a step closer to Pixee.

"Iridium." She veered a step or two away from Rustle.

"Huh, an interesting name." His glance kept darting back to her. "Got it from the story about that one horse, fabled to have been created by Death in mockery of Life's artistry? The first living being in existence, the tales say."

"Sure," she said looking not at Rustle, but at the shambles of a town.

Rustle stopped and stared back at the equine cluster. "Wait, so that *is* the fabled horse?"

Pixee gave Rustle a single nod in reply to his question.

"How...? When...?"

"Why?" Pixee offered in mock support. She moved along after Aster, but all her attempts at ignoring Rustle proved futile.

"I mean, it's supposed to be one of those tales you hear about the history of Life and Death. But, it's real?"

"Shhh—" Aster halted and turned an ear to the perceived sound of stirring. "Pretty sure someone just moved."

"Besides Rustle?" Pixee stilled and watched Aster.

Aster nodded as he took a couple timid steps towards the nearest structure, which took on the shape of a dwelling. A porch of warped boards wrapped around the front of the house ending on either side. Aster tested the wood, lightly tapping it with his toes before pressing a little more forcefully. First, he placed his right foot fully against the board and when it felt secure his left foot followed.

A window peered back at Aster darkly. He cupped his hands and examined the house's guts; what he could see of them through the years of grime coating the glass. He swiped the side of his fist across the pane to clear away some of the muck. It was as he expected to find it: a disheveled space with no life, no character. It was merely a house, not a home. Not anymore. Aster turned to report to Pixee and Rustle.

"Well—"

Rustle lurched back away from the window, punching out a chorus of creaking boards with each hurried step.

"What?"

"A face," Rustle wheezed.

Aster looked again through the window: grimy, empty, glaring back at them with deadness. Pixee joined him on the porch, striding across the wood, which hardly acknowledged what little weight she added. Even she cast a dubious glance back at Rustle.

He hurried up to the window nudging aside his companions, anxious to prove, perhaps more to himself, that he had seen what he claimed. "It was peeking out, I swear."

They stared into the hovel, occupied with discovering if Rustle had actually seen a face or if the destitution of the town played tricks on his mind. In the midst of their inquiry, it all came crashing down.

The boards gave way and admitted them into a pit.

14.

OF WITCHES &
THEIR PYRES

Ivory skulls, every iota of flesh and skin peeled away, ran up for many feet like rocks lining some deep, empty well.

Pixee collected herself off a floor of femurs and tibia. Which was just a guess, but a surgeon would have had a better idea of exactly which bones constituted the flooring upon which they all now stood, rubbing out the pain and stretching away the shock.

"What in all of the Death-tilled world is this?" Rustle peered at the nearest skull, lobbing a dubious glance into the vacant recesses that once were home to a pair of eyes.

Pixee took a lap around the cylindrical pit carefully prying at her surroundings for any sort of clue, or feeling, about what kind of trap into which they'd been dropped. "Whomever built this prepared it well. There's a curse keeping out magic."

She winced in the most consternated way as she attempted to commune with an element or two. Not a single grain of dirt shifted. Nor did the telltale shimmer of Primul magic escape Pixee's skin. The skulls peered at their guests dispassionately musing on the plight of the trapped creatures.

"Can we climb out?" Aster began to test his theory even before he received consensus.

He jumped, securing a grip into a pair of vacant sockets. The skulls held as he pulled up his full weight. His right foot scrambled to find some sort of leverage, but each time he placed it there'd be no secure footing. His fingers blanched with the effort of holding his sturdy frame in place. The muscles along the sides of his body and up his forearms tightened until they were heavy like stones, a bone deep edge of pain creeping to fill every thought. Just as the pain and the fatigue dug in and sweat coated his palms, Aster found a foothold upon the prominent brow of one skull. Relief tickled up his arms and along his upper back.

"Well," he called to his fellow captives, "this could actually work." Aster took a moment to wipe the dew from each hand, one at a time. He pushed up with his right foot to the next finger hold. The edges of the empty sockets scraped and cut at his skin as he secure his grip.

"Oh, isn't that quaint." A voice rained down from the opening above.

They all craned their necks to the source of the comment. A circle of eight faces peered into the pit. The sight of figures that had not been there a moment ago loosed Aster's grip, sending him to tumble back to the femurs and humeri. Were there ulnae in that mix?

"Oopsie daisies," called down one of the figures in a rather blithe, almost familial tone.

The bones at Aster's feet vibrated. The floor broke free from whatever foundation it had lain upon, and a slow ascent began. Pixee and Rustle looked none-too-relieved at the change of fortune, for the change seemed rather unfortunate. Misfortune compounded as the skulls rattled with tension, thick with the trauma that had brought them to be part of this malignant trap.

The skulls squealed at the captives a sound too pitched and eerie for description. Pixee bent, hands cupped over her ears. Rustle fell to his knees as if the cries from the skulls had pushed him over.

Aster trembled with effort to keep his feet under him. The wailing persisted, teasing the blood in his body as if daring it to expand beyond the confines of every vein and artery. It was all too much to resist. Aster folded to the ground, letting the pain push him as far as his body could go until he gave up consciousness.

"You smell it, too? Oh, well, right pretty to have the confirmation from the illustrious nose of Yarrow."

Chatter broke through the wall of sleep—which only loosely applied to the situation—as Aster climbed back into consciousness.

Their backs were turned as his captors poured their attention exclusively upon another figure. Rustle laid next to him, still withdrawn into the bliss of unconsciousness. Either that or the cursed skulls had actually killed him. It was Pixee who mattered more at the moment.

Vines of indomitable strength—barbed, at that—caught his wrists and ankles, pinning him to the dirt. Each feeble attempt to find some freedom only made the thorns grope deeper. They bit with a vengeance as if the plant had a will of its own, a will to take pleasure in mocking a prisoner's defiance.

The circle around Pixee was thick, with no gap for a peek. The persons hemming her in were just tall enough to hide what transpired amongst them, with their halter dresses in shades of dingy white.

The shapes of their bodies varied—some with wide hips and plump breasts while others were narrow of frame—as did the style of their hair, but all were wild and thatched-looking. Pixee's voice hadn't escaped the clique formed around her.

Was she still out? Was she staring up at her captors with her usual indifference?

"What serendipity," one of them said with a measure of glee. "Yarrow, get her out of those bonds and to the cottage."

"Hey, beasts," Aster called out, mostly in desperation. The spells he knew escaped his power of recall as the thorns pinched and dug into his flesh.

The one who had been doing all the talking sauntered over to Aster. She bore an aged face and a hefty-looking bosom which her clothing barely contained. She had maybe a few centimeters in height over her cohorts. Her hair was like faded black yarn. "Young man, you needn't interrupt."

"Iris," one of the other women called, "the Primul wakes."

"The poor dear reeks of it." Iris winked as she returned to the brood of witches.

At least Pixee was visible now. She struggled against the restraints that bound her arms and legs, but not a single note of discomfort or fear escaped her lips, even when then lifted her off the ground.

Iris oversaw the whole affair calling out directions, her fingers pointing to this person and that witch, as if she were conducting a troop of musicians in one song. From what she shouted there was some sort of plot of vengeance to be executed. An ugly plot long in the crafting, it seemed, despite the twittering voice she used to order the coven.

The time for scheming or strategizing was at an end. Iris preached to her contemporaries: "In the days that follow, this blood will power the magic that will bring witches out of obscurity at last. Those petulant Stewards will no longer shackle us and our practices. Our true magic."

So her tune ran as her fellows laughed and celebrated the as they bore Pixee away, her tiny frame barely a burden. Into the old house out of which they had originally gathered went the coven, followed by Iris, gaily trotting and twirling as she went.

Not being able to keep an eye on his friend sent Aster's arms writhing and yanking against his botanical fetters. They tightened again, in response to his agitation.

Of course, signs were all about him—literally on his face, as he licked at the flecks of dirt that had landed upon his lips—feeding his mind the idea of earthen spells. He filed through every possible chant he had committed to memory.

He employed the most obvious choice, first. He licked his lips and swallowed. Barely more than a breath, Aster called to the earth around Rustle. His focus traced about Rustle's body. Aster's words, no more than whisper, snaked into the soil and toyed with the grains. Rustle sank, just a dimple in the dirt. The plant reacted. He yelped awake as his skin was pricked by thorns.

"What in all of Life's tragic kingdom is this shit?"

"Shhh, shut up. I don't want those witches to hear you." Aster cast a furtive glance at the doorway leading into the dilapidated house. "We've got to figure this out soon or they're going to carve up Pixee."

Rustle wrested with his botanical-bonds, but learned it responded unkindly. He exhaled and a curse or some strange expletive through clinched teeth. "What's your bright idea then, because I tried mine?"

"I don't have one." Aster's eyes whirled to any point but that house.

"Better wring that brain of yours quick." Rustle nodded towards the house out of which dumped the shrill voices of that conspiracy of witches. "Aster, any ideas?"

Wring.

"Yes," Aster replied.

Spells of earth were impotent against the pernicious plants, as if they weren't rooted in the dirt nor made with ingredients from the soil. Perhaps the witches had wrought some change upon them? There was one other option, worth the time and breath: an attack on the plants from the inside and hopefully the words and cadence was right. Aster settled his mind blocking out the danger closing in on Pixee. He denied Rustle's braying for action. There was nothing in this world but those plants. Not even their biting thorns registered. The pain was but a whisper of a myth. At first the chant plopped out like a calf fresh from the womb, wobbly, uncertain:

Whispers true fawning
Secret paths falling
Habits untying
Let fly heart's renown
Free til newly found

It was time to trim all doubts. This would work. Look at those plants, having their way and relishing the blood they drew, staining the wild green stems with ruddy swirls. Rustle was saying something, shouting words, but he was a mountain on a far-off horizon. His wild calls were a bird passing high in the sky.

Aster mustered his voice for another round of the spell. This time, he muttered the incantation with a force and intent that made the plant to take notice. He dished it out a third time. A fourth. Each repetition bled out darker and thicker than his own blood.

That was when it happened.

"Aster," Rustle called. Again. "Are you making any progress or what?"

"Shhh," Aster replied, trying to grip his own focus like the edge of a cliff.

It was happening. He kept up the spell and with each utterance the plant oozed; beads of water eked out from stem and leaf. The thorns eased away, intimidated and bullied into submission. The plant shed more water until it shrunk to a wrinkled crisp.

Aster flicked his right wrist snapping what remained of the plant's grip. He cast away the other bonds and hurried to free Rustle. The rush of escape sent Aster's pain into oblivion, for the moment.

"Let's get her out of there!" Rustle looked ready to bolt into the house.

Aster couldn't let him betray their advantage. "No, Rustle. Settle."

Rustle breathed in and out louder than a bull.

"Get the horses ready. I'll get Pixee and send her your way. We'll make it out of this. All of us. You take care of the getaway, yes?"

Rustle nodded. He hesitated before following Aster's plan.

"Be ready with the horses at this spot."

Aster stalked to the corner of the building. He watched Rustle dash away to collect the horses. It had to be timed just right. One misstep and they'd all be toasted bread. A final check on Rustle: he stalked back down the lane. A good pace. Aster scurried around to the back of the house. Whatever was supposed to happen to Pixee hadn't. Yet. It was time to raze this Life-less house to the ground.

The room to build up surety didn't exists. Each step in this plan needed to be tightly woven together. He knew the words. He knew how to say them. He uttered the spell as fast as he could, twisting the chant with gale-force clarity. He stepped back as the air between his raised arms twirled and swirled into a cyclone. He couldn't hear the women but through a grubby window he saw their shapes turn in his direction.

He unleashed the conjured cyclone, pushed it right into the house. The rapidly twisting airs smashed through the brittle wood snapping the back wall into a collapsed heap. Screams rose to match the howling winds.

Pixee was there, barely conscious, laying among the wreckage. Aster hurried in for her. He caught her up in his arms and bore her away to Rustle, who had dashed in between houses. She sat like a flimsy doll in the saddle before him.

"Ride now," Aster commanded. "Just get her as far as you can from here. Don't look back."

Rustle spurred his horse towards the river. The steed bolted. Aster looked upon the witches who appeared more agitated than a disturbed colony of ants.

Their dithering was cut short by Iridium's approach. Their admiring glances turned to fear when the black-beauty bucked at the air and released from his throat a harsh, almost metallic-grating, bellow. His hoofs landed upon the earth, beating out shock waves that made the very buildings tremble.

Aster fell back, both from the tremors and from awe of the creature before him. That dark-coated beast let loose its full speed to race after Pixee.

Had his wits been sharper, Aster would have grabbed onto the horse before it careened away and ridden to a safe distance, but the horse nearly flew away and now the consequences marshaled around Aster, circling him with their menacing grins.

"Grave mistake, lad," Iris pouted at Aster.

Before he could make a move the world shuttered into darkness.

There was silence for some time. Hopefully it was silence, because silence at least was a sensation, and could be tabulated in a sort of tactile way. The ears heard sound or they didn't but if they didn't mind grasped that, and if the mind was grasping then it still pulsed with life. Aster's mind grasped, all right.

A noxious fume assaulted his nose. His eyelids flung open. Pain was something of which the mind too readily took hold, as well. Pain aplenty raced up Aster's arms, neatly tied behind his back, secured to a felled tree trunk as tall as himself. Rope dug into his skin as he wrestled and tugged.

"You meddle with witches, and your outcome is just," Iris explained, tersely. "You've made a mess of our ritual and so to assuage our disappointment, your death will suffice."

A final statement for which there really wasn't much to combat. It showed on all their faces, in the lines along their eyes and about their mouths. Except for the one who had been called Yarrow. She beamed as blithely as a summer sun. She was actually the one who ignited the wood congregated about Aster's feet.

The heat of it crawled up in puffs like an open oven waiting for a roast, to cook. Streaks of sweat raced each other down Aster's face, seeing which one could ride the contours of his cheeks fastest without getting hooked on a hair or stuck in a dimple. All the while, flames devoured their way closer.

A close intimate relationship with fire would have been perfect in a pinch like this, but Mr. Oleander had to hold secret the final phase of the rite of the Martese. Flames of red, orange, yellow—with hints of white that seemed imagined at first, fighting to be noticed through the other colors—were heedless of what they ate. They could have been subdued but now they were going to dominate every pound of flesh, wither every inch of skin, and fry away every strand of hair. Those witches milled about as if they were waiting for the sun to finally set. There was no urgency in their faces, no tension in their posture.

Think. Think. What words were there to chant away this menace?

The heat intensified. It was impossible to tune out this variety of danger. It wasn't on the edge. It didn't knock at the door; it erased the door and crawled forward.

"Utter any last words while you still have a throat, young man." Iris said. "Except a spell. The witch's fire is not beholden to songs or chants."

The coven's chorus of laughter taunted Aster to dare any and all spells he had stored away in his memory. He driveled random snatches of rhymes, no so much spells as fearful, hurried ramblings. His attempts to defy conflagration. Among all the babbling a rhythm crawled out from somewhere between Aster's nasal passages and his throat. It may not have been the right one, but any spell was better than standing there being chewed away by flames:

> *Dawn of desire*
> *Pulsing mightier*
> *Let the blood splatter*
> *Touch the four corners*
> *Stained, new attire*

It was more of a desperate prayer to someone, or something, that the flames wouldn't touch his flesh. The words rushed out into the world with such fury that they sounded like the voice of some ancient creature, beyond the skill and capability of a mere mortal man to make.

The spell Aster called out swept down upon the fire as it began to lick his boots. At his words, the witches paused their glee and took notice of the chant Aster had spit at the fire. He repeated it with more intention, more surety. The fire took no notice, but the witches did. Their gazes latched onto Aster, who remained undeterred by the creeping flames.

The inferno may have persisted, but its progress had slowed every time Aster lashed out with his words. He flung them down like a curse. Curse it seemed too: flames rolled away as the words hit them over and over again. Some of the witches reacted quick enough to avoid all injury, save being merely grazed, as the magmatic waves pursued their path. Others were not so quick.

15.

OF TREES &
A FLOWER

Their bodies writhed as the flames mounted and conquered, pulling at the skin, looking for longer burning fuel. The witches fought against the pain, screaming back at it with wretched lamentations. Only the heart could hear what words lay beneath their sounds.

The scene relaxed into a haunting silence; the fuel had been spent and the flames could no longer abide. The crisp bodies added a special sense of destitution to an already destitute town. Aster struggled against the rope. Yarrow collected herself to her feet. After shaking her orange, straw-like hair free of ash she stood glaring at Aster.

He stopped breathing. Stopped fiddling with his bonds.

"You're proud of this?" She sank to the ground and watched the last bit of fire sputter and dwindle.

"No," he whispered.

"I suppose one could understand your impulse to preserve your own life," she remarked, a wisp of sadness bleeding into her admission.

"I didn't mean—" No explanation felt adequate enough to summarize the scene.

There's a certain expectation for violence out there in the world. It's not alien. To see it carried out, no intent or planning, made it all the more ugly, and he was at the epicenter.

"I didn't want to burn them alive," Aster finished only half-heartedly paying attention to his own petition for sympathy. "I was just looking for Rose," he admitted hopelessly.

Yarrow's prostrate figure looked diminished, lost and forlorn against the backdrop of death and destruction, but at the mention of a familiar name she peered up. "Rose of Lamiston? You know her?" She gathered herself back to her feet.

Aster nodded.

Yarrow sauntered up to the cooling pyre. "You're still bound. I should have your life." She glanced back over one shoulder than the other, taking count. "Ten times over for the slaughter of this coven."

She kicked aside the dying embers, unbothered by any residual heat. Her hazel eyes even twinkled a little as she stepped closer, her breath laced with the odd combination of mint and smoke. Aster leaned away as her inspection of him continued.

"I don't know. The practice of witchcraft fades. Maybe," she sighed, "maybe our vengeance was too big, too consuming. Like a fire." She reached around his waist and unfastened the knots that held him bound to the stake.

There was no magic in her words to stem the regret. They may not have been exactly innocent but was it really Aster's place to say they deserved to be burned alive? He slumped forward coaxing his wrist to feel again as Yarrow plopped down upon the ground, seating herself next to what was probably once Iris.

"Iris wasn't one to let the past die. Some folk will take the shortest, quickest path to their ends. Some of us grow into our plans. Takes longer, but roots buried deep tend to endure the ravages of wind and fire."

The words sent a chill up Aster's arms. The tiny bumps erupted over his skin. Here was this stranger, this individual who was not privy to his life—the secret desires, the way his mind worked—and yet she spoke with a certainty as if she had known Aster, intimately, for most of his adult life. She left an imprint, a stranger passing barefoot across the shores of his mind.

He cleared his throat as he climbed away from the stake. "I need to find her. Do you know where she may be? I haven't seen her since she left Lamiston."

"She had the right idea, Rose. Get away from these society folk and their…structures and governments. Leave behind the plots of revenge and just keep the tradition of witchcraft alive, immersed in nature. The way it was meant to be." Yarrow shook her head before looking at Aster. "I don't know exactly where, but I can give you a good place to start looking."

The hurried pounding of hoofs cut into the conversation. Pixee slipped off Iridium's back with ease, but her determined movements were subdued by the waft of smoke alighting off the backs of the charred witches.

"I didn't mean to," Aster explained at Pixee's expression. "They were about to burn me alive."

"We saw smoke," Pixee said.

Rustle joined her in gawking. "She insisted we come back even though she was still weary from captivity."

"She knows where Rose is," Aster said, hoping to take their minds from the lumps of embers and ashen bones.

Yarrow had eyes only for Aster. "Find your way to the Wald. Navigate the woods carefully though, for creatures of ill repute stalk through those trees. You wouldn't want to fall into their talons."

"And your coven? What will happen to you?"

She was already making her way to meet the other survivors crawling out from the shadows, but at his questions she paused. Her eyes roamed the skies above for a moment before she met Aster's gaze.

"We're a powerful people. Sometimes you make it to the end and sometimes the end makes it to you."

Pixee and Rustle waited, looking at Aster with expectant faces.

"To the Wald it is," he said to them.

They took to the river and followed its dark waters. The sun died behind the mountains taking with it all the splendor of daylight. As the sky cooled into deeper shades of blue, up came the moon from behind the very same mountains, bringing with it a soft glow, gentle in its reminder that the abundant moon was two nights old and the ripened moon approached with dire consequences just on the other side of its setting.

"Did he say how long?" Rustle stoked the fire.

"Two cycles." Aster sat himself near the fire, a neat distraction from staring at the moon in anticipation of betrayal.

"Too close for comfort," Rustle said pushing his anxiety into the fire with quick stabs.

"The forest isn't that far off though," Aster said to his companions. "We'll make it," He added, almost into his chest, as he drummed his fingers upon his knees.

"What happens if you don't?"

He didn't want to answer Pixee, knowing how she already felt about his association with Mr. Oleander. Instead, Aster glanced quickly back at Rustle, who fortunately caught the look.

"Oh, well..." Rustle decided to offer some farce of an explanation. "I'm pretty sure it has something to do with the magic. Like potency or some such."

"Potency?" Pixee mocked.

"Truly."

Aster shrugged back at him and resumed watching the moon, as though it would change if he didn't keep an eye on it.

"You know witches and their crazy ways."

Pixee sat upright and scrutinized Rustle with her furrowed brow and narrowed eyes. "No, I don't think I do."

He laughed as if she had made a proper jest.

Their journey resumed before the moon had even dipped below the western horizon. Every mile solidified thoughts about the next step in their pursuit of Sedge. The river languished in its course while they had to forge theirs.

He'd have to talk to Rose. His mind stuttered at the thought, for behind the veneer of this mission to locate Sedge there was a crusty past Aster wanted to address. Not that he was eager to, but how could he look upon her and not see the tumult and the lost-love between them. It made his tongue thick with too many feelings and opinions.

The riders pressed their horses onward for another day and half. They eschewed any and all towns along their way opting, rather, to keep the momentum going. Not until the next morning, the third out from their encounter with the coven at Cannaville, did trees emerge from the horizon: the Wald.

Perhaps not a forest of any great import, it was, like all other wooded areas, simply a collection of trees within a measurable area. The trees of the Wald stood clad in chalky bark slashed with darker lines, tiny but perceptible. Their crowns, punching into the sky, spread out like the tips of mushrooms donning leaves of fiery orange and pale green, as if they were unaware if the seasons were coming or going.

They at last approached the edge of the wood and observed the still leaves waiting for a stray breeze to tussle them. The whole forest appeared empty, soulless, merely painted on to the world. Aster shifted in place.

"Do we lead them in or leave them out here?" Rustle vacated the saddle, holding the reins to his steed loosely in his fist while his eyes scanned the eaves of the woods.

Pixee pursed her lips. "This is a non-question. Leave them out here. They'll heed Iridium. We'll go in, find Rose, and be back." She strode into the trees, breaking upon the scenic view.

Rustle followed.

Aster carefully lowered the reins to his own mare. He watched for a moment. Iridium stood with proud bearing, dipping to clip some grass but always returning to stand with his head high as his pearly blackness glittered as the other horses milled about.

"Aster," came Pixee's summons.

The call distinctly lacked any note of frivolity. It didn't quell the hesitation coursing in Aster's mind, heart, and feet. Moving forward past the edge of the forest was the easiest part. What wasn't easy was keeping that momentum going because standing on the metaphorical edge of actually finding Rose bred such insecurity which was supposed to have been burned away by the urgency of this endeavor. Aster's history with Rose, deeply personal and rife with emotion, dwarfed the primary goal, but they had to find her and persuade her to help, which meant talking to her.

What does a person say to their first-love? A first-love who vanished and didn't even bother to leave a note? Not a single warning—written or otherwise—of the end.

Just the end.

Although it had been Aster's idea to seek her out, that didn't make the task any easier. It was, simply put, necessary.

Aster trailed behind Rustle, who followed Pixee, who peeked left and right, up and down. The forest floor was a carpet of plush moss, a lively green color like...like Sedge's eyes. Aster shook away the recollection.

It was a forest unlike most in Thuidium. Closer to a well-tended garden than a random host of trees, shrubs, moss, and whatever else grew in the spaces between. Fungus and lichen, probably. Was some greater force at work tending to the neatness of this wood? It was just too orderly and tidy to be natural.

Aster had been lost in all his musings and observations when the silence announced itself. His glance darted around, peering about the white boles of heedless trees. He stopped breathing when he found himself bereft of companionship.

"Pixee?" he whispered. His voice shook with a hint of panic. He cleared his throat. "Pixee?" he called again, louder.

His voice didn't carry. It fell heavy, at his feet. Nary an air stirred the leaves above. A perfect silence wrapped itself around Aster. He placed each step against the plush, mossy floor in a delicate manner.

As Aster shifted, his gaze darting, a shadow impressed his attention: the svelte figure in silhouette with an appealing curvature. Could this be Rose? That thought came on with such ferocity that Aster almost yelled her name.

A finger tapped him on the shoulder before he could sound off. He spun, almost losing all sense of orientation. "Don't wander." Pixee fixed Aster with her narrow eyes.

Aster heaved a sigh. "Fair, fair." He looked over his shoulder. "Is that her, you think?"

Pixee glanced around him. "I don't know. Too far away to tell. Rustle?"

He arrived at her hushed request. "What's going on over here then?"

They stood shoulder to shoulder and watched the distant figure pick its way around the towering trees. The individual took a step or two then paused to sniff the air and peer about before resuming its odd gait. Its every motion provided doubt but the desire to find Rose contended the creeping feeling that sat squished right between mere apprehension and outright alarm.

"I don't think so," Rustle surmised. "Rose!" he bellowed. "Is that you, sis?"

The figure paused.

"You really are dumber than you act."

Aster nodded in agreement with Pixee.

"So we take on another witch," Rustle argued. "What's the big deal?"

"You mean I take on another witch," Aster corrected as he turned to emphasize his point to Rustle.

Rustle looked ready to debate everyone's role at Cannaville, but as the mysterious figure sauntered in their direction, he let the argument stand where it was.

A voice drifted between the trees like a tickling breeze, of the sort that cannot wait to get in and through every layer of clothing meant to ward off such intrusions.

Aster's uncertainty was mirrored in Pixee's own face. The idea that they had found Rose so quickly, without any struggle or much searching, was pleasant. It was too good a thought to relish and Aster knew it. The figure ambled a little closer, its form still hidden by shadow and distance. Fear loomed, casting a shroud over their hopes.

Aster followed up Rustle's exclamation, in an effort to spur hope. He inhaled and cast out a confident "Hello?"

16.
OF BOUGH, EARTH, & SKY

A strand of garbled sounds returned Aster's greeting. Pixee shook her head as she began her retreat. Who knew what it was. Those sounds crossing the empty space lacked a certain humanity. Unless this undefinable figure was Rose, who could have picked up a strange, ancient tongue indecipherable to the modern ear?

The ever-present deadline, for one, that approached regardless of where the moon hung gave Aster the resolve to press through the fear prickling in his legs. The potential to at last receive an explanation to the sudden dissolution of his romantic relationship with Rose was another. Plenty of reasons to think those sounds were not the call of some wild creature.

"I don't think we're talking with Rose," Rustle admitted as he strayed away from Aster.

The figure took slow steps, barely making an impression upon the ground, emerging from the shadows and into a shard of lingering day.

"On Life's eye," Aster exhaled as mystique was replaced with fact.

That bit of fear bubbling in the corners of his mind turned into roiling boil, an avalanche of reality. It rolled through his whole body as the light from above flaunted the cruel details of the creature.

The vision before him left Aster momentarily transfixed: a snout-like nose pushed against an almost-flat face, adorned with pointed ears, and milky marbles that were its eyes. No arms, just wings folded close to its body almost hugging the curved silhouette like a leather cloak colored in hues to match bark, leaf, and soil. The creature twisted and turned its head like a blind owl as it ambled closer upon talons that uncurled with each wobbly step. An innate sense of danger coursed into Aster's limbs and sent him racing after Rustle and Pixee, both of whom had already begun their flight to safety.

The voice—of undecided temperament only seconds ago—screeched through the air, rendering the once peaceful mood of the forest into a nightmare its. Here, surely, was one of those creatures of which they were warned. Aster glanced back long enough to see it trot after them like some sort of flightless bird, wings spanning nearly two meters from tip to tip, flapping with every yard it covered as talons tore up the moss. The creature hopped and glided through the empty space between the ground and the canopy. The wings were not so useless after all.

Aster dove left as the creature swooped down into his path. In an actually companionless state this time, he picked his way amongst clusters of trees. The forest floor had changed from plush moss to a golden carpet of discarded leaves. The trees were tighter in this stretch of wood.

"Hello?" Aster ventured in a voice no louder than a whisper. "Are you there, Pixee?"

Even a whisper sounded too loud in that moment. Aster clutched at the bole of a tree. The heaving breaths and the thudding of his heart would betray him to that beast, Aster was sure.

In all of this Death-tilled wood, where was safety? Where was Rose?

Aster wiped away the sweat now coating his beleaguered features. The air between the trees grew cool and stout as the sun bowed out of the sky, filling the Wald with deeper, foreboding shadows as though the impending night was a trap the trees themselves were setting with glee.

In a short time, there would be nowhere to run. The land looked and felt the same, no matter the direction or how fast he walked. Aster jogged, hoping to feel a change in topography. It was just tree after tree on a flat plane that spread out like some giant hand. The Wald was too big while still remaining too small, wherein danger was present yet unaccounted for.

Another wild call tore through the darkening forest, stilling Aster's breath even as he fought to keep his pace. The sound of the high-pitched wail tempted Aster to look back, but to venture even a glance, no matter how quick, was to invite disaster.

The sounds crawled after him. Aster shivered as each cry hit his body. He stumbled. The creature gained on him.

He hit a trunk and spun around in time to catch a glimpse of the stalking menace.

It ambled closer, something entirely not human, and decidedly unsexy, because a violent death was decidedly unsexy, especially via the slow rending of claw and fang. The wings were unfurled and blotted out the boughs and bits of visible sky. Aster normally liked breasts but the firm, fur-coated pair closing in on him warped any seductive thoughts into a fiercely unpleasant fantasy.

He pushed off the trunk in time to see it splintered by a claw. Aster stumbled back and refocused his sight on a lane cutting through the trees, letting it guide him away; maybe not all the way away but at least to anywhere relatively safer, and free of that peeling shriek that polluted the air. How prolific was this species? Could this really be the only one in this whole wide wood?

More screeching chased after Aster. The last cry ended on a fading note.

Then, silence.

He ventured a quick peek and saw only trees. That wasn't a cue to slack. Before this encounter the only thing Aster really feared was the tight grip of his grief as it dragged him right over the edge of a seaside cliff and falling, like his mother, until the rocks below opened his body. Like his mother. Fear was now dressed in a new silhouette—an unpredictable form that came with agency and intent as it walked on claws and flapped its wings of skin. This new fear had a voice, harsh and predatory; far less soothing than the ebb and flow of an ocean current.

Aster propelled his legs, abandoning the linear route. He wound around trees and doubled back. It seemed the most productive way to lose the raptorial pursuer.

Another call rent the stillness, drowning out Aster's labored breathing. He raced in his confused path, then pulled up short as the creature descended just feet away, cinching Aster's limbs into a rigid state. He shuttered his lungs as the decrepit face closed in, its snout plucking and pulling at the scents in the air. A walloping cry hurled towards Aster. That was the signal. It dashed right for him as its lower lip bisected, making way for a pointed tongue. Fangs, wretched and coated in saliva, came into view. Acrid breath spilled out, stinging Aster's nose.

He threw an arm up across his face, against the immeasurable weight of danger lurching at him. His heartbeats rattled in his chest as his breathing thinned while pain invaded his arm. Tears clouded his vision as the beast's fangs sank deeper, un-tethering bits flesh. The world slowed, but Aster's heart raged on the longer he looked at the bite marks. No amount of staring damned the blood effusing out onto his skin, soaking into his clothes. Those fangs clamped down on his arm again, sending a wave of shock through Aster's body. A response prickled from his brain.

Aster reached out, ignoring the impulse to wail in pain and dug his finger into its fathomless eyeball. He pressed on through the squelching sound as he dug his finger in deeper. The greasy, almost snail-like, feel of the eye tempted Aster to abandon his mettle but on he drove through the moist, gelatinous matter until the creature was the one to wail. It fell back, taking with it a sampling of skin and muscle from Aster's arm.

Aster skirted the creature as it scrambled back onto its clawed feet, blasting the forest with high-pitched scream after scream, the echoes of which shook the leaves and branches above. He wanted very much to glance back, a move that didn't pay off last time, so he kept his attention forward carving as true a course as he could manage. The trees always seemed to close in.

All those trees. They stood around taunting Aster with an eternity trapped below their glossy leaves with that monstrosity shrieking after him. Trees blurred into smudges of green and gray as he attempted to pursue a linear route.

The air rang with a piercing call, an even pitch to signal the end of this wily chase. Crouched in a hollow, Aster cradled his wounded arm and coated it with what little mud he could find. Blood had stained his sleeve and the leg of his pants. Aster wiped his sweaty brow with the hem of his shirt. The scent pluming out of the pit under his arm caused Aster to crinkle his nose. He stopped.

Smelly shirt.

Bloody pants.

Aster shed his soiled clothes and ducked out of his hiding place. It was risky, but the notion of safety had been torn away like the skin from his flesh. It took most of Aster's mental capacity to cordon off the pain wrapping around his arm—the shivers and warmth crossing paths—and to still the erratic breathes. They pried at his attention even as his trap came together.

Aster sank low to the ground behind a cluster of trees. The beast appeared, turning its head as it followed the vocal blasts. Seeming to have latched onto the scent, it crept nearer then paused just feet away from where Aster hid.

The scent was there, carefully laid out in the form of trousers, shirt, and boots. For an extra kick, to really bring the illusion of presence home to this grotesque nose, undergarments had been included. It stopped in front of the discarded clothing which had been tied between two saplings. It sniffed. It bleated and clucked, appearing satisfied that it had found its prey. The tongue glowed as it licked at the fibers. Another harrowing call was let loose into the air.

Aster's heart wanted to burst. It strained hard as he repeated the thought *be still. Be still.* Those fangs. Aster clenched his teeth as he gently caressed his muddy arm. His wound seethed with a fever that danced with shivers crawling out to the rest of his body.

Only slivers of moonlight found its way through the forest roof.

The creature, a general shadow once again, went to work on the clothes. The thought of stumbling about in a strange forest naked, too many places for dirt and debris to invade, was about as unpleasant as the sounds the creature made. The ravenous snorts, like some unearthly swine coupled with a wound that burned in anger were reminders that threats more imminent threats than a dirt-covered bum needed attention.

Since there wasn't any meat to be got, the attack on the clothes was abandoned. It sniffed the air with that hideous snout, stalking closer as Aster shrunk behind the trees willing himself to be as small as possible. He lowered his hand to the ground. The sniffing was close enough to drum in his ears. Aster pinched his eyes shut. One chance to get it right. The words to the spell trembled at the back of his throat like the most powerful sounds he would ever utter.

This particular spell was chanted more with the throat and less with the lips and tongue, requiring the vibrations, instruments instead of mere vocals. The earth rattled with each hurried syllable.

The beast caught the sound of Aster's hurried chant. Too late. From the freshly riven earth, past the cushioned turf and maybe even deeper than the roots of these trees, came a scream to silence all others. The tone of predation peeled into a call of betrayal that echoed out of the earth, finally devolving simply into a violent fit.

Aster emerged from hiding, his hand still connected with the ground, still chanting to the soil and rocks to cooperate, leading the creature deeper and deeper to where only Life and Death knew. Aster retracted his hand from the ground and the gash he'd opened shut, leaving behind a small stitch and a few leaning trees.

He licked his dry lips and lifted his wounded arm closer to his face, trying to see the details. The moonbeams weren't thick enough to reveal the exactness of his injury. There were only signs and evidence to feel: a localized warmth that shouldn't have been present on such a cool night and a slightly sour tinge to the scent of his skin.

Aster pawed at the ground for what remained of his clothes because there wasn't any way in Death's dark shadow he was going to stumble around naked. He fell as he reached for his shirt and kept reaching until he gripped the familiar fabric. A bandage for the wound. There was just enough remaining of the pants to hang over his manhood.

All the movement sent the world on a tilt. His hand missed a nearby trunk and he met the ground in a rough embrace. Slowly, Aster regained his feet and careened on with his journey even though he hadn't a clue where to find Rose. Or anyone, for that matter. It was just him and the trees along with whatever else crawled and stalked the night.

"Anyone?" he whispered to the dark, cradling his wounded arm like a newborn babe. He slid down against a trunk until his bare ass touched the ground.

The forest was asleep, draped in beautiful sounds: no sound at all. Despite the tingling burn conquering his wound, Aster smiled grimly as he accepted the stillness, folding himself in with the hushed wood.

17.

OF A JAUNT INTO THE PAST

Nothing could summon light. Not even rapid-fire blinking dispelled the murk and piece together a coherent view. At least one hand still perceived textures and temperatures, enough to anchor Aster so he could crawl another yard.

Whatever blasted poison lived in the beast's fangs slowly ate away any feeling in his left arm; it was just meat hooked to his body now. Still, it was important to press on, if for no other reason than because the habit of living.

Aster realized each breath with the labor of persuasion, convincing his lungs to stay rather than drift away, as if they were bubbles and no longer cared to be party to a system keeping this man alive.

The same spry trees—or maybe it was just one tree playing tricks on Aster—looked down upon his lone prostrate form, offering no help. They were an assembly of slender nobles who deigned to acknowledge the lowly ones ambling by.

Joke was on them: they were stuck. Aster wheezed out a bit of laughter at the trees. He coughed and pressed forward. Or backward. Or sideways. Who knew? Every direction looked the same and felt like no direction at all, until a minuscule grade interrupted the landscape.

Aster shuffled along on his naked knees, trudging against the earth leaving tracks in the dirt and carpet of leaves. Up he went until the little hill crowned. The forest stopped and, like a curtain, parted to admit a view of the sky.

The feel of the cool soil was a kiss on his cheek, a kiss goodnight at the end of toil and labor. Whether or not this was the end of the journey, or the intended destination, it was as good a place as any to stop.

It might have felt like any other night of rest, whose embrace smothered away the brutish parameters of time. Deeper than necessary was the void of unconsciousness, un-punctuated by dream or nightmare. How could the slate be so clean when the poison flowed without mercy, without rebuttal from an antidote? Shouldn't there have been an attending fever-riddled vision at least, of a vastly cryptic, elegant nature?

"Right?"

There had to be a way to put this burning, catawampus world into shape? Detailed shape, not the muddled nonsense that presented itself at the moment.

"Right, what?" Aster nodded his head forward as light fought its way into his eyes.

A human shape hovered over him, but that wretched creature also had looked human before it attacked. It could be forgiven as Aster curled away from whomever, or whatever, loomed. He bit back a cry as a burning sting whiplashed across his chest.

"Settle back down, man."

Even with that annoying edge, Rustle's voice was a relief to hear. Aster blinked some more. The sky came into clear focus and the dry earth was right where he'd hoped to find it: beneath him. The world made sense once more.

Numbness clutched Aster's arm, all the way up to his shoulder, and began proselytizing its way into his torso. His dry lips cracked as he tried to speak, but words would not be summoned. "Lost. Attacked," were all the words Aster was able to produce.

Anxiety and annoyance mingled across Rustle's face as he stood beside Pixee, who glanced at the bite marks in Aster's skin. "What was it?"

Aster looked down at his arm along with Pixee. "Don't know." There wasn't a reason to herd out the details of the creature, hopefully suffocated beneath the weight of so much earth.

The wound looked gross, but not fatal. No bandage had been plied but it was dressed with some sort of paste. About a dozen pending questions were packaged in the look Aster served to Rustle. The reply to all the implied queries was a glance Rustle cast back over his own shoulder.

She breezed across the clearing with naked feet, her dark bronze hair flouncing with her easy steps. She brushed a few strands from off her face, away from her high cheek bones and petite nose. Her dress was simple, earthy in color.

That unadorned presentation gave Aster the illusion that he looked upon a different person, someone he had not yet met. The face was unmistakable. Unforgettable. She had been this sort of pastel-looking person, with a satin sheen, but now she existed in rustic hues with a matte finish; a different sort of beauty.

"Rose." Aster said her name as he would utter a prayer, wrapping his lips around the shape of it.

She knelt down and her eyes came into focus, shades of olive and walnut swirling in and out of one another. She bent slightly to examine Aster's arm, giving the wound a thorough yet tender prodding. He withdrew from her examination; withdrew from her as she had from him years ago.

"You never explained." The words had been pressing into Aster's skull since Rose arrived at his side, bursting forth before he could rightly think about them, ingredients thrown into a pan without so much as a consideration about what the resulting dish would be.

"There's a lot we didn't share with one another. There's a lot you never learned about me nor I about you."

"I loved you." An instinctual reply, like flinching at bright light.

"I never doubted your affection for me." Her attention, which had been glued to Aster, slipped and found Rustle for a brief moment before she looked back. "There just wasn't enough time for us to be like others, to dive into one another's lives."

"You just disappeared on me." The words weren't carefully chosen, obviously, a fact acknowledged by Rustle's emphatic throat clearing.

Aster ignored Rustle's dire warning, and heeded none but Rose. In her eyes there was a sense of depth. A glance at them and Aster fell, past the swirling earth tones of her irises, down into her pupils. What was going on in her eyes that there was no arriving, no landing? Just…space.

Had no one else not noticed that Rose's once alluring gaze was amiss? All the contours—textures of personality, of perspective—scooped away.

Maybe by someone?

She didn't react—nothing of summer's warmth nor winter's frost emerged from her—so Aster ventured on: "Where did you go? I had breakfast waiting for you."

"You made wonderful breakfasts." Her slender fingers rested lightly on her knees, her were nails clean and pearly. It surprised Aster how clean they were. "An artist in the kitchen."

He looked at her hands with a frown. "Not good enough to keep you coming back though."

No amount of pointed staring from Pixee or Rustle stopped Aster from exploring for reasons.

A crooked grin came onto Rustle's face. "She was always bailing me out."

The questions must have ticked across Aster's face, as much as he may have wanted to affect stoicism.

"It was kind of a debt. She…" His voice dipped almost to a whisper. "She paid it for me. Paid more than I should have let her."

That clearing lurched into silence, in which all attention poured upon Rustle. How much mint did this debt cost? His sullen tone made it seem like some price beyond the reckoning of numbers.

Instead of supplying more detail, Rustle pointed at the onlookers. "This thing that we're doing has nothing to do with this—" as he dragged a pointed finger between Aster and Rose. "So, let's have on with whatever is not this."

For many moments, no one made a sound. Aster cleared his throat to dust away the mounting tension. "So…" He cooked up some words to season the inert conversation. "Looks like you've been doing well for yourself out here in the woods."

"Thank you," Rose replied.

"Nice to see the foul creatures of the forest haven't marred your home."

"Oxalis," she named the beast. "They're territorial and vicious about it, but tend to only stalk the parts of the forest they've claimed. It's a wonder you got away." She rotated his arm. Her lithe fingers pinched the skin around the bite. "The poison is subdued. You should be fine." Rose released Aster and strolled away.

Rustle shrugged an *I told you* so at Aster before meandering off himself, as if he were exploring the little clearing.

"The least you can do is hear Aster out." Pixee stood and called to Rose. "You owe him that much. And more." She squatted back down and watched.

Rose scrutinized Pixee, in return. She looked at Aster. Her impassive glance didn't simply rest on any one person; it pried away at all who were present, as if she would peel away their mortal coils and reach their very souls. It was a matter-of-fact kind of look; no judgment or evaluation, just cold observation.

Aster sighed because her stare pulled the point right out of him. "I need to find a guy who stole from me. I've made a trade with an individual by the name of Mr. Oleander. I take care of him and then he takes care of me."

Unearthly silence saturated the gathering so thoroughly Aster plugged up any other words and just sat. The entire group was motionless. Except Rustle. He loitered about inspecting the trees that encircled the ground.

Rose appeared to be gathering up an unequivocal *no*. It certainly looked like the word dangled upon her lips, waiting to be thrust out into the world. Then she replied; not with words, but with a polite, ghostly smile before drifting away, her unshod feet barely impressing the rich soil.

Pixee helped Aster up and they followed her to a small pool not far from her tiny dwelling. She inspected the languid heavens peering down upon creatures too stupid or too timid to understand the breadth and depth of existence.

She glanced back at the planate water, the pale blue sky playing on the surface. "You are too early," she said in a tone as calm as the sky itself. "For the spell to be of enough use, we must have an abundant moon, which is still two nights away."

Her decree left Aster exchanging uneasy glances with Rustle. That abundant moon would be the last before the ripened moon graced the sky.

Rose walked back to her hut, which she made to enter. Rustle moved to follow. "You're free to wait for the abundant moon," she repeated, "but you will do it out here with your fellows, not in my quarters."

Rustle looked back over his shoulder at Aster and Pixee, a stone's throw away from the rectangle of water. "Really? Come with it, Rose. I'm your brother."

"My hovel is my own. Your friends are yours." She slipped inside.

Rustle sank down into the gap between Aster and Pixee.

"A warm welcome," Pixee observed.

"Truly," Rustle agreed. "Weird. So, you must have about a million thoughts right about now." He nudged Aster's shoulder.

Aster nodded. "They're all about how to get the gem back to Mr. Oleander before his deadline."

"Sure, that's all you're thinking about." Rustle chuckled.

Pixee looked sidelong at Rustle without a crack of expression upon her face. "You're an ass."

"Reliable. Durable. Loves the outdoors?" Rustle laid back with his fingers laced behind his head. "Yes, I'm all of that."

The banter mashed together for Aster and his mind only caught one word; it wasn't even one spoken in the conversation: *moon*. It rang in his mind both encouraging him and taunting him. Reclaiming the last bit of the Martese was just another step in the process of a larger pursuit. The magic was merely the wings upon which a desire caught wind, took flight, and melted into the eternal sky, while in a more grounded sense getting the fire fruit to seed, to be present in all corners of Thuidium, was the true goal.

Creation encapsulated all those steps. Thinking about it, saying it over in his mind, brought a smile to grace Aster's lips.

The change in expression did not go unnoticed, by Rustle, at least. "You're thinking about her," Rustle declared.

The emphatic comment from Rustle did not dismiss Aster's smile entirely. He just calmed it down a bit. "Rose? No. I was just thinking about something else." His smile flared again.

Pixee joined him. Maybe she guessed the source of the mirth waxing upon his lips. Maybe she just smiled to see him smiling. She didn't say which. The moment was unto itself, observed, and enjoyed.

Not Rustle, though. "Out with it, then. If it isn't seeing your old flame, why are you grinning so much?"

Aster tucked away his grin. Why Rustle couldn't just silently smile along with Pixee was, in short, annoying. That is what happens when other people are included on the journey, other people like Rustle who are perpetually chatty. There was such a thing as silently observing or minimizing contributions.

"Since you're insisting I share—"

Rustle sat up, posture in perfect form, hands in his lap with his lips draped in a smile. "I am insisting. You know," he said, relaxing a bit, "our paths have been crossing for a while but I can't say that I actually know you."

Pixee, who had been sitting at the edge of the conversation with her little grin, drew in at Rustle's admission. Their glances pressed upon Aster, scratching and pawing for some kind of peek beneath the surface. Well, Rustle seemed to be mining more than Pixee, but a wisp of curiosity glazed her eyes. That was what made her and Aster so compatible: she wanted to know, but wouldn't show it. He wanted to open up but wouldn't show it. Somewhere it would all come out naturally, like the eventual rise of cream.

"What's got your mind all twisted up?"

The reinstated smile felt like a confession, a tear in the façade that would leak every intimate detail. Not even hints; a full flood of unmistakable truth and information. Aster tried to patch up the grin so he could get away with saying only so much.

"Pizazz," he told Rustle.

"Pizzz…" Rustle tried to emulate the word, but his face merely crinkled as if he had been offered a freshly excavated earthworm for a snack.

"Like you're going to say piss, except you keep that last S-sound going for a little bit, then throw in some ass at the end." Strange explaining a word that had been wheeling around deep in the bedrock of Aster's imagination. Here it was, sprouting up, being introduced to the world.

The world heard it for the first time, but didn't seem so sure.

"Man, I don't know," Rustle commented, as if he had spat the word out and refused to try it again. "You are talking something crazy over there. That's really what's on your mind? Not Rose?"

"I'm not thinking about Rose. She left me and didn't say why, so I'm trying to not make room for her in my thoughts. As much as I would like her to explain things, she's not offering so I'm thinking about—"

"What is pizazz, then?" Pixee scooted in a little closer, almost touching Rustle, but being careful not to actually touch him.

The corners of Aster's mouth drew up again after hearing another voice speak that magical word. "It's the sparkle in a gem." Really, it was something he felt more than he knew. Defining it was elusive at first, then: "It's music stealing away silence. It's when your food speaks up and the flavor just sinks into your tongue." Aster nodded, more to himself than his companions who stared, frozen.

Were they even breathing? Their eyes seemed to be swiveling over Aster's face, calculating how far adrift he had gone, mentally. Obviously that their minds had some pretty sharp boundaries.

"You all look like you've never used your imaginations before."

"Oh, I've imagined plenty of times," Rustle said. "I've imagined how to sell some shit. I've imagined myself with a pile of mint that never shrinks. I've imagined kissing this charming individual over here." He winked at Pixee, who drew away from his forward proclamation of attraction. "But whatever you're using your imagination on, Aster, I just do not get."

"And that's fine," Aster replied, crunching dried leaves between his palms. "You don't have to, but I'm going to keep on imagining it."

"What do you imagine?"

Pixee's question turned the entire audience on Aster again. He gaped for a moment unsure about the authentic interest circling his ideas. If he wanted to really go for it—and he did—this is the kind of moment he would need, over and over: people inquiring, wanting to know more about this...pizazz.

"Since you're so keen to know, I imagine a new world of flavors. I imagine cooking up a taste that hasn't been experienced before. Fire and earth coming together in a small fruit I call fire fruit." He paused, reading the faces of his audience. Where Rustle looked a blank page. Pixee appeared more uncertain. What the look boded for Aster didn't matter. She often displayed that expression to him, when his ideas came out the frying pan.

The goal may have started as a lark, a bit of a distraction from grief. The longer the idea of the fire fruit stewed—the more it was shared, and the more Aster invested into completing it—the process became infused with passion and excitement, taking it all from amusement to survival: that which had to be done until it couldn't be done any longer.

Aster cleared his throat. "A little berry-like food that has a smoky-sweet flavor and releases a feeling of heat when you bite into it," he explained.

"But why fruit? Of all the things you could have created or invented," Pixee asked, giving room for curiosity.

"That's just where my mind goes: food and flavors. You know my mom she—" His voice caught at that word. The faces of people he knew so intimately—even the ones he didn't necessarily like—were too detailed, too heavy for his eyes to hold. The ground between his feet received the rest of the answer instead. "—she always smiled when I would help her bake or cook."

Pixee nodded. The approval of the idea wasn't necessary. Approval or comprehension didn't propel Aster's imagination; he'd carry on with or without it. Now that this idea had been shared with someone other than Oren, it felt all the more real. Aster smiled once again.

Rustle gave Pixee a last glance before laying back. Aster stared up at the sky like it was the last phase of the Martese dangled over him According to Aster's understanding, the key to making the fire fruit a reality hinged on those words.

The sky wheeled, rotating from day to evening, and into night. Gone was the sun. Slowly the moon rode the same arc, in reverse. Were they the same object, the sun and moon? It could have been one rock and behind the mountains sat a practitioner of immense power lighting it or snuffing it out. Aster chuckled at the little story his imagination produced as he watched the moon peer down into the clearing. A new moon blending neatly with the black sky.

The abundant moon could not arrive quickly enough.

18.

OF WITCHCRAFT
& A BREEZE

Rose had not been seen at all that day. They waited patiently, content to remain within the safety of the clearing watching the sky dim in its methodical, precise way; the sun eventually passing beyond the canopy signaling to the shadows it was time to creep out from between the trees.

"I'll get started on the fire," Pixee said.

While she gathered wood from the ground, Aster watched the forest beyond Rose's hovel. There was nothing to be seen moving in shadows between the trunks and under boughs. Aster felt Rustle's gaze on him. "What?"

"Getting anxious or something?"

"Yes." Aster trudged over towards the merry little blaze Pixee had brought to life. "I know she'll make good. I'd just like to get going. This waiting feels like time wasted."

Night surrounded them in its fullness, draping a bolt of darkness over the shape of things. The strained glow of a meager fire beat back somewhat of the intrusion. Rose emerged from the night, passing into the ring of firelight as if it were a tent. Cradled in her left arm was a clay ewer, about forty-five centimeters tall, and in her right hand she held a metallic tray upon which was a collection of what looked like phials. She directed that the fire be extinguished as she sat near the pool.

"We need no other light intruding upon the moon's beams." When the clearing was void of light, and but a lingering smell of smoke perfumed the air, Rose set the ewer on the ground. "It's time."

They gathered closer to the pool's edge, peering at the water. Not a single ripple disturbed its surface until Rose emptied the ewer. The agitated water glittered as it reached up to the very edge of the pool. "You need a personal item of the individual for whom you seek."

Everyone glanced at each other. "I, uh, what?" Aster felt the tingle of failure brush against his hairline at the mention of this unanticipated ingredient. How was he to know how witchcraft worked?

"I can't use your memory of him. We need a physical connection," Rose explained.

"A bandage with some dried blood?" Pixee drew a swath of used gauze from her sack. "What?" she said to Aster's surprise. "I had a hunch."

The bandage passed before Aster. "A weird hunch if I've ever heard one."

She shrugged at the comment. "That could be because of your fixation with the destination and not thinking about all the little steps before you get there."

Aster rolled his eyes at the sentiment. He was a goal-oriented person. He knew about steps and processes. Creating an entirely new fruit wasn't accomplished by mere impulse.

"Just because I don't know all the ins and outs of witchcraft—"

Rose ended the debate with a glance as she accepted the used bandage with its rusty stains and offered it, in turn, to the water. For a moment it lingered at the surface until the blood gradually livened into a ruddier shade. Fully saturated, the gauze sank into the depths. All three tenths of a meter.

Rose took a phial from off her tray and tipped it over the pool. Oil met the water. "All things from the earth have function and a purpose. In this rosemary oil is the purpose of remembrance."

The air about the pool tingled with an aroma, slightly spicy but mostly earthy. Aster breathed in the all-too-familiar scent and as it settled in his nose he was back in the kitchen, simply living. The others also drew in the redolent air.

"Is that part of the spell?" Rustle asked no one in particular.

There was a little bowl sitting on the tray, from which Rose took a scoop of a powder. Into the water she then sprinkled what looked like ashes.

"Of tarragon," she explained without answering Rustle's inquiry. "That the waters may maintain interest in the blood being lifted from the bandage." Rose turned to the water. Her voice, in tones softer than a boiled potato, joined the brew she had created.

In the dark water small pellets of red gathered, as if pulled off the bandage and told to seek out the other drops of freed blood. Without hint or warning the moon rode over the bulwark of the forest canopy spilling a frosty glow into the clearing. The abundant moon peered back from the water's surface, a duplication of the sky sitting in the ground. It embraced the blood into a disk. Hugged it, read it, interpreted it, and spat back an image.

Perfectly rendered nicely within the sphere of the moon's reflection was Sedge's likeness. It was an eerily accurate vision. The light creases, like little crescents around his lips, just the way Aster remembered. He pulled away from the pool, and attempted to focus on any part of this situation that would be less jolting.

Rose presided over this magic as if she loved every ingredient. It was something to see the details of witchcraft were fascinating, so far from the magic of Life or even Death. This practice was all over the place, but humble at the same time.

"The one you seek?" Rose asked of the luminescent image floating upon the now still water.

Aster cleared his throat, feigning disinterest yet at the same time unable to deny that some aspect about Sedge had impressed itself upon him. A sense of admiration, mingled with relief, was welded there, and possibly, for reasons beyond this search. "Truly. Him."

"This doesn't seem to show us where he is." Pixee scrutinized Rose across the enchanted pool.

Rose uttered not a word. The singular wind grazing over the water, creasing the still surface, was the only response she had to offer, and one sufficient enough to bottle all of Pixee's skepticism.

They all let the phantom air trace across their blank stares. Rustle even gave the breeze a sniff like a dog, uncertain about what this all meant for their pursuit. Rose broke her stare with Pixee and turned to Aster, who also sniffed at the moving air. She queried him with a look.

The scent was Sedge, sure as Death stalks the life-after. Ever since Sedge's convalescence it clung to the bedding just another fiber woven into the whole, and couldn't be washed away. Couldn't? Hadn't been washed away was more to the truth. There was a note in the scent, an unexpected serenity that stole over Aster on first whiff, that persuaded him something fierce to erased any reason to purge Sedge's lingering aroma from the linens. Aster decided it was the scent of confidence. Even in the short amount of time spent with Sedge, it was clear he filled with it, but not in over-bearing rude amounts.

Every breath of the aroma dredged up Rose's spell intensified interest in Sedge: from his façade appeared and every iota beneath, right down to the dubious behavior.

"The gale will fade," Rose warned. "We'll need to follow it quickly."

The leaves that twisted and fluttered—along with those that stirred not—plotted a course through the forest. The visible signs were accentuated by his essence, dripping from the air. Maybe not to the others who hadn't lain with that smell, but it was an undeniable tell to one who had, like catching a whiff of freshly baked bread in a room full of cats. Who hadn't been let outside in weeks. The others didn't need to know how acutely Aster picked up on the trail.

They pursued the breeze all through the night, leaving behind the homely clearing. The journey started easy enough until a shriek peeled through the forest, rattling the scent right out of the breeze. Aster halted, hugging his still-healing arm closer to his abdomen.

"Keep on," Rose assured them. "The moon will not wait."

The group proceeded through the trees at a clip. The wailing sounded again, but closer. Aster stopped. Rose paused beside him as a shriek hit them from behind. Aster stumbled forward, his bandaged arm slamming against the ground. He clenched his teeth, stifling a yelp of pain. Aster scrambled back up to his feet.

"Onward," Rose commanded the rest of the group as the creatures drew near.

Aster licked his dry lips, ready to utter some spell to help. Another cry reached up into the canopy.

The Oxali—for not one, but two—stopped and looked in Rose's direction. No screams were issued, but some guttural reply bubbled up from the throat of one of the beasts. Between the witch and the predators, a moment transpired. The creatures sniffed out the air, stamping their clawed feet and beating their wings in a cascading pattern.

In the face of these gestures, Rose stood true with her chin out. She closed her eyes threw back her head and unleashed a rending howl. The screech pitched higher than the squeal of the their attackers. The forest itself acquiesced to sound. The pursuing Oxali slowly retreated. For good measure, Rose squawked again at the creatures.

Aster finally let out the breath he had been reserving through the whole confrontation. "You learned to sound like them?"

"Survival skill," she replied. "It's how I've kept my clearing safe and free of them." She held out a hand.

Aster caressed Rose's fingers as she helped him up, almost too soft for one living alone in the woods. Too perfect was their shape and proportions, like an unattainable state of being made manifest. Was she even human anymore? Or maybe she just wasn't what he'd always made her out to be in his mind.

The Sedge-scented breeze flurried between Aster and Rose. Without thinking, he inhaled.

"Come. The spell ends when the moon sets." Rose said.

The horses beat out an unceasing song against the earth as the forest dwindled into the background. Rose sat behind Rustle on his borrowed mare. Aster kept tabs on the guiding wind as he rode at the head. Pixee followed upon Iridium.

After crossing the river, they raced to keep up with the telltale wind. It wasn't an encompassing breeze of the world, moving like a giant blanket, to fill all available space. This conjured waft passed along the grass like a singular thread. Aster held onto that string of specific air with every available sense while it rolled on ahead.

The graceful strand of scented air now bent in a westward direction. Aster guided his steed to follow racing with the night, but not too fast. There was the matter of keeping feelers—and his sniffer— out for any shifts in this pneumatic guide.

With his focus on the goal at-hand, Aster rode slightly perpendicular to the mountains. They were bulky shadows that reached out for the darkened sky while the gossamer orb retreated towards the sea, a sign that the spell would break soon. If that streamer of air, laced with scent of Sedge, vanished before they met their destination...

No time for *what if*'s and *oh no*'s. Time was a simple cup with room enough for the possible. It was too precious, too finite to waste even a single drop.

As Aster led the group along, prodding himself to focus on the chase, the moon had been sliced in half by a horizon waiting to swallow it completely. It was close. Too close.

Their hunt lasted until the moon dipped completely out of the sky, taking the aura of Sedge along with it.

Aster checked his horse glancing about in sort of a stupor, for all of Thuidium lay still. Not one blade of grass stirred. It was the time of night when no light dominated the sky. Unlike the sun, the moon left no lingering trail, a teasing wink of radiance dying slower than the source. The chance for any more progress was killed by the sun as it was slowly exhumed from behind the world's farthest edge.

"It will be back," Rose replied to nothing Aster had said, "when the moon is back."

"Let's rest. Allow the horses a break," Pixee added as she let Iridium graze.

It wasn't easy vacating the saddle when they were there and Sedge was not. There was nothing for it.

It felt as though the night had blinked. Aster fought back a yawn as the sky along the western edge of the world blushed ever so slightly.

Pixee let go and was soon asleep. Rustle and Rose sat together, not a word passing between them. It was a painting, so still and silent they sat. No point in disturbing the scene with another unnecessary visit to histories, bitter and confusing.

The intrusive ball of fire peered over the horizon and swept away the night in a fit of sunshine.

The day passed much slower than the night. Hour after hour of light loitering in conspiracy against Aster and his intentions. After a fitful rest ushered away what remained of the day, Aster sat in anticipation as night bled back into the sky. The moon broke upon the world, a little duller than the night before. The guiding air took more effort to follow on this leg of the chase.

So it went on the third night. They guided their horses slower with each passing moon. The trail stayed true, rolling farther north.

Asters spoke less to his companions as the venture stretched on. Conversation was stifled by the unease proliferating in his mind.

The moon, both guide and clock, lent a crushing dread with all its implications. The duller it became, the heavier those they pressed.

Ahead loomed the Copac, another forest that could be found on any common map of Thudium. It was as though the trail flowed out of the clustered wooden realm, much more densely crowded than the Wald. An arm of trees stretched away from the main body of the forest, a sort of wall to block the view of the land beyond. The forest was a mere hundred yards off when Aster suddenly brought his steed to a docile trot. While the other riders huddled about, he kept his nose to the open air peeling away background scents from the intimate smell of Sedge, which was now a faint trace. So faint that Aster had to check his horse altogether as he attempted to discern which way his bearing lay.

A confusion of night sounds distracted Aster's focus while competing odors obscured the path. His own musk—growing stronger with each day of riding and the pressure of the dimming moon—along with the dewy grass, and his horse plagued their advancement.

The enigma of which way to proceed wrapped up Aster so completely he hadn't noticed the moon escaping from the sky; it was the final stage before the ripened moon would ascend.

All these musings about deadlines muffled Pixee's attempts reclaim Aster's attention. As faint and uninteresting as they were to Aster, her persistent calls took hold and he eventually turned in his saddle. "Huh?"

"Aster," she said calmly. "It's over."

The sound of everyone dismounting grated against the calm night. Aster breathed deeply to assuage the headache throbbing from his temple to his neck. It was a cudgel to his hope, these acts of resignation performed by his companions.

Until, lo! The approach of galloping hooves signaled a new tune. Aster smiled as he once again twisted in his saddle, certain this time he'd glimpse Sedge approaching on horseback.

19.

OF PARLEYS

Aster vacated his saddle as the rest of the camp froze in anticipation. They collectively stared into a mass of darkness, out of which came the rapid approach of a rider. The hooves of a bronco cut the expectancy with thudding sounds.

He sat there mounted upon its back. "Don't look so petrified." He dismounted, his lips dressed with a faint grin, probably in admiration of the stunned silence his appearance effected, a form of spell neither teachable nor comprehensible.

Aster dusted off his hands. They were clammy. The dirt clung to his palms with an annoying amount of insistence. He brushed harder. "Uh, Mr. Oleander. Um, what are you doing here?"

He stood beaming at Aster. All his levity looked out of place between Rustle's cocktail of fear and shock and Pixee's blank stare. "Our agreement was to have that gem back in my hand by the ripened moon. Since we're merely hours away, I thought I'd meet up with you. You'll have to pardon my excitement."

From nowhere he produced a rose and presented it to Rose. She took the gift, cupping the base of the petals. An odd scene, but all at once familiar. Aster furrowed his brow as he tried to recall where he had seen this play out before. Silly was that thought because he hadn't seen Rose in years and had never seen her interact with Mr. Oleander. Didn't even know they were familiar with one another.

Pixee's blank stare cracked and out seeped sneer. "Was it that kind of enthusiasm that got you kicked out of the Order?"

He looked her up and down. "Whomever you might be, where did you hear such stories?" He tussled her short, brown hair.

Pixee wrenched away moving closer to Iridium. She crossed her arms over her chest. "Oren and I have had some pretty long chats. The ill fame of a Thanatist travels fast, besides." She declared the title with a boldness that no one else dared.

"Clever little lady," Mr. Oleander noted with a condescending chuckle. "Let me set the record straight, since you seem insistent on visiting the past. My only crime was being too curious. Curiosity leads to questions, and apparently asking questions was heresy. For that, I was excommunicated. You can tell Oren that the next time you and him have tea. Or whatever you two do." He moved about making himself at home, as it were.

The others tried to follow, relaxing as best they could.

"And you want this red gem to fix all that?"

"No, Aster. It won't fix a thing." Mr. Oleander situated himself upon the ground, looking almost out of place. "There's no point in looking back. We must be ever moving forward. This red gem will provide me with the sort of power that I am lacking, as much as I hate to admit it."

"Power for what?" Pixee's eyes narrowed.

"To change the scope of existence. To bring mortals to the next stage. Life and Death, mostly Death, perfunctory deities they are, just outright refuse to give an accounting of the horrors and wonders that are existence. You get a blink of time to figure out as much as you can and you end up with more questions than answers. Add to that, Life and Death are the ones to determine the fate of your eternal soul. Are you enlightened enough to spend eternity in the warmth of the sun? Maybe. Maybe you're only good enough to linger in the soft glow of the moon? Or, you could be deserving of some place among the stars. Or worse yet, your soul is smudged into the cold void that is entirely without light or warmth. We deserve more. We deserve as much time as we want, to learn as much as we want. Our fates should be our own to carve out. Don't Life and Death owe us that much?"

Either no one agreed or no one cared to argue since they all just settled in for the day.

"They do," Mr. Oleander declared to his captive audience, namely Pixee and Aster. "You're expected to play this game, which you didn't even start. The bastards setting up the board should be answerable to the players." Mr. Oleander punctuated that last statement with his devious smile, a sort of snaking leer rooted in hunger.

Was that the sort of expression he wore as he talked about the fire fruit with Rustle and Pixee? Was it what Oren saw when he had been presented with a newly concocted samples?

Aster shuddered to think he ever presented such a look.

Mr. Oleander raised himself off the ground. He met Aster on the other side of the fire, looking him up and down. "I'm going to guess that since you're halted out here in this uncultivated spit of Thuidium that you've yet to find the gem."

It was a fight to not belie the truth. Aster was unable to conjure up a façade resilient against Mr. Oleander's piercing gaze.

The man chuckled. He looked at Rustle while pointing at Aster. "This guy, right?"

Rustle offered a half grin, like he was ready to vomit or even just scream, at the sight and sound of Mr. Oleander's sick jocularity.

"Man, Rustle. If only you had half the charisma Aster does."

The slight grin fell from Rustle's face despite all the laughter being offered Mr. Oleander.

All of this supposed-mirth pouring out of Mr. Oleander even kept Aster's muscles taught and wrenching against his bones.

"Uh, truly," Aster stuttered as he tried to free an explanation from the tension grinding up and down his body, "Rose here...uh, she being witch, and all, was helping us, um, find the thief." It felt like a babbling account, but the gist was tucked in there amidst the fillers.

Mr. Oleander leaned in, almost touching Aster's ear with his lips. "Since you're so close, I can only assume you won't mind if we get that gem together. If you're not, then I'll let Rustle explain the consequences." He returned to his seat as the sky filtered into a pale , golden morning. The horses clipped at the grass, unconcerned with the notion of deadlines.

Aster dared not sigh, dared not experience the un-knotting feeling of relief. Even though he sat a few feet away, the shadow of Mr. Oleander loomed, his threat still pressing against Aster's ear. There would be no swallowing those words. One either choked on them or held on to them, letting their acuteness burn like pieces of fried meat that simply would not cool.

Aster vacated the camp mumbling something about hunger. No one bothered watching him as he shuttled off to hunt or gather. It was anyone's guess.

The camp had fully settled by the time Aster returned an hour to two later. Mr. Oleander, after having given his horse some attention, sat down beside Aster while the others rested silently, letting the fatigue from the hard ride slough away.

"What is this that you're making?" Mr. Oleander leaned in to steal a glance of the contents: a splayed fowl situated in some sort of clay bowl set upon amber embers that twinkled like jewels.

"Just a bit of a meal before we rest." Kept with care, down below an extra change of clothes, the single blanket, and inside a small box of wood was a blend of seasoning which dusted the meat as it began to percolate with the rendering of its own fat. The rural notes of bay, thyme, and sage were coupled with the punch of pepper and dried onions. Those little individual aromatic profiles danced upon the smoke and still there was something missing from it all.

It always came back to that word: kick. No amount of days or miles could put that moment far enough in the past. It was a seed unto itself germinating, worming roots into every recall and speculation.

Mr. Oleander looked at Aster—ignoring, for the moment, the playful scent of a crisping bird—and Aster looked back at that ponderous stare.

Guessing the intent behind the meaty gaze Aster said, "That ripened moon hasn't risen yet. There's still time." In the space between the asking and the answering, no breathing was allowed. Aster tried to will his heart to be still.

Mr. Oleander grinned in an amicable way. "In a finer sense, that's true and I hope you're right for the sake of this—" From some pocket, undetectable in all that black fabric, Mr. Oleander produced the page, the words for which Aster lusted, and dangled it just out of reach of the fire. With a brief flurry of laughter Mr. Oleander tucked the paper away. "But also for your sake, too." He patted Aster's knee. "Because I'd hate to execute the dire consequences upon such a promising young man."

Young man, said the person who looked as many years as Aster himself.

Pixee had rolled over and taken to sleep. Rose gave her attention to the forest. Mr. Oleander rested, too, near his horse. Aster ignored the deeply even breathes of his sleeping companions and gave himself over to the minuscule meal. The creature he found to supply meat was barely enough to feed two, but the need to prepare and to cook stung at Aster's hands, tingling in his fingers waiting to be exercised.

Not that this was about filing a belly, really. This had been more about purpose. The practice of flavoring, the movements of creation. From the earthenware, a small bite was plucked. And another, to savor the texture, the consistency; the sapidity rolling across the tongue and whispering away into a fond memory.

The need for a kick of flavor, of a new essence, beckoning from Aster's tongue would have to wait; albeit, hopefully not much longer. With that hope, Aster let sleep envelop his senses in forgetfulness.

"Time to get a move on."

Mr. Oleander's voice yanked away the tenuous slumber, which basically amounted to a nap. "Already?"

"Come along with it," Mr. Oleander replied. "The night is young and the moon approaches." He looked down upon Aster, who was rubbing sleep from his eyes. "Before the deadline expires."

Couldn't argue with that. Their camp was alive with activity as everyone readied for the final leg of their hunt, whether that ended with locating Sedge or not. Would they be venturing into those knotted, ancient-looking trees? Their trunks and limbs grew into twisted shapes of the sort Aster hadn't before seen in trees. Did their destination await them beyond the Copac?

The foretold moon climbed up from where the sun had set. Over the mountain tips, it hovered, and well had its name been given Not the stark yellow of a sunflower, but a simple iteration of the color reached out of the sky. It didn't glow so much as it looked dyed. That clever hypothetical-practitioner had painted over the new moon in the most innocent child-like color a person could concoct. Aster had no memory of ever seeing such a moon before.

Just beneath the wonder and curiosity evoked by this rare moon, panic stirred. No illumination meant no guiding wind, or so Aster assumed. His querying glance at Rose was received in kind. Her static response felt like confirmation, but Aster still picked at the air for any hint of Sedge, but his senses were left wanting.

The group stared, their unblinking gazes squeezing the breath out of Aster like a tree had fallen across his body, not that such an experience was one that he had actually ever had, but this moment couldn't have been much different. Coupled with the blatant absence of an obvious path to follow, the whole situation added up to a crushing sensation, the pressure to provide an answer smooshing harder and harder against Aster's whole body.

There wasn't time for more windings and wanderings. A quick glance at a smirking Mr. Oleander made it clear that a decision had to be met. Aster stood by his horse, scouring for even the faintest trace of a clue.

Deciding he sensed a bit of stirring in the air, Aster mounted and urged his horse along. The others followed, keeping a step or two behind. Aster rode around the outcrop of trees because going through them felt an unnecessary use of time.

Whether the gargantuan rock had been dropped there or grew out of some series of naturally cataclysmic events while the world was still being ordered, no one knew. There it sat, eternal and proud, like it was a fixture of the little valley. Humans obviously saw the usefulness in it, so it was formed and fashioned into a habitable structure. With each new occupant, features were added: catacombs below, towers above, defenses all around; a series of accessories adding up to what was affectionately referred to simply as the Keep.

The Keep appeared foreboding enough. A few torches hinted at a gate and attending guards.

"Your thief awaits?" Mr. Oleander nodded towards the Keep while eyeing Aster.

The simple, honest answer was the clue had dried up. Finding himself before a fortress was simply good fortune. Had they rounded those trees and found only more uninhabited scenery, well Aster swallowed away the dread-hypothetical reaction that would have spilled from Mr. Oleander had that been the case. All that was left to do was hope this particular structure was the right one.

"If this is where the trail ends," Pixee turned her eyes up to the sky before she slipped off Iridium's back. "We'd still need to wait until sunrise." She trailed away and began to establish another camp. No fire, just a place to sit and wait out the night.

After the deadline, of course.

Mr. Oleander must have deciphered the fear rolling across Aster's face. To hide any hints about what percolated behind his eyes, Aster focused on the tiny fires burning along the Keep's stone walls.

"After the moon passes and with no gem to hand over." He patted the spell hidden within his garment.

Did this moment call for pleading and begging? Mr. Oleander didn't strike Aster as the type to give two-shits about either. In fact, he probably loathed the sound of pleas and supplications.

"Fine. Do what you will," Aster replied. As he went to join Pixee and Rustle he stole a quick, undetected glance at Mr. Oleander, who looked to be trying to quell a smile. Maybe Aster understood Mr. Oleander because the slip of paper, that essential spell, remained tucked away safely in its hidden pocket.

Mr. Oleander remained to himself, apart from the group, while Aster joined the others in their haphazard arrangement.

Rustle tore at the grass near his feet as he shot a glance towards Mr. Oleander. "What was that about?" He whispered to Aster, who shrugged.

The current proprietor of the Keep was one Rowan, a warlord, which was how he declared himself to the visitors who called at his gate. There wasn't anything of surprise written with the lines of his rough face, capped with a shorn head. He glared under thick eyebrows while his thin lips remained unmoved.

"And your business here being?" Rowan called down. One hand clasped the hilt of a sword while the other hung at his side.

"This would probably be better discussed," Mr. Oleander replied, "if you weren't up there and we down here. Come from off your battlements so we can converse, not shout."

Rowan turned and held council with his own folk. Peeking our from among those with whom he conferred, Aster spotted that familiar face, casting down quick glances.

Sedge. Ran home to daddy.

"Spotted the thief, have you?" Mr. Oleander asked across Aster's silent musings.

"Up there, standing just behind Rowan." He leaned towards Mr. Oleander. "What if they don't come down and talk with us?"

"Ways and means." He gave Aster a pat on the shoulder. "Ways and means."

"Not likely." Rowan replied as he tightened the grip on his weapon, ready to unsheathe the blade. "Such a one as a Thanatist is better left outside my gate."

The word had a crude and uncouth cadence, the way Rowan pronounced it. However it was said, whoever uttered it, Mr. Oleander remained unfazed by its use. Who was Rowan to lambaste with certain labels, anyways? He made a living off gross unethical practices like usury and extortion. He usurped the agency of his fellow humans, and did so with pride. No moral high-ground had he.

"Shout your purpose. We can hear you just fine." Rowan leaned against the wall and waited.

Sedge stood back though. If he meant to blend out of sight, he failed. His presence was plain as day to Aster, who took a few steps closer.

"We're just here to restore the property your son acquired unethically from this poor, destitute farmer." Mr. Oleander used the most aggrieved voice of which he was capable.

Mr. Oleander's partial embrace—an uncomfortable mockery of the paternal—was not to be wasted and, therefore, would not be shrugged off even with a bit of wiggling. He carried out the effect with a taut grip. Everyone there knew just enough about Mr. Oleander to dismiss his attempts to project altruism.

Rowan raised an unkempt eyebrow before casting a brief glance back at Sedge. Between them, a discussion transpired. Cross words, perhaps?

"Well, if you haven't already been informed," Mr. Oleander called to the audience upon the wall, "a precious stone. I'm surprised you haven't had it whittled down and stuck on the hilt of a sword or some other. Aster here was set to sell the gem to me, and he'd like it back. Seems it will fetch a steep price. Right m'boy?"

M'boy? Mr. Oleander roused up a folksy drawl. No point in interrupting the characterization since it might work on these knaves. They were just fighters, as far as Aster was concerned. What could they know of art, beauty, of the world beyond their swords and arrows?

Rowan held aloft the gem in question. The morning sun poured through the red facets, leaking sharply crimson coruscations. "Since you've come calling for it, Thanatist, I no longer have to doubt my son's claims about the great power of this gem. It's as he said then. We have claimed the fabled Truce Blood." In that moment Rowan's laugh snaked down the wall and echoed through the valley. "Yes, thought you were the only clever man in Thuidiuim, didn't you?" He clapped his son on the back. "Then we are done here."

It was curious that, for a moment, Aster possessed that potent artifact. Of all the historical objects of legend, the fossilized blood of Life and Death had been dug up out of his own plot of land. Not that Aster had an inkling of how to wield the power within or even what sort of power was stored up in that crystalline rock.

Through the armor and weapons, past the other surly faces, could be seen a man who was not just an average thief. Sedge proved to be more substantial than that, the sort of person who recognized the red gem as no mere garish trinket. All that stature was obviously run by a well-exercised mind.

Sedge connected glances with Aster, each seeing the other outside of this conflict. Of course, Sedge could have been looking elsewhere. There was no telling exactly upon which person or object he chose to focus.

"We're done with the parlay." Mr. Oleander offered up a cheeky grin and turned his back to the gate, to the wall, to Rowan and Sedge. "Time for some appropriate, proportional action," which he said so quietly that only Aster caught the words.

Aster, with one last look back at the resolute face of Sedge, hurried after Mr. Oleander, who remounted his horse and trotted away from the wall. "Wait," Aster called scrambling back up into his saddle. "How proportional?"

20.

OF THE COLOR RED

"You're going to realize, my good sweet Aster, that to reach a goal, to produce the results you want, you've got to strike with certainty. I'm not talking about acquiring a mere fancy either." He stopped and put a finger to Aster's chest. "I'm talking about an imperative."

The reins on the situation were firmly held by Mr. Oleander, in whose unwavering gaze was scribed intent: he wouldn't be handing those reins over to anyone; he wouldn't even relax his grip in the slightest. Everyone else was just a passenger, including his adversary. To see such certainty in action was admirable and disconcerting at the same time.

"This is a new strategy that will secure my gem." Mr. Oleander explained, as they advanced away from the fortress, back towards their little encampment where the rest of the party awaited.

"What's the story?" Rustle asked as Aster and Mr. Oleander returned from their conference at the wall.

Pixee, who had been convening with her horse, joined the group. "Is there some sort of escalation planned?"

Aster nodded, still unsure about exactly how Mr. Oleander intended to escalate the situation. It took a moment of searching among his belongings, but Mr. Oleander finally produced an answer: a jar.

"And this," Pixee peered into the glass container, " is your plan for getting back Aster's gem?"

She spoke for them all. Aster couldn't have been the only one on the edge of anticipation, so to speak, curious yet afraid about what Mr. Oleander plotted.

"My gem," Mr. Oleander replied as he slowly surveyed the contents of his jar. "We are going to clear house and once the Keep is destitute, we'll walk in and collect."

"Nice plan," Rustle nodded in agreement. "Has a sort of comforting vagueness to it. Now, if you wouldn't mind a few specifics: what army will be clearing house? I surely won't be marching against a warlord. Pretty sure Aster and Pixee aren't armed for combat. Rose?"

She raised her eyebrows in mild interest.

"Are you going to lend us some nifty magic to storm the Keep?"

Rustle's sarcasm was met with confusion.

Mr. Oleander waited for Rustle to finish and once the tirade ended, he offered another view of his jar in reply to Rustle's snark. Held inside was but a cloudy-looking mass. Perhaps he thought his precious schemes, with all their intricate details, were just too much for the group to grasp?

"What are we looking at?" Aster pressed.

"Our army."

Rustle, Pixee, and Rose opted to wait at a distance, while Mr. Oleander and Aster ventured back towards the gate and, once more, called for an audience with the master of the Keep. They waited until Rowan appeared high above with his dutiful son by his side.

"Come to apologize, Thanatist?"

The word was hurled again with ample contempt but Mr. Oleander smiled with an authenticity that left no room for sardonic conversation and rudeness.

"No," Mr. Oleander replied prodding Aster in the ribs with an elbow. "Nothing of the sort. We're here to give that young man—" He directed a finger at Sedge, "—a chance to apologize and return the property he stole."

It was hard to tell for certain, being so far away and all, but Rowan's face twisted into an expression of amusement. No quips or verbal jabs were returned but a set of prepared archers arranged themselves along the wall, bows bent. Their arrows were summarily released. Aster just barely dove out of range as the arrows sped towards their targets.

Not Mr. Oleander. With a flick of his wrist, he brushed aside the arrows those archers dared to aim in his direction. He looked up at the men on the wall. "Alright then, Rowan. Your answer is clear. Then I won't regret what I'm about to do."

"Are you even capable of regret, Thanatist?" Sedge called out as he leaned hard into the battlements, fists grinding against the stone.

Mr. Oleander took Sedge's question as rhetorical as he fidgeted with his jar. From the unstopped opening wafted red smoke. Looked smoky. Could have been fog. Or cloud. One thing was certain: it was red, creamy with hints of pink. Always red with this guy.

Mr. Oleander set the jar in the grass and with his arm around Aster's shoulders, he ushered them away. A quick look back and the red smoke seeped out of its container.

After arriving at what Mr. Oleander called an 'appropriate distance of safety downwind', he turned and blew, his breath urging the fog towards the wall of the Keep.

The mist pressed upon the grass, bending the blades and withering the fresh green color into a forsaken brown. With every inch gained by the rolling fog the cloud grew to human-height.

Aster blinked until he felt less dubious about what he saw. Yes, they looked like the shapes of people. Mr. Oleander's army, a cluster of phantoms crafted from insubstantial mist. The details were positively beyond comprehension. Perhaps that was the limit of Aster's own magic? He wouldn't have been able to imagine this spell-craft that wafted under the naked light of day. Mr. Oleander's power reached beyond the mundane, the practical, because he could envision a wraith-army; he could see the events and the phenomena unfold, a sight that most probably couldn't—maybe even wouldn't—dare.

They marched on, more individual shapes joining the congregation as the jar emptied, until the first wraith arrived at the gate. At least Rowan was smart enough not to send an entourage of his men to meet the cursed fog.

"What are they?" Aster whispered, afraid to cut into the silence that blanketed the little valley.

Mr. Oleander grinned as wide as his lips would stretch. "Just a bit of Thanatos, performed right before your very eyes, my good Aster."

The gleeful admission dressed the situation in an entirely new garb of sobriety. This wasn't just some jaunt across Thuidium. They weren't just wheeling and dealing, making threats, and rattling swords.

His companions were not far away physically, but their distance from the events unfolding was enough that they maintained a certain innocence, while the innocent horses grazed upon grass that hadn't been wilted by what were the spirits of vengeful warriors. Pixee clutched Iridium's mane, as if she were ready to abandon the situation. Rose looked away while Rustle clinched his fist but didn't approach any closer.

At the sound of Mr. Oleander' cackle, a slightly jocular sound, Aster turned back to witness the Thanatos playing out before him, not sure if he wanted to see what would transpire.

The ghostly shapes pooled around the gate. Rowan and Sedge barked orders to the men at arms. Their words were indistinct but their tone reached like mountains. More arrows were let loose; they swam through the crimson incorporeal forms, planting into the ground until a thicket had sprung up at the base of the wooden doors that served as entrance to the Keep's courtyard.

"Can't they float through the gate?" Aster gave the red soldiers an appraising look.

"If they were really nothing more than fog, they wouldn't be much help in clearing out living soldiers. They've been incorporated, in a way. It's blood they seek. Not wood or stone. Against blood only can they do damage. It's quite a sight."

Complicated magic, this.

A congregation of nearly a hundred shapes, all silent, all menacing in their wisps of armor and helms, were stalled at the gate which stood firm against the gentle brush of seemingly insubstantial beings. They held their ghostly weapons with an air of purpose, as soldiers well-versed in the art of combat would. There were spears with tips towering high. Some held board axes while others gripped the hilts of long-swords.

Mr. Oleander took up the empty jar and positioned himself just a little closer to the Keep. Not Aster though. His feet were heavy with hesitation. A desire to be like his companions sprouted: innocent of what was about to take place.

"Aster, I will need some assistance for this next part," Mr. Oleander called as he held aloft the empty jar.

The chance to hesitate, to excuse himself from being part of the next phase of action evaporated. Aster sighed and trotted over to Mr. Oleander.

"Since the gate stands as one solid piece of wood, wedged impossibly tight into place, my army won't be able to simply slip on into the Keep which means...I need some fire," he instructed Aster as he handed over the jar.

Aster searched about, waiting for someone to deliver the flames. A quick look from the Thanatist told him to hurry and produce some fire.

"If you had finished the Martese with me, this would probably be going quicker," Aster said as he prepared some fuel.

Mr. Oleander stood, an unceasing gaze upon the gate. "If I had would you really be here right now, holding up your end of the bargain?"

It was an accusation that rattled Aster's sensibilities. He swallowed the insult, though, and ran back to his stuff. He retrieved flint stones and a chip of steel. After a few strikes a sufficient little blaze sprang up.

"Now," Mr. Oleander instructed, "keep it going while I help the red soldiers get past that gate." His words manipulated the flame into a thick, trunk-like shape. It snaked its way through the red phantoms. "Keep that fire fed," he commanded with a wisp of thrill in his voice.

Aster shoved more grass and twigs into the jar, anything he could find in his immediate vicinity. Aster dropped the jar as the mounting heat bore up on the glass. He sucked at his singed fingers while his mouth was agape. The fire approached the gate in form and drilled into the stalwart wood, which splintered and cracked until it was an obstacle no more.

Mr. Oleander beamed as his summoned host drifted through the newly charred entrance.

Rowan was already scrambling, ordering his men in panicked, hurried shouts. Those stationed upon the battlements focused on the interior. Aster looked on, mildly curious about the effects of the foggy army. As he watched, the remainder of the gate crumbled. Sedge remained above the fray. Even as the first screams erupted from behind the wall, his attention remained fixed on Aster. There was something so easy in their eye contact, flaunting the devastation piling up around them. Nothing hard or soft. It was just happening, even as more shouts leapt over the Keep's wall.

At last Sedge turned away, unable any longer to ignore the crescendo of screams ascending into the sky, shrill prayers and pleas in a perfect blend of pain and fear. More wretched than most cries because the voices of warriors—trained to kill and dominate—had been reduced to pitiful calls, slimy and putrid as they tore apart the serene green valley.

Mr. Oleander closed his eyes and he tilted his head back as he let the twisted song—desperation beyond the reach of every iota of hope—sing back to him of every soul released from its mortal raiment. He took a deep breath. Could he sense the copper aroma in the air?

It took some time, but at last Mr. Oleander signaled Aster to join him nearer the gate. "Let's go have a look. Maybe even get that rock." He gave Aster a nudge and a wink as he passed through the smoldering entrance.

Aster searched the faces of his companions for signs of approval, hoping they'd be on their feet and ready to tread past the decimated gate in strides of victory. They all remained where they stood. Rustle held on to Rose's shoulder. Pixee shook her head in reply to Aster's silent request. He was truly alone in this deal. He made it and his friends would leave him to fulfill it.

Without anyone by his side, Aster followed after Mr. Oleander. A neat sun dominated a fair sky, its warm rays spilling down upon a now silent Keep. Aster tried his darnedest not to picture what awaited on the other side of that wall. Whether it was gruesome—the most likely scenario—or just an absence of life, the outcome was going to be startling.

Aster took a wide step over the charcoal remains, a step that proved most difficult, into the courtyard which was an arrangement of flagstones expertly laid to cover the space between the Keep and the defensive wall. The first few bodies were just on the other side of the gate, unavoidable, splayed out in full view and Aster had to maneuver between their tangled limbs.

Mr. Oleander bent down alongside Aster who had his blanched face tucked between his knees. "Never seen a mutilated corpse before?"

Aster breathed out slowly. "Nope," he said between breaths. "Not a human corpse, let alone a mutilated one."

Mr. Oleander perked up. "It's all perfectly natural We have all this stuff inside of us too. I guess it can be a bit jarring to see it strewn across the ground though."

Aster up righted himself. "You think?"

The courtyard was a halo about the main structure of the towering rock which had but one way in and out. It bent in an arc as it neared that lone entrance and exit, around which the bulk of the red fog amassed, cleaving through those who still drew enough breath to seek for refuge with in.

"And still they fight. Those sad sacks." Mr. Oleander gingerly stepped away from Aster, navigating his way about the bodies.

A meaty carpet woven out of the guts and muscle of Rowan's foot-soldiers wound down the courtyard until it ended where the evil fog was now gathered.

Aster stumbled his way to where Mr. Oleander stood, whose face was stained with an expression of glee as he watched his red minions search for joint or crack that would give them passage to invade. Hoping to at least avoid stepping on faces, Aster kept his eyes on his feet. He nearly collided with Sedge and had to quickly shake away the sight of that chest, as appealing as a woman's breasts for some reason.

"You survived." The statement came out in a sigh.

"I did. Wasn't sure what this thing was actually capable of. That fog wrapped itself around me and drifted on." He stopped explaining and lobbed an obdurate gaze. "You maniac bastard," he said, a fleck of spittle spilling from between his gritted teeth.

The accusation must have been meant for Mr. Oleander though, right? There was no way that those words applied to Aster, in any sense, at any time.

"I assume you're talking to me." Mr. Oleander kicked a leg out of his way as he approached Sedge. "I am the one who unleashed this carnage on your people, so it's must be me. You can't possibly mean Aster here. He hardly had a hand in all this."

But Sedge kept his gaze fastened on Aster. Not a single blink of his eyes interrupted his accusatory stare. "Him too."

"Or maybe you mean yourself?"

Sedge's roiling gaze stabbed at Mr. Oleander's smirking face.

"Do you mean yourself, Sedge?"

Sedge drew a long-knife and held it to Mr. Oleander's throat. "No. I don't mean myself. I mean you. To a lesser degree Aster."

"Even though you stole his property, and then refused to return it?"

Sedge opened his mouth, but when the response failed to materialize he shut his lips tight until they blanched. His eyes narrowed as he steadied the nine inch blade closer to Mr. Oleander's skin.

"But then why didn't you own up to it?" Mr. Oleander smiled at the steel.

It was a grimy situation and no one offered a breath of clarifying honesty. A simple admission, from everyone, would have swept away the tension, fear, and anger. Mr. Oleander made the only offering, in the form of a nearly-sinister laugh, a sound that added an oily sheen to the silence that only turned grimier the longer it lasted.

"You don't even know why you're afraid," Mr. Oleander whispered.

"Petty accusations are so unbecoming of you, Thanatist."

After seeing the carnage of the red fog, it made a little more sense why someone uttering that title looked as though they were choking up a slug that had been inadvertently swallowed, if such a thing was possible to accomplish. Inadvertently.

"No, it's just that you reek of fear." He ushered a whiff of air into his nostrils, like a feast of smells. "Pungent like a ripe cheese. No reason to be afraid though."

Not what the survivors holed-up in the Keep must have thought, what with their screams peeling through the very walls of that monolithic building. Aster looked past Mr. Oleander to the Keep's door, shut tight, but not tightly enough. No red fog.

21.

OF AIR, AFTERMATH, & BLOOD

Sedge followed Aster's gaze; muffled shouts preceded his comrades-in-arms as they escaped back under the sun. Mr. Oleander's smile suspended Sedge's impulse to run off and support the people hunted down by the menacing cloud. The tension between those choices must have been a wrenching every muscle in his body. Aster imagined thick quadriceps and long calves, all flexed in preparation to bound towards the yelling and screaming.

"You know what you should be afraid of? It isn't me." Mr. Oleander pulled the grin away from his lips as he leaned into the slick knife edge until it pinched his flesh. A drop of blood appeared from beneath Mr. Oleander's skin.

Sedge returned the statement with a snort. "You're probably worse than my father's racket. Worse than any tyrant."

"The real tyrants aren't of mortal kind. This layer's oppressed by Them. Think about it. The end of the division between this layer and the life-after."

"You're mad."

Mr. Oleander's beaming face clouded. "No, Sedge. It amounts to living without fear of the end. Eternity on our own terms. Aster—" Mr. Oleander gave up explaining his vision to Sedge. "—how successful would you be without the dread of what if? How far and wide would you dream?"

What if? It stung, badly. The idea that something could happen and the fire fruit would end up just an idea, a draft, without the rest of the world tasting it, was unacceptable. Every day that dream wasn't realized was just another day spent trying to outrace fears, doubts, and inevitabilities. Mr. Oleander knew right then he had converted at least one person.

But just the one.

Sedge's expression evened out as he swung back his arm, blade poised to fatally stab. A worthy warrior he must have been in his own right, but blood is slick and there was plenty of it—plenty of bodies and body parts to stumble over—and Sedge moved heedlessly, focused only on his target.

Sedge's face was streaked in blood, like some kind of war mask. He pushed up from the muck into which he had fallen and sprang at Mr. Oleander again, who quickly discarded his flowing outerwear. He stood with his tightly wrapped cross shirt and in his billowing pants. Aster stepped away as they met in a surprisingly fierce clash. Mr. Oleander had always seemed more of a mentalist than a fighter, yet here he was keeping a trained fighter at bay.

The tussle shifted as the two men grappled for mastery. Aster evaded the oncoming conflict, avoiding the pieces of humans strewn about. Under the sun's generous light, blood and innards winked back as if they were freshly polished gems. The battle was but a distant song to Aster as he scanned the faces of those hewn down by the red fog. Their eyes still looked at the wide world above. Aster squatted and shuttered them, one pair at a time. He scoured for more, anything to put his back to the fighting. He stepped into a puddle of tacky blood and that's when he saw it peeking out, that glossier shade of red among all the shades of red. Aster scooped up the gem, coated in someone's mucus.

It was then that Aster spotted Pixee hopping over the charred gate, followed by Rose and Rustle. She picked her way through the bodies, hurrying towards Aster as fast as she was able.

"Blood," he muttered to Pixee.

"Lots of it too. The blasted rock is coated in it," she responded.

The wrestling continued. The two men grappled and fought among the corpses. Their fists swung. Fresh blood flowed while bruises blossomed. Their ferocity came in waves. The only sounds were the huffs and grunts of the two contenders.

"No," he whispered. "This is not just some gem." He shook the rock at her. "Truce Blood," he whispered.

Understanding flooded her face and her eyes glittered with something akin to fear. "Hide it. Quick," she hissed. "He can't have possession of it, Aster. You can't let him have it!"

A nervous look clouded Rustle's visage while Rose maintained her placid expression.

"You knew about this gem the entire time?"

Rustle averted his eyes, refusing to provide Aster with any explanation.

"Sedge just happened to know he had stolen the Truce Blood?"

"It was a hunch, okay?" was Rustle's flaccid reply.

"And that hunch is what you sold to Sedge? Maybe you could have shared that with me first?" Aster knew full-well that such a disclosure wouldn't have altered his decisions.

Rustle had naught to offer but a silent gasp as he struggled with the urge to dispatch his usual smirk. "You didn't seem to care," he said once he had smoothed away the humor from his face. "And now you know why he was the first choice."

"Funny that you tried to sell it at all instead of handing it over to the Stewards." Pixee shot a suspicious glance at Rustle.

He looked ready to defend his actions when the kerfuffle between Sedge and Mr. Oleander came to a pause. They bathed the recovered gem with all manner of attention; not all the attention was of equal make: Mr. Oleander's gaze leered unflinching as if his eyes were mouths ready to devour the gem while Sedge's eyes spun, looking for the next move, but always returning to the stone as if he were placing it at the center of his strategy. Neither registered the soured confusion writ upon Aster's face.

He was inclined to let the thing fall back into the gore. Better yet: shove it back into the earth and pretend as if it had never come to light. It wasn't essential to his plans. Too late for such daydreams.

"Well played, Aster." Mr. Oleander said. "Looks like you've gotten what we came for."

By Sedge's account, the thing which Mr. Oleander claimed to have gotten was not, in fact, got. He injected the altercation with new vigor as he landed a strike with Mr. Oleander's dagger. The jab was deterred, leaving a mere cut to Mr. Oleander's hand. The knife had been wrested away from Sedge and flung far out of reach. They were down to fisticuffs. After only a few rounds both men were bent and huffing, painted in sweat and blood.

"You're quite pugnacious," Mr. Oleander complimented, right before he delivered a severe hook to a winded Sedge. The final effort looked to have drained Mr. Oleander. He bent with his hands on his knees as he drew rapid breathes.

Sedge raised himself out of the gory refuse into which he had fallen. His eyes were fiercely green against the red that covered his face. "Hold." He labored some deep breaths. "Hold on to that for me."

"No, he'll keep it safe for me. Right, Aster?"

Under the sun, the dismantled bodies infused the courtyard with an acrid stink that insisted itself into the olfactory in a draught so offensive and heady that Aster couldn't help gathering the putrid aroma through his flaring nostrils. His timid backward through the muck steps were a song that squished out with careful deliberation.

"If you're trying to carry that thing out of here—" Mr. Oleander coughed as he slid up the wall. "I will make sure the rite of the Martese isn't the only thing you'll be missing. Don't forget our deal."

Rustle's wide-eyes pawed at Aster, pleading *please don't forget the deal. In all the layers, please keep the bargain.* Sweat dribbled down Rustle's temple, squeezed out by the approach of either doom or relief. Rose stared vacantly as if the words meant nothing to her.

"I don't know what in Life's mind he's talking about," Sedge declared in undaunted sobriety, "but if you don't take that thing away, I'll kill you and I won't regret it."

Aster shrank between the immensity of threats hefted at him with a surprising amount of ease. What was one to do between two men armed with so much motivation? "I mean…" It was all he could muster to say.

"Life's lips, you're naïve." Mr. Oleander approached, but only just; he didn't want to startle Aster. "You need me to have it too."

"Don't listen…" Sedge warned, seemingly out of fight.

They both looked bleary. With the Truce Blood back in Aster's power, diplomacy was now their flavor. "There must be a less violent way?"

"But there isn't," Mr. Oleander replied, his tone as serious as a lover's declaration. "There will be too many willing and ready to stop me, us, from changing their familiar, blithe little world. Isn't it worth it though? Obtaining perfection? Finding all the answers to every question. Having the autonomy to call the match is a power worth fighting for, worth stamping out the small-minded opposition. Is it not?" He hurried on: "It's all I've ever wanted. I've wanted understanding, knowledge. More than riches. On Life's eye—" It was a comment for inspection by no one but himself. "I'm greedy for wisdom. Nothing will impede my journey to understand as much as I can.

Mr. Oleander looked over at Sedge. "And you would want to deny me the chance to end this divide between mortality and eternity.

To end the biased judgments of Life and Death over the souls they themselves created? I just need the Truce Blood and it will all be very real. Eternity on your own terms. Forever at your own pace. "

It was a gentle, euphonious speech, and Aster lowered the stone at the sound of Mr. Oleander's proposal as his lips twitched, the prospect making them dance nearly into a complete smile. It always did seem a trifle unfair that people only had a finite number of years to figure out themselves, their place in the greater picture, in such a small window of time. Why should anyone be denied the chance at growth and cultivating their own fate?

Mr. Oleander watched Aster's hand sink to his side and it must have eased him. He stopped being cautious and approached wantonly. "Atta boy, Aster." He reached out his hand towards the jewel which he so ardently craved, sure that he had won the moment.

Pixee placed a steady hand at Aster's elbow, before Mr. Oleander could secure his prize, and without a single utterance repeated *no* over and over. She was so certain about the correct thing to do. Why was she so confident in any given course of action?

It was magic that couldn't understand because his internal compass didn't work like that. There was ever that swoosh of the sea muddling and confusing what was right and wrong; good and bad; best and worst. She might understand his desire to see a process through to the end, to feel the rush, cleansing and clarifying, of accomplishment.

Then again, maybe she didn't need that sensation, that form of validation. Was there any truer form of validation, though?

Pixee's visage hardened as she watched Aster clutch tighter at the Truce Blood. She'd never understand.

Sedge dove at Mr. Oleander's legs. They crashed into a heap of remains, ending diplomacy. Their scuffle broke out anew, sloshing through the muck of life snuffed-out. Sedge gripped Mr. Oleander's neck and squeezed. Spit dribbled from Sedge's clenched lips. A swift knee to his groin gave Mr. Oleander room to flip the advantage. He stood and hauled Sedge off the bloodied ground and fastened his hands around Sedge's neck, straining but still smiling. He licked the foreign blood from off his own lips as his hands clasped tighter.

His fingers, and muscles, stopped doing the work. His magic took over. "Just a few moments, Aster, and we'll be able to get back on track. Both of us."

Aster shuddered at the wink and smile, friendly gestures radiating with undertones of vulgarity as they rode the waves of gem-lust rippling through every fiber of Mr. Oleander's body.

All while Sedge flailed against Mr. Oleander who seemed to be sucking the air from Sedge's lungs.

"Shhh, shhh. Easy Sedge. Let it go. You lost."

"No—" Sedge croaked back with such labor.

"Just—" Aster hesitated. Sedge's blood-sotted eyes and Mr. Oleander's focused gaze both found Aster. "—we can leave him be and walk out of here."

"No, Aster. That isn't how it works. You smite your enemies and then you get to carry out your plans. Otherwise they just—" He inhaled deeper, while Sedge's chest barely rose and fell. "—keep. Coming. Back. Don'tcha?"

Aster held the gem tightly to his chest, watching the violence play out.

Mr. Oleander noted the motion. "Don't do anything silly Aster. This will all be over soon." Mr. Oleander, not being prone to hyperbole, meant it.

The failing of Sedge's breath was enough to spur Pixee into action; she maneuvered over the bodies, two small blades in her hands shaped almost like little steel stars. Her attack, though fierce, was wild and rolled like an unchecked fire through unsuspecting trees. The same ferocity which Mr. Oleander used to send her tumbling away.

He regained his purchase upon Sedge's neck before the warrior could crawl away and siphoned the last bit of air flowing through Sedge's lungs. Through all the confrontation, Sedge didn't show a flicker of fear. His face had no room for a look of defeat for, Sedge's courage was beyond the reach of Mr. Oleander's onslaught. Given how dire the situation was, his bravery must have been engraved upon his very soul. Courage did not keep the heart beating and soon Sedge's proud eyes were shuttered.

Mr. Oleander pulled himself out of the discarded bodies, brushing his hands against his dark pants until they were as clean as he could manage. He exhaled deeply and silently as he examined his ruined hands, stains that would need extensive exfoliation. The Truce Blood rolled from Aster's palm into Mr. Oleander's.

There was no denying the gleam of satisfaction that highlighted his dark eyes. His fingers closed hungrily around the stone. He slipped a small note, the bargained price, into Aster's now vacant hand, patting him on the shoulder.

He made to exit the courtyard, stepping round about the human-litter. "Rose, dear," Mr. Oleander called.

She heeded the summons without a smidgen of resistance Her hand slipped out of Rustle's as she drifted over the remains to be at Mr. Oleander's side. Her movements proceeded in a silence as thick as dried blood.

Aster's protestations sluiced into the quiet: "Rose."

She spared him a portion of consideration, the fleeting kind that lingers about as long as a single wave touching the shore.

He tried to remember the first time he said *I love you* to her, which was the first time he had said it to anyone. All he recalled was the sound of the surf crashing into the towering, rocky cliffs. That one memory erased all the others that had followed.

"Rustle," Aster pleaded. His own voice came out riddled with confusion, like a child's voice, as his lips turned down and his forehead scrunched. All Rustle offered was a shrug.

"Go on," Mr. Oleander nodded to Rose. "Explain."

"My soul. It's his." She shrugged impassively. "The settled debt." She spoke the words in a haunted voice, distant and without the volume of emotion. It was a fact and she didn't determine its value.

Aster sank into the muck. It not longer smelled. It not longer felt slimy or repulsive. It was just there, staining his skin.

Mr. Oleander donned a smirk as he looked back, one last glance at the handiwork he left strewn around the Keep. His eyes narrowed at Pixee kneeling beside Sedge, who stared up at the sky never finding purchase.

The odd rite in which she engaged captivated the Thanatist. Her hands pressed insistently against Sedge's sternum, pumping several times before she switched to urgently breathing into his mouth. She repeated the process of mimicking the motions of a living body, checking now and then to watch Sedge. She went back to work, pumping and breathing, and waiting.

In that moment, she was the most interesting thing in the world to Mr. Oleander. His keen glance lingered until he made to approach until Rose spoke. What she said, only Mr. Oleander heard. He looked up to the moon. He shook his head before calling out some word in a strange tongue. Limbs and torsos rose from the ground and detained Pixee, pinning her to the blood-stained stones. Disparate organs crawled into her mouth reaching with the muculent fit of an octopus tentacle to pull her away from Sedge.

A morsel of bravery tingled up Aster's legs. He rushed to Pixee's aid, as she writhed and fought. That's when he noticed it, the subtle rising and falling of Sedge's chest. Just how long was the space between the death of the body and the release of the soul?

Aster looked up from the lively entrails with which he wrestled, teeth gritted and tension crawling along his jawline. He gave a silent plea—to Death. Maybe Life? Some entity that had more power than Mr. Oleander—that the faint breathing exercised by the revived Sedge would go unnoticed.

By some grace, or luck, Mr. Oleander departed without catching the tiny signs of life emanating from Sedge. He simply turned and led Rose away from the Keep, offering a slight wink in Aster's direction as he stepped beyond the wall.

The bodies and limbs subduing Pixee relaxed and returned to their inanimate state. She clawed the gore from her mouth, chunky streaks of various glossy hues plastered over her lips and obscuring her teeth making her look as if she had none at all.

Aster shrank from the fury stabbing out of her eyes, clutching at his shirt, staining his clothes. No words were deployed. She just shoved him back, right into a heap of dismembered bodies. Aster scrambled, slipping his way back to his feet.

Sedge gulped in the air flowing back into his lungs. Aster smiled at this revival, yet quickly reeled in his relief and presented a more modest reaction. "Pixee saved you," Aster said, feeling compelled to explain the situation.

Sedge examined Pixee, taking in the sight of her. He offered her a slight nod which she accepted, patting him upon the shoulder.

"Did he—" No pause to savor the alkaline scented air, the little intricate details of being among the living, Sedge wanted to pick up right where his life had seemingly ended. He took survey of everyone's expressions as he initiated the question which appeared to be answer enough for him. His mouth drooped and his eyes, once softly inquisitive, flashed darkly. "You let him take the Truce Blood out of here?"

What was there to say to Sedge's mounting fury? "Truly," Aster's voice felt small, diminished by the carnage all around him. "I did." He clutched at the small page.

Sedge shoved his way to his feet, but apparently being revived from death takes a toll on the body. He crumpled back to the ground. He shut his eyes hard for a moment, then: "For what reason did you have to hand that weapon to someone like him?"

All the expectant glances pouring down upon Aster gave him the distinct impression of sinking. Of being buried alive. The earth closing in, like these ponderous stares, eating up the light and slowly shutting off the air. The world above still moving on, making sounds that turned into mere vibrations.

He escaped their pile-on. They continued to stare while he took some deep breaths and paced around bits of bodies.

The darkness, though, wasn't an experience that stopped at the senses. More than the wetness, the grittiness, and the tickle of wriggling worms the darkness seeped into the very mind and multiplied until it polluted even the memories fashioned before and after the moment that the earth closed in. That darkness mocked Aster even on a bright day.

"Aster?" Pixee left Sedge's side and approached.

He shrugged away her touch. "You know," he said with a dark chuckle, "if this is such a big deal, and Mr. Oleander poses some sort of universal danger, then why are the Stewards not intervening?" He looked about, scanning the piles of flesh and pools of blood. "I don't see any of them here."

Sedge found his strength and stood. "Any of you know how to summon them?"

22.

Interlude: Life & Death's Latest Confab

The firmament was especially thick, almost congealed. There had always been an airy quality to it, a sense of openness, like it could be pushed aside and the other layers would be in plain view, complete with dimension and texture. What was this change?

It was time to confer with Life and see if the feeling was mutual or if it was just Death being Death.

"Have you noticed how dense it feels?"

Life, with a dreamy expression, looked Death in the eyes. "Huh?"

Why was Life never serious? The layers could be colliding and Life would probably just sit there clapping at the pretty colors.

"You don't...the layer doesn't feel off to you?" Death put a stop on the question of layer-stability and looked at Life's hands. "What are you doing?"

Speaking of 'pretty' colors, there was a smattering of them oozing out of Life's fingertips. Both terrifying and attractive.

"I've not created anything new in eons. My hands, the hands of an artists, are restless. So let me paint in peace while you continue to worry. As you have. For eons."

Death stood akimbo, digesting the somewhat scathing rejoinder. Quite accusatory. Maybe even a little troubling. There was no harmony in that response. Where was the harmony?

Death swiped at Life's hands, scattering whatever Life had been working on. "Will you focus on the present for just a moment? We've responsibilities of which I have the distinct impression are under assault from nefarious forces."

With a sigh Life set focus upon Death and waited.

Death hemmed and hawed. Postulating was easier than explaining.

"Will you get on with it, Imfa."

Death twitched. The employment of the old name was a sign Life was in no mood for jest. "I don't know how to put it. I just feel cut off. I've not been able to reach my mind past our layer."

"And for what possible reason were you reaching?"

"The Truce Blood."

Life snorted. "Are you still on that?"

"I thought it prudent to finally have the Stewards go check on it. Make sure it hadn't fallen prey to any ill-intent."

Life chortled and resumed the display of colors. "You and your fretting. It's fine. Everything is fine. Has our layer collapsed? Has the Universal Energy stopped flowing? As if such a thing were even possible." Life looked around, tabulating the possibility. "Not likely so you…" Life met Death's strained stare. "Put away that scowl and find a project. Oh, I don't know, go record some history or another."

Life checked out from the conversation. There was no point in pressing the issue, so Death strolled off to some other corner of their world and fretted in silence.

23.

OF HOME, HEARTH, & HELP

The journey back to Lamiston was a somber one, made under the carnelian glow of the fabled blood moon which had finally graced the sky.

It rode the moon-arc, dropping a sense of expectation upon the world, though no one would have been able to compose the specifics of what was expected. Each hour just felt heavier, longer, each one grinding into the next.

Their route took them alongside the traditional path of the moon. Pixee rode fiercely. Rustle's shoulders slumped while Sedge sat with the posture of determination, eyes swimming against the swarthy glow. The rusted orb in the sky peered down like a spectator hanging about to observe this little band of travelers. Even after several hours of riding, a curious event happened: though they charged ever closer to the coast, the moon did not fulfill its arc. It hung, pinned to the apogee of its route across the sky, a revelation that kept Aster from the embrace of sleep when Pixee finally called a halt to their riding.

Aster perked up out of his pelt, wrapped his arms around his knees as his curiosity about the moon lingered. By the looks of everyone settling in for the night, it was a curiosity he alone bore.

"After all the hard riding, you can't sleep?" Sedge sat up. He rubbed a hand back and forth over the prickly stubble that covered his head.

No blankets for the tough guy, apparently.

He crawled over and sat next to Aster. Not immediately beside him, but close enough to be considered intrusive. He stared.

The question wasn't rhetorical. Alright then. Time to find an answer for him before he clawed away the silence with his staring. Couldn't be an authentic, vulnerable reply because Sedge wasn't privy to that kind of personal musing.

"Guess not," was all Aster had to offer.

Sedge's chuckle was a deep baritone rumbling that sounded like the echo of rocks falling out of place. Not a whole rock-slide, but just a few stones tumbling into the earth. "Alright." He looked up at the moon, too. "He's in it for himself, you know?"

A lecture? Maybe a good strategy would be to feign sleep. Aster forced out a yawn, stretched his arms above his head and let his legs unfold.

"Whatever romantic notions he's sold to you about immortality, better just forget them; he isn't going to do anything selfless or good-natured. I've know people like him my whole life his ambition keeps him from seeing the real consequences of his action. I can see the danger as clearly as I can see the moon. He won't stop and he won't care how many people he has to cut down to get to what he wants."

Sedge's offering was serious. Didn't make it acceptable or beyond reproach, so Aster denied it and threw his attention back up at the sky. "Is it me or is the moon just sitting there?"

"Huh?" Sedge paused his warnings and glanced up again.

"It hasn't moved along the sky. You ever think that the sun and moon are the same thing?"

Another deep chuckle rumbled out of Sedge. He shook his head as he used Aster's shoulder to brace himself as he stood. "Anyway, I just hope you're with me and Pixee on this because I'm not about to let Oleander tear our world apart."

Sedge loomed like a mountain of surety. Where did he get it? He was like Pixee; a taller, more muscular version.

"I'm guessing," Sedge ventured, "this is the onset of Oleander's scheme."

Aster was immersed in stillness once again. The rhythmic breathing of his companions was the only sound that night. No insects. No frogs or toads. Nothing. After a quick glance at that suspicious moon, Aster wrapped himself back up in a fur and slept.

Lamiston's archway welcomed them, as it welcomed everyone who passed under. The horses were returned to stable. The remainder of the journey was made on foot. Not that there was much distance left to cover. Oren wasn't too far outside of town.

"Must be pretty exciting, having a father who was once a member of the Order."

Aster shrugged. The lack of a sunrise made Sedge's chattiness more nuisance than pleasant.

"All those exploits and all that knowledge."

"Truly," Aster replied.

"You have a favorite story from his life as a Steward?"

Aster sighed. "None that I can think of."

It wasn't a lie. It was just a vague way of telling the truth without actually being honest. Aster looked at Sedge for a brief moment. Nothing in the man's face inspired Aster to crack open his personal defenses, the walls that kept history and feelings private, and let vulnerability flow freely at this man's feet.

Sedge grinned into the silence before he offered a slightly confused, if not hopeful, shrug at Aster. "I'm certain there must be one story that you think about?"

Aster stopped walking. Rustle and Pixee continued on ahead, seemingly unconcerned about the rest of the party. Once they were a good deal down the road, Aster turned to Sedge. "Even if that were the case, I don't know you like that. I'm not going to open my whole life to you."

Sedge's smirk fell apart. "I was just making conversation."

It was all well and good. Nothing wrong with that. People made conversation all the time. They asked each other about the weather. They wanted to know how someone did this or that. Sedge may have thought his inquiries were idle chit-chat, but he was wrong. Did he not realize that he asked about Oren, about family? He couldn't know how much that meant, but Aster was not in the mood to give Sedge the benefit of the doubt, to pardon this intrusion, even if the intruder was oblivious to his offense.

Sedge jogged ahead to catch up with Rustle and Pixee, who would feed his need for communication. He'd probably complain about Aster being resistant to the simple pleasure of exchanging ideas and thoughts.

They strolled down the dusty path and only sound traveled back to Aster, shadows of words without distinct form. It wasn't motivation to catch up with them. It was confirmation to keep at his own pace, the one at which he decided he wanted to move. For a brief moment, Sedge glanced back. It was a quick look that wasn't for the scenery. It was clear where his eyes had been pointed. He turned forward again, too quickly to make out the expression he wore. All the possibilities were negative in Aster's mind.

The group carried on, with Aster a few paces behind like some stray creature tagging along, smiling to himself as he thought about filling Oren in on all the adventures. He bent his fingers giving the paper in his pocket a bit of a caress. That twinge of betrayal he felt when he found out his father had hidden his life as a Steward evaporated. Thinking back, that was truly a petty response. Facing a lot of death and danger put it all into perspective. And the Martese! Showing off that bit of magic with his accomplished father was going to be like sharing the fire fruit for the first time.

Aster picked up his pace a bit until he was a step behind Pixee. They turned off the main path and strolled down the scion that took them to Oren's cabin. He was there, alone, standing with his face to a sea that stretched out in an endless swell. The group walked right up to him, unconcerned if Oren was meditating or crying, or just standing and staring.

He was most certainly standing and just staring, a habit he and Aster shared, and that, in and of itself, was something of a consolation. It had been more common between them before Aster lost himself in the task of concocting the fire fruit. At the sound of their approach, Oren detached from his reflections and took in the tale the others, namely Pixee and Sedge, had to share.

Oren surveyed his audience until he caught sight of Aster, standing ten yards or so away from everyone. Away from the cliffs.

"He's been a little distant," Sedge offered. "Physically and mentally."

The tattletale. Aster crossed his arms over his chest.

Oren walked past Sedge and up to Aster, arms spread open. Aster untangled his own arms and leaned into the embrace.

"I've heard a thing or two from your friends over there. How about you give me your take?"

Aster looked past Oren at Sedge and Pixee. "Since I don't know what they've already told you—"

"Doesn't matter what they've told me. What do you have to say?" His voice had a smile in it, even as his face remained perfectly placid.

There wasn't going to be a way to tell Oren all that he'd experienced, not with the sound of the surf beating against those cliffs. Aster walked towards the cabin. They entered and sat down: Aster on the couch, close to the armchair wherein Oren situated himself. Anyone else but Oren would have found that seat unbearably lumpy.

"So," Oren began, "how'd you fare?"

For some reason it was tough to simply list off all the events of the past couple of weeks, the many kilometers that passed under foot. The smell of death. The heat of fire. Oren's eyes neither begged impatiently nor languished in apathy. He simply waited.

"I mean…" Aster began thoughtfully. "Do you want the point or do you want a travel log?"

"I'd just like to hear what you have to share." He folded his hands into his lap.

This would have been so much easier as an interview type situation. Oren's shifting meant it was time to just dive into the conversation. Aster drew forth the paper from his pocket and handed it to his father. Seemed as good a place as any to start.

"Let's see what you've got here," he said unfolding the proffered page. He quickly scanned the contents before folding it up handing it back to Aster.

No reply. He stood, went to the fireplace, tossed some wood into the grating, and built a fire. He returned to his seat with a fixed and serious expression.

"I bartered for this. He delivered." The tone was almost haughty, almost *I told you so*. "I can finally see the fire fruit to its full potential."

The flames sprouted as they latched onto the wood. "I'd like to know how that will help you and I'm even more curious about the price you paid. From what the others have said, it was pretty steep."

The others, as Oren had referred to them, hadn't entered yet. Not even Pixee, who was so well acquainted with Oren and Aster. She knew well enough to leave Oren and Aster alone.

Oren waited for his son to explain and Aster waited for his mind to vomit some sort of densely logical reason his father wouldn't be able to refute.

"Well," but the mind wasn't giving up any secrets, like it was its own separate entity that Aster had to coax into sharing. "I think that's a matter of perspective," Aster finally spat out.

"And you don't think ripping apart the layers will lead to dangerous consequences?" Oren said, all snug in his chair.

"How could eternal life be so bad? Even the growing pains to get there?"

The sigh Oren offered in reply was devastatingly loud, and for a moment there wasn't anything said. He just idly examined his hands. "Your mother would probably side with you," he said at last. "She'd see this situation from your perspective. It's honestly a little scary to hear you talk like this. It's how she sounded before—"

The sound of Oren's voice cracking turned Aster's eyes moist. His lips felt like they would slip off his face if they continued to tremble, while a little dribble of clear liquid trailed from his nose. It was like it had taken no time at all for his body to react, reactions mirrored in Oren's face.

His voice sank to a whisper: "—before she tried her little burial experiment on you." Oren placed a hand on Aster's knee. "I may not have been the best at helping you cope with your mother's death, but this isn't going to bring her back—"

"I know, Dad."

"And," Oren continued, "it's not going to help erase seeing her leap off that cliff out there. You'll always have to deal with that."

"I can deal with her suicide." That word hadn't passed his lips in…ever. He'd thought it many times, but had not once allowed himself to name the act. He sniffed up the emotions before anymore could run down his cheeks and out his nose.

"And what about the other stuff? Can you deal with that?"

The other stuff. Daring of Oren to mention that incident in its entirety. Profane even. Every orifice felt dry at the mere hint of that moment. His lips were sealed shut, backed together into a pale strip.

Just as Aster cracked his lips apart to summon a reply Pixee entered, thankfully, followed by Rustle and Sedge.

She offered Aster an apologetic glance. "We took a moment to talk things through out there," she began.

"Pixee, hold that thought," Oren interrupted. He turned back to Aster. "What about it?"

"What do you want me to say? In front of these people about one of the most painful memories of my life?" The room was ten times smaller now, as if everyone was buttressed up against one another.

Oren had no mind for anyone else but Aster. They would all be denied attention, and so would the weighty matters Pixee bore into that cabin. "You can be mad at her, about what she did. I just don't want it haunting you anymore."

"Dad, please. Don't." Aster's chin crinkled.

Rustle and Sedge looked everywhere in the room except at the couch and armchair. Even Pixee had developed an aversion to the scene playing out in that living room. They heard it all, though: the most private, intimate, ugly, and honest part of Aster's life. They heard his voice racked with pain, quaking on the edge of tears. Their witness to this display of emotion felt more embarrassing than if Aster had accidentally shit his pants in front of everyone. Oren just allowed it to happen, too. He didn't clear the room. He let everyone sit there and partake in the rawness, let their eyes poke at Aster's vulnerability.

"I don't care, Aster. We've needed to have this conversation for a long time and we're going to now. Anymore putting it off and it'll never happen." He paused.

No one in the room dared breathe.

"You see why I'm worried about all this? I have a feeling Oleander infected your mother with this idea of eternal life. She never broke free from it. And she couldn't escape—" he swallowed a sob.

Oren went silent as the whispering ocean found its way into the cabin, heaving and sighing. Over those natural noises came the fading shriek that would find a way to clambered up from the sheer rocky cliffs.

"I'm sitting here watching him and his dangerous notions infect you too," he plead, as if he were seeking agreement, or perhaps forgiveness, from his own son.

Aster had none to dredge up. There wasn't a whole lot to say to Oren's confessions. "Just because it drove Mom insane doesn't mean it's a terrible idea, in principle."

Oren shook his head. "That's not it, Aster. She didn't lose her will to live because she couldn't master some spell or end death. It was seeing what she did to you. The lengths she went through to realize her desire. Your expressionless face staring up at her every time she looked at you. Never calling for her again after she tried to bury you alive, as part of some maniacal rite."

Aster dared to take his eyes off the floor and let his gaze roam around the room, but the roaming stopped when his eyes stopped at Sedge, who stared back wide-eyed, mouth slightly ajar. He wouldn't look away either, incapable of continuing the charade of giving Aster and Oren privacy for this heavy conversation.

Aster offered a smirk, chilling and dark in a way. Sedge had wanted Aster to open up, to be less distant. Instead, he was dragged into this blighted family history. Hopefully Sedge enjoyed the twisted tales.

Aster packed away the smirk and removed his attention from Sedge. Was he becoming like his mother? In a moment, all that he had been working towards—seeing the fire fruit come to life and multiply—felt tainted. The joy of creation, with all it's flavor and color, drained from the idea.

Aster unfolded the last verse of the Martese. Aster pondering what it meant for him, he wadded it up and stuffed it away. It wasn't a victory, just another link in the chain tying him to a past that would not stop wailing.

Oren held out a hand, one with callouses, lines, and sun-baked skin. Aster took it and followed his father out of the cabin and down towards cliffs he would have rather avoided. The sounds rushed up the rocky walls, all too eager to greet Aster.

They stood a small pace apart while Oren inhaled deeply. The corroded moon spilled its light upon the edges of waves and ripples. "I don't know if you can ever enjoy this view again. I want you to be able to." He turned and faced Aster. "I can't change how I handled your grief. I'll never stop trying to help you though. We'll do the best that we can while the ocean sings. And when we hear that note for the last time, I hope we can smile with little, if no, regret."

He spoke of dying in a way that made it seem so natural. Of course it was natural. Ideas died. People died. Water and wind took rocks and mountains into dust. There wasn't a being in the world of which Aster could think that lived forever. No, natural wasn't the right word.

Oren made dying less mysterious and sinister.

The thought tugged a smile from Aster. For the first time since Mr. Oleander spoke of immortality, Aster forgot about unlimited time alive and grounded himself in the here and now; this layer.

"Thanks Dad." Out of the corner of his peripheral vision, he saw Oren's mouth twitch with a smile.

"Alright, kiddo." Oren's eyes gleamed as he draped an arm around Aster's shoulders. "How about we take another look at what's on that paper?"

24.

OF FLAMES & MUSIC

Words saturated the rough, fibrous page, closer to the feel of linen than paper. A gentle caress told Aster that page and ink went beyond the state of mundane tools. As soon as the words had stained this page, their power soaked into the fibers, as if the spell lived first in form before it lived in function.

"Fire's ready," Sedge relayed to the group, bathing each of their faces in a twisted dance of warmth and shadows.

Aster removed his longing gaze from the verse and handed it over to Oren who silently mulled over the chant. Maybe what cadence or inflection he should apply to these sacred words? One last sweeping look at the paper before handing the spell over to Pixee.

She took it without question.

"I thought you were going to conduct it?" Aster, on the other hand, was not privy to whatever had been unsaid between the two.

Oren smiled at Aster. "I think Pixee is going to handle this."

"Why?"

Oren studied his son for a moment. "Is there a reason you need me to do this instead of her?"

The answer as a question meant this wouldn't be turned into a whole investigation of what was a pretty simple request. Apparently. "No. No reason."

"It was only supposed to be an oral tradition. One Steward at a time was taught the rite." He watched Pixee study the words. "I shouldn't be surprised that Oleander had the spite to steal the words and record them." His eyes narrowed at the mention of his former companion in the Order. "It feels strange to be saying these words, like I'm saying a prayer that wasn't meant to pass my lips. Some beliefs we never fall out of." He patted Aster's shoulder with a bit of a laugh. "Pixee will do just fine."

There was nothing to say against Oren's words. Oren stood back. Pixee stepped forward. For the first time in the years of friendship, Aster saw her smile. It was just a little thing, blessing Aster with what consolation and comfort she could offer.

Aster sat looking at the fire and suddenly Pixee spoke without signal, gesture, or preamble. Her voice slid out from between her lips like a long forgotten song:

The world sings in a hallowed melody
Rise in a new key
Wander 'til you discover harmony
Chords struck fearlessly

Can there be music without an ear to hear?

An actual physical ear. That's the question.

A curious phenomenon, but that doesn't take away from the reality of the sweet notes wrapping their way around it all, because there is context this time: all the familiar pillars of the environment holding aloft in an immeasurable sky. More sky than in any story ever told: wide-open, listening to the melodious voice that rings through every bit of creation. It reverberates stronger than a heartbeat. More finely tuned than the chatter of a stream. Even more pervasive than the wind off the tips of mountains. This is what magic is all about, no?

Out of every component of existence seeps a measure of this heat, contributing to the symphony. Despite the torrid heat swelling into a crescendo, there's nothing to feel except appreciation.

This rock? Not much to add in and of itself, but it cradles the heat for a long time.

The trees and grass? Food for the heat that it might abide.

The stream? It kisses the heat with an absolute hiss.

The little flame, just a single note quietly singing, and then the voices multiply higher, taller and wider, an entire chorus eating up the earth's crown—munching right through the foliage—until all is devoured. When the music is this powerful, who cares where your feet are or if they are at all?

Can fear abide where hope is? Can a person say mistake and lesson at the exact same time? Surely not. Surely, this is a tune that makes all things right and gives the world a clear conscience, even though it shines not like water, smells dour unlike fresh air, nor is textured like earth.

Purity. It is purity reaching out for an embrace…

When the world was the world again, the whole group was huddled closely around Aster, looking almost panicked.

"What?" Aster glanced about as they moved back.

His pants were blackened and tattered, almost half eaten away with the unmistakable mark of fire. His exposed legs were unmarred, though, as if the fire had passed right over them. Not even a single hair had been harmed. The realization tickled alive an understanding until Aster brimmed with satisfaction. And perhaps even a slight sense of power.

Aster stood, dusting away the ash. "Fire it is."

No one responded as Aster squatted by the fire. Did they know how? Oren must have. Which element was his? None of the others could know what it meant to journey into each of the elements, if it could be called a journey; sure felt like one. In each instance, the world, physically at least, had been taken away and replaced by the idea of a world.

The flames still danced and waved along with the breezes wafting in from the sea. Sedge was closest and he stared at Aster with something like concern on his scruffy face.

Aster smiled back as he speculated about this newfound connection, this power. How to use it, though? The question pressed at his mind, like an otter trying to crack open a clam. It really shouldn't be this perplexing. The Martese was all about bonding with an element, an intuitive connection. Maybe like a relationship, it took time to get to know the element well enough to direct it?

The flames jumped. Sedge did, too.

"Was that...was that you?" He glared at Aster.

"I think so." Aster focused on the fire again, this time imagining a vine tracing up out of the ground, reaching higher.

The flames elongated, twisted, and climbed.

"This is going to come in so handy," Aster said.

"Now that your Martese is all settled, can we get back to Oleander?" Sedge kicked dirt over the flames, ending them.

"The Stewards have probably already noticed the sun not rising," Aster remarked, "but we should make sure they're aware that Mr. Oleander is walking around with the Truce Blood. Can you help us find them?"

They waited for Oren to give them the next step, hoping for an answer that would wrap up the danger and anxiety in a fairly uncomplicated way.

"I wish I could," he finally said, to the sea.

Aster closed his eyes. He could feel the sighing behind him. It ceased to be mere sound a long time ago.

"You never really leave the Order," Oren explained. "You know, the whole flock concept came about because of the great truce Life and

Death made with one another, eons ago." Oren peeled his attention away from the ocean for a just a moment, long enough to make sure his audience was attuned to his words. "And that truce," he said pointedly back at the water, "included no direct contact with us mortals. I never understood that. Seems like the least responsible approach." He sighed and relinquished the vast, dark waters from his unwavering gaze as if he no longer found it interesting. "It's the way of existence and it's the reason the Stewards are so focused when it comes to how they use their energy. When you're the only conduit to Life and Death themselves, best not to crowd that path with menial tribulations. Even though I'm no longer in the Order, I always felt them: their success, their failure, the comings and goings of their members. Something stuck, like feeling the sun even if I was unable to open my eyes to see it; call it the energy of the Universe."

Oren shuttered his eyes and turned this way and that. "And now that I think about it, seems like it's been a while since I've noticed even a hint of them." He opened his eyes again, giving each person equal attention. "They've all dropped out of the sky. Like the sun has gone down on the Order. "I don't know where to find them," Oren said in answer to the question, "but I do know how to find them."

Oren held his hands out away from his body, tilted back his head, just so, and sang to the sky:

I see you no longer

I hear you no farther

I feel you in my mind

The memory of you I unbind

Flow freely like blood

That the earth may judge

The incantation left Oren's lips in a breathy whisper and draped over everyone as a fine, silvery mist that settled like a cloud of dust that had been kicked up.

That was it. The sky was dark above, decorated with naught but the blood moon. Nothing about them or in them stirred.

"Get a move on then," Oren directed. "The answer will be discernible for only so long."

There was a moment's pause as Pixee stood trying to read an explanation on Oren's face. All he had to offer in return was a shrug. In that short time Sedge was already striding away on his thick legs.

For some reason, Aster didn't feel pressed to follow at all. "Sedge is on the prowl, so I doubt there's going be much trouble keeping tabs on whatever that stuff is."

Oren chuckled, dismissing the subtle inquiry. "You've landed yourself in quite the adventure here."

"You make it seem so lighthearted, Dad."

Oren gave a moment's thought to Aster's words. "That's because I'm not as worried about you as I used to be. Talking about your mother and all that took a lot of the worry away."

Aster could only nod. His dad was right. That conversation purged the parasite weighing down each step and every decision. Instead of saying anything, Aster leaned in and wrapped his arms around Oren's shoulders, burying his face against his neck.

Oren returned the embrace, giving Aster a squeeze. There was a moment between father and son beyond classification, before Oren broke away from the hug. "Don't keep them waiting. Get this all fixed up and come back so you can bring the world your fire fruit."

25.

OF PUSHY ANSWERS

The answer at which Oren hinted—because he apparently did not, or could not, offer any direct details—hopefully came in an obvious form, a crack in the ground, perhaps; maybe a tiny range of mountains? However presented, they all just wished for direct. Life willing.

The hope eased over Aster, the sort born from the clarity that fire often brings after consuming the detritus or loosening the dross. His clarified mind perceived the perpetual tune against those seaside cliffs no longer in melancholy register, but detected a more mellifluous song. With his life now swirling in harmony, Aster trotted along with the others.

Pixee walked at the head. As usual. Not that she had caught the answer.

"You're certain they're not anywhere on this peninsula?" Rustle asked as they approached Lamiston Proper. "I'm just curious as to how you're so certain, is all. He shrugged back at Aster and Sedge.

No support from his fellow travelers. Just more grins.

She kept her response, if she even had one. Who knew? When it came to interactions between Rustle and Pixee, she took the approach that he hadn't asked. Clearly she had not yet learned how this approach was a failure since such neglect had always been, and still was, met with only more questions.

Aster and Sedge chuckled at the small comedy playing out a few paces ahead of them. In their moment of mirth, Aster met Sedge's glance. They both kept their smirks fastened. Not tightly; they sort of just hung there upon their lips as if uncertain whether or not the circumstances still called for such displays. At the sight of Sedge's smile, Aster's own grin failed. He quickly cleared his throat and smiled again, a little fainter, unsure about wading any farther into the current of Sedge's amusement.

They walked along side one another, their postures relaxed, as if the tension braided together on their way to Oren's had been forgotten. Perhaps it was just stored away after the pitiful display of emotion and tragedy between father and son? Aster cast furtive glances at Sedge, trying to see if any pity lingered in those green eyes. Sedge walked with his lips in a perpetual grin, shaking his head at Rustle.

Aster sensed more than sympathy in Sedge's vibrant countenance. He detected a chance to treat Sedge as more than a companion of happenstance. Aster's discerning eyes perceived room for more to exist between he and Sedge. He let go of the self-examination, for the moment, and resumed watching Rustle interrogate Pixee.

She deigned to reply. "The incessant questioning has got to stop. You sound like a child."

"Not an answer," he stated.

"It is an answer." Pixee walked on without removing focus from the road ahead. "Just not the answer you want to hear."

They crossed the square, and made their way out of the town altogether. Had the earth offered its answer by the time everyone had passed under the eastern archway? None that could be detected by anyone in the group. Not a single chink in the ground. No strange rumblings. Not even a Death-tilled flower to mark the way.

"Did he do it right?" Rustle looked at everyone in the group before continuing on.

Looking back meant entertaining doubt in Oren, so everyone looked everywhere except over their shoulders. Oren had said it would be discernible. He'd also mentioned earth in his spell, so Aster squatted down and grazed his hands across the dirt—bald of any vegetation after steps uncounted—inspecting for the prophesied clue. His eyes picked through the dark, taking in every iota of moonlight that they could. His hand filled in the rest of the detail as it caressed every crevice. Rustle's surprised grunt got him back upright.

Then came the curious noise from Pixee, a pitched *yeep* like a squirrel finding an acorn. Sedge made no sounds, which was a wonder since he too must have felt the same sudden tugging that had taken hold of Aster in his bones. The movement of his body without any conscious direction yanked a shocked sigh from Aster's lungs.

Puppeteering was the answer?

"What in Life's left eye is going on?" Rustle called as his body was directed north, along with the rest of them.

"The answer Oren assured us," Pixee replied in her imperturbable tone.

"But I'm not doing any-blasted-thing." Rustle watched his own legs and hips bearing the rest of his body away. The panic in his voice was almost comical.

Everyone, save Rustle, accepted being passengers in their own bodies as the force conjured by Oren's spell took control and directed their every move with the insistence of a toddler who found something wondrous yet common.

There was naught to do but let the muscles fall into gear and follow the urging that literally shook in their frames. To what end the earthen materials of their skeletons drove them was the new question; probably not just only in Aster's mind.

Rustle was riddled with alarm while Pixee wasn't giving away any of her thoughts. Sedge just strode along, letting the momentum carry him at its will, his jaw set in determination.

Their path was familiar with each passing step, as if the undulating ground were a song Aster had heard before. The unreliable light from the blood moon failed to give any hint as to how accurate his guess was. No one dared stop to rest, nor even attempt to counter the force crawling through the innermost parts of their physical being. For the longest time they just had to keep walking, no variations; no twists or turns. After what felt like hours there came that first jolt since the reply took over.

Pixee, of course, noticed the change first, all the way ahead of the group. Aster reached a certain point when a shudder wrenched his limbs, sending tension from his skull down to his ankles. The answer letting him know there was a change in direction.

Someone bumped into him. "What? Where are you...?"

"Sorry bud," came Sedge's voice. "Just following the thing."

Aster shifted his feet slightly east. The tension abated and that one turn, that simple alteration in direction, was all he needed to understand where this answer was taking him.

Fatigue set in, turning a simple hill into more of a mountain. He couldn't tell his muscles, worn out from the hours of walking without a break, that they faced only a slight grade; the earth knew nothing of limits—no sense of exhaustion or stress—save one: the spell. They filed along and even a sigh escaped from Pixee.

The land was draped in the satin night. Far off, the Mountains of Lune stood, a darker darkness against the night that. "You think anyone's ever scaled the mountains?" The question wasn't directed at any particular individual. It was just a way to stifle the unrelenting movement and let everyone's minds latch on to some other theme.

"Not that I've heard of," Sedge replied to Aster.

Aster was growing accustomed to Sedge being beside him. Maybe intentionally. Maybe just coincidentally.

Was there even such a thing as coincidence? Whether randomness existed or not—and to what extent, if it did—had never occurred to Aster. Yet, in the face of many new circumstances, new people, and new concepts, those questions had a place here and now.

Aster looked in the direction of the mountains, mysterious bastions of rock that poked at the sky. There had to be secrets locked away in those peaks and on the other side of their slopes.

The unknowns. The wonders. All of it sent an ache through Aster, deeper than the ache of moving non-stop hour after hour.

The spell invoked by Oren still inserted its power into their limbs. They kept the pace set by this other force until it slipped away at last. The sudden absence of momentum caused Aster to stumble and nearly topple onto the ground.

After regaining balance and savoring the control he had once more over his own body, he looked up. "Of course. It would be here."

Even as a mere shadow the building was unmistakable. Rustle's sigh was just another piece of evidence which told Aster he wasn't the only one thinking how it was a rude fate to be at Mr. Oleander's villa once more.

"We're all seeing this, right?" Rustle looked at his companions. "Fair, just making sure I wasn't the only one with that sinking feeling." He wandered on up the path to the front door, unwary.

Pixee wandered after him.

"So he isn't going to check for traps? Maybe make sure Oleander isn't home?" Sedge asked.

"From the looks of it, I doubt Mr. Oleander is around, and apparently, Rustle thinks so too," Aster replied.

Rustle pushed open the front door and stepped in as if he were some expected guest. Since there was no reaction to the invasion which Aster took it as a sign to follow.

A long assortment of shadows greeted them. They stood, huddled together all looking down the short hall, waiting for a light source to present itself.

"You're a fire guy now, Aster. How about a little help with this darkness?" Rustle said.

"You mean conjure fire out of thin air and then what? Carry it around in my hand?" Such a feat might have been possible. This bond with fire was new, so new that all ideas about fire were possible but still impossible.

Pixee took Aster's hand and directed it to what felt like a lamp protruding from the wall. "Light it up," she directed.

"How?"

"Feel out the fire. Find it and tell it where to go."

She made it sound so simple. How about she finds it, without a flame in sight, and tell it where to go. This wasn't just about lighting a lamp because if it had been, one of the group would have done something by now instead of standing there in the darkness. They wanted to see the power, maybe even more so than Aster.

Feel out the fire. The fire. There wasn't any.

The element has to come from somewhere. Aster curled his slightly dewy hand closed, perspiration juiced by the pressure of expectation heaved upon him. The warmth was all there, in his palm. In him.

Aster put his hand to the lantern, feeling for a wick of some sort. When his fingers made contract with a fibrous surface, he pinched it tightly. His body had a ready supply of the element, which he just needed to get onto this wick. Stop thinking about what to do and just do it. They were affixed to one another, this element and him. Fire was now like a reflex. An encouraging thought. He knew how to flex a muscle, bend a joint. A bit of concentration—detailed concentration, not a generic wish—saw the heat of his body gather and slide into his fingers in long, amber tendrils.

A chill fluttered across his back as his fist nearly sizzled. There wasn't pain, just the sense of a growing divide between the sensation in the tips of his fingers and the other parts of his body as they relinquished their store of warmth. The wick ignited.

The other lamps sprang to life, like they were all connected. Enough visibility had been instituted to show off the array of sketches lining the wall.

26.

OF INVESTIGATIONS ON THE EARTH

It came as a surprise to Aster how uninterested his companions were in the drawings that lined the wall.

Pixee simply carried on, turning the corner at the end of the hall without a second glance at the sketches, as did Sedge. Rustle gave each a partial scoop of consideration as he followed the group down the hall.

Despite having already viewed each one already, they still proved to be curious and provocative. That last drawing though. This one image had excavated for itself an undeniable impression, the sort to reach down into the psyche.

The frame was light in Aster's hand, almost too light. It should have felt heavier than the Truce Blood, for some reason beyond his grasp. At the very least, the image was deserving of a more durable case. Maybe should have had some glass over it for an added layer of protection against dust and other invaders and contaminates.

"Aster." Sedge peeked around the corner. "You coming?"

Aster nodded while Sedge took a moment to observe Aster before disappeared back to some other part of the house.

It didn't literally say his name, but there was a voice in that image and it sounded like it knew him; it spoke, if spoke was the right word for this feeling, with an essential familiarity. Such was enough justification to keep the illustration instead of returning it to its place among the other. Bearing his plunder, Aster turned the corner into another, longer hallway.

The group had assembled in what looked like a room used for studying: books shelved and a desk littered with papers. Why Pixee had led them here was her guess alone. Sedge glanced at the volumes standing firm. Rustle shifted the papers about.

"For whatever reason, Oren's spell brought us here, so here is where the Stewards have to be. Let's divide and search. This place isn't so big that we can't cover every room in a reasonable amount of time."

Pixee's plan was heeded only by Sedge, who ventured off to some other part of the house. Rustle meandering about the room, hesitant to explore this house of ill-repute on his own. The fear of Mr. Oleander's wrath must have been seared right into his soul. He decided to offer help, in the form of scrutinzing the few delineations adorning the walls

"Just feats of magic, apparently," Aster explained over Rustle's shoulder.

Pixee started leafing through volumes plucked from their restful slumber on the shelves, shaking out the tomes as if she would somehow dislodge a clue from amongst the pages.

Rustle's wandering eye was snagged on a specific image, as abstract as the others hanging about the halls of Mr. Oleander's home. Aster paused his own search and observed alongside Rustle. The background was inverted while the main subject, a group of creatures on four legs canine in likeness, were upright. They pointed their snouts towards the base of a crescent moon, which had the appearance of being buried deep in the earth.

"More like Hortlak," Pixee said after a halfhearted glance.

"Come again?" Rustle asked.

"Creatures of the earth, " she said as she returned to feeling out the room. She tipped another book upside down, shook out its pages. "Known to be associated with death. Their appetites are rumored to be like that of goats: willing to set their jaws to just about anything, especially the remains of soulless bodies. They have a bite that can turn bone into grit."

Having satisfied her hunch that the Stewards were not to be found in this particular room, nor were there any clues as to their whereabouts, she took her leave down that same hall. To the kitchen, perhaps.

Aster walked away, towards the left wing of the villa, wondering what sort of secrets—which is to say, treasures—Mr. Oleander kept to himself.

He came to a room on his left, mostly empty: sparse furnishings and a small contingent of books set neatly on a shelf. He approached and slid the first volume off its perch. *Elements of the Elements* said the first page. Not really a clue about the Stewards, but with three other people looking for them Aster could spare a few moments to see what the book had to say.

Of what sort of tale it told Aster was unsure. There were a good two inches of pages through which he scanned, looking but not really reading, hoping the right words, those most germane to his aspirations, would fly off the page and slap his attention.

His eyes caught a smattering of phrases:

Spawn of Death's whimsy.

Servant of Life's ingenuity.

Walls on the wheel of time.

They spoke of the history of histories, all the way back to when elements were primitive, probably before any living and speaking being learned how to manipulate them. To grasp their meaning—to absorb their intent—would take a new level of analysis for which there was no time, as intoxicating as that would have been. He shut the book and returned it to the shelf. Alas, this wasn't an expedition for words and this room didn't hold the Stewards. He left the other books—titles like *The Full Tale of the Forest* and *Earth Bound: The Struggle to Counter Earth Magics*—unopened.

The next room was emptier than the last. Not a single book to be had. A lonely drawing, situated on the wall farthest from the door, prevented this room from being literally empty. Such a small distinction, like a single smudge upon a canvas.

Aster took a few steps closer and the image came into focus. About as magical and fair as any of the graphical depictions hanging about the place: rather wilted-looking figures, five of them, their arms stretched over their heads, as if hung up by some undisclosed rope. With a sneer, Aster set his back to the image.

The next room: longer than wide, with skylights above that probably flooded the interior with so much sunlight during the day, if such a thing were to happen again. There were a couple couches, plush and well kept, and a chair or two surrounded by books sitting untroubled upon cases standing floor-to-ceiling. Smug with those stiff spines, the volumes hosted an army of little Ts and Ls, set like spears marching, daring anyone to conquer their meaning. Dare to search, they heckled. Well, since there didn't appear to be any Stewards in this room, why not dip into those writings and see if they didn't contain a useful spell or two? Maybe an earthen spell would help ensure his creation would be able to proliferate on its own.

On Life's lips, there were multiple editions covering each element. Their binding felt like cuts of dehydrated beef. They must not have been opened in some time. Mr. Oleander read them once and didn't bother to ever pick them up again, apparently. Maybe he didn't need to?

Aster slipped a book from its place in line, no longer even pretending to be interested in the hunt for the Stewards. The dry spine issued a crackle as he flipped the cover opened.

The pages fluttered like butterfly wings. A dry paragraph about the intricacies of various types of rock. A few more pages flipped; not so much dry as muddy was this section on the power of pacing words to match the density of earth, which was interesting, but too theoretical for Aster's need. The next page touted a chapter heading: *Earth, In All Its Forms.*

He took his hand off the page and let his eyes graze along each line to casually chew on the sentences.

No longer threatened by the profuse amount of letters, Aster waded through the paragraphs about the iterations of the earth element, the flavor from the last sample of fire fruit echoing across his tongue; saliva seeped out of every nook in his mouth at the recollection. He somehow knew, on an instinctive level, he needed the knowledge of earth to match his deep connection to the element of fire.

The chapter drew to an un-satiating close. Five pages yet remained though. Aster put all his focus to paper, not skipping over a single word. Earth in every sentence, the solid facts of it. They were faceted at times, chunky at others. Then came a sentence that shook Aster, an earthquake of an idea coming on unexpectedly, as earthquakes do: *...the final form of earth is found at the end of life. Living draws to a close, the soul carries on in another realm freed from the scope of elements. What remains behind is given to the earth, willingly or not.*

Given to the earth.

Burial.

A morbidly common word in and of itself, but that was for the folks who hadn't seen spades of dirt thrown over their body by a mother with a mad obsession seething in her eyes.

A quick glance about to make sure the world was still in one piece: walls were upright as air moved freely through empty spaces; One deep breath in, held for a moment in an attempt to tell the body how to react, to not let a memory infested with negative emotions overcome the hear and now.

"Burial," Aster uttered with a delicate breath.

When he had ever said that word before he couldn't remember. Now that he'd summoned the courage to actually utter it, with his own voice, there was a power in its syllables. She could have been on to something. Not the maniacal pursuit to cure dying, but the power of the rite of burying in and of itself. There had to be special words that would make a burial more than just hiding and covering.

Aster scoured the pages for the necessary song. He riffled through the book one more time. He missed it. The answer was in here. A third time. No spells. Just more gibberish about earth. He slapped the cover down before vacating back to the previous room, with its manageable collection of volumes. An appropriate place to start.

"You found something," Pixee claimed as Aster passed her by in the hall.

Without any amount of reply, Aster breezed into the room, perhaps a little too hopefully, but that was neither here nor there. Pixee's presence barely registered as Aster tore into a pile of books, investigating their titles, tossing aside the ostensibly irrelevant, evenly the loosely relevant.

Sedge joined Pixee in looking over Aster's shoulder at the growing pile of discarded books. "Books? They're in a book?"

The useless question plied by Sedge was fit to ignore. Finding the Stewards was the primary quest, of course, but other purposes could be fulfilled along the way. Out of the pile came a book with potential. Just inside the black leather cover was the title: Songs of the Obscure.

"I think I may have found a clue," Rustle said with his head peeking in the room.

He vanished, followed by Sedge and Pixee. Aster looked up and for a brief moment caught a lingering glance from Sedge before he left entirely, for which Aster was slightly thankful now being able to lean into the book without the ruination of all the silly questions and prying sighs.

This book felt heavier than it looked, a feeling of lead buried deep between the covers. Or maybe there was a heftiness in each individual page. They were the color of tea that had cooled ages ago, a sign each one needed to be lifted with the utmost care.

Pixee's voice peeled through the hall, a summons that had an edge of urgency. Aster himself let exasperation escape his lips as he nestled a couple of fingers between two pages.

With his discovery cradled against his chest, Aster joined to his cohorts in the next room over. He paused at the door and waited for someone to disclose what was so important that he needed to be present. There was nothing going on, except a lot of looming about that eerie drawing.

"What are you looking at?" he asked, hardly looking at them, hardly acknowledging aught but the pages at hand.

That was the extent of Aster's involvement. He inched into the room with his eyes glued to the words in his treasured book. He halted and refocused on his own, personal inquiry.

Sedge turned away from the drawing for a moment, examining Aster, his thick arms folded across his thick chest. He pursed his lips. "Aster, I get that you're excited about finding some nifty spell, but a little help would be nice."

Sedge's politely framed demand provoked barely a glance. "Truly, just a minute." The book of spells beckoned. Aster sunk to the floor.

Sedge approached. "Don't mess with that book too much. Something about it doesn't look right," he said with a sneer.

Sedge, the all-knowing, all-strong warrior with a heart and mind of gold. If he knew so much, the Stewards would have been found by now. He was just too sure about being right and his tone announced it. Granted the book was aged, but beyond its faded cover and tired ink, there was nothing else about it that looked specifically vile. The pages felt a bit unlike paper. It was as they had been cut from….dried pig's skin.

Aster shrugged away the implications of Sedge's comment and resumed gingerly scouring the contents. The stanzas were mixed with no apparent order, as if they had been collected over decades like a personal journal. Stanzas about fire followed those about earth which preceded other songs of fire. Among the various incantations, there had to be the one. It lived somewhere nestled between chants of air and water.

Aster set the book upon the floor. He took hold of the page in a most genial way ready to turn to the next.

Sedge clasped down on Aster's wrist. "No. The Stewards first."

Aster welcomed the touch with all the serious menace of which he was capable. His version of menacing may have been laughable to such a one as Sedge, seasoned in techniques of intimidation, but his chuckling was really uncalled for. He let Aster's wrist slip from his grasp as he squatted down beside Aster.

That look was on Sedge's face, the one that said *what am I going to do with you.* "This is more important than finding the Stewards?"

"Since we're here, I don't see any harm in picking up a few trade secrets along the way," Aster replied without a trace of guilt in his voice.

"Trade secrets?"

"Spells and techniques that might be of a benefit to certain persons in the pursuit of certain magical outcomes."

"Let him do his thing for now," Pixee said with a roll of her eyes, leaving Aster—reluctantly—to his business. She resumed questioning Rustle: "You think this is a hint, because...?"

Rustle began his defense. Their words warbled over Aster as he fixated on the text in his hands. Three people looking was plenty. A fourth compatriot would be excessive, especially for the task of staring preponderantly at a drawing.

The letters on the page were barely a whisper. How long ago had they been written down? It took a stringent gaze to bring each title off the page. *The Talking* something something. Nope, not right.

Miasma...not? Yes, *Miasma Not*. Seemed like a good chant to know, but not the right one. On he pressed through the spells, each one marching past Aster for an earnest inspection. Most of them failed to pass muster; either the words were all wrong or they were just too faded to read.

Then came one: Rite of Internment. Aster's hands fell to the sides of the book as the spell practically lunged off the page. Upon reading over the words a second time there was a strong familiarity about the stanza even though Aster was sure he'd never read it before.

Their breathy syllables laid waste to all other sounds. No amount of whispering or calling from Sedge, or anyone else, would rein in this moment, the cusp of a realization that needed to take place.

Where had this exact arrangement of words been spoken before?

His lips moved soundlessly for a moment, in a desperate bid to place them. They rolled over his mind, right over the mystery, arriving right at the most sacred memory he had; sacred because it branded his psyche with trauma that sung as clearly as the ebb and flow of the ocean tides. Did he really want to admit to them what he had stumbled upon?

Out of the corner of his eye, Aster could see that Pixee and Sedge stared at him. A little concern, even a bit of confusion, strewn across their countenances as they witnessed him withdrawing from the book to which he had been clinging so ardently merely seconds ago. Rustle maintained his fixation with the drawing, lifting it away from the wall to have a closer look, but not removing it.

Pixee knelt down and waited.

"This. The one she used on me."

Pixee turned the book more towards her, giving the page a quick read through. "Why did you want this?"

"Looked like it would help me with the fire fruit," Aster said fumbling to produce a convincing grin. "A backup plan, in case the bond with fire didn't help."

She dispensed a knowing look but didn't say *do this* or *don't do that*. Instead she patted his shoulder as she pushed herself back to standing and resumed discussion with Sedge and Rustle gathered about that random drawing.

What was the real purpose behind this incantation? Was it the use his mother applied? Her mania clouded Aster's eyes, but he blinked it away.

He'd give this rite new purpose. He'd use it on the fire fruit so the magic would no longer belong to the obsession of a woman manipulated by fear. Was it just natural, like a weed, or did someone plant it there?

With the discovery of such a personal connection, the book felt heavier; as if a certain energy, or power, coursed through the page itself. There was more to this moment than simply the passage of time consumed by events. This was ceremonial. The sound of the fibers being detached was more of a claim; anyone with the will to take power was claimed by that very same power in return.

Pixee's raised voice cascade to where Aster sat. "You want me to take your suggestion seriously?"

"None of us are an authority here," Rustles said. "We're all guessing in this situation."

"They're here somewhere." She paused for a breath. "We need to keep that in mind, no matter how frustrating the search seems so, better suggestions. Not connected with the drawing."

The spell was almost physically his.

"Have to say, I agree. Leave it alone, Rustle."

"Listen to me," Rustle insisted in a slightly whiny register. "We can't ignore this. It's a clue."

The page was nearly free. Just a few more centimeters left to pull away. Aster cast a quick glance over towards the wall, where Pixee and Rustle debated the meaning behind the sketch. Then, Rustle yanked the framed image from the wall.

The floor gave out from under their feet.

27.

OF INVESTIGATIONS
IN THE EARTH

A floor inserted somewhere in the earth rushed up in an excited embrace.

All the air in Aster's body was forcibly exhaled. Grains of dirt clung to his teeth and tongue which Aster evicted as best he could before opening his eyes. But had he really? A darkness no less than absolute draped over Aster's perception, like black cotton, thick and dry and even a tad prickly in an unfamiliar way.

Aster inhaled deeply. His skin tingled and small bumps raised along his arm making it feel like a freshly plucked goose. He ran a finger down his forearm; the hairs stood upright. A shiver followed the caress. These reactions were the sort his body would display had he been dunked into a river.

He shifted and relaxed just a little when he felt the spell in his hand. That and the drawing. Both had survived the fall, along with Aster. He secured them in the waist of his pants and underpants, against his back.

It was time to make sure everyone survived the plummet into this destitute place. At the moment, he had heard no other sounds but that of his own movements. His own breathing was barely audible.

"Sedge?" In the dry, still air Aster's voice was less than a whisper puffing lamely out from between his lips. The black cotton soaked it up, as cotton is prone to do. The chill rose then abated.

"Pixee?" More stillness. "…Rustle?"

Aster was finally up, so it felt, sitting there with nothing to hear but his own wheezing. Was he even looking? There certainly wasn't any seeing taking place. He rolled his eyes over and over while blinking aggressively just to assure himself he was conscious and not lost in some abysmal dream. The one sensation nonplussed by the robe of dark was under assault by a mustiness. There was another odor subtly woven in and out of the general stale aroma, befouling the atmosphere of whatever sort of place they had landed. Aster pulled at the stagnant air with his nostrils and, yes, there it was: a sour bouquet tingling in his nose, yanking and prying at his throat: the stench of meat that had gone sour.

It had to be a dungeon? The ground was raw and undeveloped. Aster's hand detected the rough caress of pebbles and dirt. No polished surface, cool and smooth, nor the grain of wood.

"Everyone alive?" Pixee's voice inched through the thick darkness.

"Present," Rustle said, the sound of his shifting cutting into the stillness.

Their voices barely traveled, like they had to be shoved out in order to be heard. Moving in the unfamiliar pit was like learning to walk anew; no sight to guide foot and leg, just fear thwarting balance. Landing each step, and evenly at that, proved a struggle. The feel of only slightly yielding flesh told Aster the person he'd bumped into wasn't Rustle.

"Oh. Sedge." Aster took his time, letting his fingers fall slowly away from Sedge's proud body.

Sedge cleared his throat. "It is kind of tough, uh, to navigate in here." His hands slipped down Aster's sides.

"Do you feel that?" The question plopped out of Aster's mouth.

"I think so," Sedge replied, almost in a whisper.

"Like the air in here was dipped in a...deep river. Or spraying off the ocean," Aster said.

Sedge didn't agree or argue right away. His reaction was shut behind the dearth of light. He sucked in a breath. "I think I see..." His laughter eased the encroaching blackness. "I get what you mean."

Aster smiled, to himself of course, as he scooted back hoping to give Sedge a little more space. He tripped on his own step. His arms went out in some form of defense and were greeted with a meaty mass from which Aster decidedly lurched away while a shudder coursed up his body. The response found expression in a strangled sound that straddled the line between a yelp and a grunt, loud in that cotton atmosphere. He landed right back into Sedge's chest.

"What? What is it?" Sedge asked as his hands set upon Aster's shoulders, holding him steady after that run-in with...whatever hung there in the pitch-dark.

Aster had a guess, teetering on the cusp of utterance, but all that his mind allowed him so say was: "Something's over here." Aster eased away from Sedge's tender grip.

"A way out?"

What was in Aster's words led Sedge to believe he had found an exit? "Something, like, I don't know. Just come look—"

Look. See. That was a lark. There wouldn't be any seeing. There would be a tactile investigation, however, into the malleable surface and the ostensible source of the tangy scent, as much as Aster denied that the two were connected.

He extended his fingers to their limit, wanting to avoid coming into too much contact with the mysterious object. His eyes were shut tightly against, what? The sight of gore? He'd had his fill of that and survived. Something horribly and oddly out of place? Even if this was the case, the fear of such a situation was laughable in this impermissible blackness, so aster chuckled. Aster stood rooted on that packed dirt as he tried to milk even just an iota of light with his pupils but was only left with memory of light.

His fingers met the substance in a bit of a caress, sliding his fingers up one hesitant centimeter at a time until there came a bump, a bit of a protrusion, followed shortly by an arch.

He froze. "It's a body," he declared to the dark, yanking his hand away.

The hurried crunch of multiple feet shuffling closer filled the stationary air. A semblance of warmth started to cut at the chilly air as everyone's breathing and body heat combined into something like a sober chorus.

"Are you sure?" Pixee's voice hung, disembodied, in the dark.

Aster turned to where he thought she stood. "Pretty. If we had light I'd be nothing but."

"Let's get some light going then," Pixee offered with un-pilfered conviction.

For a moment, the room resumed a frothy stillness. Everyone waited on a response, for compliance with the directive issued by Pixee. A little light would be a helpful addition to the situation. The darkness was heavy, penetrating until it ate up the recall of color. It had been easy enough to light those lamps hanging in the villa's entry hall. A little bit of concentration and poof: flames.

"Uh, well I'm gonna need some fuel for a fire. Then I'll have to figure out a way to keep just the light and not the heat." He didn't mention the possible sources he held in his hand. Too precious were both the page containing the Burial Rite and the sketch to use as kindling. He wouldn't be able to explain why the sketch, but he was going to follow his intuition on this.

There had been a moment's deliberation before Aster heard the sound of fibers tearing. Hands, hefty and well-used, draped a strip of fabric clumsily across Aster's palm.

"Thanks, Sedge." Aster knelt down while more fabric had been bestowed by Sedge. "This should work," he claimed, though the words felt wobbly as he said them. Thankfully, no one gainsaid him.

"Primul magic?" Aster suggested.

The crunch of shifting dirt told him someone moved slightly. "You need the practice more than me," Pixee said. "I know my connection to the elements. Better you figure yours out while we're not in any danger. Immediate danger, that is."

It was a fair reason. Aster sighed. "So, hold your hands over here."

Aster directed his compatriots, arranging their sets of hands into a sort of clump just above the cloth, which he had knotted into a little ball. He cupped his hands together and slipped them just below the web of fingers offered by this fellows.

It was all guess work. This notion that heat would simply do his bidding still didn't feel natural, especially under these strange, frigid circumstance. Weird to assume that an entire element was at the his beck and call. That was the thing though, wasn't it? Knowing it would all work according to the assumption drummed up in his mind, even without proof?

Aster shook away the incredulity worming its way in his thoughts, and pulled heat from everyone's hands. It was there in his imaging, a string of some kind, or what he thought heat looked like: translucent, oily, and yet light. Someone shivered, it was a clarifying gesture, giving the notion of heat-as-a-thread more substance.

The warmth continued to fall from the congregation of hands until it felt like weeds dredged out of a pond, lank and flaccid. Aster opened his cupped hands, spilling the heat upon the fabric. It glommed onto the fuel, reacted, and up sprang flames. The light bit at Aster's eyes.

Rustle huffed and rubbed his hands together vigorously trying to regain warmth.

"Those sleeves going to last?" Sedge asked.

"Let me think for a second," Aster said while the flames engaged in feasting upon the fabric.

Aster ignored the sudden visual of Sedge's arms, segmented with defined musculature. "Yes. Got it…"

> *Wake to the world in an unexpected shell*
> *A livery wraps around your sacred heart*
> *Naked you become, leaving behind the brightest part*

Aster pinched at the fire and tossed aside the heat leaving behind light that pushed back against the dark.

"Did that spell do something?" Sedge inquired as he, for some reason, clasped a tiny blade in his hand.

Aster took Sedge by the wrist. "See for yourself." He Sedge's hand toward the fire. There was a natural resistance, but Aster urged Sedge's closer until he touched the flame.

Sedge swiped his hand back and forth through the fire. "Look at that." The fire highlighted his whimsical grin.

Aster clasped a hand around Sedge's wrist. "Careful. You can still put it out."

The meager light reached out as far as it was able, and the dark yielded to reveal Sedge's hand slowly retracting out of Aster's grip. Aster watched the motion play out before turning to give the chamber a scan.

What he could see of it appeared narrow. There would be time enough to interrupt even the most benighted corners of the dungeon, but one matter took precedence over the search for an exit, a mystery more disconcerting than being trapped. A dose of light would put to shame the enigma of that meaty substance. For better or for worse.

Aster exhaled slowly, walking even slower, eulogizing the situation with as much reason as he could muster—as much as his imagination allowed—which barely reached the level of substantial.

Aster's stomach lurched when his paltry flame shooed away any concealment, which might have been a mistake. The dark peeled back to reveal the bare skin, dry like a patch of soil that had long been without the company of rain. He raised the light a little higher peering at those shuttered eyes. Aster licked his lips. He glanced quickly back over his shoulder at Sedge, whose face offered nothing. No one's expression had any inkling of a reaction. Aster brought his merry little fire closer to the naked body. The light bore upon that face and the orange glow fell into cavities where eyes should have been.

Shadows returned to the face as the light fell to the ground. Aster swayed, back into Sedge's steady hands.

"Life's left eye." Rustle breathed. His retching punched at the quiet. "Who is she?"

They all stared at the relatively intact corpse hanging a meter or two off the ground, arranged with her arms extended above her head.

Sedge stepped around Aster and grabbed the light source off the ground and pointed it at the dead woman. The heat-less flames danced across a face that wasn't young but neither was it aged. Her eyelids looked to have been removed. "Strange, the missing eyes are the only sign of violence."

"How in Death's Realm she ended up like this…" Rustle let out a low whistle.

"They." Sedge cast the humble light down the wall. Other figures came into view.

All dangling against the wall, naked and without detailed examination, probably eyeless like the first. More worthy reactions there were to serve up at the sight of five bodies dangling in iron shackles with their eyes scooped out. All that Aster could summon at the moment was a beleaguered "Why?"

Though a twisted mural of light and shadow painted Sedge's face, his eyes shone clear. "Why didn't the Stewards stop Oleander from possessing the Truce Blood?" He looked in earnest at Aster. "And why did Oren say all that shit about not being able to sense them anymore?"

28.

OF A SENSE OF SENSE

His statement demanded no vocal response. Not that anyone had breath to offer one; the discovery robbed them of air the same way a plunge into icy water would have.

Pixee pushed through her cemented companions. She took the light from Sedge and craned her neck to see what they were seeing. The light was a little dollop upon the cloth; she edged closer. The fire wavered under the silent gasp emitted by Pixee.

She reigned in her shock. "This is not what I wanted to find but it's not completely unexpected."

"All hung up to dry here in Oleander's basement," Rustle added.

The darkness filling those hollowed-sockets was denser than the darkness in that pit. There was no end to it, stretching deeper to some other place and time. Out of those vacant sockets crept imaginings. It wasn't so much that they had shapes—creatures with form or face—it was more like an unease, broader and heavier than any that had touched Aster's mind before. Shadows, with all of their menace, charged from those lifeless faces containing a wrath that ended in more than death. The chill they had all forgotten came back, sinking deeper somehow, from touching just skin to hitting joint and bone.

"How long will this last?" Pixee's voice retrieved Aster from the languid despair that nearly drowned him.

She held the light up like an offering. The benign flames, dithering as they are wont to do, swirled and chased one another across Aster's field of sight.

"I'm not…not sure," he finally replied as he grasped the sight of Pixee, her serious eyes insisting on him. "I've never done this before. Hopefully, long enough for us to find our way out of this Death-tilled chamber."

There were only four walls in the rectangular space. The corpses, all lined up with their eyeless skulls looking everywhere and nowhere, were shut back up in the dark as Pixee bore the light away to investigate other parts of the chamber. Just knowing they hung there, defiled and decomposing, was enough to stir up shudders that passed like winds over a plain. How long until, of their own volition, they slipped from the cuffs and crumpled on to the dirt-floor? How long until they joined that dirt?

"Here," Sedge squatted down. "Get up on my shoulders and see if you can feel for a trap door or something."

Pixee saddled Sedge's shoulders as he stood. There was the initial wobbling about, but Sedge found his footing. Pixee held the light up and pressed her hand against the spot through which they had fallen.

"Nothing."

"Push harder?" Rustle offered.

"It's not budging."

Sedge walked Pixee along while she investigated every inch of the ceiling—and every inch withstood her insistence—avoiding the bodies for as long as possible, but it was time.

He stood near the first one as Pixee knocked, not even hesitating to brush against their skin as she felt the entire length of the floor-turned-ceiling, moving from one corpse to the next.

Sedge lowered Pixee back to the ground. "Looks like we're really stuck."

The search for escape had settled and the room once again filled with that cottony blackness, an inevitable suffocating stillness. It was too much, just sitting there waiting for the exit to present itself. It felt wrong to leave them hanging there, naked and violated. The first body was heavier than Aster expected.

"You're going to rip her arms off," Sedge said.

Aster released the body. The metallic shackles rattled and chimed into the silence. Aster took a step back, wiped his nose. "Can you pick the cuffs open with that little knife of yours then?"

Sedge's voice crawled through the dark that separated him from Aster. "Why do you need to do this?"

"Because I do," Aster said to the meager orange glow that reached up to the corpse's chin.

"Sweat is the answer. It works on grief." An admission, addressed less to Sedge and more to the figure latched to the wall, dangling in eerie calm. "It works on sadness, confusion." He half-turned towards Sedge. "So I've found."

He faced the corpse once more. The feminine features—wide hips, breasts, and a decided lack of external sexual organs—chilled with the absence of a beating heart and flowing blood. This was an empty vessel, no longer conveying an entire consciousness, accomplishing deeds and executing vision.

Aster resumed fidgeting with her body, trying to be delicate but still assertive.

The light flickered and sputtered before it evened out enough for Sedge to watch. "Wait," he said, following Aster to the body. "Pixee?"

She resumed her perch upon Sedge's shoulders as he carried her small frame high enough to reach the bonds holding the dead

Stewards in place. She picked the lock. Aster heard the click. After a second click the body thudded against the ground.

"You feel better now?" Sedge wiped his forearm across his brow, the little drops of sweat made to glitter by the light which now burned a bit more humbly.

Aster didn't answer as he scooped up the lifeless body and bore her away from that wall. A pitiful, ignoble end for someone who probably had a lustrous life. Her dirtied breasts and exposed genitals needed shielding. It was at least one small dignity to clarify this indignity.

On to the next body: a man who looked much denser than the lady, forearms thick and hairy. He also sank into a mere pile of meat. Aster took him by the wrist and dragged him over to lie next to the first.

The third body slipped to the ground and as Aster made to move this corpse: "Shhh." Sedge paused as he faced away from the remaining bodies dangling at the wall.

Aster dropped the skinny arms he had grabbed and paused with his hands on his hips. "What?"

"Stop breathing."

"What now?" bemoaned Rustle. "Getting tired of carrying Pixee?" His chuckling shuddered from outside the light's vicinity where he sat, observing the project.

Sedge turned and shot a glare to wherever Rustle sat, not helping. "No…jackass. I heard something."

"If you're going to stop the process," Pixee said as she shifted upon Sedge, "then at least set me down. This isn't exactly a comfortable spot to be sitting on."

"Get the last one real quick." The dirt crunched and shuffled under Sedge's determined steps as he lined up with the last body.

Pixee unfettered the wrists. Aster heard it, then: the clack of metal slipping out of metal. The wall against which the bodies had been hung rumbled; it was the slightest gap, just enough for a breath to pass. Sedge quickly unburdened himself of Pixee; they both rushed to the small joint that had been released. Sedge pushed it back, some kind of broad door on a pivot joint.

Everyone hurried through the opening, except Aster. His gaze prodded at the exposed bodies. They were with Death now; hopefully. The brightness of their souls evaluated, Death would soon know about the misdeeds that ferried them away from the mortal layer. When Death learned about the failing of the Order would anything be done about it? This wasn't his fight; it wasn't Sedge's fight. Or Pixee's. Those bodies, laying in the dirt lost to darkness, were a testament that Mr. Oleander's machinations reached beyond any one mortal.

No, this was started with Life and Death, leaving their blood just lying around for some malicious person to dig up. Let them sort it out with their infinite knowledge and power. Mere mortals had enough to worry about without taking on such nefarious plots: warlords, the slow decay of time, and the complicated dance of love and relationships.

His head bowed as he continued to count the fears and worries that came with being mortal. With a sigh, Aster turned his back upon the expired Stewards.

He drew out the framed sketch and the piece of stiff parchment with his prized spell, this Burial Rite. He folded the later carefully and tucked it away in a pocket. The former was easy enough to free from the frame which he discarded. With an unexplainable amount of reverence, Aster folded the drawing and stored it with the spell.

He slipped through the opened wall, gently patting the paper in his pocket. Hunched over, he traversed the narrow tunnel back up to ground level where the cold of the dungeon slowly slipped away.

The others stood waiting. They were all caught-up in the act of taking in as much of the untainted air as possible, ushering in the scent of grass to drown out the residual musk of rotted of corpses.

When Aster emerged, their expectant eyes pried at him in the hope of answers to questions they hadn't asked.

"What?" Their puzzled expressions, a surprise.

"We have to tell him," Pixee offered. "Oren needs to know."

Aster dropped his chin. "I know. He was right. I honestly don't think Oren will really care."

"Why wouldn't he?" Sedge asked.

Aster shrugged. "He will be disappointed but he only really cares about the things he can change."

There was a certain excitement bubbling just below the surface of Aster's somber expression, stirred by the potential of finally being able to fulfill his pursuit. First the Martese and now these instructions. With all these pieces, he couldn't fail. Wouldn't lose, this time. The excitement threatened to crack open on Aster's face. Fitting that it would be brought about by the very same words that had broken his family into pieces.

"He'll know what we need to do next," Pixee said with a sort of shaky certainty.

Even though she wasn't entirely convincing, they all followed along. Aster didn't blame her. She was fighting a plot that was probably old as time itself, but for them it was a new danger. Who was Aster to tell her what the next step should be? He wanted to show off his newly acquired magic, though. Whether Oren would approve or reproach Aster for dabbling with this particular ritual, he was about to find out.

Sedge walked alongside Aster in silence for a moment. "Pretty important magic, huh?"

Where was he going with that question? Aster huffed. "Truly."

"Big time solution?" Sedge glanced at Aster, eyebrows peaked.

Each statement was cryptic if not slightly accusatory. "I suppose?"

Sedge's prickly questioning—not thorn or brier prickly but more like thistle prickly—was just noticeable enough to be annoying.

"Well, good." Sedge nodded as he resumed walking in silence.

Aster welcomed the dearth of questions, but kept taking quick glances at Sedge as they matched pace with one another.

"Magic is great and all," Sedge added without precursor, his hands dancing with the words. "But sometimes it causes as many problems as it solves."

Aster slowed his stride. "I get that." He leaned away from Sedge, with a shrug. "What are you getting at, exactly?"

Sedge didn't respond immediately, as he fished around in the sky for his exact intent. He turned his eyes upon Aster, the red moonlight causing the green in them to diminish into some dark, unnameable shade. "I guess I'm just curious why you would be tinkering around with magic like that, after all the issues it caused."

It sounded like concern. May have even been genuine, but Aster couldn't rightly put it on a scale to determine just how much was authentic and how much was dross.

"No reason to be worried," Aster assured. His next thought sprang up, but his voice felt heavy: "She used it in a terrible way. That was her."

Sedge nodded unwilling, or maybe unable, to dive deeper into what Aster had just shared; how he shared it. They continued to walk under the dark sky without any more conversation. After a few more hours of silent travel, Aster began to question the existence of day, as though that phenomenon was now just a legend. A giant ball of fire lighting up the entire sky? How incredibly mystic and preposterous.

Oren would have an explanation. He knew things. Deep things. If he didn't know them, his gut was to be trusted. That instinct of his had kept him and Aster alive and comfortable long enough.

Oren was right where Aster expected to find him: standing at the cliffs, watching nothing in particular. Maybe he even heard the voice of his beloved, long since dead, in the sigh of the tide. It was almost a travesty to interrupt his meditation.

There was no need. He turned at the sound of Aster's approach, steps that were pushing into the ground with the fervor of a man being pursued. Not quite a run, but not a calm stroll either.

"You found some clue to explain all this?" Oren gestured to the night that had lingered for days, without crack or sliver of sunlight. It was supposed to have been a direct question from a father who knew a thing or two about the world, not a plea or a prayer to a son who knew much less.

They didn't wait for the others, but walked straight away into the small cabin. Aster sank onto the couch as the adventures of the past few days slipped away and metaphorically fell to the floor. With their pressure absent, Aster sighed. Fatigue invaded his whole being. Oren kept the door open before planting himself into his usual seat.

Pixee, Rustle, and Sedge admitted themselves into the small house, filling up the available space that remained in the main room. Pixee shut the door and leaned back against it while Rustle sat before the fireplace, unburned sticks of driftwood stacked in a grate in anticipation of a warming fire.

"If you can manage, tell me what you found?" His inquiry was imbued with a hunger to understand, to expel the mystery of the novel goings-on that had fallen upon the world.

Aster rummaged through the store of details in a search for the relevant, the necessary; what he considered such. One look at Oren's face—the lines that usually bunched up about his eyes now smoothed by the curiosity pouring out of his wide, richly blue eyes—and there was no boundary that defined necessary.

Instead of a curated selection of information Aster drew out whatever popped into his head: "We, uh, ended up at Mr. Oleander's. They were shackled up in some secret dungeon…" which seemed like the perfect starting point.

"Go on, kiddo." Oren lightly touched Aster's knee.

"They were, um, naked. They had no eyes, Dad."

"Aye," Oren said, as if it hadn't surprised him. "The eyes are the key, the portals to the soul. Life and Death communicate directly to the Stewards' souls. No eyes and pathway between this layer and the next is shuttered."

"But they're with Life and Death now," Aster said, as he searched Oren for confirmation that the statement was sound. There was a need for assurance that such violence would be answered with real justice. "Their souls are in their layer and so Life and Death will know about the mess here."

Oren peered back at Aster. "There's a lot I learned as a Steward. Some of it from study, some from experience. There's much that remains a mystery. The souls of those Stewards may have found their way or they may very well be lost, wandering in a way we don't even know about."

Aster shivered. His skin prickled. "So it's as bad as you thought?"

Oren chewed on the question for a moment. "You know who wanted the hands-off approach?" He turned his glance upon each person, one at a time, waiting for one of them to return his questions with a bit of conjecture.

Sedge and Rustle just stared, letting weariness have its way with them. The insightful Pixee could only shrug in response.

"Life." Oren nodded sagely. "Yes, all the old tales and lore name Life as an artist. Every being is just a project, a clay pot or filled canvas to the being we call Life." He cast his eyes down at the floor between his feet. "Troubled by no thought beyond the act of creation. Now Death," Oren said with a bit more brightness to his voice. "Death looked for purpose and wanted the same for us so he demanded, as part of their truce, that they would provide some guidance for mortals. Hence the indirect contact through the Stewards…for those special cases. There's no other way for them to touch our layer." He chuckled grimly as he surveyed his audience. "Oleander behaves a bit like Life."

Aster sat and bit absently at his thumb nail as the story unfolded before them.

"You, kiddo, are a little bit of both Life and Death." His father winked, as one corner of his mouth turned up into a half grin. Oren slouched in his chair which was so worn and contoured to the old man's topography. "I'll tell you what, you can speculate with all the certainty in the universe about someone and what they may or may not be like, but that doesn't mean you're prepared to be proven right." He tried to smile through the news, but only managed to not grimace.

"What's your next move?" He directed the question to Pixee.

29.

OF DEBATE &
DECISION

She sank to the floor pressing against the door to make sure the unnaturally long night was shut out. "I don't even know where we'd start."

For a brief moment, she hid her face in the palms of her hands. When she faced everyone again, there was a ripple across what was usually a set expression. Frustration fluttered across her jaw before she relaxed and let the confusion drip from her eyes as they roamed the room for comprehension. A familiar mood for Aster. It wasn't hard to guess how it felt when there was a problem waiting to be solved but where or how to find the solution?

Why were solutions always so slippery? Or mysterious? Maybe the solution here, that which confused Pixee most, was just too big. Being as clever as she was, she probably knew what needed to be done but her mind couldn't get purchase on it. It wasn't elusive, just too girthy. Aster instinctively flexed his hands as if he were trying to grip a thick tree limb.

No one blinked. They all just stared, at the floor, the ceiling. The tension and the pressure was written so clearly on each of their faces; Oren glanced absently at his hands. Sedge looked at Aster.

"First step, find Oleander," Sedge said into the whirling vexation.

There was a wave of nodding in agreement with the statement. The group was in general agreement over this initial step.

"As an overall strategy, yes." Oren leaned forward and scrutinized Sedge. "Then what?"

Sedge met Oren's glance. "Kill him."

Such a plan didn't necessarily require an entire counsel or much debate. It was a standard approach with which to meet any nefarious force. A grin stole across Oren's face and a chuckle seeped out of his mouth. Sedge looked sidelong at Aster with a shrug as if he missed the joke.

"Well, then you've got it all figured out neatly, don't you?" Oren leaned back in his seat and waited.

The two men challenged one another, not antagonistically. The back-and-forth was more productive in nature. Aster sat back and silently admired those two men and their confidence.

There were so many similarities between them, not the obvious sort. Their likeness was found deeper and it came to the surface as they looked back and for at one another, trading questions and answers. Iron-clad wills. Reason and logic, their guiding lights.

"So, where is he then?" Oren focused solely on Sedge, his hands folded in his lap.

Sedge looked down. Seemed he even had the confidence to admit he had no clue. He just shrugged and shook his head.

"He's going to need to actually find the seam, a point of connection between the layers," Rustle said. He looked up, brushing the hair from his forehead. The cast of incredulous looks put to Rustle stopped him from saying more. Rustle had been more clown than sage through all the years Aster had known the man.

"Where is this coming from?" Aster asked, but they all had to have been thinking it.

"I have some rare books that have passed through me inventory and I pick them up from time to time and, yes, I know how to read," he huffed. "Like magic so much knowledge is attainable if you know where to look."

"Yes, but the magic you're claiming to know a thing or two about," Oren commented, "is one that few people seek after. Hopefully you've merely dabbled in the practice of Thanatos."

Pixee stared at Rustle, her face twisted in consternation as if she saw Rustle as some other person, a creature with whom she hadn't just spent weeks traveling. "You're a Thanatist?" Her tone sounded injured.

Talk about expressing betrayal. Aster simply folded his arms across his chest. He looked quickly at Sedge before staring at Rustle. "Where did you find the Death Tooth mushroom?"

"How…?" Rustle looked like he had been caught stealing.

"Mr. Oleander explained that bit of knowledge." Aster said to the confusion bubbling on Oren's face. "So, where did you find it?"

"I'd rather not say," Rustle replied, with airs if not slight embarrassment. "Yes, I've merely dabbled, but how about we get back to the problem of Oleander."

"Truly, like why does he need to find this…seam?" Sedge asked.

Rustle shrugged as his eyes peered blankly at Sedge.

"Seam," Oren practically spat the word. "The layers may be separate but they are so close together like butter spread over bread. The realms of Life and Death are the bread. Our world is the butter."

"And if Mr. Oleander takes down the divide? I mean, general sense of dread and foreboding aside," Aster asked the group.

"There is no way to separate them," Pixee offered in a tone of finality. "Once the butter is smeared, can you take it away? Does the bread survive? Even if he finds the seam, he'll still tear apart creation."

No bread. No butter. Such a domestic scenario, but it was an image easy to understand: an aggressively wielded knife tearing the bread into shreds in an attempt to peel away the butter, like it was some sort of mistake.

Aster's mind wandered into the realm of food, as it so often did when he was grappling with concepts too hefty and too broad for his shoulders to bear outright.

Fruit preserve made for a better dressing, especially on toasted bread. The fruit preserve so mired into the nooks and crannies of the bread; maybe even absorbed. It didn't strain the imagination to picture how disastrous that outcome would be for both bread and preserve. It was truly impossible to picture the devastation.

"He could just as easily take a peek between layers without that rock, but with it he'll be able to actually manipulate them. Do some severe damage," Oren said.

"So, that's it then? He has the Truce Blood. He's started whatever plot he has in mind and we're too late?" Queried Sedge.

"No, I don't think so." Rustle gave another moment's consideration to his own reply, testing out his hypothesis silently as his lips shifted back and forth. "All this darkness and the Stewards, is just set-up. I don't think he is at the main spell yet."

It unsteadied the mind to think about the complexity of the magic being cooked up. Aster almost whistled at how impressive the feat of it all. This was more than manipulating a part or portion. Mr. Oleander was out there trying to play at being a deity.

Sedge slapped his hands on his knees and made ready to take flight right then. "Enough talk. Let's go find him."

"How?" Pixee's pointed tone matched her pointed stare.

Sedge swept the others with his glance. He had a sideways grin. "How did you find me?"

The solution lighted upon everyone in the room, save Oren who peered at Aster, seeking an explanation. Aster was too wrapped up with Sedge's thought process to provide elucidation.

"Would she be willing to help us, after all that talk about her soul belonging to Mr. Oleander?" Aster pointed the question mostly at Rustle.

The mention of his sister's plight made Rustle's features droop in a way that appeared all too sincere. It almost erased his penchant for reacting with sarcasm, jocular bravado, and incessant flirting.

"It's the only plan we've got," Pixee said as she stood. "If she can repeat that same magic on Oleander than it will be worth the trip."

"If not?" Sedge sat back and waited for the alternative.

"A waste of a question," Oren injected. "Trust your instinct and it will lead you down any and every path, as sure as water finds its way to the sea."

Aster smirked at the wisdom.

Sedge leaned forward in his seat. "We've got our plan for finding him. Does anyone have any idea on how to kill this maniac?"

He was more than maniac. His intentions were deep, carved out of logic, albeit a twisted form of the stuff. He had the knowledge to back it up, too. Bastions of wisdom, with foundations as deep and broad as the mountains themselves. Yes, taking Mr. Oleander out would be akin to chipping away at the Mountains of Lune.

Thoughts that must have been had by everyone in the room for no one else looked particularly bright-eyed about the prospect of trying to end Mr. Oleander. It was a question that rattled everyone's minds more than any idea proposed thus far.

"If you can't think of a way to end him," Oren said into the silence that hung lank upon the situation, "then think of a way to capture and end the Truce Blood."

Pixee perked up at the suggestion. She looked at them all. "Hortlak."

No one indicated that they grasped how interesting or helpful that was.

"It's blood, right? We get it from Oleander and feed it to a Hortlak and that will be the end of the thing."

Sedge looked at her as he drank in the suggestion. He nodded, a serious, slow movement of his neck. "Where are they?"

An amicable knock at the door cut across the discussion before Pixee could explain the specifics of her plan. Naturally, everyone looked at everyone else for an explanation. Anyone from whom Oren could expect a visit was already seated in that room.

The knock sounded again.

30.

OF EYES & PAIN

O ren's eyes were set as if to say that there was nothing to be afraid of. He gathered himself up out of the comfortable chair, strode to the door, signaling Pixee to move out of the way. She hesitated, shaking her head as if she knew what awaited outside that door. Their silent exchange ended with her removing herself.

Oren stepped outside and off the porch, with Aster just a step behind. The others remained crowded in the doorway as father and son went to meet the visitor.

"Isn't this quaint?" Mr. Oleander stood a few yards away from the wood-plank porch, his voice naturally carrying over the ambient sounds: the crash of the sea and the breeze that alighted off those waters.

"I'll never need more than that," Oren replied, conversationally.

"Ever the man of small ambition."

The conversation hit a lull. The two men, once associates, waited on the other to reach the point of the exchange.

"""

Maybe Aster finally heard him the way everyone else did? The snide narcissism tingling each syllable he uttered. In light of five naked bodies without eyes, his voice had less of a fraternal ring to it.

"By Life's light, we were just talking about you. Seems we don't have to go hunting you down after all," Sedge said over Oren and Aster.

Mr. Oleander grinned. He made a quick gesture. The door of the cabin slammed shut to a chorus of surprised yells. "Have you been practicing your Martese powers?"

Aster gave no reply. The question seemed too casual.

"Have you?"

Aster shrugged, his eyes and jaw set.

"That's what I was hoping for." He wove a wind from the thought of his malice, a wind sharp like the edge of a blade, wrapping the cabin with an incessant buffering.

The wooden structure shuddered under the force. The windows trembled in their frames, threatening to break. Muffled shouts tripped over the press of active air. The display of Mr. Oleander's bond with the element sent Aster a gawking surprise that was quickly supplanted by fear.

Mr. Oleander's voice carried above all the ruckus "Beautiful night, isn't it? What better place to enjoy it than from these seaside cliffs."

The conjured air groaned on, pressing against every side of the meager cabin, like an invisible fist squeezing a ball of dough. Wood snapped and cracked, like Aster's thoughts, making it nearly impossible to settle on a single idea or notion on how to help Sedge, Pixee, and Rustle. The danger encroaching upon his dad tugged all the harder at Aster's focus.

He ventured a glance back: Oren and Mr. Oleander stood almost nose to nose. They appeared vastly different in age, Mr. Oleander looked almost the same age as Aster, but that couldn't be; he rode alongside Oren before Aster had been born.

"Tell me, Thanatist," Oren said, "how did you subdue them all? Was it one at a time? The cold void awaits your soul once it departs mortality."

"Listen to you, talk about mortality." He chortled as though he and Oren were brothers caught in a joke. "There won't be any such thing."

Deeds too evil for the word drained Mr. Oleander's voice of any inflection, leaving his words anemic of charm revealing just how dangerous his ideas and plans really were. He looked down at both their feet before again meeting Oren's staunch gaze. "To be sure, I better subdue every Steward."

The words seized Aster's attention away from the tousled cabin, the threat Mr. Oleander levied as plain as the sky above. There was but a sliver of night between him and Oren, not even the sigh of the ocean intruded on their dueling glances.

Oren flinched first, which was far scarier than Mr. Oleander's friendly voice or his penchant for scooping out eyeballs. Aster was afraid, but not so much for himself.

Aster tried to match Mr. Oleander's movements, but he was no trained fighter. His momentum betrayed him, right into the sand at Mr. Oleander's feet. The distraction gave Oren enough time to engage Mr. Oleander. The sand about his feet depressed, with the sort of grace that came as natural as an earthquake. No manipulation or compulsion brought about chants. It was just a simple pit that opened up to swallow Mr. Oleander.

Before the earth could take him, Mr. Oleander rode a draft above the ground. He wafted to close to Oren to rob him of any breath.

Oren fell under the assault. He managed to regain at least his knees. He drew his arm back and drove his fist into the ground. The sandy terrain convulsed, right down to the very foundations of rock.

The rebuttal sent Mr. Oleadner stumbling back, loosening his strangulation on Oren. A moment of silence prevailed wherein Oren and Mr. Oleander.

Pixee, Sedge, and Rustle exited the cabin, also released from Mr. Oleander's persuasions. Their cautious steps and cagey glances directed them closer to the two remaining Stewards. A preeminent of air and of earth both looking worn but still burning. It was in their eyes, in the torrents of sweat being squeezed through their skin. It tasted thin, but sharp, a nectar of determination.

Sedge signaled Aster to convene with them but that meant leaving Oren alone to conquer and eliminate this purveyor of terror, this sower of darkness.

Aster picked up a scent wafting off Mr. Oleander, through his pores and mingled in his breath. What was that? Faint, but distinct. Aster pinched it with his nose and after inhaling again, it became apparent that particular burning was passion and it would be the accelerant he'd ignite.

Until Mr. Oleander turned slightly in Aster's direction. "Thanks for the gem," Mr. Oleander chirped in Aster's ear. "I want you to know that you made all this possible, especially what's about to happen next."

It was a taunt, and Aster bit. He charged. Instead of lighting up the passion oozing out of Mr. Oleander, Aster lit his own ferocity. His skin glowed in seething, coruscating red and amber. He'd melt the face off Mr. Oleadner's skull.

The intended target twitched eliciting a reaction from Oren. The earth was but a giant blanket in his hands. He flicked his wrists and the cliffs drooped. Waves of dirt, sand, and rock curled out of place and rolled inland.

The others hurried back, away from the approaching cataclysm. Aster stumbled to the earth. His fire went out. Only Oren withstood the tremors wrenching through the earth while Mr. Oleander fought to balance. It was clear, in that moment of chaos, that those two were matched in power and daring.

While Oren held the mastery, for the moment, he looked at Aster, unconcerned how it would feel to die. His father, the pinnacle of all things good and worthy in this world of darkness and uncertainty, offered a final message to his son. His lips moved without dropping a single sound: *I'm so proud of you.*

His father's eyes smiled, glittering with all the words he had yet to tell Aster, even as Mr. Oleander's finger slipped past Oren's eyelid, babbling inane words in a tongue only he understood, the sound of which was abrasive, severe.

Aster made to lung, but the rocks were already complying with Oren's wish, the one he sewed into their every crevice, each tiny grain. The rending and crumbling clawed up from some depth in sober tones. There were crashes or bangs. The earth shifted and cracked in solemn tones.

Sedge grabbed Aster at the wrist.

Oren nodded. Aster looked back at Sedge who returned the look with a sober nod of his own before he dragged Aster back, away from the devastation Oren wrought upon the land. But Aster did not go willingly. He screamed. He kicked against Sedge's hold. He would stand by his father, just as his father had stood by Aster's.

But the earth was in motion. The towering cliffs shuddered and deteriorated until they utterly failed. Oren grabbed a hold of Mr. Oleander. Their tussle persisted even as they both fell along with great chunks of earth. Aster fell back against Sedge watching as the two men were soon lost in a cyclone of rock and dirt.

Plumes of dust climbed into the sky as the tumult settled down. He peeled out of Sedge's embrace and scurried to the edge; it was a new margin. The collapsed cliffs sloped to meet the on-coming surf and where the on-coming waters kissed this new shore was Oren's cabin, just a pile of sticks now. There weren't any signs of his father among the rocks. Aster scanned with a fervent eye but all he could discern in the wretched light was the foam easing onto and off of a jagged shoreline. Who cared about what happened to Mr. Oleander, whether he survived or was crushed. Was Oren buried under all that rubbled? Had he been crushed, broken into a crooked heap?

Like Mom?

A salty breeze brushed Aster's face. He faced it only to see Mr. Oleadner making an adroit landing. He sighed looking almost mournful as he surveyed the changes wrought by Oren.

He looked down at Aster. "I really just wanted to harvest his eyes, like the others. I'd feel more confident had I gotten them out."

The better part of Aster wanted to strike Mr. Oleander after hearing him speak of Oren in such a way. He made to extract himself from Sedge's arms but was forced back, pressed into ground next to Sedge. The invisible pressure kept them both pinned, rocks biting into their backs.

"I don't really have time to go digging for the old man," Mr. Olenader said. He looked over at the edge of the world, bobbing his head back and forth in consideration.

Aster gasped, but the words wouldn't come. He couldn't inflate his chest enough to utter the angry, spiteful curses. They would fall utterly short of just especially against a minstrel of evil.

"I know," Mr. Oleander cooed. His brow flexed in pity. "You won't be able to stop this, so please don't try again," Mr. Oleander straightened up and lifted a foot above Aster's face.

The world stopped, going utterly black for a while.

Then a call crawled tut of the prevailing darkness. It was a wobbly sound desperately tugging at Aster's ear. *Aster.* Yes, that was the sound. It was the name Aster.

"Aster," came the call again.

"Welcome back."

Aster should have said something—*thank you* sounded pretty fitting—but when he thought about what words to speak they just drowned in a reservoir of other emotions, more profound and dominating. Fortunately, the feelings were dammed. For the moment.

A bandage had been applied to his head. It was wound tightly as pain radiated from the upper left part of Aster's forehead.

Aster prodded gently at his tenderized skull while Sedge puttered about the familiar room, picking up clothing and organizing in a general sort of way.

There was plenty for which to be grateful: being in his own plush bed, being whole, even Sedge and his assistance, but all that fell under the shadow of a looming, buttery grin slathered across Mr. Oleander's face. The memory was an infection, retarding concepts like gratitude, or hope. Any attempt to force out the words failed; they felt too thick to say like a handful of oats shoved into his mouth without so much as a drop of milk to accompany them.

Sedge lingered near the chest of drawers, opposite the foot of the bed. He wound up the unused bandage, casting glances at Aster now and then.

All Aster managed was: "How bad is it?" he pointed to his head.

"Well," Sedge approached the bed, setting the roll of white gauze down on a bedside table. "You probably don't need to see a surgeon now." He went to touch the offended flesh, and then retracted. "But you probably don't not want to go see one. He hit your head pretty good."

Aster's shoulders sank. He punctuated his weariness with a well-earned sigh.

Sedge removed himself from the edge of the bed and observed Aster from a distance. "We haven't found him, but when you're ready," he said with labored effort.

The dam holding back all the emotions was decimated. In the silence that followed there existed a new pain, beyond the scope of bandages and surgeons. Every muscle in Aster's body was taught under the ferocity of this new wound.

Could an uglier face have existed? His chin wobbled into little wrinkles, like it had been submerged in water for hours. The lights in the room blurred as an elixir of fluids drained freely over all the little folds and tiny pockets of skin.

Oren was just a word now, a sound that Sedge wouldn't even bother to make. A shuddering cry raced out of Aster and into the bed. The room had been still but now it was flooded with unabashed sobs, wailing and bemoaning. How embarrassed was Sedge sitting there, bearing witness?

Was Pixee also present to observe the perverse outpouring of emotions? Death-be-dead if Rustle was party to this scene. Aster cracked open his eyes, concerned about who would be standing there watching him. After his beleaguered vision confirmed it was just he and Sedge, Aster buried his face in a pillow.

There was room for every shade of feeling in this moment. Dense anger over his inability to stop Mr. Oleander burned, as fairer appreciation for all that Oren had meant to Aster sluiced into expression, yanking at every facial muscle or melting away behind closed eyes.

The air was wracked with crying when Oren's final words, delivered silently, played in Aster's mind. Unlike his mother, his father had actually came to know, had discovered, the deepest parts of Aster. The sounds Aster shoved out into the room matched the loneliness occupying his psyche, vaster than the night sky outside.

The cries eventually ran dry—maybe there wasn't enough water in his body? He was probably just worn out?—and his eyes felt pasted shut from the tears. He sniffed away the dregs of his grief before he managed to pry open his eyes.

Sedge looked away as he rubbed the back of his neck. Shock and pity whispered from his gaze. "You okay?"

Aster nodded as he wiped his face with the back of his hand. Breaths escaped in small whimpers as he collected himself.

Sedge approached a step or two and peered down. He didn't recoil at the sight of Aster's ravished eyes, pooled in threads of red. "If you're up for it, come outside." He showed himself out.

The decision was left in his lap, to stand witness to Oren's remains or to ignore his demise, already fixed as a looping memory:

the ground breaking apart and then he fell, like his mother fell. At the recollection of the sight, Aster crumpled into his pillow and poured out more sobs. Guess his body had more water to spare.

Aster peeled himself out of the bed, rubbed away the crusty, dried tears before emerging into the living room.

Everyone, except Rustle, cast their glances toward the kitchen table. There were no remains, no body over which to stand and mourn. A burial had already taken place. What had been him. Pixee, possibly with Sedge's help, had created an effigy from sticks. She managed to find a couple pieces of familiar clothing. At least Aster didn't need to fear looking down into empty eye sockets, leaking oblivion like the other Stewards.

"May your soul find its way to the sun, leaving behind the moon and distant stars." Thus Aster whispered, a sort of benediction to his father's life.

Aster stepped away from the representation of Oren and gave Sedge a nod before walking from the scene. He could hear the shifting and movement but Aster didn't have the strength to react, to worry. Perhaps the surgeon should take a look at his injuries, which throbbed with every step. Aster blinked hard to steady the world as it teetered back and forth under him. He managed but a few steps until the ground rushed to meet his already aching head.

31.

OF BLOOD IN THE SKY

There's a moment before the eyes open and light spills in, even before light is perceived to exist, because everyone gets the light before they actually get the light. That moment when it's time to swim up from the mercurial dream-scape that is imagined light, imagined shapes, and hints of colors; it's all symbols. Well, not every time. There are moments when a thick velvety nothing wraps all around the mind, and there isn't room for symbolism. There's no telling when the drape is pulled back and…

Aster opened his eyes in an uneven, wonky motion. The light he received was the subdued light of candles. He still had to shield his eyes though. After a moment of considering the light's potency, Aster decided it wasn't all that potent. He ventured a glance and noted the familiarity of his surroundings. Ah, yes: all this furniture, the shape of the room—probably quite a common shape—and him.

"Welcome back."

Aster shielded his eyes again.

"Do you have a thank you for me this time? If you keep passing out then I'm going to have to start charging you for my help." Sedge sat down on the edge of the bed showing a surprising amount of sternness. "Especially if you refuse to say thank you."

With the initial shock of grief cried out, managing a couple of words felt less taxing. "Thank you."

Sedge mulled the gesture over in his mind.

"What?" Aster asked at the stoic Sedge.

"Nothing. You're welcome." Sedge patted Aster on the leg. Twice. No more. No lingering touch; just a hardy pat, of the type that a father might give a son. Neither one were fathers nor had fathers, any longer.

"Why did you go back?"

The question put a halt on Sedge vacating the bed. "Hmm?"

"You were running from your father, or maybe life as a warlord's soldier—"

"Captain, actually," Sedge corrected, belying a sense of pride.

"But you went back?" A question that had actually been stewing for some time and in the absence of fathers it seemed an appropriate time to fish for an answer.

Sedge didn't respond immediately. He could have been considering, like Aster had, how much to actually share which seemed moot after the amount of he learned of Aster over the past few days: the ugly crying, the most intimate memories and feelings.

"He wasn't much of a father," he finally said. "But he was a damn strong man, and if that Thanatist dared to follow I had a better chance behind the Keep's wall than wandering about in the wilderness." He looked away, down at the blanket. "Or so I thought," he said with a forlorn smile. "There was also the chance you'd never find me, which I was pretty confident about."

"Confident?" Aster sat up a little taller.

Sedge was smiling a little more but without looking back at Aster. "Convinced is probably a better word."

Sedge's explanation was mostly expected, but still comforting in a way, as if it made Sedge approachable. That bit about being convinced they'd never see each other again was a curious revelation.

Sedge must have caught the lost look in Aster's eyes. He considered for a moment, looking at the bruises on Aster's face. "What's your favorite memory of your father?"

"Mine?"

"Yours." Sedge shifted, folding a leg up on the bed. He faced Aster more in this position. Their legs touched just so. "All the memories of my father are of drills and training, being one of dozens of soldiers learning to follow commands." He looked at the blanket hiding Aster's legs, and picked at the stitching for a moment. "I bet you have cozier memories to look back on," he said chancing a glance into Aster's beleaguered eyes.

It was Aster's turn to let a sense of pride eek out across his face. There were dozens of memories packed away. In this moment of grief those memories stirred a much-needed warmth that hurried away the saltiness of grief.

"Lesson, explanations, and laughs," Aster said without preamble. "I mean, he had a way of treating me like a friend but making sure I didn't forget that he was my father. The first time he took me down to harvest mussels with him." A faint laugh, accompanied by some tears, escaped Aster. "You should have seen me trying to finagle that water bucket. Later on I found out that Dad had just filled it with a little water. No mussels. Good thing because by the time I reached the top of the cliff the thing was nearly empty."

The memory was so full of joy and fondness, it hurt to recall in a way, but Aster wanted to share the point, the anchor that kept that special moment alive in his mind; not only alive, but vibrant.

"And once I set that nearly empty bucket down and looked up at Dad, so sure he would be disappointed I spilled all that water, he smiled down at me and told me 'you spilled a lot of that water kiddo, but you made it all the way back without giving up on yourself.'"

Sedge placed a hand over Aster's shin and gave the calf a squeeze. "That's the cutest thing I've heard in a while."

Sedge withdrew his touch and left the bed. When he turned to leave the room his back almost filled the doorway. It was broad and powerful-looking, with strength enough to bear the adventures crossing his path. Sedge just walked through them with his head high, gaze burrowing past the contingent of dangers, both those he predicted and those that were unforeseen.

How did Aster's own back compare? It was the natural thing to compare and contrast? Thinking back on all that had transpired lately, didn't feel like there was much power back there, just enough strength to tend to the little personal dilemmas that came day to day not carry the fate of existence as a whole.

Sitting in the comfort of his own bed, the decision came as a sigh. In that sigh was all the grief and insecurity that had been cracked open when he saw Oren disappear over that rocky ledge.

"What's that sigh?" Sedge turned at the sound. Aster had not been muted enough apparently, by the look writ upon Sedge's face.

Aster threw back the covers. The rampant amount of skin on display gave him pause. Shocking to be naked when it was Sedge who left him thus. He rapidly replaced the covers, hiding his nudity from Sedge, for some reason, though all the secret parts had obviously already been displayed.

The embarrassment bloomed warmly over his cheeks. "Um…" Aster looked away from Sedge. "The sigh. Yes. It's just that—"

Sedge nodded. Not the amicable nod of understanding—nothing amicable about it—but a nod acknowledging what Aster let escape: an intent fleeing his mind and maybe his heart. Sedge left the room.

"He's just going to stay?" Pixee's voice crawled under the door.

The contention in her words was enough of an indication that it was time to go out there and confirm his intentions. Aster peeled back the covers and dressed. He finished adjusting his shirt and examined his face and head with a light touch. There were sources of pain and then there were sources of perseverance. Neither one matched.

He ventured into the living room, greeted by the stare of every available pair of eyes. His mouth opened, ready to say the words, but their stares put a strain on his voice. "I'm well enough to get to a surgeon," Aster began. "I'm not up for any more adventures."

They all froze. Pixee's face in particular knotted into an expression that could curdle cream.

"You don't understand."

"What is there to understand?" Pixee said.

There was an answer, a worthy retort to volley right back at her. Maybe it was being continuously exposed to her perpetual aplomb, but what was once simple, admirable confidence now took on the shape of smugness. It was enough to snuff out any inclination to verbally spar. Instead, Aster walked to the front door and pulled it back.

"You're right. Nothing." He stared out into the night. "You don't need to understand my reasons. You just need to leave my house and leave me to myself."

Pixee cut into the ensuing silence with a huff. "You have that right." She swiped her pack from the floor and swiftly made egress without even checking with Rustle or Sedge about leaving, or waiting to see if they'd follow. Such was the extent of her self-possession.

Rustle stirred first, appraising the open door before he considered Aster. "Well, I'm going to follow along before she gets too far ahead and I have to triple the pace of my walk." He donned his own traveling gear. "Aster—" he paused in his salutation and smiled a wan grin. "Living is shitty sometimes. Not just for you. For all of us. Enjoy the darkness." He breezed past Aster.

Then there was Sedge, seated at the table watching the departures from a distance, reasonable but not too removed. His keen stare insisted itself upon Aster, who didn't even have to look back to know how intently Sedge examined him.

Aster watched the departed figures blend into the night before closing the front door. "Going to stay or follow them?" He asked without turning to meet Sedge's gaze.

"I'm not staying. Whatever this mood is that has suddenly scared you from the goal of—"

Those words: did he choose them with any deliberation or did Sedge just throw out the first thought that came to mind? A pretty irresponsible approach.

Aster spun around. "You're being kind of a dick."

Sedge scooted his chair out from the table and stood there, a great warrior and all. "And you're being a child."

Their insults clashed. Neither one flinched.

"You'd be too if you had just watched your remaining parent, your hero in all the world, brutally die right there in front of you." The admission felt crooked, like it shouldn't be shown to anyone.

It was out there now, so Aster continued: "And you weren't able to do anything to stop it. I thought I could help fight this but I'm not capable of stopping him. So, I'm going to spend my time doing something that is in my power." He nodded toward the front door. "You better get going if you want to catch up to Pixee."

Sedge took the dismissal in stride.

Now, with the house empty it was finally time to put all the pieces together, pieces to complete fire fruit.

But first, to Lamiston.

Getting a handle on the pain still throbbing across his skull was the aim. He long legs carried him towards the solution. Lamiston was littered with only a little light as windows spilled the muted orange-yellow glow of hearth and candle. Aster made his way through town, the expressions on most faces were clear: no one knew whether they should be asleep or awake.

Thankfully, the surgeon was awake.

"That doesn't look at all pleasant," Serenoa said as she examined Aster's head. "Not one bit. Did you slam your head against a rock or something?"

"Close enough. I fell" Aster leaned out of her grip. "Now that you've finished gawking could you do your healer-thing and handle it?"

She glared at him.

"Please?"

"It won't be immediate," She perused her assortment of medicines. "But I'm sure I've got something in my collection that will get the process going," she said with a chirp.

"Just what I came for."

After she finished shifting through an assortment of jars, Serenoa returned with the one she sought. She salved along Aster's hairline and down towards his left eye. She handed him the jar filled with a paste that was the color of wilted mint leaves. Speckled was a good way to describe it; lumpy and speckled.

"Stop touching it." Serenoa swatted Aster's hand away from the cream slathered over his bruises.

The paste was cool against the wounds. Aster held his hands tightly at his side, fighting the temptation to respond to the tingling that erupted against his skin.

"How long does this have to stay on?"

"I would normally say until first light…" She turned and let her glance stray out the window. "I don't know if that applies anymore."

It didn't sound like the simple longing for diurnal hours, but for understanding, for surety in patterns that were once predictable and reliable. That longing was probably in the minds of every person under this sun-forsaken sky.

She turned back to Aster. "Leave the cream on until it's well dried. Then rinse off and reapply as necessary until the lump is gone and the bruising clears. It will heal any internal damage, too. As long as you use it just as I've prescribed."

He slipped from her exam table and shot her a wisp of a smile as he gave a mumble of appreciation.

With a jar of the medicinal salve in hand, Aster walked back through town under the mess of darkness. A few days. A couple of weeks. It was tough gauging how settled the unassailable night was. The question pawed at Aster as he crossed the square, vacant save for one individual who had ventured out. The person sat there as if market had not ceased, devoted to a pattern that was now in jeopardy.

Aster recognized Barkley, a farmer of roots, loitering beside a full cart. "Hey there, Barkley. Trying to get the market up and running again?"

"Eh?" came somewhat of a disjointed reply.

His voice had an odd, aged quality to it. He sounded lost, between learning how to speak and forgetting. Considering he wasn't much older, that was disquieting. "Selling off the last of your roots?"

"Eh," he said again.

Barkley's eyes rolled back and forth, and around in their sockets, never settling his focus on one particular object and certainly not giving Aster an iota of attention, as was expected among polite company.

The roots, what should have been roots, were revealed by the stingy light of the blood moon to be mostly a pile of sludge, chunky and sloppy. Barkley's harvest looked more like a heap of compost than an edible crop. The sight of which caused Aster to shrink away. He picked up hints of rot among the pile, and grimaced at the aroma.

The moon looked down up on the scene with an indifferent glare. It was just a small evil, and just the first of many consequences to be wrought by the unnaturally evil night.

"Well, good luck with that," Aster said as he hurried away from the cart.

"Eh," was Barkley's reply.

Aster wanted to put as much space between himself and this announcement that the world was beginning to sicken.

It took a few tries—the bond with fire was still so new—but Aster managed to suspend a ring of fire just above the little pit at the back of his house. Not quite like sunshine but the circle of flames overhead lit the patch of property as well as could be expected.

The bond with fire made the process of conjuring up an oh-so-perfect heart of heat easy as making tea. Words weren't necessary, just eyeballing the size and intensity of the element. He draped the right dose of the right mix of fruits and vegetables—the bounty of the earth—around the heat and bonded the two with just the right words. The fire fruit: waxy gems, in their own right, endowed with the flavor of the earth and the heat of fire.

Into the pit went the little botanical miracles. Now the Burial Rite would play its part. How, exactly these words and gestures would combine to make this creation fruitful was deeply mysterious, it almost ached to try and reason through. But that's just how magic is, sometimes.

Aster simply accepted the results as a gift, as he gave the page from Mr. Oleander's book special handling, out of the way of any stray spark likely to fall from infernal halo.

After so many failures and misses, each attempt started to feel like the last opportunity to get it right. Aster took in a deep breath before he ventured a glance at the words on the page. Seeing them meant the process would be started before he was truly ready. It was a natural reflex for most practitioners.

No, one does not simply start. Not when it's this important. One slips into the process. No belly-flops.

With his mind attuned, Aster aimed his gaze down at the page upon his lap. The lofty flames shed light down and revealed the Burial Rite, spell and instructions all lined up neatly down the center of the paper. The stage was set. It was time.

The words flowed with the slow roll of deep intention:

Earth cracked open as in a sigh

Each line was accompanied by a scoop of dirt, soil so rich and dewy it looked like it had been dug right out of a starry-night sky.

The words sounded sweet, like a lullaby. At least, that was how his mother had spoken them as he watched her perform this very same rite on him.

Trust the dirt, the lights in the sky.
As they fall down kissing your eyes

Aster buttoned up his voice. He glanced up. The only light coming down wasn't really of the sky. Those little creations sat on the ground and waited for their creator to bless them with seeds, with scions. The rest of the words were there, to reward all the toil and anticipation.

"Life's dangling jewels," Aster hissed.

Whether Life—or Death for that matter—possessed dangling jewels on their persons was an utter mystery, but those were the words Aster found to best express his frustration. Here was the end of a long tunnel of queries, guesses and failures, and just all the shit—there had been so much blood to deal with and wash away—and there was no Death-tilled light.

Aster carefully folded up the page, thicker than most paper he'd ever handled. He made sure not to hold it not too tightly, the mechanics of his hand directed to respect its delicacy. He collected the precious samples from the pit. He stood, singed his hair on the forgotten fiery light.

The Burial Rite was stowed in a pocket out of sight and reach of flame as Aster stepped out from under the thing before he stomped out the source of fuel. The rest of the configuration simply fell into smoke. A scent of burning wreathed the yard before slinking away, blending into the other scents pollinating the air.

He was truly back in the dark. It was a nasty, unnatural night that would kill any perpetuity with which Aster would have endowed his fire fruit. Barkley's cart of rotted vegetables was a severe reminder that the shadow of Mr. Oleander's plot lay over all the land.

Aster peered in the direction where the Mountains of Lune abode, questioning all that was taking place. Over the leagues, as far as his sight could carry, Aster spotted a gleam above the craggy peaks, a small sliver of light, like a wound had been opened in the dark.

It looked odd, felt wrong. It was a sense that the situation was far from resolved. Actually, events appeared to be racing in the complete opposite direction of resolved. This was just another crack in the façade.

As much as he wanted a simple life exercising his creativity and feeding the people around him with food that ignited joy, that wasn't the case anymore. For who could be creative in the midst of a world confused and on the brink of ripping apart, the end result according to Pixee.

Aster filled his pack with fresh clothing, a couple of blankets, his flint and steel; pretty much the same inventory he'd been lugging around Thuidium. He paused at the door giving his abode one last sweeping glance. He shut the door. The adventure began anew. As if he knew what he was doing.

He truly didn't.

Sitting and waiting for others to put into motion a course of action would have disappointed Oren. Aster needed to be involved, to try and help Sedge, Pixee, and even Rustle.

32.

INTERLUDE: DEATH'S PERSISTENCE VS. LIFE'S PATIENCE

"Are you on board now?"

"You're asking again?"

It couldn't happen again if it had never concluded the first time. "Wrong. I'm still asking."

"The answer was, as it has been since you first asked, you're worried over nothing." Life slumped into a relaxed posture letting the sheen of the layer curl about his form.

"First, that isn't an answer to my question. That's your opinion about the situation in general."

"And second?" Life sat up. "I assume if there is a first point that there will be another. Possibly a third?"

"And fourth and fifth." Life was not going to sail this question down some metaphorical river again, especially since said-non-existent river had run out. Metaphorically speaking. It was over, the edge had been reached. "And a sixth. And it keeps going until you actually address my question."

Life's placid demeanor showed not even the tiniest ripple in a face that was like rain-washed marble. "Technically, you have one point. The subsequent numbers are just repetitions of your request to tune into the Stewards."

"You're splitting hairs."

Life stood, donning a full smirk. "I haven't any of those."

It wasn't a big deal before, but the carnelian sheen peeking through from the mortal layer was cause for concern. Who had set a crack in their opal atmosphere, Death wondered?

"Nor I, but the saying applies. If you'd just stop dodging the question, then this whole conversation would not be so futile."

"I'm glad you've finally realized that your entire inquiry is for naught."

"You are being obstinate to the point of suspicion." Death stabbed a finger in Life's direction.

Life redirected Death's finger away. "You are being paranoid. If you have an accusation, try throwing it around rather than all the innuendo."

Death took the invitation. "You are part of this."

Instead of appearing affronted, Life had the airs of an artist whose work has just been discovered. "And can you tell me exactly what I'm supposedly a party to? I'm rather confused by your flimsy attempt at dramatics, old friend."

The familiarity of Life's tone, even the vague wisp of pride, did not deter Death. "You've forestalled contacting the Stewards to retrieve the Truce Blood and now look at the Mortal Layer. It's shrouded and the seam it sticking out."

Life nodded. "Yes, I see. That's a good point."

Death shrugged and glared heavily at Life with eyes shiny and black, like gold-flecked . Perhaps, after all the debates—attempted debates—Life would finally acquiesce.

Life nodded. "I'm sure it's fine." Life emitted that strange laugh. "You'll worry yourself back into the void, Imfa."

The pat on the shoulder was not assuring. Life's laugh was not pleasant. The redness bleeding across the Mortal Layer was not normal. So much that was not; it felt like the void already.

Death wondered: even if Life had agreed to it, would it be possible to contact the Stewards? Would breaking any part of their truce mean the end of all existence?

That appeared to be the direction regardless of the consequences.

33.

OF DESPONDENCY

It was weird seeing Sedge once again in that booth; the same one where they met for that first time, when he had tried to procure the all-so-important Truce Blood.

Aster expected all of them to be many-a-mile from Lamiston by now. Yet on a whim, he stopped into the Hart's Den to offer up assurances to Twiggy that he was still alive and would return—eventually—and there they were as if they had anticipated Aster's actions.

Aster made his way through the sparse crowd populating the tavern. Most patrons had that same sullen expression hanging upon their faces: the uncertainty, the glum consternation tugging at the muscles in their jaws.

Aster took a wide berth of a couple tables, occupied by denizens wide-eyed, chewing on either crockery or their own fingers.

Best not to make eye-contact, but focus on the booth. When he arrived Sedge glanced up and made room for Aster, who acknowledged the stares as he settled in. "Looks like a few crazies came out for a drink."

"We've seen a few odd ducks, too," Rustle said. "Guess this blood moon is really making some folks sick.

What remained of the crockery had been saved by the proprietor himself, Twiggy. His large frame loomed over the mad patrons. "Out with you nutters. Now!"

Without waiting for compliance—or contestation, for that matter—Twiggy handled the oddities right out of their seats and through the door. Hardly a peep emerged from the recipients of Twiggy's special attention, but when the commotion settled all eyes veered back to their own tables.

Sedge grinned. "We were going to give you another hour," he said with a tone of triumph.

"What, you all took bets on if I'd rejoin?"

Pixee remained stern. "Sedge caught up to us, practically dragged us back to this tavern and had us wait, wasting precious time while you hemmed and hawed over your role in this important endeavor. I'd be halfway to the Wald by now." She took a noisy drink from her earthen tumbler.

It was a struggle to keep her potent gaze. She knew what she felt and not a trace of remorse for it was to be found in her stare. Aster eked out a meager apology for the delay.

She set down her cup, smoothed out the features on her face. "It's fine. Let's put this delay behind us and get a move on. It'll make this plan a lot easier with another person on board."

That was as gentle a reply as Aster could have expected. He knew her well enough to know, so he gave himself a little smirk. "Alright. First a quick word with Twiggy then off we go."

The night was neither cool nor warm when they ventured out of the Hart's Den. Beyond the town proper, the mountains stood darker than the night. Aster watched them for a moment, just making sure he still saw it.

"I take it that doesn't bode well for us." Sedge stood just behind Aster, peering at the sheen outlining the mountain tops.

"I'm certain that Oleander has found the seam." Rustle slid next to Pixee and causally placed a hand on her shoulder.

She threw her elbow against his ribs. "You're probably right. But that doesn't mean he can start ripping."

Rustle, still recovering his breath shrugged. "No?"

She glared at him. "I don't know the mechanics of this whole process. He probably doesn't even know exactly. I'll wager he's done enough research to think he knows. Even just a hint of uncertainty gives us time."

Each new hint melted into a puddle of questions. Aster decided to eschew the expanding puddle as he leaned towards Sedge. "This is great and all, but how about we get moving."

"To the Wald it is," Rustle said casually.

They had ridden as far as they dared push the horses, just passed Cannaville. Pixee's horse actually seemed without limitations, as if it could ride as long as the night lasted. The constant gallop left no effect upon neither its limbs nor spirit. The other steed, that bore Sedge and Aster, did not take the press with such dignity.

"It's getting to you too?" Sedge asked.

"What is?" Aster replied, as he pulled out a pelt.

"The lack of daylight? The unnatural night sky?" He looked up. "That moon."

It was up there, same shape as it had always been but now looked more like a scab on the sky that had been picked open by nature and left unhealed Mr. Oleander's scheming.

"You know," Aster said to the sky as much as to Sedge, "at first I didn't think Mr. Oleander's plan was all that devious."

"I remember," Sedge commented.

"It's looking pretty gnarly now. And this constant night..." Was he about to state the painfully obvious? The pending words felt so apparent that they'd be practically stupid to say out loud, so Aster simply left his thought to be only partially expressed.

"I began to wonder what would happen to people who don't see the sun. In their heads, I mean." Sedge explained. "How much more of this state until we all start to go mad, or whatever is happening to people's minds?"

There was no answer to that question, as much as Aster wanted to be the one to solve the riddle, to be in the know. "Well, truly, that too. In their souls, probably."

Sedge turned to Aster. "What were you going to say?"

"Not to be completely self-centered, but I was thinking that nothing would grow in this darkness. Even if this Burial Rite made the fire fruit seed, no sun means no sprouting. No growing. It would all be pointless."

Sedge's gaze was gentle, like he wondered what Aster would say next and Aster, in turn, considered how Sedge would react when he said it. "The Martese, the burned fingers. Facing the past. I don't want all that to just go the way of the sun, painted over by darkness."

Sedge gave a laugh, a light sound. "Even if we don't manage to stop Mr. Oleander and get the sun back, those things still will forever be a part of your personal history, lessons that only you can choose to kick out. Just because this creation of yours doesn't exist, doesn't mean you've failed. Your value is more than your productivity."

"So I've been told." Aster tugged at the grass, tossing it into the fire. "I like that sentiment. For others."

Sedge shrugged. "I mean, live your life as you will. React how you want."

"Do you not ever feel the tug of certain desire? To create? To imagine something and then bring it into the world?" A lite smile on Sedge's face gave Aster the answer. "See. I knew most people felt that pull."

"I always wanted a family," he said. "A normal one. Not another soldier, but a child to teach and guide in appreciation of life." He sat there, mouth slightly ajar, poised to continue sharing some thought. He look at Aster, hesitation apparent. "You know, to be like Oren."

They sat there silently for a moment and, actually that admission was a beautiful sentiment. They shared so many qualities that it made sense. It was even quite possible and inevitable.

Aster gave Sedge's shoulder a slight bump. "You get it."

"I suppose I do. In a way."

"So there, we both have our reasons to see this through," Aster declared.

Silence followed as the two sat and traded smiles at one another.

"That sky, huh?" Rustle plopped down on the opposite side of the fire. "Can't tell whether I'm coming or going anymore."

Aster and Sedge leaned away from one another, as if Rustle's appearance has rocked them apart.

"Where's Pixee?" Sedge asked.

"Getting some water." He shook his head, sending drops to scatter here and there. "You guys should go have a dunk. Feels pretty good after all that riding."

Pixee wandered into the ring of light, her own short hair pressed down with wetness. "Are we talking about the darkness?" There was a general consensus of nods from the party, as Pixee set her clothing out to dry, if such a thing were possible without the sun's light and warmth.

It might have been the next day. There was a chance that it was still the same night. The line between one day and the next was no longer so obvious, leaving behind a mess of uncertain hours, resisting the old names.

Aster yawed. The others appeared to have been up for some time, their gear already packed away, horses at the ready.

"No one woke me," Aster said as he sat up and threw back the blanket he had slept under. He felt his final application of medicinal cream crack and pinch at his skin.

"You still need a bit more rest than us," Sedge offered as he handed Aster a skin of water. He waited as Aster rinsed away the cream. "Looking much better."

Aster had to take his word for it. No mirrors. He stood there while Sedge smeared the cream over the diminishing lump that had sprung up where Mr. Oleander had struck him with a well-placed kick. It all felt less tender and swollen under Sedge's delicate touch, as his thumb glided gently with Aster's hairline, smearing a generous helping of healing-cream. Sedge's eyes locked onto Aster's as he swept a few strands of hair back off Aster's skin. A smile flickered as Sedge finished and his touch lingered just a tad longer.

The packing was done and the journey resumed. There were two pauses before reaching the nearest crossing: a bridge of little design but much function. Thankfully, it was unguarded. After passing over with ease, a hurried pace was ensued. The moon hung above the world offering little light as they reached the eves of the wood. The moon was lost to view under the congregation of slender trees and their limbs, which were still at the moment for not a single breath of wind disturbed them. Their feet padded along the once mossy floor. Instead of simply yielding under foot with a slight spring, the plush carpet now squished and oozed with each step. The branches above sagged, as if siphoned of the superior woodiness that had once made them erect and haughty.

"The sun hasn't been gone long enough to do all this, has it?" Sedge asked of the group.

"Pretty sure it's more than just that," Rustle offered, but offered no more as he walked the slowest, stopping even at the sound of his companions' feet, whipping his head about expecting to see the ghastly figure of an Oxalis.

"Guess we get to see what it's like when someone pulls at the seam of creation." Pixee took up the lead, practically dragging Rustle.

"This way," he whispered as he strode ahead of the group, his sense of purpose stoked by Pixee's insistence.

34.

OF ETERNAL CONCEPTS

The trees and their droopy limbs fell away as they traced up an incline, and soon Rustle had brought them to the familiar bald crown. The tiny hut and a quaint fire were all that populated the exposed hilltop. Aster gave the sky a quick review: no stars and just the moon set upon an onyx canvas.

She waited by the fire, wrapped in a plain linen garb that loosely swept the ground around her. She hadn't stirred, not even a twitch of her fingers, as they approached. Aster silently signaled everyone to halt. Her stillness was almost blaring.

"Rose?" Aster said as he stopped a few feet away from the fire. He examined her without moving any closer.

She looked lost with her gaze hooked on the flames tossing and dancing across her view. Where was she? Because she wasn't here, with them. Her chest expanded with breath but there was an anemia to her complexion, which Aster hadn't noticed last time he saw her, calling into question her vitality. Ashen lips and nails dull as sun-dried shells all hinted, in unison, that the Rose was alive in the most basic sense of the word. He wanted to reach out and touch her, feel her warmth. Give her some of his, if she needed it. From what he saw it wouldn't have surprised Aster if he found her skin cold.

Rustle ignored the hesitation and took a seat next to Rose. "Where are you, sis?"

Her glance lifted. She looked first at Aster before glancing at her brother. "There is so much blood in me right now. Watching the flames is soothing." She caressed the fire, at ease with the flames between her fingers.

Aster took a seat on the other side of Rose and pulled her unscathed hand from the flames. "What's going on?"

Her words were a cryptic weaving, and they piqued his concern, but her eyes, mazes to wander in, alarmed him most.

"Why are you here again?" Rose drew her hand away from him.

With his arm wrapped around her shoulders, Aster implored Rustle.

Even as Aster and Rustle continued to consider Rose's state, Pixee strode up to the fire and laid her words out, as plain as skin. "We need your help locating Oleander and to stop him. We all know his plan and can't let him fulfill it."

"Then what you really want isn't Oleander, but this—" She traced a finger down her neck, over her collar bone until she stopped between her breasts. Rose pulled the neckline of her garb away from her chest. A red glow spread across her skin like a luminescent rash.

"The Truce Blood," Sedge said, with a certain breathy reverence.

Judging from the silent gazes heaped upon Rose and the glow emanating over her skin, the sight wasn't a trick of Aster's mind.

She let her garment relax back into place and the red glow was veiled again. "It's safe. Secure." No hint of irony adorned her words. "All petitions, regardless of how endearing, would wither even as you spoke them."

"I know," Rustle said as he laid his head on her shoulder, "but it wouldn't hurt to try."

"If you can't give it up, then how about if we took it?" Sedge pronounced as he took a step towards Rose, brining a dagger to point at her chest.

Before Aster or Rustle could get their hands on Sedge and hold back his more forceful solution, Rose grasped his dagger-bearing hand and squeezed and twisted until Sedge winced. She forced the dagger right out of his grasp.

"You don't have the means to let me defy him."

Sedge sunk away cradling his crushed hand. She had stunned her audience into silence by the demonstration of her strength.

"Because he has your soul?" Aster's gentle inquiry caused Rose to crumble into herself as if she would cry, but no sob escaped her lips. Her cheeks were as dry as bones left out under the sun.

There were many other questions that Aster desired to pose to Rose, namely how could she be alive if she was absent a soul? It looked like neither the time or place for personal curiosities, so he kept his queries more relevant.

"Do you know where he keeps it?" The question felt like a plea to the sky, to the moon. To any soul that was still a soul.

"Then what? You would have come to my rescue? Stolen it back? You're sweet Aster, but you're also naive sometimes."

Her indictment stabbed with the force of a spoon: blunt, scathing, slow to penetrate. Rose couldn't have meant it; she was just emotional. A quick check with Sedge offered neither agreement nor disagreement with Rose. Sedge—ignoring his aching wrist—pulled Aster away from Rose and led him from the fire. Pixee joined in on their conference.

"She's just emotional, right? I mean just because I offered to help doesn't mean I'm naive." The sense of urgency in his voice was unintentional, but it was there all the same. Right along with it came a certain tone of defensiveness.

"Let me explain something that may help you understand, Aster." Pixee mulled over her next words. "Without a soul, she is just dry earth. No oceans, or rivers. Not even a trickle of a stream."

Rose looked so different with this new insight, sitting there on the ground looking like she was trying to put some sort of expression on to her face, but she was frozen with that one look: no flow, nor current passing across her visage, as if she had been replaced by a mere sketch.

The sketch.

He rushed to his pack and drew out the paper. The vague familiarity now made sense. It depicted the rape of Rose's soul.

"I took this from Mr. Oleander's," he explained as Pixee and Sedge glanced over his shoulder. "I didn't know if it would actually help, but—" He fell silent.

Pixee took the drawing from Aster's hands and deposited it into Rose's lap. "Is it in there?"

Rose handled that page as if it was the most fragile thing in existence, caressing it like a new born baby. Her hands said more than the features of her face which sat perfectly still as her fingers intimately traced the lines of the flower.

"That's a yes." Pixee retrieved the sketch.

"Then," Aster said as he grabbed the drawing from Pixee, "let's crack it open and get her soul out."

Pixee swiftly reclaimed the drawing from Aster's pawing fingers. "It doesn't work that way. It's not a damn egg. Rose, you were right about him being naive," she concluded while eying Aster.

He eyed her back, unwilling to relent to the slights.

Aster yanked the drawing from Pixee. "I'm not the idiot you both make me out to be."

"If that's the case," Pixee commandeered the drawing again. "Stop handling this like it's just some piece of dead wood."

Rose's fingers found the edge of the drawing and, with the ease of a leaf falling from a branch, slipped it away from Pixee and out of

Aster's reach. "Aster, you're not an idiot. There are just some things you haven't learned yet. You haven't learned of souls. You fear death more than you appreciate it."

The word *death* wrapped around Aster's throat; it constricted his breathing enough to push briny drops down his cheeks. He gazed at Rose with his glistening eye. "Hard to appreciate something when you're taught to ignore it," Aster replied in a whisper.

Rose looked to the others for an explanation of the torrent of emotion seeping over Aster's face.

Sedge clasped Aster's shoulder and gave it a squeeze, watching Aster brush the tears from his skin. "He's had to get reacquainted with grief since he saw Oren die because of Oleander's plans."

His hand swept to and fro across Aster's back with just enough pressure to ease the fear of loneliness that attended every mention of his father's passing. Aster leaned slightly into Sedge's contact. There was a brief look between the two, some sort of exchange of appreciation for that touch both for giving and receiving it, before Sedge stepped away.

Rose looked up to a sky that sagged with the excessive darkness and the blood moon, an open sore upon the somber atmosphere. "I truly wish I could help you stop him from pulling the world apart. I do."

Aster slowly stilled his sniffling. "How do we get your soul back to you then?"

"I don't know," she replied. "Souls have special requirements to be able to exist when unfettered from a mortal robe. Oleander is clever and depraved enough that he found some way to contain the soul outside its intended vessel."

Souls. Moons. Blood. How did they know so much about all of these topics? Where was the education to make these ideas less mythical? All he had was this virgin bond with fire; in the midst of these grand plots and eternal concepts, that seemed of little import.

Pixee sniffed the air. "It's actually evening now." She meandered away from the group, despondent in their stagnation.

"How do you know?" Rustle asked, a little too late as Pixee's small figure became a shadow among all the shadows surrounding the trees. "How does she know?"

No one answered because no one really cared about hours.

Sedge yawned. "Feels about right to me. I think it's time we took some rest. We'll be safe here, Rose?"

She surveyed the trees that lined the clearing. A once sprightly wood now looked wilted showing, in their way, the defeat many people must have felt as the night carried on without shrinking. Leaves shriveled without falling. "They may be fleeing this blight, so you will no longer find Oxalis a threat. Make yourselves comfortable and keep the fire alive, just in case." She retreated back into her hovel, leaving them to the silence that infested the Wald.

Sedge worked on feeding the fire while watching Rustle loiter about the edge of the clearing, peering this way and that. "He is one odd fellow. He's either smitten by Pixee or still afraid an Oxalis will attack in the night."

"Why would he be afraid? Rose would know if they were any danger here." Aster scooted to within reach of the fire. He tried to accept the heat the flames spilled but only the light touched him, giving his eyes a point on which to focus.

"Who knows," Sedge said as he sat beside Aster.

Then came a pregnant silence, so pregnant that Aster started to kick at the ground. He looked to Rustle to deliver them from it, but he was too preoccupied watching the darkly coated forest.

"You know," Aster began awkwardly, "it's too bad that gem is stuck in Rose."

"Terrible situation."

"So close, but so out of reach."

"Just awful for her."

Aster considered, seriously, for a moment—not just a way to fill the quiet—because he genuinely wondered. "It can't be comfortable for her to have such a hard object poking at her insides."

Sedge gave the fire a good stoking. They both sat silently. Sedge had to have been thankful the smoke wafted away from his eyes.

"I imagine not." Sedge finally said. "She's probably pining for a release from that and Oleander's dominance."

"He is the only Thanatist around. I mean, if Pixee doesn't even know how to free her soul, then who can?"

"What are we talking about?" Rustle lowered himself to the ground with a sigh.

"Talking about why you were so focused on those trees over there," Sedge replied with a smirk.

"That, my good men, is my business." But in his usual way, Rustle couldn't help but prattle on: "I mean, she's is out there with Life-only-knows what sort of creatures crawling around in those trees. I don't care what Rose says." He shuddered.

"Well, Pixee seems more than capable."

Rustle accepted Sedge's assurances. "Now, what were you really talking about?"

"Just how sad it is that there isn't someone who could help us free Rose's soul. Pixee didn't know how." He looked away from Rustle and appraised the little hut that stood sentinel, a lonely dwelling. "Seems only a Thanatist can."

"Right you are, Aster."

"Aren't you a bit of a Thantist?" Sedge stopped messing with the fire and stared at Rustle.

"Not the kind of Thantist that tinkers with souls, no."

"Well," Sedge threw his stick into the fire. "Seems like the only one that is the right kind also happens to be a megalomaniac in the middle of a very specific plan so I guess Rose is stuck. And so are we."

Rustle leaned in, letting the heat wrap around him. "You're wrong about that, Sedge."

"Medlar?" Pixee glared at Rustle after he had finished weaving a tale about another Thanatist out there in the world. Or outside it. His reporting wasn't exactly linear. "A real one, not a dabbler like you?"

"Yes," Rustle sighed at the dubious assessment towards his own magical abilities. "That was his name. Is his name." He peered at the confusion adorning his audience. "I don't know. To the best of my understanding, he is somewhere between living and dead, the poor fella."

"Rustle, don't get sidetracked. Are you saying this Medlar-person is accessible?"

He stopped fidgeting. "That's basically what I'm getting it."

Pixee looked the group over. Hunting for a maybe-Thanatist would not be easy. Many more miles would be added to their quest if they took this route, all while Mr. Oleander continued prying and pulling. Buried in her appraising glance must have been the question of whether there was some other way to secure the Truce Blood.

"It won't hurt to check it out," Aster offered, timidly. He examined Rose, a blank page with neither opinion nor recommendation on the matter of her own soul.

"Well then," Pixee replied. "Rustle and I will go get this Medlar and bring him back."

Rustle garbled some coarse sounds. "Small problem. He is kind of locked in place."

"What does that even mean?" Sedge asked, probably what everyone had thought.

"It means what it means, Sedge. He can't go anywhere. Is that easier to understand?"

Sedge drew his lips in tight as his hand curled into a fist.

Pixee smirked as she glanced up at Rose. "I take it that Oleander's will regarding where your person goes is probably not defined?" Pixee's reasoning felt like a solitary breeze rattling the forest canopy: the group's stagnation shaking with comprehension and hope.

"Off to Alder we go." Rustle smiled. "You all are going to love how quaint that town is."

35.

OF A DISTANT LITTLE-KNOWN TOWN

The Mountains of Lune ran almost the entire length of the world hugging all the lands in an embrace and only the vast ocean, proved even more mysterious than the mountains. The head of the range was commonly known as the moon-hand and the base was known as the moon-foot.

Alder was near the moon-hand according to Rustle. All the way past the Copac which was as far north as Aster had ever ventured; it sat in a land of bald, rocky terrain. From Rustle's description, Alder was a place little inhabited. He spoke of a small civilization free from the desecration of any warlord. The people of Alder were their own, with their own rules and way of living. This report gave everyone the impression that Alder was as far out-of-the way as any populated settlement.

"Why all the way up there?" Aster inquired as they ventured away from the homely clearing.

"There are a great many mysteries to the workings of Thanatos," Rustle said in reply. "I'm not about to pretend to know even an iota of how such magic works."

"Yet, you dabble," chimed in Pixee as they walked in a line, their steps flattening the moss into decomposed mush.

The blood moon. The Mountains of Lune. That thin and silvery, almost opal, light at the mountain's peak. Which one wilted the world? Which one had swallowed the sun? Mr. Oleander's plan had so many parts; guessing the role each played, whether perpetrator or crime, was murky at best.

"I'm just a lowly shopkeeper, m'lady, who happens to meet interesting people as they embark on their own little adventures. And I listen to their interesting lives and tales."

Pixee wasn't to be patronized. "And so this Medlar just happened to wander into your curio shop?" She looked sidelong at Rustle. "In a little-known seaside town?"

Rustle came back at Pixee's incisive observations with all the silence he could muster.

Pixee refused to go unanswered. She levied her query against Rustle once more: "So Medlar just happened to be visiting Lamiston and he wanders into your establishment. And—?"

She wasn't the only one who found Rustle's connection to this other Thanatist, one of little notoriety, a bit dubious. How could anyone in their group not want to explore the nature of this relationship, especially Rose? She walked unconcerned, it seemed, about what happened between the people in her life, rather more interested in examining the world around her.

"You okay?" Aster asked her in a quiet voice as they made their way closer to the edge of the Wald.

She nodded.

"Just..." Conversing with her wasn't the same; not anymore at least. Gone was the Rose he had once loved. "You seem uninterested in what we're trying to do for you."

Her attention pawed at the sky, seeking purchase upon anything. And yet, the sky was absent anything but the ruddy moon. So her gaze fell to the undulating ground before she scrutinized the horizon, the expanse of all things, or nothing at all which she seemed to find far more interesting than her soul.

"There were times after dressing a wound or delivering a child that I'd be cleaning my hands of blood or afterbirth. I know such moments took place. I can see the events in my mind, but I wonder what they felt like. Was there a sense of satisfaction seeing a bandaged person walk away? Was there happiness in a mother's face as she embraced her new offspring? My memories are there; they're just lukewarm behind my eyes. So, you'll have to pardon me if I'm not enthusiastic, or any other kind of flavor or color."

She moved on while Aster almost slowed to a stop. For a moment the tang of her words left him without breath. Nothing of a gasp, sigh, or hiss was able to depart from his lips, even though he really wanted to express his reaction in some physical way. Did she realize how bitter she had sounded?

Sedge caught up and paced Aster. Just a couple of steps and their movements synchronized: arms and feet locked in motion, together in one little pod of space and time. In the pause that attended their steps, Aster was sure he felt a breath of tenderness lingering about them.

"How is she even alive if her soul is not a part of her?" He finally confessed the confusion that had been buzzing around in his head.

Sedge chuckled at Aster's honest inquiry. "I'd guess some magic keeps her animate even though she doesn't have a soul. Think of it this way, Aster, she's just a steak at the moment and if she had a soul she'd be seasoned steak, cooked in butter, garlic, rosemary."

Aster grappled with the concept, though the food metaphor helped bring the lofty idea down to a level that was much more digestible to his mind. His gaze wandered away from Sedge, as his mind chewed away on this new information.

"I get it," Sedge continued. "You're like things of the earth, or you want to be." Sedge went on as they came out from under the eves of the forest: "You want the past to be present, abiding like the trees. You want to see change come about as quickly as mountains move. But Aster," Sedge paused both his words and his steps for a brief moment, pulling in Aster's attention from thoughts of meat and souls. "You're not earth. You think you bonded with fire for no reason?"

Sedge had a slight tilt to his head peering at Aster as if he wasn't sure what he was going to do with him—too complex and uncertain, perhaps—but not necessarily exasperation. Sedge looked upon Aster as an enigma to be embraced, not to be remedied or tolerated. It was as if his sat rested contentedly on Aster. The only missing element from his look was the mossy green color of his eyes, which had been dulled by the red glow of the moon.

He draped an arm over Aster's shoulders. "Don't take root when you're meant to burn," he concluded with a firm squeeze.

Sedge trotted away to catch up with the others, leaving Aster steeped in cogitation, a scud of concepts to sort through. All the words which Sedge had shared were hearty truths, baring more preponderance than niceties.

Ascribing to be one particular element never appeared in the magical training; not even Oren had delved that deep into the theory of magic. In light of recent events, it all made sense. The outcome of the Martese now had an explicit reason. All because of Sedge, rousing this new understanding.

Ah Sedge, with his stride and perfect posture; he was something else, more than he appeared especially at their first encounter in the Hart's Den. The emotionally intimate moments between them piled up, rising to heights beyond casual.

The word that applied to the relationship forming with Sedge slipped away, like smoke, so Aster left it unlabeled as he rushed to catch up with the group. Everyone seemed focused on whatever Rustle gabbed about.

They milled around as the horses were made ready. Pixee's horse, Iridium, had dutifully kept watch over the borrowed mare, grazing peacefully near the riverbank.

"It's hard to explain unless you've met him. Most people have notions about what a Thanatist is supposed to be like." Aster heard Rustle say. "But he really was nothing like Oleander. At all,"

Pixee, who had dared to push back against Rustle's schemes, hints, and innuendo, asked the boldest question yet. "And is your association with Medlar in any way tied to the debt your sister paid?"

Rustle distractedly patted Iridium's flank. Sedge prepared the other horse, a paltry ruse to mask how genuinely interested he was in Rustle's reply.

"Uh, nah, not really. No." Rustle moved about trying to dodge their glances. "Not directly. I mean, he may have been a factor in the situation."

Unconvinced by Rustle, three sets of eyes were turned upon Rose for some sort of rebuttal. Or affirmation.

"He needed help with a debt," she said matter-of-factly. "As to the nature of the debt I did not ask."

Rustle fell back and wrapped an arm around his sister's shoulders. "Not my proudest moment, but I've done my best to make amends, thank you very much. Hence the dabbling in Thanatos."

There were opinions about Rustle churning in everyone's mind—there had to be—so it reasoned that everyone would have a corresponding take on whether or not his self-proclaimed efforts at penance were lip-service or sincere gestures, but Rose kept her thoughts on the matter closely to herself. She stood beside her brother, resting a hand against her chest.

The party was situated thusly upon two horses: Pixee, Rose, and Aster upon Iridium while Sedge was blessed to ride along with Rustle. Fortunately, Pixee's small frame left just enough room for Aster to fit snugly behind Rose; possibly a grace made in token of the relationship that had long since vanished.

As they arranged themselves, Aster glanced over at Sedge. Sitting still as Rustle fumbled in the saddle to get comfortable. They grinned at one another, giving this small moment of humor time to shine while the night reigned.

They followed the River Crest back down until they found safe crossing again. Once over the water the real race began. The horses were put to the paces. There was no hard deadline this time, a defined event or enumerable bundle of hours which signaled the end. It was more intuitive, knowing that someone out there had a well-defined plan to tear existence into pieces and was proactive about making it happen. Where was Mr. Oleander in all this darkness? What sort of new deviance was he working on at that exact moment? The questions bounced around in Aster's mind as he jogged upon the horse's back.

The bastioned towers of the Mountains of Lune lurked on the edge of sight as the trek carried them farther north and farther away from populated towns and cities. There was a brief stop in Utricularia, looking more monstrous the closer they approached. There they stocked up on supplies and left behind the city of wooded buildings. The mare that bore Sedge and Rustle stumbled to keep up with Iridium.

The world stretched out larger than Aster had conceived. All this wandering put the breadth of Thuidium into a new perspective, and his voice felt little more than a whisper in the midst of so many new places and faces.

That was when it dawned upon him: the fire fruit was going to change the world or at least be tasted by thousands more than Aster previously imagined.

"We need to give this dame a rest." Sedge checked her gait until they came to a stop.

Rustle vacated the saddle and limped away, rubbing his thighs while Sedge gave the horse a break from bit and bridle.

Pixee tugged upon Iridium's mane. The horse slowed to a stop and she slipped to the ground. "A quick rest," she directed, a slight edge in her voice as if she anticipated all manner of possible dangers.

Aster helped Rose dismount. They made themselves comfortable, naturally forming a circle around nothing in particular. Aster dug out a small pit in the center of the ring. It looked like a good place for a fire.

Pixee arrested his movements. "We won't be here long enough."

"We'll need a longer rest," Sedge contended.

"You'll have to deal with less. Oleander is on the move whether we are or not."

"No one's ignoring the signs." Sedge sat back, watching Pixee.

Pixee had said all that she intended on the matter and anyone looking at her knew that any further arguments were futile. She abandoned their little cluster and attended to her horse.

"You seem awfully anxious, Pixee."

The way she looked about, it was as though she could not let the shadows be shadows. Any object untouched by the moon's light earned her scrutiny.

"Where has all the confidence gone?" Sedge patted the neck of his own steed.

"I'm not confident, to be honest. I just…" she lost her voice; it shrank away like a breeze moving on. "I just want to know that we can actually undo all this."

She moved to escape the attention of so many people, small group though it was. Pixee's confession yanked at Aster to the point of discomfort. She wasn't allowed be insecure because at least one person among them should have absolute confidence.

Aster buttoned up his expression to keep the discomfort from escaping through his face. For the first time since this ghastly night blanketed the world, the impulse to blame Life and Death, or even the earth for puking up that cursed rock, sputtered and went out. A dispassionate coating leaked all over the situation. Decisions were made to get to this point. Decisions, better decisions, would need to be made to survive through to the other side, even with what little hope remained, a thin seam of it.

Rustle hugged Rose tightly. "It's not you," he assured her as Pixee departed.

"It is," Rose pulled away. "It's me. It's him. It's all of this darkness. That harbinger of danger in the sky. You can't escape the fear that nighttime inherently brings and when it's perpetual…"

They left Pixee to stew in the shadows. Everyone else tried to collect a few moments of rest, mentally and physically. No amount of time felt sufficient as danger hugged the entire world.

It had only been a couple hours since Aster fell into sleep. Sedge was already up, dusting himself off and signaling Rustle that it was time to ride on. Aster's bones and joints still rattled with the miles of riding they had already experienced. There would be many more put under the hooves of their horses before they saw Alder on the horizon.

Through the thick nocturnal hours, the party carried on with the blood moon and Mountains of Lune as their constant reminders. Aster cocked a glance up now and then towards the sky, just to make sure the moon still bled. Bleed it did, tarnished light hemorrhaging down on the mortal world, both unfathomable and familiar all at once.

How did Mr. Oleander do it? How did he interfere in such a grand cycle, that seemed so out of reach from mortal hands and minds? Much more of this perpetual darkness and who knew what would happen to life on Thuidium. This was not just a curious event, but a life-altering—a life-ending—occurrence. No sun. No crops. No fire fruit. To have been only one of two people who tasted and appreciated its flavor, the ingenuity of it, was a personal calculation that brought an evil so vast into more comprehensible terms. Otherwise, the magnificence of the situation would have been easy to push off as an issue for others to combat.

The remaining leagues to Alder closed, one gallop at a time; there had been rests, but no fires. A shape, darker than the surrounding night, rose up far in the distance.

"Is that Alder?" The question announced a pause to the group, a much needed pause that Aster felt in his back.

36.

OF HORSING AROUND

"There it is," Rustle said as he slung an arm around Aster's shoulders.

"Is it…" Aster squinted, "big?" The vague shapes that lay ahead didn't give away much about the town. From what was visible, the place looked no more than a long-term campsite.

"Nah, not at all. Smaller than Lamiston, if you can picture such place. Which works, for being on the cusp of the civilized world."

"What lies beyond then?"

"You ask so many questions." Rustle gave Aster a sturdy pat on the shoulder. "I don't know, man. The uncivilized world? It doesn't matter because we just need to get there. The rest is incidental."

Rustle peeled away and joined Pixee as she started a fire, tuckered-out from all of Aster's curiosity, likely.

"He's right, you know." Rose stood where Rustle had been. Together, they watched the flames kick up. "You always had this need to know all the parts, like it would help you solve problems easier."

"Ha," Aster grunted in reply. "All the parts. I didn't, and I don't." Rose and her assumptions. "You weren't around long enough to know me that well."

"No, I suppose I wasn't. Though, I still understand you better than you realize, even from the short amount of time we spent together."

"Which was your fault." There was an extensive, incriminating speech waiting in Aster's lungs.

How he wanted to issue the unanswerable evidences that she was, inconclusively, to blame for the demise of what would have been a blissful coupling and a heedless love capable of withstanding any erupting threat. Yet here they were, practically strangers in a strange part of Thuidium, just sitting in the dark and breathing absently into the night air. Alas, there was plenty of conflict to fill the days to come, so Aster exhaled away his shapeless speech.

Maybe when the sun shone again and Rose had her soul back, he might bother to hash it all out with her, but until then the matter seemed so…stale.

Aster went and sat beside Pixee, examining her in silence. "Are you going to be well? I don't think I've ever seen you nervous," he commented with his own nervous laugh.

"Not nervous."

"It's fine if you are. We all experience it."

She huffed. "I'm confused."

It was a surprising answer and one that Aster didn't buy completely. "Pixee, we've known each other a while. You can level with me. Be real."

He nudged her. She returned the gesture with an authentically aggressive shove of her own.

"Our history together doesn't give you automatic insight into who I am and how I feel from one moment to the next."

Sedge and Rustle sat quietly, exempt from the scathing introspection and inspections Aster had with his fellow traveler.

"I just want to make sure you'll be well, is all." Aster stood and rubbed her aggression out of his shoulder. He gave her one last look and relocated closer to where Rustle and Sedge sat.

"Sometimes you just have to let people do what they will do. Give them time to work things out for themselves," Sedge advised.

"I was just trying to help. I don't see why she became so defensive."

"No, Aster she wasn't. But then again, you could just not try to make everything neat. Let stuff ferment. Let it stink for a bit. It's how you get a good drink. Some things can work themselves out."

Like Pixee, Aster drifted away from the group with his pack. He found a spot apart from people and their moods. Aster let go of it all and gave himself over to sleep.

The amount of time that passed wasn't measurable, not without degrees of lights in the sky. Sedge shook Aster's shoulder.

"Time to get a move on."

Aster rolled into a sitting position greeting a world that looked exactly as it had when he fell asleep which was disappointing, even if it was what he expected. In the time that Aster slept a false hope germinated that something would look different after a few hours of rest. Cheated by hope again, Aster resigned himself to simply gathering his belongings and continuing on with the darkened world.

The others prepared to depart. Rustle adjusted the saddle. Rose stood and seemed to converse with Iridium and there was Pixee, on the ground fidgeting with her pack. Aster glanced at her. She tossed him a quick look.

Aster plopped down beside her. "What can we expect? What are the people like up here?"

Pixee shrugged.

He drew himself up, but examined the ground between his booted feet. "I'm sorry I pressed you last night." He smiled weakly. "I just needed…"

Pixee looked sidelong at him.

All the possible responses filed by and they all started with *I*. Pixee's face held no clues. She just waited. "If you ever want or need it, let me know how to help." Aster sat with his legs crossed as he dodged the looks from his other companions.

She stopped fidgeting with her belongings and her lips parted in preparation to say something. Instead of words she simply clasped hands with Aster, an embrace constructed of just hands and fingers, pressing around each other until both hands blanched white.

Alder grew before them as a collection of dwellings. Nothing in the silhouettes spoke of commerce. Most of the buildings were single-story with flat roofs. Their specific make, the materials used in their construction, hidden from discernment. A few torches offered light, but it was hardly enough to give the visitors a clear idea of what awaited them. Prudently, they slowed their mounts as they drew nearer the light.

Standing at the onset of the town was a contingent of figures, mostly hidden in shadows. The fires burning at their backs only gave hints as to what these people looked like.

Sedge slipped to the his feet and stood between the guards of Alder and his companions with Rustle Pixee being closest.

"We'd like to pass through peacefully, if you're agreeable," he announced to the general assembly.

No one from the other side stepped forth.

"That we are not," came the reply. It was a disembodied voice of character and authority. Not so deep, but not exactly a tenor either.

Neither Aster nor Pixee or Sedge could pick out the speaker who took delight in denying their passage.

"You could have hinted at an armed guard," Sedge whispered to Rustle.

"Had I known," Rustle replied back.

"Care to make yourself known?" Sedge twitched to keep his hand from the hilt of his weapon.

A burly figure, an inch taller than even Sedge, emerged from the group. His right hand clung to a spear almost the same height as his person, the diamond-shaped head of which was fashioned as if two or three blades had been forged into one. A wild beard tumbled off his cheeks and chin, hiding the exact shape of his face. His rotund belly insisted itself over the waist of billowy pants, into which a dark shirt was securely tucked.

"I do care, but in the interest of courtesy s'pose I'll make an exception," he said with a spry tone, as if he were chatting with a neighbor. "Crag's muh name and this here is our town." He gestured to the people and buildings at his back. "What manner-uh business has you strangers out this way?" He leaned forward examining the visitors before him.

Sedge gave the tall man a glance. "Just looking to pass through."

"For what purpose need you cut through Alder rather than go 'round? Or rather, how 'bout you just leave us be, all ta'gether?"

Sedge looked at Crag. Looked at his companions. It seemed an obvious explanation, yet this Crag person insisted on a more detailed response, for whatever reason. Sedge invited Rustle into the exchange, hoping that their purpose could be spelled out clearly.

"Truly," Rustle stepped up next to Sedge. "We need to get to the Gury."

Crag narrowed his eyes as he pondered the requester as much as the request. "You been ta' tha' Gury before have ya'? A mighty specific request. You strangers spring up outta nowhere askin' about some place that's never visited by strangers. I don't know a single face amongst ya'. I'mma level with you all, anyone daring to travel so far under this hapless moon surrounded by this here gnarly night has my suspicions tinglin'." He continued to gauge his guests. "Y'all have aught to do with this infernal darkness? It ain't natural." He eyed the sky as diligently as he surveyed his visitors.

"The only thing we have to do with this Life-less night is trying to end it," Pixee offered.

Crag's face piqued with interest at the statement. A mild form, as if someone had just told him the average lifespan of a meal worm. "You don't say?" His gaze bounced from person to person. "We ain't come this far out of the way to be mired in squabbles and troubles of others. Yet here we are. This blackness," he said to the sky, "been heavy on our hearts. Makes us trust the world even less."

"Great," Rustle said. "Then you'll want us to pass and handle this business." It wasn't a question. It wasn't a continuation of their request.

Crag presented his full height, his barrel chest seeming to expand. He held his spear across his body. "Not what I said, fella. I like the thought of this wretched night being snuffed out, but I can't say as I trust you folks. Haven't said much to convince me uh that, your pretty words aside."

"What's it going to take to get us access to where we want to go?" Sedge placed a hand on the hilt of his dagger, secured at his belt.

Crag responded with a tightened grip on his spear, planting it firmly against the ground. "First off stranger, it's going to take more'n a ragtag group of hardly armed folk to get past me and the fellas."

The men supporting Crag were a wall of thick bodies, most of them also bearded, and all armed. Most stood with tall spears, like their leader, while others bore crudely forged swords. Beyond them the goal waited. One of the goals, at least. Rose's freedom was blocked by this pack of country whelps.

Aster bit back his thoughts and instead tried to focus on a solution. "How about a trade?"

Crag's posture relaxed.

"Is there something we can offer as a sign of trust?" Not that Aster had a single iota what possession could possibly constitute an emblem of trust. Maybe he could perform fire spells for them? He opened his mouth to offer the service.

Crag spoke up first. "I've an eye on that there horse." He stuck his chin out toward Pixee. "The steed with them amber eyes."

Pixee recoiled and placed a hand upon Iridium. "No, no, no. This is not just a horse. This is a friend. I'm not going to let him go with a band of extortionists."

"You wound me with your words, little lady," Crag said, his soft face tightening. "Whatever you may be looking for is going to be stuck in that there Gury. My terms are set." Crag made his way back in the midst of his fellows who closed in around him, like a gate.

Rose set a hand softly on Pixee's shoulder. "No one can blame you." She traced gently against Iridium's glistening hair as she sniffed at the animal. "The scent of immortality lays upon this beast as it does you, Pixee. It'd be a travesty to part with such a creature. I think he would have no other partner."

Iridium stood with his head held high, as if he understood all that had been said. For the first time Aster noticed the eyes of the horse. They may not have been exactly amber but they weren't dark like the other horses'.

As he admired Iridium's peculiar eyes, Aster wanted to talk Pixee into making the trade. They were so close to helping Rose, to getting to the end of this wretched ordeal; it was all there, beyond the smattering of rooftops. Or so Rustle hinted. He hadn't been specific. There had been no other viable plan, though, and it all hinged on this one step. Now that step was slipping away.

The way Pixee clutched at Iridium was enough to dissuade any attempt at persuasion. They withdrew from the band of countrymen and a conference commenced.

"I suppose we could risk going around," Rustle offered.

"Just suppose?" Sedge eyed Rustle with a slight sense of humor to his question.

"I'm not intimately familiar with the geography up here, alright. I've been here one other time and took the direct route with Medlar through the town. Trust me, these people were more welcoming then. We go around then we could very well find ourselves wandering into a pit or far out of our way."

Iridium bent down to receive whisperings from Pixee. The creature slunk off, away from sight. Its dark coat blended so well that it looked as if the horse melted into night itself.

"He'll see what's what." She watched where the horse had vanished.

"You two can talk to one another?"

"I wouldn't call it talking," she replied to Aster. "More like silently understanding one another."

"A meeting of the minds," Rustle said. "I get it."

Did he really get it, though? To Aster, his words felt more like play-acting rather than a sincere understanding of the communication between Pixee and her singular horse, a laughable attempt to impress her. Either way, his levity helped the mood as they waited for the return of Iridium.

They languished under the timeless night in anticipation of some kind of report; any news would do. The fires at the threshold of Alder waved at Aster, mocking the distance that yet remained between him and his destination.

In that moment of consideration, Aster's mind was lost watching those small torches flicker wondering, what he would do with the element: maybe a surprise attack, or a stunning display of light. A squeal shot out of some dark corner of the world extinguishing the thought. Pixee sprang up and ran towards the sound.

The group was suddenly confused like a hive doused with water, the sense of cohesion and purpose melting away as everyone responded to Pixee's response in their own way. Sedge tried to hold the group in order, but Pixee had been conquered by the danger etched in Iridium's call.

Rustle chased after Pixee. Aster kept his place by Rose, who stood with a rigidity of one untouched by the discomfiture of the people around her. She gave the scattering figures an appraising nod, then turned on her heels to walk back toward the torches of Alder with a graceful, confident gait.

"Rose," Aster called. He turned and glared at Sedge imploringly, because if anyone was capable of reeling everyone back into order, it was him.

"Go after her," Sedge groaned. "I'll follow Rustle and Pixee. Let's try and get everyone back to this spot." He was off before the directive could be questioned.

Whatever counterargument Aster thought to make was still being worked out even as Sedge hurried out of sight, burying himself in the darkness. Aster released his confusion, his fear, and trotted after Rose.

They gained the line of torches, where the guards still milled about in a disorderly manner. Even in the weak light, their menace was apparent. It was more than visible. It was palpable. They turned and glared as the strangers again approached their territory. Aster gave them a nervous wave as Rose stood without a lick of fear. No determination. She just stood. The guards must have noticed for none drew near to threaten or question her. Instead, they offered the bulk of their menace to Aster.

"Back at it again are ya'?" Crag stepped around his fellows. His gaze lingered upon Rose. "She don't look too happy."

"She's not," Aster said. "She isn't sad either, which is actually the reason we need to pass through Alder."

Crag considered the words, looking back and forth between Aster and Rose. "Curious fella. Well, how's about I let y'all on through."

Aster gawked. "Really?" He gave Rose a spirited smile. She simply looked onward.

A snorting broke Aster's gleeful mood.

"Truly. Yer offering of peace is accepted," Crag said, followed by a boisterous laugh that sounded entirely too forced to be taken seriously.

He even snickered as Iridium bucked and kicked at the figures around him, men trying to direct the animal while avoiding his wrath. They looked about as comfortable with the task as the horse.

"We didn't technically offer the horse to you…" Aster began.

It was a vexatious situation all around, especially not knowing for what purpose they wanted the beast. Sure they said "offering of peace", but that was just pretext, right?

"No," said Crag. "Not directly I s'pose. Sending the creature snoopin' around in the dark, I took more as an indirect offer."

Iridium continued to fight against the tethers that had been fixed to his body, stamping and snorting. He began to gnaw at the ropes. Out came the weapons, a language every living being understood. The tips of spears pecked at his flesh; pecked but hadn't pierced yet. Though, one sudden move and Iridium would be a pin-cushion. The message was communicated and the black horse stood stock-still.

"That was a dumb move. Quick tip, slick," Crag leaned on his spear. "Only one accessible point into the Gury and it's right through this here town."

The crowd of guards parted. To venture into the town and enter this Gury-place without Rustle would have been pointless. Just as this thought passed, and as Crag waited for Aster to accept the invitation, Iridium began to whiny and stomp. The motion shook the ground, a tremor ran up Aster's legs.

Crag held his feet. With a word, his men plied their weapons more insistently. The threat quieted the beast.

"Cretins," Pixee shouted as she ran up.

Crag stood between the horse and Pixee, grinning. "Thanks missy for the peace offering."

Even with the meager light of the torches and a stingy moon, it was apparent that tension wound tightly around Pixee. How could it not? Her friend-steed was bound up, his very life threatened.

"Now," Crag said in a husky voice. "You wanna venture into that tumble o' boulders or not?"

37.

OF A ROCKY ROAD

The next move hinged on Pixee's approval. There was a distinct impression that if she had said no the guards still wouldn't have released Iridium. They were in it now and Pixee must have realized that. She didn't reply. She didn't flinch. She filled the breathless moment with a long look at Iridium. The amber eye peered back at her, a look meant for Pixee alone to understand.

Others could infer at the intent in that jeweled-looking eye, but those would only be guesses, projections of what some thought a spiritual bond between horse and person would look like, at how such two being communicated.

Pixee nodded back at the horse as her fists uncurled, slowly, until her fingers were splayed.

Crag rumbled with a chuckle the erupted deep from his gut. "Relax, little one. You're free to enter now."

"I'm more relaxed than you know." Her voice, darker than the sky, wafted towards Crag, who clutched at his spear.

To Aster's knowledge, no one else in this cadre of on-lookers had seen Primul magic at work. The opal tendrils oozing off her skin startled those who noticed. The snapping and cracking of wood broke the still night. Not that the loss of spears threatened those guarding Iridium much. Crag stormed towards Pixee, undeterred.

Sedge readied his blade, but Pixee was too ready, too full of menace, to need his help.

Crag evaded the gaping fissure that Pixee had opened in the earth by slices of a second. Some of his fellow Alderians were not so lucky. The yells rose up all around Iridium, but Pixee's voice summited them all.

"Run!"

Iridium bucked and kicked, taking some of the captors out. Their bodies thudded against the ground that still crumbled and broke open. The horse fled. The people followed suit.

The danger that was Pixee's wrath chased them in the air and upon the ground until the phantom limbs reaching off her skin retreated, vanishing like steam. Aster reached out and grabbed her before she collapsed to the ground.

All stood silently before the re-sculpted landscape stretching out before them. The weariness must have passed for, she shook off Aster's supportive touch, nodded at him to follow as she moved in a wobbly stride into Alder. After Pixee's display of power, the place took on a mood more akin to Cannaville.

To even call the place a town, and these structures buildings, would have been an overestimation. Such words implied certain qualities: craft, design, organization; a particular feel. This place, well, it just looked too rustic for any of those titles.

To either side of the lane upon which they trod homes had been erected in no distinguishable pattern. They were low to the ground, about tall enough for a man of average height to enter. They looked a bit on the round side, like balled-up clods of dirt. This must have been the way of the people of Alder: eschewing the conventions practiced throughout much of Thuidium. But then, that is what made the world what it was, variety in people and in their ways.

The land sloped down gently. Boulders of various sizes, and in a number too plentiful to count, littered what had to have once been some expansive body of water by the look of the environs.

Rustle surveyed the land. "Medlar's in there somewhere."

Somewhere? That did not sound comforting. The vagueness of Rustle's assertion perturbed Aster and possibly the rest of the group.

"We might want to flood the place."

"Why?" Sedge stood beside Rustle, his gaze hopping between the mass of boulders and his companion.

"Keeps the Plagioclase docile."

"Plagioclase? What's a Plagioclase?" Sedge looked over at Aster.

"No idea," Aster replied.

"Nothing you want to meet," Rustle offered. "You hear them before you see them. The cursed things are creatures of fire. I thought Oxalis were bad." He shuddered.

Pixee crawled down the small lip of turf and in between the mess of rocks. She knelt on the ground and remained motionless for some time, her head turning left and right with her eyes focused down. The moon's rusted light dyed her short hair almost copper.

After a few minutes she reached for the dirt, but the opal sheen hit the ground first. From beneath the earth she had drawn out a single drop of water which rested upon her fingertip. Under the gaze of a corrupt moon, the small helping of water looked more like a drop of blood.

With the delicate touch of an artisan, she pulled and pried at the liquid. Before long, the drop exceeded the room upon her lithe finger. Now she held it like a lump of dough, pulling and stretching the one drop until it was the size of a bed sheet. Wisps of opal continued to swirl around her hands. Was this the energy that flowed through all of creation? The very same silvery light stitched across the tips of the Mountains of Lune? Aster cast a quick glance north and then east, trying to pull aside the darkness. Somewhere, off in the distance he thought he could see that strange sight.

A splash brought his attention back to the scene at hand.

"I'm not sure how big this—"

"Gury," Rustle said.

"—is, but I'll fill it up as much as I can." She let out a breath before taking in another draught of air.

She screwed up her face, a little bit of her tongue peeking from between her lips as her fingers wrapped around an intangible fabric. The energy upon which she had purchase, she tugged and tugged, heaving it as if it were either immense or immensely heavy.

With wonder in their eyes, the group leaned in and witnessed the rising water level. It was imperceptible at first, but after long enough they noticed boulders shrink as the water crawled up their faces. Some rocks disappeared entirely. Others became but caps sticking out of the inky liquid.

With a final tug, Pixee dropped her arms and sat back, almost falling, onto the turf. She passed the back of her hand across her forehead to relieve her skin of the sweat that had been squeezed out by her efforts.

"How are we to travel?" Rose asked.

"Safely?" Rustle grinned crookedly at his own jocular reply, unsure about the use of humor in the moment, but unable to surpass his natural inclination.

The twin stares—of pursed lips and narrowed eyes—from Pixee and Rose quelled any further attempts at levity from Rustle.

He cleared his throat. "I don't know. Boulders are still poking up, so I imagine it's not terribly deep." He cocked a glance at Pixee, eye brows peaked.

"It's really not, to be honest. Just enough to hopefully keep the Plagoclaise at bay." A note of exasperation tinged Pixee's words, probably born from the effort of the magic and her fear for Iridium.

"So we can wade through…carefully. We don't need anyone slipping between the rocks and breaking an ankle." He paused and threw a distrustful glimpse at the water. "Or worse. So, let's get on with it."

The water lapped gently at the rocks, giving the darkness a bit of an inviting character. It was a soothing sound, or would be if they didn't have to find their way in and through the mess of rocks and pools.

Pixee, more so than the others, moved slowly and unsteadily. She plodded on through the doubts and weariness, leaping onto a nearby boulder. The priority was the Truce Blood—and by extension, freeing Rose's soul—as much as it must have pained her to not seek out Iridium first.

Aster gave himself a running start and leapt over the small watery gap, landing upon the nearest boulder; albeit, not as gracefully as Pixee. Soon the crown of the boulder was filled with the entire party. Barely.

"Alright Rustle," Aster directed. "Lead the way."

He hemmed and hawed. He looked ahead. He looked left. He didn't look right. "See…maybe…I think that…" He nudged and shifted into Pixee and Aster as he debated within himself.

Sedge rolled his eyes at Aster.

"Last time I was here, there wasn't water. Oh, and there was light. It's throwing me off," Rustle admitted.

"Just guess," Aster urged.

With a deep sigh, Rustle slipped down the north-face of the boulder and scurried across a few smaller rocks before clambering up the next large stone. With that, the group was in action, cutting their way across the Gury like lizards, slinking up and down the sides of rocks. The going was slow, the soreness in their limbs the only measure of the passage of time. Admittedly, not a precise indicator, what with the amount of scrambling in which they had to engage just to travel even a short distance.

After the first sign of fatigue crept up into his eyes, Aster called for a halt. Everyone had stopped on separate boulders. "Anyone else need a break?" There wasn't a single audible reply. "I'll take that as a yes," Aster concluded.

Everyone sunk into a sitting position, almost in unison. "Any idea of much farther?" Sedge inquired.

Rustle swept the blackness with an addled glance. "No."

Pixee's attention continued to slip back towards Alder. It wasn't exactly like losing a child, but it had to be akin. As much as she tried to keep her mind on the journey, it was consumed with fear for the horse she called friend.

How long would it take for her to emerge and resume her role as leader? Just postulating on the outcome ate up precious minutes. It was troublesome to see Pixee distraught, her head turning at every sound as she lingered behind the group. Larger, unanswered questions and vexations dwarfed even this deeply personal tragedy. Pixee would understand.

Aster scrambled over to the rock upon which Rustle sat. "Think," he said trying for his most encouraging voice. "You probably can recall the general direction?"

Rustle stared, looking a bit vacant. "I mean, kind of." He looked down at the water below, as black as the sky, but with a glossy sheen.

"You see her over there?" Aster directed Rustle's attention at Pixee. "She's showing us the meaning of sacrifice by continuing on this path. All to help your sister. You want to stop feeling guilty for Rose's state? Then you better pull it together."

They both saw Rose in their own way—sister, former lover—but with equitable potency of fondness and longing for her freedom. Rustle was sure to have added traces of remorse to what he saw, but best not to mention that.

"Set aside what you're afraid of, all those doubts, and just go." Aster waited for the words to sink in, to wrap their way around Rustle and squeeze him into realization.

Rustle opened his mouth, but instead of expending energy in responding with words, he stood and, with a quick look about, made his way to the next rock. Rustle's movements stirred the group, purging the fatigue from both limb and heart.

The scrambling and leaping soon came to an end as Rustle halted. He peered down at an enclosure: tall boulders arranged in a circular fashion around an open space.

"There," he said pointing down towards the ring of rocks.

"Alright, good stuff Rustle." Aster slipped down the boulder upon which the group had paused, slipped and landed in about three feet of water.

What manner of creature these Plagioclases were that such little water could subdue them, Aster didn't care to guess. He sloshed into the opening and explored, feeling out the ground.

Sedge was soon by his side, kicking around before each step. "Seems to be pretty even. I'm only meeting sand and small pebbles."

"I'm not feeling any large rocks either. Let's get Rustle on over and do whatever needs to be done. Rustle," Aster called.

The others waded into the circle. The water stirred and rippled away from each body. Pixee remained dry upon the top of the boulder, knees tucked under her chin, beyond forlorn as the worry for Iridium captured what little energy remained to her. Somehow the night looked especially thick around her.

"I'm going to need her," Rustle whispered to Aster.

38.

OF A PEEK BEHIND THE VEIL

"Why? She's going through a bit of worry and I'm pretty sure hopping from rock to rock sapped what little energy she had left. It's probably best if you just do this down here and she stays up there."

"No can do, captain," Rustle said as serious as Aster's ever heard him sound. "This bit of magic needs her blood."

Aster seared the dark with his shock and repulsion. Blood. Her blood? "Why?"

"Primul blood, man," he said as if that was the key to every mystery in life. "Most magic dealing with the path between this layer and the others requires it."

Rustle shrugged at Aster's incredulous stare.

Primul blood. Rustle wasn't asking for the blood from some bit of refuse, dropped by the burdened limb, or left by a dying stag. He wanted to cut into a friend and spill an essential part of her. Every twist and turn of this slow crawl over these Death-blessed rocks squeezed out an inescapable sigh. Was this how Pixee had felt throughout this entire ordeal? Aster had only been at the helm for a few hours and exasperation already clawed at his wit.

"Just a few drops. I'm not asking to drain her," Rustle said at Aster's sigh.

Aster leaned in closer, dropped his voice. "Magic between the layers? Does Mr. Oleander know she's Primul?" he hissed. "The void take you, Rustle. How could you have hidden this?"

His gaze was unwavering and emptied of humor. He actually looked insulted. "Whether I had told you then or not, it doesn't change anything. You though you'd be able to hide her heritage from Oleander until he died?" He exhaled a sober laugh. "Oleander doesn't know. At least…" He peeked over Aster at the lone little figure, stone-still. "No he doesn't know. So let's be done with this entire mess."

Sedge had already waded his way back to the rock upon which Pixee lingered. She was turned three-quarters away from the circle. Aster watched him scale his way to the crown and sit with her. Their voices fell back as inaudible mumbles chasing one another.

He had woven some sort of spell with his words; they both returned to the circle of stones. Pixee was there in body but her expression, still twisted in concern, left little doubt that she was no longer in this expedition.

Rustle surveyed her. "We are in business." He took her hand, no hint of flirtation was to be seen in his touch as he led her farther into the ring.

He directed everyone to stand close, with Pixee in convenient proximity to himself; it was always circles involved in these deep bouts of non-elemental magic: sun—when it was still a character in this tale called existence—moon, or people standing round.

Aster sidled up next to Sedge who leaned against a rock, already unburned of his travel gear. Even through the paltry light the fatigue was clearly whittled across Sedge's face. Until this dip, the dried mud of thousands, maybe millions, of steps clung to the soles of his boots.

They let the movements and banter unfold before them like a play, relishing this respite from puzzles, attacks, and threats of doom. Sedge cracked a smile. Aster nodded in agreement. The ease of communication between them warmed the coolness lapping at their legs.

"We should find the trapped soul of one Medlar, Thanatist of subtle fame—"

"No fame you mean," Sedge commented. "No one has heard of him but you."

"A good thing too." Rustle cleared his throat and paused, waiting for all extemporaneous comments to be subdued before he proceeded. "He knew enough and lucky for us he got stuck between mortality and any of the posthumous layers. Aster, the drawing?"

Aster unslung his pack, placed it on the boulder, and retrieved the sketch from its depths, surprisingly exempt from the water's touch while all the other contents in his pack, and the pack itself, felt sodden. Rose watched her trapped soul being passed from Aster to Rustle, her eyes colored with aloofness.

Soon she would care again, care about more than the presage of Mr. Oleander's will. She would cry, and laugh, and she would love again. He wanted he soul freed, so she could experience the textures of life. On her own terms.

"And you know enough to summon him, or whatever it is you need to do?" The fog had lifted and Pixee's penchant for astute observations shone again.

"Summon. Cute." He tapped her gently on the nose, which only caused a twisted expression to bloom on her face. "No, we don't summon him. We find him."

A discontented groan issued from both Sedge and Aster when Rustle intimated that the desired results would not be immediate, that the process would be indirect, possibly extensive. Aster replanted himself against the closest stone as he waited for Rustle to commence. The rock was cool to the touch; another reminder of the sun's absence.

Rustle bequeathed Rose with the drawing of herself, which she cradled against breast. "Now then, all ready?"

Aster and Sedge shut down their exchange of looks at Rustle's announcement.

"As some of you may know, while others probably don't, there are layers to this whole thing." He gestured in concentric circles around his head. "The Realm of Life and Death. The layers prepared for souls in various states of enlightenment, represented by sun, moon, and stars all as deep and as wide as eternity itself. Let's not forget about the dreaded void of nothingness between and surrounding the other layers. And maybe ones which we have yet to learn about. To find Medlar we just need to find out at what depth he got stuck."

"Your plan for doing that?" Sedge asked.

Rather than explain, Rustle gathered himself up to execute whatever ordinance he intended to utilize to peel away the elements and search the realms beyond.

"Why does this remind me of Oleander's plan?"

Even when facing Pixee's brutal, unsweetened honesty, Rustle still responded with an unabashed amount of grinning. "Dear Pixee, don't you fret. This is not even close to his scheme." He addressed the group: "Let's get on our way."

"You sure?" She wouldn't let her argument go until she reached a satisfactory level of understanding.

"It all comes down to scale," he said.

Her gaze was relentless, so much that she didn't even need to say more. She just stared, and he knew.

"Digging into this small little patch won't bring ruination upon the entirety of existence. It's the difference between a small cut and removing someone's head, savvy?" Rustle's usual blundering demeanor cracked away allowing for actual profundity to seep through as he made his explanation.

To even conceive of this type of magic—of manipulating layers, sideswiping the here and now—was deeper than any power

Oren mentioned and he was the most profound person Aster had ever known. It came as something of a shock that Rustle, this often waggish individual, didn't succumb to the maddening effect the Death Tooth mushroom was reported to have oft times. For the first time since meeting him, Aster had to wonder what sort of sternness lay under all of Rustle's humor?

Beneath the rusty beam of the blood moon they resumed a circular formation and waited for an incantation, perhaps? Was there some sort of motion that would peel away the layers? Rustle maintained a perverse amount of mystery about the whole exercise.

"Well then," Rustle announced. "Alright." He cleared his throat numerous times while he shifted, sending ripples out against the boulders. "Now. Ahem. Fair."

It had to be performance anxiety. He was nervous with Pixee right there, her speculation tempting him to drown in the complexity of this magic. The skeptical looks and slight snickers were not new for Rustle.

"Kind of getting cold just standing here," Pixee chided.

Rustle mumbled and dithered some more.

"I'd like to be dry again," she added. At last, a grin stole across her lips.

As the delay persisted the group lost interest in the whole spectacle. The standing-circle they had formed wobbled and wiggled into something oblong. Sedge and Aster escaped the water's chill upon rocks. Sedge wrung out his pants and shirt as they watched Rustle fumble his intentions.

"Oh, for Life's sake!" Pixee lifted her hand from her side sending a cascade of water droplets into Rustle's face. "Will you just take some already. Stop making us wait in this water."

He whipped out a small blade and paused, the tip of it hovering just out of reach of her skin. "Well, I'm not used to asking for blood, so pardon me if I'm hesitant to intentionally wound you. Just a few drops, mind you."

The circle of spectators reformed its proper shape and shrank imperceptibly as the blade's tip sank into Pixee's palm. Rustle's breathing broke the stiffness, as he tried to put his force somewhere between effective and violent. When the crimson ribbon twisted its way out of Pixee's skin Rustle was there cupping his hands together to collect the sample. She curled her hand into a fist squeezing out a thicker stream of blood without caring how much he actually needed.

He nodded at her.

"You have enough there?" Pixee inquired, none too kindly.

He smiled and held his hands as steady as possible. The back of his thumbs received the smallest threads of her donation. The circle waited as Rustle dredged up a mood, a temperament forged from his experience with the Death's Tooth mushroom.

His focus rolled out under the moon's pallid light. Pixee's donation of blood danced to the vibrations of his thought, reeling and curling on itself in a serpentine jig. Rustle sunk into utter concentration, of perfect stillness, which was probably absolute requirement for this more demanding branch of magic, Thanatos being as demanding as magic got.

The lack of chants, tangible and fixed sounds, gave Thanatos an eerie feel. The use of blood didn't help the image much. It was like having to imagine a type of fruit that never existed; not a task for the faint of heart or for the timid of mind. All this creative work put Rustle in a new light, one brighter than the corroded moon beams dressing him, as he executed his spell-craft.

The blood responded to the presage of Rustle's will, thinning into a sheet, a sort of curtain hanging in the still evening sky. Rustle's eyes went completely white and looked, as it were, through literal objects—shapes, colors; all the parameters detectable to human senses—and saw the essence of the thing, the intention woven into its being. What did his sight perceive? How many layers did he search through until he caught sight of Medlar? He stopped. His eyes resumed their mundane appearance.

The curtain thickened, but only slightly. Rustle looked mighty pleased as he waded closer to the bloody curtain, under the bloodied moon. So much blood.

"This should do it." Rustle reached up, gathered a handful of the blood as if it were a literal fabric, and then tugged.

The silky bolt of material slipped down, fluttering to rest in the water before dispersing into memory. *Ooo's* and *ahhh's* rippled around the circle. Not literal sounds but the expressions of everyone, save Rose, said as much. Aster smiled for it.

As common as magic was in the world of Thuidium—like so many tools and discovered processes—the wonder of seeing the world bend and fold in unexpected angles wasn't dulled in the slightest. The magic of magic itself couldn't end, wouldn't submit to monotony. Not to say that such was Rustle's only motivation for adding a bit of flourish to his display, but an unmistakable look of pride infiltrated his face, showing that he relished the effect his spell had on his peers. No one watching seemed to resent Rustle his moment.

That effect increased many-fold when everyone looked up, along with Rustle, and saw the personage who hung in the air, like some half-finished painting that had been started on the surface of a pond.

"Medlar." Rustle named him with the familiarity of a good friend.

"My dear Rustle, you meddling knave. I see you somehow managed to remember where you left me. And found yourself the blood of a Primul?"

Rustle slipped an arm over Pixee's shoulders. "Truly, happened to have one hitch her wagon to mine."

"Wrong interpretation." Pixee ducked out from under Rustle's embrace. "In any case, we're here for a specific reason."

39.

OF CONVERSATIONS BEYOND THE PALE

The unincorporated Thanatist moved only his eyes as he scooped in the sight of his audience. "Quite an association of confederates," Medlar said, mostly to himself. "Yet nothing ostensibly links them all; no insignia, no colors, no armament."

"We're not from any clan," Sedge offered. "We're just concerned citizens of the world."

"And what has you all riled up enough to venture to this Death-tilled spot?" Medlar queried his guests.

Or was he their guest?

"Her." Rustle held out a hand to Rose, not in any signaling way, but an offer of unity.

"She, being?"

"My sister."

"I don't see her too well. She's not all the way there, is she?" A grim laugh echoed from the depths, like a memory because it took so long to fall into the present.

"Since you're pretty versed in Thanatos, I thought you could help with that."

"Do tell?" Medlar said, humor stealing into his voice.

Rustle sighed and released Rose's hand. "You remember that deal we had?" Discomfort oozed out of his voice as he shrank away from Medlar's grinning visage. "Well, when you didn't come up under a shroud Oleander didn't take the double-cross with much humor, so Rose did what she has always done." Rustle looked her up and down with his dewy gaze. He stopped at her eyes, vacant without horizon or topography.

Rustle pinched back the tears that had pooled in the corners of his eyes. "She took the fall for me," he finished.

Rose's soulless stare dried up his tears of regret and cemented his gaze into something that looked more responsible, more focused.

"Oleander reduced her to this soulless shell standing beside you? I knew the man had a pair of stones on him, but never did I guess he would swing them around. Sad."

"So you're saying you wouldn't have?" Sedge folded his arms against his chest.

Aster glared at Sedge.

What? Sedge replied with his wide eyes before carrying right along with his point: "If you hadn't been relegated to this unincorporated portrait-in-the-sky, you wouldn't be showing-off your stones either?"

"That's neither here nor there at this point, is it? What is substantiated is that I never took my practice of Thanatos so far."

"We can talk about the merits of Thanatos later," Aster said.

"Fair enough." Medlar sighed away the rest of his story. "Pray, tell: to what purpose have I been fished out of limbo, then?"

Rustle nudged Rose. She held aloft the sketch, presenting it in a sort of dignified plea.

"Can you free her? Or tell us how to?"

Medlar's phantom-head tilted as he gave the image due appraisal. "Stones indeed. That man and his Life-picked ways, hiding such a treasure in a childish etching. No tact, at all. What I can do is give you the steps to pry her soul from its cage. Getting it back in where it belongs, I don't know how that would work exactly."

His free-floating form retracted from the gasps and ticks of disappointment. "See here now, taking a soul is easy, relatively speaking. Rejoining a soul to its mortal shell? Not so much, understand? Do you suppose I'd still be relegated thusly if I knew?"

"Did Oleander ever figure it out?"

Aster shook his head, put a hand on Sedge's forearm. "Why though?"

The misty glance of Medlar narrowed in on Sedge. "How in all of Death's Realm should I know what that brazen fiend knows!" His phantasmal shape shivered, almost went out like a candle flame being pushed around by some tormenting wind.

"Just asking," Sedge commented to Aster, out of the corner of his mouth.

"Not the time."

"We will take whatever help you can give us. If we can free Rose's soul, then that will be enough." Pixee said into the tense circle.

The wrinkles ironed out and Medlar appeared more ingratiated. "That I can work with, charming little Primul." He beamed down at Pixee. "Take notes, here's what you want to do…" and he rambled off a list of items, made comments about their arrangement, priority, and purpose.

Every point of instruction was addressed directly to Pixee. For the best. A clattering of stones cut into the thanatological lesson. Medlar's voice carried on without a hitch, his explanations about the acquisition and stages of souls distilling upon the circle like soft sheets of rain.

Aster felt a nudge. He looked at Sedge, as if the man had interrupted an important prayer. *What?* his said with a look.

"Did you hear that?" Sedge looked back trying to pry open the deep, deceptive shadows that lay all about them.

"Look at Pixee over there. Pretty sure we don't have to understand all this jargon right now."

"No," Sedge persisted, still looking about the gravely still boulders crowding around the little open space. "I'm not talking about Medlar. You don't hear that?"

The exchange between Pixee and Medlar—her requests for clarification; his patient repetition of concepts and instructions—rested into muddles of sound as Sedge's hints took the foreground. The darkness yawned back, as pervasive a stillness as the water in which they stood, unsearchable because it was the same as far as eye or ear could discern.

"What am I listening for?" No sounds, save the present conversation, could be heard.

Aster fought against the imperturbable mixture of night and shadow, hardly penetrated by what little light did fall from the moon. There was no disturbing force to be seen, or even detected.

Sedge turned, cocking his ear in many a direction, as if to secure the sound he thought he had heard.

Aster nudge Sedge. "Let it be," he whispered.

"Aster," Sedge hissed.

When Aster turned to serve up an annoyed, if not benignly menacing, glance he found Sedge staring down at the water. Naturally, that amount of interest needed scrutiny, especially considering the presentation at hand, which should have been the most important object of focus in all the world. Instead, Medlar's instruction turned into mumbling; Sedge's agitated state left little room to comprehend complex magical rites and.

Aster watched for a hint of any variation in the water. It looked like the same water just sitting there. A slight sheen provided by the moon's stingy glow waved around Sedge's thighs moments ago. No, it was just above his knees.

Aster grappled with what he saw, trying to measure and affirm the water's level with his naked eye. The new level should have been more fascinating than it was, as demonstrated by the self-satisfied expression listed upon Sedge's face.

It was almost too easy to shrug away Sedge's paranoia, of which he presented so smugly even with that slight twinge of anxiety. Surely the water would eventually drain of its own accord, sucked back into the earth, back to whatever spring from which it had sprung. That's how it worked, right?

Aster still managed to offer Medlar's lesson snippets of attention, tiny little morsels of concentration. The water's apparent recession gave way to thoughts about the strange creatures of which Rustle had warned them: images of scaly beasts leaking out of dark nooks, intimidating bodies endowed with claws and teeth, all manner of weaponry beyond the strength of defiance, and speed beyond reckoning. These imaginings drooled all over Aster's sense of caution and survival with sick persistence.

"Now, any more questions, little Primul?"

Pixee looked to be making sure all points of the process had been clearly understood. She shook her head.

A splash, like the plunk of a single rock from somewhere amidst the congregation of boulders, reached Aster's ears. Sedge and Aster looked back over their shoulders. The feeling of watchfulness again leaked into their little stone circle, as if the darkness itself breathed.

Their silent bartering continued for a moment, which negotiations concluded with Sedge turning his back on the group and doing his best to pry apart the dark. No one else appeared to have noticed the sound.

Medlar hung there, relishing his audience as he explained superfluous details to Pixee, who took genuine interest in the added information. Rose held the sketch in her tender grasp as Rustle only feigned interest in the chatter of the trapped Thanatist.

It was difficult to imagine that none of them perceived the sinking water level. How could it escape their detection? Had they not felt the cool, wet hemline slipping lower down their appendages?

Surely Pixee noticed. Yet she prattled on with Medlar, ignoring, or oblivious of the fact, that more of her body showed above water. His tales and lessons couldn't have been so interesting as to obliterate considerations of safety.

"Aster," Sedge whispered again.

In the direction indicated by Sedge there was a sound. Aster stilled his breathing to give more room. It wafted his way: a voice, a river of words cutting across the stillness.

While the voice reached from they knew not where or how far poured out of the shapeless dark, the water retreated until Aster saw the foot of his own boots pressed into the mud. A querying look discovered Sedge's face dressed in a similar cocktail of confusion and alarm. Then a whirl of events dumped all at once until Aster was left nearly breathless.

Medlar wrapped up his instructions as the intrusive voice dripped out of the air and down into their gathering. The water vacated completely, every drop, leaving behind cracked and crumbly dirt.

A hiss issued into the circle—a sound of heated metal plunged into water—muting all other sounds. Medlar paused. No one dared exhale. The hissing leaked out of a crevice again, closer, stronger.

The circle collapsed, and Sedge backed everyone behind him as he drew his daggers. Pixee forgot about Medlar for the moment and stood alongside Sedge as another threatening hiss, escaping from a different crevice, reached the group.

Even as everyone clumped together, proximity and numbers didn't add a feeling of security. The nudging and jostling sent Aster right through the wispy apparition of Medlar, who felt like a breathy kiss with cold lips.

"Plagioclase. They're are coming to see if we're edible," Rustle explained in a grimly humorous tone.

"And the water just happened to drain on its own while we were here?" No one's face gave support to Pixee's theory. "So who drained it?"

"Probably irrelevant," Medlar said with airs. "I will just hang around until you've shaken them."

The creatures slunk from out of the shadows and into the clearing, dressed in moonlight that revealed somewhat of their details: they crawled lizard-like enough, but looked to be robed rather in skin than scales, like plucked chickens. A plume of feathers collared their necks as their faces came to a point. Their jaws fell open and the hissing resumed. Thick saliva sizzled against molten tongues glowing with angry tones of orange and yellow.

Tails, like leather thongs, thrashed at the air cracking louder than thunder. Boulders shook and tumbled at the display.

Rustle tugged at Aster's sleeve, but not insistently enough to distract him from observing the lithe movements of these naked creatures.

Even with danger circling, not a slathering of fear smudged Sedge's countenance. His wink and smile outpaced even the selfish light seeping from the jaws of these Plagioclase. The corners of his mouth were more than muscles on which to hang a smile. They were the tips of heady confidence that brightened until Sedge's visage shined too thoroughly.

Rustle offered a more substantial insistence, so it was time to yield.

Faith in the strength possessed by Sedge, and Pixee's cleverness, had to prevail. That was the only way to leave them to face the creatures while finding a place to hide Rustle and Rose.

The steep uneven path reduced fleeing to a series of silly movements. Through a narrow lane running past some giant boulders Rustle, Rose, and Aster stole. The hissing and cracking sounds died as the massive rocks huddled tighter, shutting away their view of the clearing. They scrambled atop the rocks finding some form of a trail among the domes. Their going slowed. Signs of battle failed to keep pace with their escape.

40.

OF A HEART-
WRENCHING MENACE

"Keep up Aster. They're going to be fine."

He hurried after Rustle who was leading their escape. Aster threw glances back to where they left Sedge and Pixee, like he was some meager insect stuck in a world much bigger than himself, where danger appeared in an instant, from any direction. Aster slipped down the face of a boulder and rested in a hexagonal-shaped space between massive stones. Rose and Rustle stood facing him, breathing in gasps. Rustle stopped mid-breath. Rose turned her gaze up. In expected fashion, everyone looked up to see at what she stared.

"We're in something of a plight, aren't we?" Mr. Oleander swept down from the top of a rock, forcing them into a tighter huddle. He stood there and pointed a raving grin at them.

"You—" Rustle could but gawk at the appearance of Mr. Oleander. "Guess we know who drained the water."

Mr. Oleander's smugness felt dirty, like that layer of dried grime accrued at the end of a day of hard labor, palpable in a textured way. No amount of self-imposed distractions could rinse away his attention.

The desire to strike was clearly etched on Rustle's face and the same seething anger burned under Aster's own skin. They were so close to unlocking Rose's soul from its shackles. Yet here he was, as if he had dropped out of the sky. Every heartbeat was a billows that stoked the rage broiling within Aster. With Rose was enslaved to this madman, the intensity growled and roared in a way that only a forest fire can.

It was the only weapon Aster had to combat Mr. Oleander's obscene arrogance, so he let loose a roar; it was not merely a sound. A wave of heat rolled out before him, like he had opened a furnace. No flame. Just blistering air. Well, it would have been blistering to someone.

The chill rolling down his body told Aster he had expended all his elemental store. He eased his mouth shut as the unflappable Mr. Oleander stood there, not a blister upon his skin or hair out of place. His skirting of harm practically glittering; it was hard not to admire him even in the midst of so much evil.

"Part of me thinks performing the Martese wasn't a total waste after all, but seeing that you couldn't stand up to those Life-less Plagioclase keeps me in doubt. What is the point of elemental mastery if you dissolve into a puddle of nerves and emotions?"

"And Rustle," Mr. Oleander stood with his nose almost touching Rustle's cheek. A grin fluttered over his lips. "You have got to stop this. Nothing you do will make up for your sister's plight. Had you thought about it sooner, much sooner, then this whole situation could've been avoided. Here we are though."

Mr. Oleander winked as he took his place behind Rose. Perverse was his touch as massaged her shoulders. The enmity ignited anew deep inside Aster. Silently he cursed himself for not carrying some weapon, any weapon.

What if he had actually practiced harnessing this connection to fire? What if he had stayed with Sedge and Pixee and tried to use it to help them against the Plagioclase? Theses…regrets came in a cascade, dousing the ferocity within. It was over, though. His shoulders slumped, his gaze fell into the dirt. Only if.

"And you, my dear, have you learned your lesson about trying to betray me? There isn't anywhere you can go that I can't follow. Such a distinct scent." He slipped the drawing from her grasp, without the slightest opposition, inhaling the scent of her hair all the while. He stowed the prized image into some hidden pocket. "You must miss your quiet refuge in the forest. Your fungi. Your trees. The mud over there. This isn't for you. Not to fret. We'll get you back. First, the loose ends."

Mr. Oleander peeled away from Rose. In a flurry he was gone, snaking his way back from where they had just escaped.

"He's going to do something to Medlar."

There was no arguing against her observation. It was nakedly obvious. Mr. Oleander must have seen them conversing with the Thanatist before he launched his attack. Couldn't have competition spoiling his plots.

Rose gathered Rustle's hands into her own, enveloping them in sweet earnestness. "It's time."

No request. Not a supplication. It wasn't a command either. Rose just stated a fact, like taking in air was a fact. At one point the sunrise was fact too, but looking at the sky now there seemed to be room for facts to change, to evolve, or, as in the case of the sun, just go away.

"Are you sure?" Rustle's voice trembled.

She nodded.

"What time is it?" Aster beckoned, of Rose. Of Rustle.

Their mysterious contingency plan wasn't allowed. Not now. Not until they had given a complete explanation. Every gesture, the tone of their voices, teased a finality. This was not this time or place to just accept half-truths and riddles without question.

"I'm only alive because of Rustle," she admitted

"How?"

Rustle tapped his sternum. "Without her soul, her mind would go cold and her body would become a useless slab of meat, so I guess it was a blessing and curse when Oleander made a copy of my heart and placed it in Rose. It tethered her to life, kept a fire burning in her mind, preserving her thought and memories."

Aster looked back and forth between the siblings, the wonder and questions pouring out of his face. "And he just assumed that wouldn't come back to haunt him?"

"He had it right, though." A bleak smile streaked across Rustle's lips. "My sense of self-preservation makes for decent armor."

"Though Rustle's heart keeps my body preserved and my mind functioning, my agency is under Oleander's providence. He has written his will over my soul. The route with Medlar failed. Oleander found us, and he always will, so there's one option left."

Aster shook his head, determined to end this debate. "There is going to be another way. We've outrun him this long. Even if he does something to Medlar, Pixee has the process down. That's the sort of Death-sotted thing she does. A steel-clad memory. We'll get the sketch back, and, and—"

And there was more to say, thousands of possibilities. They had but to decide and in the end there was going to be a pleasant, agreeable outcome.

Rose slid a hand up Aster's cheek and, for the first time since they entered each other's lives again, something of a smile crossed her lips. Faintly, but it was there; heavier than the most intimate secret, so heavy it couldn't be endured for long.

"Dear Aster. You're no less wise for being so fool-hearted."

Rustle gave them his back.

"You remember," she recalled, "that first morning, when I woke in your bed?"

Aster nodded, and he felt the tear slicing its way down his grime-coated cheek.

"I half expected you to walk out hinting that I should be gone by the afternoon. We stayed in your bed grazing on berries most of the day." She sighed. "You had me convinced that there was room for love not just for the sake of benevolence, but for the sake of simple cheer and merriment. No amount of evil can ever take that away."

Aster sniffled. "We can fix this."

She smeared away the tears washing down his face. "You and Oleander are a lot alike. You're both so fixated on accomplishing." She kissed him, just under his eyes. "Just make sure you don't end up completely like him." Her hand slipped away, leaving a phantom of her caress to haunt his skin.

Rustle guided her gently atop a nearby boulder, above the dirt and muck. They felt far away though they were still near.

Standing there, face to face, Rustle drew forth a knife.

Aster fell to his knees, grinding into the dirt with a heavy sob poised just within this throat. It needed to be liberated because he could choke on it. Something about watching Rustle point the tip of his knife over his own heart made it impossible to cry though.

Rose looked upon Aster, pretending not to see Rustle, as she drew in her last breath, some macabre play on a tiny stage. It was such a small moment: no sound; no dramatics.

So this was how it was undone? Magic expertly wrought could not be untangled, unwoven. It had to be ripped apart.

Rustle crumpled into a pile. His hand fell from the hilt of the small blade that rested within his chest. Rose faded slower. She never turned away. Not until her face fell against Rustle.

The Truce Blood was his for the taking, once again. Aster pinched his hands into fists to try and still the tremors. He'd need them to be steady for what came next.

He climbed to where their bodies lay and with a silent apology, Aster retrieved the dagger from Rustle's sternum. He knelt beside Rose, closed his eyes, unable to witness what needed to be done.

41.

OF NO LONGER HORSING AROUND

Sedge and Pixee hopefully fought off the Plagioclase. And Mr. Oleander. Absent was the ache to go and search them out, to aid them.

They were more capable in arms, but just being at their sides felt like the right response. Yet the only impulse to move was a faint twitching at Aster's fingers wrapped around the hard gem, so coated in her; what had been bits of her. Oily blood glided down between his fingers, down a tired forearm.

While Aster picked away the gore clinging under his nails, somehow the darkness grew thicker, like a bolt of wool wound its way around his body. The moon was less copper and more crimson. The world? It lay ahead with all its majesty, all the variety. For the moment it was just boulders stacked atop of each other.

Rose was right, too.

She had unrolled the abridgments—the thoughts and hopes Aster always tried tucking away from inspection—and saw the complete story of who he was, a tale that few understood. Rose, though, studied it. Memorized it; even after the long separation she just knew even when Aster was unsure of himself.

With a handful of words, she had decrypted what he barely understood: there wasn't some linear path that had to be tried. This revelation swept entire notions about how life was supposed to be lived clean off the board, and in the fallow space that remained a new fear took root, less dense than the fear of surviving. What was life supposed to be?

How could someone really be living if they didn't walk a line of objectives leading straight to an accomplishment, every hour of every year filled to the brim with productivity? With well-defined purpose?

Trying to picture it left Aster clutching the Truce Blood, his palm pressing into the hard, uncut edges. It bit into his skin, and when he finally allowed his hand to relax he knew there would be little dimples left by this gem, this fossil.

There were some undeniable commonalities between Mr. Oleander and himself. Getting to a goal was all Aster was good for and any means to arrive seemed justifiable. It's why he even bothered with the Martese. It's why he let Mr. Oleander take the Truce Blood in the first place. The promise of reaching some end looked far more appealing than trying to figure out the consequences that may or may not come about.

Feeling the mucky gem told him that there were ways and means better left untouched. The evidence stained his skin.

He wiped away the streak of blood, mingling it with dirt. The importance of simply arriving, for the sake of arriving, being wiped away, too.

The point of the fire fruit started out as some wild experiment, to douse grief with a bit of imagination and invention. They were twisted paths that sometimes circled.

As the image of a crooked, disjointed road made its way through Aster's understanding, he uncurled his fingers from around the stone and let it tumble onto the ground; it plopped into the dirt. How freeing to enjoy the sight of these hands, empty of any implement, just sitting there bloodied but stationary. In the stillness, Aster slumped against a boulder and cried over Rose.

Somewhere in the depths of his mind burned a tiny candle of hope that there would have been another breakfast to share. Maybe just one more, in which he would convince her to have a third. Reality was, that candle had been snuffed out.

Aster scooped up the gem, wiping the dirt around without really cleaning it. He forgot about goals and accomplishments; there wasn't anything to fix. Well, there was, but who cared? There was just feeling: raw, slimy, freshly carved emotions. He cradled those, too.

Aster limped his way towards the village of Alder. He wasn't injured so much as achy, sore, and defeated. Too defeated to walk his normal gait.

Serene was the town after facing the Gury and its nettlesome residents. How many more curious creatures would there be to encounter? There wasn't anyone else left to help face down the violent oddities crawling out of every corner of Thuidium. Where were all the snakes and spiders? The generic fauna that one could answer without specialized arguments?

Sedge was one who could take on menaces both mundane and peculiar, all without a store of spells. Aster grinned. Sedge slicing into those molten reptiles was quite the image: muscles working in tandem as they drove the weapon while his face was etched with determined purpose.

The first outlying buildings—houses, most likely—crowded around. It was as simple a settlement. More so than even Lamiston. A humble little collection of quaintness that met every need comfortably, holistically.

Aster stopped and listened hard. All signs hinted that the guards, and other sort of folk of this town, were holed up in their little hovels, afraid of what other mischief this strange night would breed. In the midst of the village there was something set upon a pike. Aster swallowed. He had a pretty good idea what it was. Not human, which brought little relief.

He inched his way closer, gripping the Truce Blood with a jealous hold that drove blood out from between his fingers in tiny rivulets.

A sample of light gave shape to this hastily erected monument. Light glinted off the eye, once amber now dark as the sky. Aster whispered the horse's name to himself. He went to touch it when the sound of doors creaking open arrested his movement.

Bodies stole out into the open, worming their way out of doors. The emerging figures were revealed by the bad light of the Blood Moon. There was a look in those squalid faces, speckled with blood and stained in grime; wide-opened eyes that told Aster all was not right with the denizens of Alder.

He glanced at the disembodied head of Iridium. The horse seemed to stare back with a gaze that speared Aster with fear.

The advancing mob practically danced their way closer, which made no sense considering the demeanor they held when Aster first arrived. The pragmatics had been melted away to reveal a fierce frivolity that was, according to Aster's gut-feeling, anything but.

"Uh—" There wasn't much to be said. What could he say to minds that were farther afloat than the cursed moon?

They simply closed in, sauntering and promenading until the air throbbed with their insanity. There wasn't enough dry cloth to take away the perspiration that dribbled down Aster's face, into his eyes.

"Hi." It was a limp sound, barely a word at all, which the crowd easily ignored.

They continued their macabre advance, galvanizing the night with their smooth dance. No time to stick around and meet the locals that were, honestly, no longer. Sudden movements were never a good idea, either. Fortunately, the egress was unobstructed.

The tainted moon exposed a few smiles among the group. Crag was there, a crooked grin stretched across his face. Their number wasn't important for the insane need not be counted. They were to be measured by the intensity of their madness and this group looked well supplied, if their creamy moves were any indication.

Aster backed away from Iridium's head, still watering the ground with blood. He spared only a second to consider where the rest of the horse had been set. His escape needed more focus.

"Lizard King," they shouted in gleeful tones.

Lizard King? What in all of Life's left eye were these folks on about? The shouts and calls only grew in volume and unity.

"Come adore Him," they sang as they spun on their toes, twirling out circles with their out-stretched arms. "Let us taste the fire within."

The word *taste* initiated many bells, the internal kind that drown out the voice inside that lists what to do next. There wasn't time to narrate every action and the attending, reasonable justifications. There was only time for the quick snap and pull of muscles to put as much distance as possible between his flesh and the rantings, the snapping jaws, and grappling hands of troubled souls, polluted souls, who craved violence. In any other situation, it would be easy to just laugh away such incoherent dribble.

This was not just any situation, obviously. The way they ejaculated their nonsensical phrases—cries about some kind of Lizard King and the usefulness of its flesh, the potency of its consciousness—had texture. And their calls grew louder and closer.

Hardly a breath escaped Aster's lungs before a brazen, insane smile bore down with other-worldly fervor while the teeth behind those lips snapped shut with a dull cracking sound. Aster nearly pinched his eyes shut against the riotous assault as he swung his arm in a wide arc. The gem picked up on the momentum and clashed with the skull of the afflicted, sending the body to the ground, still jabbering in untranslatable tongues.

Aster hit the same spot as the original impact, crashing the stone with precision and what felt like an appropriate amount of vigor, given the dire need for defense; the skull fought back though, the shiver of it crept up Aster's arm. He grit his teeth and bashed the maniac again. And again, until the spot felt less staunch. One more for good measure.

Aster looked up from the collapsed skull to see another afflicted Alderian close in, perhaps more frenzied than the first.

"Make the Lizard King whole," she cried. Her teeth snapped, almost filling her jaws with Aster's flesh.

It was a new dance, this. She twirled and struck in fluid gestures. Aster responded with staccato shifts, snaking across the dewy grass, eyes fixated on the woman's flippant grin. She unleashed a piercing scream rise into the night that soon disintegrated into laughter.

The Truce Blood, coated in a new layer of gore, slipped out of Aster's hand as he tried to wield it. Instead of a fatal thud, she was met with a simple slap by the rock. She lunged; her impact sent the air clean from Aster's lungs.

Her body went limp.

Looking down was a breathless Sedge. Standing near that breathless Sedge, offering a hand, was a taught Pixee. They were plastered in dried mud, their clothes singed here and there.

"What in all of Death's Realm is wrong with these people?" Sedge set his back to Aster as he scanned the approaching mob.

"My only guess is that." Aster indicated the piked head of Iridium.

"Oh shit," Sedge whispered as he urged Aster back.

The dance had slowed and the diatribes about this Lizard King—whomever or whatever that was—poured out in growing exuberance. Pixee must have noticed the head, for she no longer moved with a well-lubricated alacrity. All while the people of Alder inched closer with their trotting,and bopping movements brought into focus madness most shiny.

Aster recoiled from the aggressive glee that pouring out of these peoples' mouths and from the corners of their eyes. There had been enough observation and confusion for Sedge's liking as he herded away his companions.

Even Pixee relinquished her grief over Iridium to the need for survival, for the time being. She hurried after Sedge, who hurried after Aster, who made the decision to duck into the nearest dwelling.

It was reactionary, not strategic, because everyone knows the best way to avoid a mob of the insane is to strike out into the open, find a live horse perhaps, and flee. The panic had been overwhelming. Aster's reclaim on logic was too late. The door began to shudder with the hostility of the poisoned mob.

"You could have just as easily not followed," Aster said in an attempt to excuse the predicament in which they were now cloistered.

Sedge shoved furniture across the door—a stoutly fashioned wooden table and a flimsy bed made up the bulk of his hasty barricade— as he shook his head at Aster. "I could have. Pardon me for believing that you'd be more strategic." As grave as his voice was, his wink belied the seriousness of Sedge's rebuttal.

The mob outside pressed itself harder and more vehemently against the barricaded door which groaned and creaked earnestly as the press of intrusion doubled.

"Now," Sedge turned away from the door and surveyed Aster and Pixee. "Anyone have any particularly helpful spells? Aster? Fire?"

"Doubt I could siphon enough heat to get anything going."

"You doubt," Sedge repeated. "Great."

The instinct to argue in tones most affronted swelled in Aster. Since he was the one who basically had trapped them that urge withered rather quickly.

"Pixee?" Sedge inquired.

She shook her head. She displayed her hands through which a violent tremble ran. "It won't stop." She sank to the floor, curling her knees up to her chest. "Iridium's gone. We'd been through so much, I just—" Her voice faltered before it failed altogether. Her grief flooded in to replace survival instincts that had been sharp, precise.

Her grasp on magic was vanquished for the moment. Aster's own mind perked up as the danger and defeat swirled around him, the sound of it began to tremble through the walls of the little dwelling. He moved Sedge away from the barricade. He knelt, placed his palm against the dirt floor.

With his eyes closed, the outside of this small hovel of a home came into Aster's mind. It was there, clear and precise: the almost roundness of the roof, the rudimentary door, and the bald patch of dirt before it, so clearly trod. It was that bald patch to which Aster's mind clung as the chant snaked its way from lips to ground:

> *Mystery now*
> *Mystery then*
> *Playing bones and skin*
> *Patient as a...*

The riot outside ceased.

"That was quick," Sedge commented as he helped Aster off the ground. "Getting good at this magic thing."

"I didn't finish."

Aster looked Sedge in the eyes as a genial rapping against the wooden door cut into the sudden silence. The casual tattoo of a calm fist added a new layer of panic to the situation. Pixee felt it. She shot up with her fists clenched as Sedge's own hands balled up at the sound of another knock, a patient knock as if a neighbor came calling to borrow an egg or inquire about town gossip. .

42.

OF BARTERING

& A SNACK

It wasn't unexpected. It wasn't a mystery. Everyone in that small enclave knew who was just on the other side of that door.

How he came to break through a crowd of clearly unstable people was the most curious part of the situation. This was Mr. Oleander, though, purveyor of perverse magic. There was simply nothing for it but to open the door.

Sedge and Pixee both acknowledged this with their expressions of annoyance, or maybe it was more exasperation. Either way, no one wanted to welcome Mr. Oleander into their refuge, such as it was.

Another knock, this time with slightly more force.

Sedge displaced the make-shift barricade with little care for the state of the furniture. Aster pulled back the door.

"I was beginning to wonder if I had the wrong house." With a genial-looking grin, Mr. Oleander stepped inside. Behind him the crowd of the insane stood, quivering against some unseen force that had them immobilized. "Interesting folks, these…people of Alder."

He shrugged. "Whatever has gotten into them has these bastards all a dither. That poor horse though. They were non-too gentle. You know, I was curious what this dark sky, that moon, would do to people. I hope Death enjoys the new arrivals. This lot should be especially interesting."

The blithe tone, shored up by a slimy smirk, rattled in that small space. It was all over Pixee's face: his boasting burned away reason, just ate it up the way flames consume dry grass, and left in its wake plumes of fear and anger; those two potent fuels for human action.

"Death's good graces, you are feisty now aren't you?" He smirked at the sneer Pixee pointed in his direction.

"It's a tricky spell after all. Not sure—" he feigned a shudder, like he would drop something delicate. "If I can hold the horde back while defending against an attack."

There were those among the crowd who began to twitch, their hands curled and uncurled, legs shook with potential, and their pious grins flickered. Their eyes strove with Mr. Oleander in silence. With the deranged crowd still too near Aster, Sedge, and Pixee all stifled any more attempts at aggression towards the villain.

Mr. Oleander shuttered his cackling. "Now, I'm here for a very specific purpose which I'm sure you can guess." He looked Aster up and down. "I'd like the Truce Blood back, friend."

From some unseen pocket, Mr. Oleander pulled out a sheet of paper. A leer slicked across Mr. Oleander's face as he held aloft that one, singular, living sketch.

"You maniacal waste of existence." Every muscle in Aster's body flexed, ready to spring into action, but Sedge gripped Aster's arm too tightly.

Mr. Oleander's hands were stained in evil—pure, undiluted evil that far exceeded unethical behavior—and now he pawed at her with those rotted fingers; even if was just an avatar of her eternal form, his very touch was a blight leaving excrement all over her memory.

Mr. Oleander's molestation of that sketch stoked Aster's indignation until it burned brighter than all his fear. Other matters were now void. The Truce Blood's destruction, the horde of afflicted, squirming in a somber press, even Sedge and Pixee dissolved into muted scenery.

"You know the way to get her back." His laugh mocked Aster, "Her? I mean her soul. She's definitely gone from this world. All so you could have your precious gem. You know," he held the sketch of Rose out in front of himself, eyed it with an unconnected gaze. "I saw what remained of her."

Pixee inhaled sharply and cast a quick glance at the stone, seeing the mess that covered it for the first time since they regrouped.

"Yes, quite a mess. I'm going to guess that getting her blood and bits off your hands was no easy task. Was it, Aster? I see a few stains on your clothes. How was it digging into your lover's flesh?"

He was right. The stains were forever embedded into the cloth. Was it sick to see them as a piece of Rose herself, to carry around and cherish? Some would call it morbid but each time his skin met those blood stains a reminder of her gentle caress stole up his body.

"Was it worth it? Rummaging through her insides for your treasure? Or was it Sedge's treasure? As I recall, you really didn't care about the thing."

Mr. Oleander caught Aster's intent, the truth frothing at the brim ready to spill. He salivated at the reaction. Mr. Oleander dug into Aster with a ponderous stare. He was cunning in his not-so-rhetorical-questions, a flick of his sly tongue had Aster ready to respond with a thought unburdened by any editing:

"I, uh..."

The flavor of that truth was vile, like holding in a mouth full of vinegar. It needed to be swallowed. Or spat out. Instead of sullying the moment, irreversibly, Aster sent every drop of that acrid truth away, into some mental recess of his mind. There was no denying: it was tempting to spew the thought at Sedge's feet before cracking every tooth in that confident skull of his. Even a quick glance in Sedge's direction would stir up the temptation to shove the Truce Blood into *his* chest. Aster clenched his jaw muscles into little knots, the pressure radiating into every tooth until his whole head throbbed with hatred, a brew of resentment towards Sedge and Mr. Oleander, but which was worse: the message or the messenger?

Pixee's smoothly adept hand slipped around Aster's, unfastening his fist. She sewed their fingers together. *Shhh* she urged, even though she hadn't made a single sound. At her bidding the nascent hatred went mute. The manipulations woven by Mr. Oleander frayed and the truth of bigger danger, the better reason for having this stone in his hand, shown clearly.

"Rose's soul is going to be immensely disappointed in you if you don't get her out of here." He waved the paper at them before he glanced over at Sedge and Pixee. "Am I right?"

That Thanatist had no right to her name after he pilfered Rose of her soul. He didn't have the right to even think her name. The stupor of bitterness towards Sedge evaporated out of Aster's mind, and in its place flood vision of wrapping hands around Mr. Oleander's neck. Aster tightened his lips together as he flexed his hand along with the desire to squeeze until this nemesis was silenced indefinitely.

"Ah, ah, ah." Mr. Oleander held his hand out. A ripple of motion rolled through the crowd, some of which even managed to grunt and growl before Mr. Oleander reasserted his power.

Aster stopped, huffing breaths like he was ready to blow out a fire.

Mr. Oleander dangled that drawing with an urgency superior to Sedge and Pixee's dissenting gestures so Aster held up the Truce Blood. Behind the piece of parchment, Mr. Oleander smirked, almost warmly. The facets of the rock twinkled even in the modest helping of light. All its glitz and shape drooped in comparison to the drawing of Rose, a depiction of what had been.

Mr. Oleander nodded at the gem, dangling dangerously loose in Aster's care. The grin fell from Mr. Oleander's face as the Truce Blood hit the floor. It tumbled until it met Sedge's foot.

"You were right. Sedge always cared more about this rock than I did." Aster directed his gaze to Mr. Oleander, staring matter-of-factly. "So eat shit and die."

"You won't even have the chance." Mr. Oleander moved with maniacal deftness as he bit the tip of his index finger clean off then drew a bloody line down the center of the image, bisecting her and the flower she held. He slowly tore along the line of that stain. The rift oozed with a glistening juice, like sweat. The soul yawned and slipped out from the paper, a caged being rediscovering freedom. The figure was a perfect copy of the Rose that had lived in mortality, or perhaps the mortal shell had been a perfect copy of the figure hovering at Mr. Oleander's side. Either way, it was Rose sure enough.

She was still a vision of morning felling the night, breaking open the sky. She was a cold dawn, a winter's morn full of light but still frozen, disconnected from all the attending memories that Aster held precious.

Mr. Oleander smiled in the self-satisfied way anyone does when they think they've wowed the crowd. "She's beautiful isn't she? I have to wonder what sort of hints Medlar gave to you." His eyebrows peaked as he scanned Sedge, Aster, and Pixee. "The man couldn't even keep himself from becoming trapped in his own spell. I don't know what caused you to think he had the knowledge to free her soul." From some fold of his garb, Mr. Oleander drew forth a handful of some pertinent treasure. "He probably didn't even mention how you'd need these."

The eyeballs still glimmered, strangely moist. The green and brown hues of her irises recalled the serenity of the little clearing in the Wald she called home. Their shades were defiled by Mr. Oleander casting a salivating leer upon them. And what did Rose's soul know of danger? Was a soul aware enough to fear?

"He offered a less perverse method," Pixee said unflinching.

"Oh, is that how he justified his ignorance? How whimsical of him," Mr. Oleander said as he rolled the eyes around in his hands.

"Delicious." He filled his lips with one of the eyeballs. Into his mouth he sucked it, as if it were nothing more than a grape. His jaw flexed with casual chewing.

The sound emitted by Pixee was obscene. Her disgust at Mr. Oleander's contempt for life poured out. Not just life but an existence of another. Rose's wailing followed, penetrating every memory, even the ones that had nothing to do with the present situation. Her screams sent a chill into the room that ate up the air. Even Sedge gasped for breath.

Into Mr. Oleander's mouth went the second eye. He let it linger between his front teeth, allowing it to stare without seeing before he snapped his jaw tight, cutting into the gelatinous organ. Bits dribbled off his lips. He sneered as he swallowed. He dispensed a wink before cleaning his mouth and chin with the sleeve of his outer coat.

Aster had collapsed, his knees pressing into the dirt as his face twisted into an ugly mask of grief and bewilderment. The aura of danger that clung to the situation was a crust against a flood of tears.

Mr. Oleander lowered himself until his lips were level with Aster's ear. "Now, you can give me the Truce Blood or for my next trick, I will give these wretched townsfolk back their mobility and you will be torn apart in the most painful and slowest of ways. Try to picture the red fog and the mess it left behind."

He let Aster pickle in the violent imagery as he leaned against the doorway; the crowd of afflicted were saturated in sweat as they fought the magic holding them in place. "Aster, please tell your pet to give up the stone so we can all go on with our lives."

The desire to be exert some grand gesture of bravery was there, even if it was just a thin coating. Alas, it was deadened by all the pungent fear, bitter anger, and sour loss. Through them all, Aster was only able to shake out a barely perceptible shake of the head.

Thankfully, Pixee was there with all that vim, all the vim they ever needed, which launched her body beyond obstructions and obstacles. A growl peeled from her lips as she cast herself at Mr.

Oleander and the two vanished into the slew of bodies now unfastened from their magical restraint. Their grins flared at once as they pressed toward Aster, and Sedge.

"Where is she?" Aster scrambled to his feet.

"I don't see her." Sedge stood up on the tips of his toes.

The minuscule selection of furniture was shoved out of the way as the people of Alder surged forward, leaving Aster and Sedge with a crust of space to defend; Sedge had his daggers. Aster peered at his own hands, curling and uncurling them in a deliberating kind of way.

The room throbbed with tension. The bodies were close, slick with sweat as their heat piled. Even Aster's brow percolated. He saw the warmth as a fuzzy cloud, which he could grasp and bundle up. He scooped and scooped like he was collecting cotton. Sedge hissed as the amassed heat touched his skin. He stepped behind Aster, whose fingers looked like iron pokers: searing orange, nearly white.

The heat grew.

Aster stretched and spread it. The advancing troop pressed the calefactive wall he had amassed, insisting their way forward even as their clothes ignited. Their flesh blistered and shriveled into crispy wafers of red, pink, and black. The flames reached to the walls and grasped the wood beams supporting the roof. Aster picked off a bit of fire and burned a hole in the back wall.

The turf felt accepting as Aster as they scrambled away from the mounting fire that engorged itself on the hut. Sedge heaved sighs of air much cooler and cleaner. A few figures managed to reach beyond the gap, their arms stretching out, skin and flesh smoldering. The blades of grass and damp soil brought a measure of comfort, but Sedge wouldn't allow for a pause as he led them away from the burning house. They scrambled in a wide bend around the consumed structure. There were others, untouched by the fire, prancing around in their erratic dance, still babbling about a Lizard King.

"Who'd think to eat a horse," Sedge commented as they hurried past the torched building. They hadn't moved quickly enough.

There was a call and the bodies that were congregated outside the fire's reach traipsed after them.

"Where did she go?" It took all of Aster's focus to not stumble as he looked for signs of Pixee while also avoiding the menace of the mad Alderians.

A wave of intensity rolled on before the afflicted, making the madness feel closer than it actually was. And still there was no sight or sign of Pixee or Mr. Oleander. To where in all of Thuidium they had been whisked away remained elusive. There wasn't a vast selection of out-of-the-way spots in which to hide in this small settlement; few buildings, fewer variations in geography. It was flat grassland, for Death's sake. There were simply no signs of her.

Sedge and Aster stood with their back against a small structure, breathing like there was little air left to them. "We can't keep dodging these lunatics," Sedge puffed.

"No, suppose not," Aster exhaled. "I just don't feel right about leaving Pixee behind."

"We stay to find her and we'll be trapped fighting off those—"

A bulky figure appeared from around the front of the house. "Yer Scaly Highness awaits the Great Placation," he bellowed.

Aster recoiled while Sedge lunged, driving steel into the man's gut.

"Oh bother. Deeper, fella," grinned the Alderian. "There isn't enough of uh tickle there yet." He chuckled before his eyes went blank.

Sedge drew back. The rotund figure toppled, but the others had heard. Their caterwauling proceeded their dancing approach.

"I see your point." Aster turned and raced away, with Sedge a step behind.

Wherever Pixee was, she'd be fine. Aster wanted to trust that. He had to trust that. Something in his gut? His soul? And yet a feeling deeper in his person, scratching at his bones, gnawed away that trust.

Aster cast one last glance back over his shoulder as Alder shrank into a collection of tiny dark blots.

43.

INTERLUDE: ARRIVAL IN A MANNER MOST UNEXPECTED

Not one passed unnoticed by Death, who stood mourning as only an immortal being could, existing outside parameters and petty measurements employed by those beholden to such limitations. Ideas like ends and beginnings, for example, were not part of the deity's understanding. On an emotional level. Nor were emotions.

This mourning was not of loss, like the mortal practice with its ostentatious displays, rife with the unpalatable aroma of fear and ignorance. Death had to wonder, for the briefest of moments, what fear felt like.

Life made that ticking sound—tisk tisk—as each maligned soul shuffled on by. "This lot looks worse for wear."

"Thank you, Elu." The old names always felt more natural, universal. "Your prowess in observing the pitifully obvious helps. It does, really."

"You've a keen eye for function Imfa, but you tend to downplay aesthetics. I'm here, old friend, to point them out when I can."

Death's shoulder felt tainted by the addition of Life's affectionate touch, so Death shirked away the offending contact. "Trust me, your commentary is not needed. Not now, hardly ever, so please take note."

Of all the souls exiting the mortal realm, this particular batch posed special interests. They marched on, Death's keen eye sluiced over each of the charges. Their haggard, withered appearance made Death wonder: what manner of corruption brought these souls to such a pitiful, mutilated state?

Magic? Some foolish mortal dabbing in the art of manipulating souls. The Stewards had given this practice a name, ages ago.

Thanatos.

"What's that look?" Life inquired of Death.

"We've been at this for eons. You could probably guess my very thoughts by now." Death sensed the exasperation radiating from crown and beyond.

"No sense in tangling your energy up into knots over events that are beyond our reach, yes? These mortals met unfortunate circumstances, from the looks of their wilted, moldy souls, and it happens." Life beamed incessantly. "I wonder if this lot is even fit for the stars."

"So unbothered by the state of our little flock. I can't help but wonder about you, Elu."

"As a creator, an artist, you have this sense."

Death raised half a brow.

"Some art is worth putting on display and some..." Life watched as another deformed soul slithered past. "...you throw out."

44.

OF ESCALATIONS

From a distance, Alder looked a bit of a smudge, with the fire spreading. The light of the flames chewed away at the darkness with a ferocity usually reserved for sunrise or sunset. As neither were guaranteed to be seen again, the expanding reach of hungry flames would have to suffice, in mockery.

Sedge padded at the turf with an anxiety that found its way up Aster's own legs.

As the fire raged on, erasing an entire town by the looks and smell of it, the distance sounds sang Pixee's name over and over. Aster wanted to ask about Mr. Oleander's whereabouts but it didn't matter until he knew what had become of his friend. The mission to end the horrid night could wait to until her safety was assured.

"We just left her." Aster hugged his arms around his knees. "I can't shake the feeling that I'm going to regret that."

Was this the time for regrets? For analyzing decisions that were beyond the reach of amendment? It was a thought, a feeling, pressing hard against every sense of self-preservation that would normally be chiming in Aster's brain and through his muscles.

"I don't like it either, but there wasn't much of a choice. We were being attacked and would've been overrun. We couldn't stand up to that many crazies."

As sound as Sedge's argument was, it didn't assuage the guilt that rattled around in Aster's mind. Nothing would, except to see Pixee safe and in one piece. It was a hope, a desire that bore repeating.

With due consideration given to Pixee's safety and the sound, logical reply from Sedge, there was now a moment of silent observation, bereft of words and the pressure of survival; it was a pressure that had damned the grief meant for Rose's violent demise. A beautifully calm moment mutated by the tears cutting through the ash and grime on Aster's cheek. They were warm. Aster didn't want to heed their presence, what they signified. That would mean acknowledging that she had not just been killed, but erased. Obliterated into just a memory.

Or maybe more like a daydream? A fantasy.

No, memory. He knew they had shared a few nights together, wrapped up in each other's arms, tasting one another's skin.

The tears rolled on and Aster let them. Silently. Sedge put an arm around Aster's shoulders, drew him in close, and gave a little squeeze. Sedge's body felt complete and firm.

The pensive moment ruptured at the sight of two figures striding away from the fire. Sedge and Aster exchanged a look, both wondering if the time spent in reflection should have been time spent moving because neither knew who approached.

Aster sucked in a sharp breath through his teeth when he noticed that one of the back-lit figures was much shorter than the other. Sedge's arm slipped away, a vacancy rushing in to displace the heft of his assuring touch.

Sedge put a hand on his waist where his blades were sheathed, but didn't draw them. Aster stood beside him as the figures lengthened. Their silhouettes gave way to identifiable figures.

"Pixee," Aster breathed.

She hadn't walked to them. She had been carried by the nape of her neck. Mr. Oleander held her like some errant pup. At the sight of a beaten, dominated Pixee, Aster was caught between ferocity and devastation. It didn't look right seeing someone so certain now crippled and detained.

"At ease," Mr. Oleander called as he halted a dozen or so yards away.

The world was drained of its song. Sounds ceased to exist: fires, bugs, animals; the wind. There was just Mr. Oleander's voice.

He held Pixee aloft, in the way a child might show off a thatched doll. Look at the replication of human life, what really isn't actually alive, of which I have possession. Isn't it nifty? For such was the gleam in Mr. Oleander's face, that tinge of pride. Yet, the gleam was muddled by an unusually disheveled appearance.

Mr. Oleander's hair was limp against his forehead, without shape. His skin, which practically eschewed dirt, was polluted with grime cut with streaks of dried sweat; there even appeared to be trails of blood along his hair line. His teeth shone even whiter against all the smudges muddling his face. He poured out a laugh that was half wheeze. After calming his breathing Mr. Oleander lowered Pixee, like she was becoming too heavy. Her head bobbed with the motions as if she cared not to hold it up any longer and preferred to let an external force decide which way she turned and looked.

"You started quite the fire. Now, if you don't mind, I'd like to know how you ignited that ravenous blaze. Was it while the grunts attacked?" He peered over his shoulder. "I'd call that impressive. Did you actually exercise some of that power of yours?"

"I did what I had to do. What are you doing with Pixee? Pixee!" Aster called.

She moved her eyes just enough to meet Aster's gaze briefly before she fell to seeing naught, perceiving less. She probably only had thought for the hand that clenched so possessively at her neck.

The anxiety to secure her release gnawed at Aster's attention, the way rain drops knock dirt away from a rock. Mr. Oleander kept right on inquiring about the fire though, as if he were slowly arriving to some point.

He lifted Pixee a bit and surveyed her full stature, giving her body a shake. The stubs, where her feet should have been, knocked back and forth. "I guess I'm just impressed and wanted to share that with you. I had hoped that you'd grow into this power and see it for what it is."

"I don't…can we talk about Pixee. Pixee?" Aster tried to summon her attention but she was too far gone, to a place where pain and humiliation didn't exist.

Thankfully, from the look of her. She wasn't in the moment with Aster, Sedge, and Mr. Oleander. Not mentally.

Mr. Oleander tucked her behind his back. "She's quite alive. Well, not quite. Just barely from the look of her. No need for sorrow as she put up quite the fight. I've cauterized the wounds. Can't be letting such precious blood spill out all over the place. I wasn't too sure at first, but after our little tussle, I could see she was indeed Primul. Which is advantageous for me. She was the final piece in my plan. Such a gift." He sighed with an expression steeped in longing that surpassed lust and hunger.

Aster mentally shook off the examination of Mr. Oleander's face and simply rolled his eyes. "Not here for any fluffy words or whatever monologue you've prepared. We are here to make sure Pixee is safe, which means out of your hands."

How they would secure Pixee, well, that was a question that would be answered as events unfolded. They'd surely find a way to take each action and reaction like stepping stones across a river, until Pixee was soundly out of Mr. Oleander's grip. That was enough for Aster to think about, on which to focus. Anything beyond he could worry about later.

Sedge stood by, with his daggers at the ready.

"Fluffy? Perhaps to menial folk of this world. I didn't think you were among them, Aster. That's a fault in the mentor and giver of gifts. I saw your desire and the potential ability. I thought *here's a guy who gets it*. Ah, well. I never regret sharing knowledge, nurturing the understanding and power of others, as I did for your mother."

There must have been a twitch, a tell, that crept through Aster because Mr. Oleander smiled and nodded. "There it is. You're getting it now. Where do you think she got that Burial Rite?"

"So I've been told." His mother's face—as faded as the memory of her was—flashed in Aster's mind. His father's face quickly followed. Memories of a family slowly chipped apart, at the hands of the fiend before him, left Aster dry like a disused well.

"Resentment towards whom, I wonder," Mr. Oleander said aloud, as if he glimpsed the mood within Aster. Mr. Oleander brushed the hair from his face. "In any case, I offered your mother a key to quell one of her most persistent fears. And now I offer you a key because I'm that generous." He hoisted Pixee so that her stubs dangled a few inches above the ground. "I'll let you nip some of this Primul blood, enough to make your fire fruit seed." His other hand was out, waiting. "Just hand on over the Truce Blood and all the answers are yours."

What was there to do in this moment of decision? The Primul blood would be a neat solution. No more hunting down silly words. No dithering about with experiment after experiment. How pristine and alluring a solution it appeared. It was the sure resolution, a promise that would not fail to produce. A hand, tried and tested, stilled the debate vexing Aster.

"Aster." Sedge's voice was a whisper, but with as much sonority as if it had boomed like an avalanche. "You don't need to."

At the mention of the gem Pixee, who looked withered and forlorn throughout Mr. Oleander's little speech, changed. Her distant eyes snapped back to the present as she cast a glance at Aster; the relaxed cheeks went taught. Her face once again drew up in confidence, in a surety that was hers for no other reason than it belonged there.

It was tough to see, what with Mr. Oleander's hand gripping tightly around her neck, but sure as the moon hung in the sky she shook her head at Aster.

Why would she say no? She was signing-off on her own death. They'd stop him. They would and she could help. She'd probably be the one to come up with the plan.

Mr. Oleander's grip tightened, if that was even possible. Her eyes widened as his fingers pressed into her skin. A small dagger was introduced. It bit at her neck as a thin obsidian ribbon ran away from the puncture. "There is only so much blood—and time. Your decision, Aster."

The answer was written all over Pixee's face, but that answer was tougher to swallow than a chicken bone; it just sat there with no intention of being ingested.

The dagger sank deeper into her flesh.

"Moon Foot," she said.

There wasn't room to question her about the final words that had dribbled out of her slack lip. Just a minimal hint about where they should head next. Should they make it out of Mr. Oleander's presence that was. So, Aster accepted them as she hit the ground with a sickly thud. Her last gasp tripped over the gash in her throat on its way to her lips.

Mr. Oleander chuckled in his usual blithe tune as he collected her blood in an earthen cup conjured from the ground. "I won't be daunted. Obviously, I'm the only one of us who is willing to do what it takes to see a goal to fruition." He sealed the cup in a magical way. "You could have been great, you know that? Now you'll never know."

Pixee laid there like a lump of clay, mostly molded, but with that extra something missing and before Aster had time to react, Sedge's grip was locked tightly around his upper arm, leading Aster away from Pixee's corpse and from Mr. Oleander, who stood with his prized blood watching his prized stone retreat into the embrace of perpetual night.

45.

OF CHANGES
IN SCENERY

"I'm sure it wasn't easy to just leave her like that," Sedge said.

He didn't say the word dead. But, then again, neither had Aster. They just carried on silently accepting the fact of her demise without the pomp of a cracking voice or the sparkle of tears.

Not that Pixee wasn't worth either of those gestures. She was worth every tremble, every drop. From both eyes. That wasn't the way to mourn a being like Pixee. None of this single-tear-down-the-cheek bullshit. A set jaw, rigid posture, and a confident gait on the way to ending this whole catastrophe would be the most Pixee-esque send-off Aster could give his murdered friend.

Aster kept his pace brisk, his strides long. He felt the flex of his calf muscles. All the while, the cavity of Rose's sternum, the one he had to open himself, and Pixee's defeated eyes right before they went vacant, flashing behind his eyes every time he blinked. To combat the threat of emotion that would suspend his action, Aster reasserted his pace, moving with an urgency that challenged his heart, thudding with such force he could practically feel the blood dispatched throughout his whole body.

But why wasn't Mr. Oleander in hot pursuit? An outright chase came across as beneath him and his prowess. He'd surely find a way to cut the chase. Aster imagined once he and Sedge arrived at the Moon Foot Mr. Oleander would be there, hand out to receive the Truce Blood.

Aster tightened his stride, vowing to get there, somehow, with enough time to rid Thuidium of this wretched rock. His hope was not cheated, for the horse that had born them to Alder was grazing not far from the town itself. The question then became: could this horse take them far enough, quickly enough?

Many a mile had passed under hoof before Sedge called for a halt. The stop was not long, despite the concern that he and Sedge both had for their animal's well-being. This wasn't a matter of convenience though. Aster couldn't—wouldn't—let the feeling go that somehow Mr. Oleander wasn't far behind. That feeling of pursuit crept up his arms. It tickled the back of his neck, playfully malicious, like a rapist toying with a victim. The resulting shudder was real and spurred Aster to insist that they keep on moving. They sat upon the horse, driving the beast to its limits.

The horse pressed on at Sedge's urging, and once they left the River Crest behind, they ventured into lands Aster had never seen; still hadn't seen, technically, since they were all draped in this stubborn night. The blood moon only hinted at features, the edges of shapes; it offered a generalness but kept the details for itself.

The movement of their steed gave the sense of a rising and falling land, of valleys that stretched on. Were there forests nearby? No red-laced tree tops came into view as they rode on. It didn't feel fast enough, not with the promise of Mr. Oleander out there executing who knew what sort of mayhem.

Sedge's guided the horse, with a modicum of care, through the low visibility. Aster felt the undulating of Sedge's muscles the steed raced on, southward. The feel of their flexion convinced Aster to hold a little tighter, to lean in closer than was perhaps absolutely necessary.

The mysterious Mountains of Lune edged ever closer suggesting the range bent inward. The towering peaks were still edged with that opal glaze, a spectacle that seemed to leak back in to itself rather than shine outward. They must have arrived at the moon foot, for which they had sought these many days, though it still felt like it had only been one.

What a useless term, days. What other norms had been blotted out under the press of the dark?

Sedge at last checked the horse's pace to a mere trot rather than an urgent gallop as they neared an outcrop of towering rock that cut across their path, a wall of stone pushed up from the very foundations of the earth, to poke at the sky, though not nearly as tall as the rest of the range.

Sedge dismounted. "Looks like the end of the line well enough."

Aster followed. The ground under his feet was barren, just a plate of crunchy, pebbly dirt without a hint of vegetation. "Didn't know Thuidium had land like this."

"Like what?" Sedge seemed preoccupied with scanning the area for any sign of Mr. Oleander.

"Like, I don't know, just dry dirt." His voice was a whisper. So quiet was that little nook that they felt like the only two beings in existence.

"Can you create a light?" Sedge inquired as he—judiciously—inched towards the bastion of rocks that formed a cul-de-sac.

Aster peered about for some sort of anchor for a fire. "Not seeing much fuel. Any fuel, to be quite honest."

"Try your shirt."

His tone was dry, but Aster cracked a smile. "Try your shirt," he whispered through a grin that wouldn't go away.

The thought occurred to Aster—more of a recall than an original invention—as something of a halo. He looked up towards the sky and trained his mind on the fire's brightness, a lasso of flame to cower the night.

He narrowed in on the concept, shaking off the breeze that rushed past him. Just as the idea of light had fully formed in Aster's imagination, the darkness reeled back and a ring of flame-less fire opened up above the little valley.

"Well played," Sedge commented as he glanced up.

Aster swallowed, unable to dismiss the dryness in his throat. "Not mine." His voice cracked.

"No, our dear Aster's not quite adept with his fire-power it seems." Mr. Oleander strode into light shinning down on the small vale, revealing a visage that was wont to be put to rest.

"I'm getting there," Aster said as he conjured up no expression at all. Though, his strained voice belied the brew of anger and fear fermenting just beneath the exterior. "Speaking of, how did you get here? I see no horse or other beast of burden."

"That's the limit of your imagination, Aster. The limit of your power," came the pointed reply. "When you don't use magic for every little thing, every time, you get a real sense of the potential you wield. I'm surprised you haven't realized how acquainted I am with air." He winked.

The wink had said so much to Aster and his mind filled with all the implications of Mr. Oleander's reveal.

"If only you had let me tutor you more, you could have felt the same bond with fire. I wouldn't be the one illuminating the sky for you."

"I thought power for the sake of power wasn't your game." Aster conquered his inclination to let emotions slip through his eyes and face. He casually hid his clasped hands behind his back, hoping the heat crawling off his skin wasn't noticed by Mr. Oleander.

His chuckle was a darkly melodious sound. "And I stand by that, but that doesn't mean I don't familiarize myself with the best uses of that power. You want your simple agrarian life and I want to explore and discover. We are both after something. Ways and means. Well then," He breathed deeply searching the valley uncovered by the lamination of a fire without flames as if he were amused by the novelty of the situation. "No more wasting each other's time. Let's finish this."

Mr. Oleander's tone offered a folksy indifference—an invitation to the pub, perhaps—but the poignant menace that stained his face conveyed the absoluteness of his declaration.

46.

OF A CLASH &
HUNGRY SPECTATORS

Sedge was inches away with his steady breathing, his posture upright and correct. He stood as a man who knew no fear. But that couldn't be, right?

His courage was a wonder. It's why Sedge could draw his bladed weapons and command the steel without a single wobble. The fortitude emanating from Sedge, wrapped all around Aster, guiding his back to straighten, shoulders to widen, and chin to stick out.

"He's right." Sedge turned to Aster. "Time to end this."

The cue was obvious. Aster nodded and ducked away from Mr. Oleander, who would not be ignored; he dove after Aster, after the Truce Blood, without regard for Sedge or the weapon he pointed in Mr. Oleander's direction, right at neck level.

Aster fled to fulfill his role in the conclusion of this wicked affair. He did not stop to see if Sedge would have the chance to cleave Mr. Oleander's head from his body. That was Sedge's role alone. The clash at Aster's back told him that the fight had not ended so neatly.

No dainty was Mr. Oleander, especially when there stood an obstacle in the way of his ambition. Whether by sword, magic, or his own hands he would fight on until all obstacles were put down. Which meant Aster needed to get a move on.

He pulled out the Truce Blood while calculating what it would take to ignite the hottest fire he could. What of a receptacle, though?

The sounds of conflict shifted closer, the only clue on how the combat fared; no way would he venture a look. That's how the game was lost. The Truce Blood held all his attention. The problem of it, to be exact, and how nothing in his inventory looked fitting in which to cook the gem.

Who knew all the ins and outs of magic anyways? Even the people in Aster's life who had a deep understanding of how to manipulate the elements weren't around. There was the chance that this moment, this need for magic, would be even beyond the grasp of Oren, Pixee, or even Rose. Like Sedge said, there was only action; trial and error.

His eyes and mind slung about, perceiving nothing of a solution. That was, until his had met a familiar sheet of paper. He exhumed the Burial Rite from a pocket and held it aloft: the last promise for a long-awaited accomplishment.

Grunts and scuffles reached out to Aster, reminding him of more immediate needs: the danger at hand, which swept away the hope that Aster had ascribed to that bit of spell-craft—accompanied by a certain degree of resentment—until it was just another page with words. Such a page that could bear Aster to another destination.

Mr. Oleander howled at the penetrating thrust of one of Sedge's blades, a move met with the force of a tempest that rushed from Mr. Oleander's anger. It clove the small valley's peace. Pebbles scattered. Rocks moved from their abodes. And Sedge relinquished his grip.

Aster held the page with the ferocity of a man with everything to lose. Against the staunch airs, he leaned as he stretched the paper towards the flame-halo. He pushed back against the torrent of wind that heaved in retribution. The halo wavered under the duress of Mr. Oleander's gale. Aster held the page aloft but the flames licked without biting, so he snatched the benign fire and squeezed until he was sure heat had returned. The page ignited.

Once the fire touched the first words, the flames burned in such a way that was beyond a mundane hearth or forge. Tongues of powder blue, amethyst, and licks of white ate away at the offering. Aster brought the burning page close to and shielded it with his body.

The fire, though odd in how blatantly magical it appeared, looked approachable enough and before it consumed the inscribed spell completely, Aster wrapped it about the gem. His hand felt neither pain nor danger; there was a nuzzling sensation, like a pet warming up to its owner. Aster closed his eyes—to give the moment the sense of awe and wonder it deserved.

Sedge's indistinguishable baritone replies answered Mr. Oleander's taunts and brags. The clamor inched ever nearer as Mr. Oleander sought the gem and Sedge followed to stop him. Their advancement halted as the two clashed anew. The air moved in a way that was dangerous. And the thought struck Aster: he'd be able to simply suck out all the breath from his foes and leave them to suffocate?

Just as Aster couldn't keep fire alight without a source of fuel, so could Mr. Oleander not defy the natural order of an element. Not in this layer. Elements had limitations. What were the bounds of air? Even in spite of that minute relief, The image of Sedge laying without a breath in his lungs lurched into Aster's mind.

Sedge kept Mr. Oleander occupied through strength of arms that such a ferocious, indisputable attack hadn't been attempted yet. No time to question why Mr. Oleander didn't just flatten them with a crushing wind or thin the air into an unbreathable ghost. The point was to give Aster time to dispose of the Truce Blood, the real objective.

The gem kept to its faceted form, hard edges that didn't even flinch at the heat. Aster cajoled the fire to burn at levels of intensity never before attempted.

Mr. Oleander, though full of evil thoughts, had at least one good point: let the imagination dictate where the magic can go.

In that moment, Aster's imagination operated with gross desperation. He poured down upon the fire all the mental persuasion of which he was capable. He fought back the intrusion of limitations. It was a strain, pulling and twisting into belief a flame which hadn't been dreamed up before, hotter than the sun itself. All the while, the magical fuel curled and blackened into ash.

"Don't you dare, you smarmy bastard." Mr. Oleander kicked Sedge back and dislodge the dagger from his calf.

He hardened for an attack until Sedge bore down with his second dagger, poised for a fatal stab.

"The cave," Sedge huffed, as Mr. Oleander doubled his defense.

Sedge fought in a noble manner, leaving a wound or two upon the smug face of his foe, and yet it seemed to be going Mr. Oleander's way, who tore and ravaged to pursue Aster.

No time to count points and assess who had the upper hand. The cave wasn't far. Already the flames licked and danced with more heat. Aster stood and carefully, yet expeditiously, maneuvered away from the encroaching fight, bearing the flame in his cupped hands.

The gem's defined shape softened and sagged as the mouth of the cave gaped larger, and darker. The paper was nearly spent. The gem finally sank into a glossy crimson goo.

Hope rose when Aster greeted the cave's maw, catching a low rumble reaching out from its depths, from things not human. Small points of light peered out of the dense darkness.

The sounds of fighting gave way to his own breathing all while his hands glowed, reminiscent of heated metal. The smelted gem rolled like soft clay. Just in time, too. The pearly fire sank into nothingness. Aster dusted away the ash of the spent page. His hands, glowing less, kept the blood pliable.

The eyes, tiny moons themselves, waited as Aster, unsure of how close was too close—or not close enough—took a step towards the waiting creatures, another species of beast that only the myths and legends could explain. Here were the Hortlak.

Then it all stopped, in an instant. Had the race ended already? Was doom imminent? Aster clutched at his charge, squeezing the melted Truce Blood. It gushed between his fingers like mud.

"You show some real promise." A bowl of air gently cradled Aster above the ground. He was returned to the earth by the Mr. Oleander's will. "Of course, you'd be dead if you hadn't brought some might along with you, but I still respect the effort you put in to resisting."

Aster scrambled to his feet, inching away from Mr. Oleander. His eyes scanned about looking for some improvisational weapon, a rock big enough to shut up Mr. Oleander. Yet the risk of dropping or losing the Truce Blood kept him on the defensive.

"Let's have a look now." Mr. Oleander traced a spell with his entirely-too-gleeful voice.

Aster located a suitable rock, which he threw. It thudded against Mr. Oleander's chin. His voice faltered but continued as blood trickled down to his tunic. Under the duress of earthen magic, the bones in Aster's fingers snapped, one at a time. Pain gnawed away Aster's composure. He bent and vomited. Still, he clutched at the tacky blood squeezing it into a messy shape.

"I will make sure it's from your dead hands that I take this if I need to." Mr. Oleander said as he caressed where the rock had hit. He approached and looked rather as if he had finally had enough of the back-and-forth, of the challenges to his designs and his power.

Aster tried to take in a deep breath, to still his trembling and his fear, but his lungs had naught upon which to draw. There didn't seem to be much air to draw upon. Aster tired again. His chest felt tighter. There was too much labor to suck in enough air for his body's need.

The tightness mounted. The inhalations were shorter, shallower. Instinctively, Aster drew his hands back. The melted gem slithered from Aster's clutches. He sat there, fighting for even just enough breath to exist.

Mr. Oleander reached for the putty-like substance, but quickly retreated his grip, suckling his singed fingers. "That's smarts."

It was just enough distraction to pause the torment for Aster, who sucked in breathes like a starved man gobbles food. Sedge was some distance away laying on the ground, passed out perhaps. Hopefully just. Aster turned back to see Mr. Oleander manipulate the air, hovering his coveted prize.

"Smells nothing like mortal blood, am I right?" He said with a deep whiff of the levitating blood. "Has an almost floral scent. Flowers and..." The blood hovered lazily. "...and wood. Not entirely sure. Doesn't matter. It's the power that's important; creation itself. Combine this with the Primul Blood and I'll have that seam ripped apart in haste."

Aster had moved. Mr. Oleander, who sounded off a spell before Aster could level any sort of attack. The pain and the sound reached Aster's perception in one moment. He cradled his broken arm before doubling over to retch. Little was left in his stomach. Only bile made its way out of his mouth. He sat there rocking in-time to the throbbing.

Mr. Oleander's breath caressed his glistening face. "I can't wait to see the look on Death's face when I yank that layer back. Oh, Life and I will have a laugh."

Life?

The statement was confusing, as were so many aspects of this whole series of events. Aster only knew that he didn't know as much about the world, or existence, as he once thought, and Mr. Oleander's revelation further pushed that word—knowing—out into the ether, like a ship without sight of land.

"A friend of yours?" Aster inquired through gritted teeth

"No," he said he stood. "Not friends. Don't make that mistake. Life has no friends. Perhaps that's why Life and I were able to see eye-to-eye on so much. We don't evaluate relationships the same as other mortals. Or even immortals."

"And why does Life want with your help?" Aster labored to ask, to put the ideas ahead of the pain that fought for dominance in his mind.

"Life was the original artist, you know. True, Death brought the paint but Life created the unimaginable with it. And when you're an artist and can no longer paint? Well, you find a way."

"And you're the way?"

"I wouldn't go so far, no. Best not to be an upstart in the eyes of Life. I'm helping carve out the way. First, we peel apart the layers. Yes? Yes."

The pain occupied every nerve making the feat of concentrating on Mr. Oleander's explanations a trial. His words cracked, faded, came back into clarity. Blood rushed to the point of damage. Aster's suffering didn't completely obscure the danger standing there, so close Aster could touch it.

Touch he did, with his foot which he drove right at Mr. Oleander's knee causing him to buckle.

Aster obtained the blood with his unburdened hand before it dropped completely to the ground, holding onto its sagging edges. He scurried behind Mr. Oleander's prostrate figure, tears streaking his face as his broken arm cried out in the most visceral language possible. Aster managed to wrap his unbroken arm around Mr. Oleander's neck, yanking and flexing his bicep against Mr. Oleander's throat as he applied the still heated blood to his skin.

Mr. Oleander's groans turned into shrieks of pain as Aster's skin coursed with anger and hatred,; all the feelings that made his body seethe were pooled into the blood. It heated like a stone pulled from an oven, that sits on the sun. Mr. Oleander's skin offered up the sizzle of pork belly on a cast iron and a smell quite similar.

Aster forced his mind to shut against the threat of his excruciating injuries. He heaved the blood away. Employing a spell proved strenuous; the words were heavy; so heavy Aster practically had to shout them.

A scud plowed over them, pressing Aster into Mr. Oleander's back, who erupted into feral sounds as the blood-disk was ushered out of reach.

The luminous eyes shuttered as the forced wind careened in their direction.

Mr. Oleander hurtled an elbow back into Aster's eye, escaping the grip. He pushed himself up off the ground and bounded after his prize, calming the driving wind Aster had summoned.

The sight of Mr. Oleander putting hand to blood wavered, blurring in fragments. The ring of fire lighting the small valley Aster latched on to the opportunity, before it too was lost. With his wounded arm dangling at his side. His other hand raised up, his fingers wiggling they swiped at the fire donning the small valley just before Mr. Oleander's preoccupation drained the spell completely and the flames wisped away.

With the single strand of fire plucked from the now vanquished halo, Aster tugged—just as he'd seen Pixee do to a single drop of water in the Gury—and pulled at the essence of the flame, at the very idea of fire, until he had a long tendril of heat and light in his grasp. He winced in agony. The fire whipped in a circle like a lassoed rope. With each rotation, heat filled the flames once more. It wasn't troubling, or painful; it was comforting, assuring.

Whether this plan would help or not wasn't a concern in that moment as Aster tossed his rope of flame at Mr. Oleander, who prepared to leap away from the cave. The fire caught hold of his clothing, the surprise of which brought Mr. Oleander back down to the ground.

Thantist fought with the flames as they shriveled every fiber and stitch. He rolled about, giving most of his attention to clutching at the Truce Blood, the last piece to his plot. Mr. Oleander grappled with the conflagration. Just as he turned to counter Aster's assault, howling broke out anew.

Aster once more pressed against the agony wailing in his arm, wanting to make sure Mr. Oleander would not escape, but a fresh wave of anguish surged through his body when he shifted. His sight went fuzzy as if a sheet of torrential rain had passed over his eyes. Aster pinched his eyes closed as his body reacted to the pain, his guts heaving, his heart nearly thrusting out blood. Stillness flooded the night and Aster planted his forehead upon the ground unable to look at the world.

He held his eyes shut, sure that mysterious signs and wonders would soon be herald the complete undoing of existence. Wasn't that what Pixee had warned about? The world unknit until utter bedlam flooded in?

Aster rolled to his back and fought to breath in a normal pattern. It might have been vain, but normal sounded delicious after the ferocious conflict.

The howling that issued into the quite cove ruptured the slender moment of calm Aster had been trying to conjure. He looked towards the cave. Gone was the blaze that had been feeding on Mr. Oleander. Just little disks of light dancing erratically. In all the commotion Mr. Oleander's voice rose above the wild calls of the creatures, a wind howling and whistling louder than the beasts. Then notes of pain, not unlike those Aster heard as the red fog attacked the Keep, joined the maelstrom of sounds.

The Hortlaks howled all the more fiercely, drowning out Mr. Oleander's screams. All manner of incongruous noises somehow resulted in a sense of surety, like a soothing lullaby, even if it sounded anything but. The cacophony—yelps, howls, screams, and grunts—sank away, into the guts of the cave. The glowing eyes vanished like stars winking out.

47.

OF MOON SET
& SUNRISE

Despite the grinding pangs biting their way up and down his arm, Aster stumbled about to find Sedge. It didn't matter if those creatures lost and went without their morsel and the whole quest broke into pieces of failure. Sedge wasn't going to be alone. Especially at the end of all things.

Aster traced his way back to where he thought Sedge had fallen. The search proceeded smoothly until Aster tripped over an unseen lump, sending him to the ground; a scream-inducing meeting when his mangled arm took the brunt of the fall. From behind Aster came a grunt, thankfully issued by Sedge. There they were, a couple of lame bodies lamenting and twisting about.

Aster kept his eyes pinched shut and let the searing agony abate. He rolled over until he faced the pool of ink above. After Aster reined in his breathing: "What...what did he do to you?"

Between gritted teeth, Sedge replied: "Broken legs. Maybe some bruising and a couple cuts or stabs. I haven't taken full inventory."

"Broken arm," Aster huffed.

They stewed in the silence, a moment sweeter than the blossoming honeysuckle or an autumn rain. There was no reason to keep looking at the world, lost in stalwart night. Whatever would happen, whatever form the cure or the fatality took, would be. It still was uncertain which to expect.

The sky remained an un-cracked slab of obsidian. So yes, this was as good a time as any to shut out what might be and just soak in the now.

"Aster," Sedge whispered feebly.

His voice sounded as though it seeped out from between a wane smile, one that barely hung on through all the pain and doubt that must surely be mastering his mind. After a moment of silence that pooled around the two men, Aster sat up and slowly peeled open his eyelids.

There was that moon, sitting high in the sky in all its unearned dominance. The opal sheen that had traced the tips of the Mountains of Lune lingered, neither growing nor shrinking. It was as if all that Mr. Oleander had enacted was suddenly paused. Noting in view intimated whether his plot would reverse course or carry on.

"Sedge?"

"Hmmm?"

"If Mr. Oleander is really dead, wouldn't all this end?"

"I don't know, bud." He laid there, motionless, not even opening his eyes. "You know more about magic than me."

"Yes, but," Aster paused and considered the sequence of events, measuring them against what he knew, or thought he knew, about magic. "No one but Mr. Oleander knew about the kind of magic he was attempting."

Sedge's eyes rolled around for a bit. "I think that if Mr. Oleander was still alive, we'd know it. The man would not hesitate to finish what he started." Sedge paused for a breath. "Do you think he'd hesitate to finish those who stood in his way."

It was more than a fair point. Someone ambitious enough to want to end the act of dying wouldn't stop unless put down. The thought released Aster from worry. He went limp as he sank back against the ground. They both stopped breathing, waiting to behold the unraveling of Mr. Oleander's hold upon the world. It was like taking a plunge into deep waters out which it would take time to resurface.

The act of breathing made it difficult to tell if that moon was set to rights or if it was all just a trick, brought on by a potent sense of hope. Ah, hope. What a terrible idea. It was like a little lie on the vine that a person watched to see if it would bloom or wither.

"I think I can figure out how to get your legs mended," Aster finally said after he tired of waiting for the moon to fall out of the sky.

"You think?" Sedge winced as he shifted, then slumped back into stagnation.

"I'm not married to earth, but I've had some practice with the element. Learned a chant or two." It was now time to laugh. Or chuckle, at least.

"I can't wait to see you try. Practice on yourself first," replied Sedge with a bit of relief in his voice, maybe even a hint of mirth.

Aster looked over to where Sedge lay. "What did he do to your hands?"

Sedge raised one off the dirt, but only just. It was enough to look at the puncture wounds encircling the nub where his missing thumb had been. "He bit me. I stuffed it in his mouth to keep him from sucking the air out of me. Again."

"Oh," Aster said. His mouth poised to make another comment about the skirmish, maybe even about the Hortlak. Instead, Aster resumed silently breathing.

"It's almost weird seeing the sun again," Sedge offered in a tone that was both relieved but also, in a way, a little confused.

There was a moment when it seemed impossible that day would return. Then the moon at last resumed its trek across the sky and finally set behind the horizon. Fear magnified the time it took, slowed the moon's progress, and made the whole sequence feel like months when it was mere days for Mr. Oleander's chaos to melt away.

"Truly, it kind of is," Aster replied, without commentary.

It was too peaceful a moment to try and recall the headiness of a perpetual night reigned over by an unromantic, blatantly evil-looking moon, with all its rusty, bloody light.

There was one topic Aster didn't mind breaching in this moment of serenity. He turned his eyes toward Sedge for a brief moment, making sure he was ready to bring this up. Again.

"We're sure he's really gone?" Aster could practically hear Sedge rolling his eyes. "We never did go into that cave and check. I just don't want to have to see the sun disappear like that again." Aster clenched his hands in his lap.

"If he hasn't come back by now, I'm confident he's never coming back." Sedge smiled at Aster with a bit of a shrug. "I'd go so far as to say that his twisted soul wasn't relegated to sun, moon, or even a star. It's just out there." he gestured at the sky. "In the darkest part of the universe, cold and with nothing but anger and regret for company."

His voice carried a level of surety that evaporated doubt. Aster relished in the assurance offered by Sedge as he leaned back with his weight braced by his hands. The earth pressed back, dimpling his palms. There was Sedge, sitting next to him, hands in lap, as he bounced a knee like the wing of a butterfly. Turned out learning to heal bones was not as trying as Aster expected it to be. Sedge's legs came out more healed than the trial run with his arm.

Before them, the sun slowly bowed out of the sky and Aster felt a little sad. Now that the world returned in full force with all its wondrous detail resurrected by the appearance of a universal light, there weren't enough hours of day to make up for that run of seemingly-unending night.

Aster tilted his head and recited to himself the names of colors and shades, wanting to soak up all that was visual. There were still so many to recall, even after a few sunrises and sunsets. The fire fruit would be something in the vein of orange once it blossomed, he was sure.

Aster's thoughts carried his focus away from his body. His arm relaxed and small bits of dirt rolled his willing hand away until his forearm grazed Sedge's leg, who pretended not to feel it, as he silently watched the aureate sky while casually attempting to fold his knee away from the unintentional touch.

It turned into a game of avoiding another brush of contact. A twinge of discomfort sent a tremor down the length of Aster's arm. A sidelong glance revealed that Sedge adjusted his body away by a degree or two before setting a hand down at his side, his fingers spread out. They both gave their hands to the earth: cool but not cold; dirty but not filthy.

After traversing across the land together and seeing some real shit—seeing each through that shit—it was difficult to believe that these touches, these grazes, were mere happenstance. Or maybe they were? Maybe, just maybe, Sedge's hand shifted for no other reason than pebbles and dirt driven by the pressure from his muscles and in their haste, they ushered it right alongside Aster's?

The atmosphere tingled with more than comfort offered by a mere friend, or the sort of kindness one would give a neighbor or chum. There was a thought—a whiff of an idea that escaped a cloud of possible explanations—that seemed to say: to end the uncertainty, one need only reach.

It was the slightest of movements; the dirt barely shifted as Aster turned his wrist counter-clockwise a degree or two, putting his hand even closer to Sedge's until they were more than grazing. Sedge met the gesture in kind. Flesh upon flesh, skin warming skin.

Sedge licked his lips.

Aster held his breath.

The sun was absent. All that remained of its light drained from the sky while a coolness stole over the little hill upon which they sat; it was not the coolness of waster running deep or the chill that crowded Mr. Oleander's dungeon, but a sigh the earth released after hours of basking in heat. Shadows crawled out to cover blade, leaf, bough, and brick. It would have been an ideal moment to insert some benign comment about the weather, another statement about how it'd be nice if the sun would linger for another hour; they'd had enough night to last for years. Here and now, with him, words seemed offensive; just sit and silently reason about intentions and results.

Aster's errant little-finger moved reflexively with a slight bend. It shook just a tad as Sedge petted it with the tip of his own little finger. He stopped caressing and held it in place. It was an invitation for Aster to occupy the little nook underneath. His touch seemed to beckon Aster, saying *come here*. Sedge raised half his palm from the ground as Aster accepted the invitation, the tiniest of embraces, from which Sedge looked away. It signaled the beginning, and dismissed any uncertainty about what sort of touch this was. This moment was to be soaked up gradually like it would never happen again.

Sedge sat without motion, hesitating to answer Aster's hand laying supine. With his gaze trained on their waiting hands, Sedge had to have been asking himself the same questions: what in all of Life's light was going on here?

The moment stalled, stretching beyond the capacity for comfort. All Aster wanted was to relax his arm, but he waited on Sedge. Just as the discomfort of being stationary radiated through Aster's limbs, Sedge's fingers spread and sank between Aster's. Their fingers folded down upon one another at the same time, a steeple that collapsed into a sphere, held tightly together. Twilight rolled on in perfect serenity. The touch was now accepted by the both of them, and everything their contact implied, or so Aster had hoped.

They were in darkness. Again. A more natural darkness, though. The window was shuttered so that not a single light broke through. Aster knew the place like he knew his own body.

"Make yourself comfortable."

The bed sighed while Sedge made himself right at home and that was amazing, in the most terrifying way. Their level of comfort with one another needed no expression. It required quiet, actually.

"I've drawn a bath for you." Light poured out of the bathing room in a sultry glow.

Sedge joined Aster beside the steaming tub. Aster smiled, as he sprinkled mint leaves on the water's placid surface causing the air to tingle with a cool, subtle aroma. He then pulled a jar from a cabinet and tipped it over the water spilling a stream of oil.

"Sandalwood oil," Aster explained. "Towel over there." He pointed to a small stool next to the tub. "And clean garments here." They sat beneath the towel.

Aster left Sedge to himself.

The candles set up around the room each sat near or upon plates of polished silver. They spilled a fair share of lambency, of the sort that pushed back the darkness just enough. Plenty of shadows hung about the room still.

Sedge stood in the doorway to the bathing room with his clothes rolled up and pinched between his arm and his side. "What do I do about the water?" His voice danced through the air with a delicate bass.

All those days and that very long night together on the road and his voice was never once harsh or lined with malice. There was reason, mirth, and curiosity all packaged in a sonorous pitch. He looked like he smelled nice, too, like he felt strong; not just the musculature rippling under the soft linens that clung to the wet skin under his pectorals, or hugging his inner thighs, but more like he wouldn't let the world in and melt his resolve.

The assessment left Aster sitting with a coquettish grin on his face.

Sedge smirked as he stated to approach the bed. "What's that look for," he asked of Aster.

"Nothing," Aster replied as he stood, unable to subdue his own smile. "I'm going to take a bath myself. Relax on the bed."

They crossed paths as Aster vacated the bed and Sedge moved to occupy it, by willing invitation this time. They stood there and exchanged a chuckle. Their smiles danced with one another as their glances slid off one another.

Aster finally detached from the flirtatious moment and went into the bathing room, shutting the door behind him, as snugly as it could be.

The water was warm, like a liquid hug. More oil and leaves were added and Aster sunk into the comfort of the bath. The water lapped away the grime of the day, the aroma smoothing over all the questions he had for himself.

From where in all of green Thuidium did this enchantment with Sedge even spawn? It was so unreal how it was more than a fire in his loins. Not since Rose has anyone been the cause of such synchronization of mind, body, and soul in Aster.

There were moments all through their travels together where it could have started: a quick glance, a consoling touch, or a faint smile. Searching out the root, the precise moment of conception, wasn't important. It was too warm and satisfying a sensation to pick apart. Best to let it unfold, like sunset and moon rise.

Ah, but even that could be manipulated. The whole episode with the blood moon attested to the fact that nothing in existence was guaranteed, not the order of the skylights nor souls.

So maybe what was about to happen felt as natural as the dance of the flame? Or it was as sure as the expanse of the ocean? The point being, nothing in the unwritten moments of Aster's immediate future felt foreign or evil. This night, this experience with Sedge, was just something that was to be. Like the elements.

With that, Aster let the residual drops escape down his thighs before he vacated the tub. He dried off, then stood debating with the fresh linens waiting to be wrapped over his skin. Aster bit his bottom lip as the arguments for and against dressing volleyed back and forth. A daring voice approved walking out of the bathing room in naught but clean skin. Let Sedge see the feast before he partook. No, he couldn't walk out with his turgid member leading the way. Let Sedge reveal these succulent viands with a slow unwrapping of clothing.

So the argument proceeded in Aster's mind as he looked from mirror to clothing and back gain.

Aster cast a quick look at the door as he held the linen union suit in his hands. A smirk crossed across his lips as he let fall the clothing.

Sedge sat on the edge of the bed looking like he was in that room, in that bed for the first time. His lips parted as if he would gasp but only exhaled in silence.

Aster leaned against the door frame relishing the effect. He left the bathing chamber behind and walked the few paces to the bed. He slowly lowered himself until he straddled Sedge's lap.

"It's getting late," Aster said in a breathy whisper. "I didn't know if maybe—"

Sedge held Aster at the waist and leaned in. Between their lips a gap existed, big enough for only their mingling breaths. "Thought what?"

"—maybe you wanted to get some rest before you leave." Aster wrapped his arms around Sedge's neck, tasting every sigh from Sedge.

"Leave?"

"Things are wrapped up. Mr. Oleander has been taken care of. I'm sure you have some place you wanted to be off to."

Their lips kept grazing as if daring one another to be the first to invite the other in. Sedge's hands roamed from their place at Aster's waist. They traced up his spine. Then back down below the hips until a tingle erupted across Aster's cheeks.

Sedge brought his hand to the back of Aster's head, strands of hair dangling between his fingers. "Leave the future to itself. Just let tonight happen."

Their lips met in prayer and lingered together until each breath escaped through their nostrils in deep, heaving sighs. There was a moment's pause, when their lips no longer locked but they touched with the slightest graze. Sedge smelled right. He tasted complete.

Sedge gave into Aster's insistence as his shoulders were directed back onto the bed, unbuttoning the top of the union suit. The topography of Sedge's torso laid naked to be mapped: peaks of his nipples, hills and valleys of muscles, and veins that wound down his arms like rivers. Hair covered it all, like a fields of grass. Aster explored every feature. Slowly, with reverence and the methodical plodding of something trying memorize each contour, every nook. The faintest touch of Sedge's skin evoked the scent of mint and stoked a prickling heat that emanated from Aster's loins, rolling out to every corner of his body in a slow crawl like the flow of magma.

Sedge sat up and wrapped an arm about Aster's waist, a gentle movement, and turned him over onto his back. He slipped between Aster's thighs kissing him lips to chin.

Chin to neck.

Neck to torso.

Each kiss that Sedge placed was a gesture of security. In the mediocre light, no one would have been able to tell where Sedge's naked body ended and Aster's began.

Sedge paused, gazing down into the shadows of their intertwined legs, the last chasm keeping their bodies as separate entities. He sank with tender insistence. There was the slightest resistance from Aster's body, but one slow exhalation and they were joined, locked into one.

Their passion kept pace with the night as two figures, wrapped up in one another, rolled together like the ocean and sky. The lights dimmed and were eventually swallowed by darkness. Light was unimportant in this situation, for sight was the sense that informed the least.

Two people, in complete synchronization, felt more than any eye would have discovered. They had seen enough of each other over the past few months. Now it was time to feel one another: the harmonious thrusting and receiving, puffs of breath, a thin coating of sweat, and the onset of climax.

Aster had no way to warn of its approach, to speak over the sudden rush that sprang from within, a perfect brew of pleasure and pain; pleasure that conquered the mind along with the right measure of pain that allowed Aster to feel himself empty of his seed. It was an immediate collapse of self-control and the slow unpacking of sensibility, communicated with breathy sounds for words had escaped him in that moment. He felt the room reel and spin as his body calmed.

Sedge's grin broke through the dark, with a chuckle that tumbled from his obviously upturned lips, as he felt the sticky opaque liquid that, in a way, glued them together. Placing his forehead against Aster's, Sedge thrust a few more times in rhythm with Aster's quivering and clenching body.

Right after that last intake of breath, but before he exhaled, the orgasm raced out of Sedge's body. It wasn't just one muscle that contracted or one appendage that stiffened. It was every corner of his frame wrenching tightly. Barely a complete second passed, maybe not even that much time, before he released himself inside Aster.

They sank into a perfectly relaxed state at the same time forgetting words existed. Sedge rolled his sweaty body off to the side laying back onto the bed before he pulled Aster in close so that their skin stuck together.

His chest was wet, but it felt welcoming; firm but just yielding enough to be comfortable. As the heat of sex dissipated, eaten up by the cool darkness, sleep overtook them both.

48.

AND ONE LAST THING

All the world seemed to sit in perfect stillness. There could have been battles raging in distant corners of Thuidium, factions warring over territories. There maybe were even infidelities being committed. Whatever happened out there, beyond the walls of Aster's home—even just outside his room—was no matter, not when a moment with Sedge still hadn't been lived out to its fullest.

The passion was excruciatingly fulfilling, but not so fulfilling that Aster would deny another turn in the sheets. With that, he reached over to pull Sedge in close so he could initiate more love-making.

His hand only found more bed. Vast and empty it felt after feeling too small just hours ago.

He sat up and rubbed his eyes. The window had been draped but some sunlight still managed to dribble into the room, just enough for Aster to confirm he was alone. This confirmation warranted slipping on some clothes and venturing out of the bedroom, that cool dark cocoon.

Not in the main room. Nor in the kitchen.

Sedge was found outside, his exposed skin almost glittered as the morning sun played against the sweat squeezing out of his pores with the exertion of a spade. He wore a pair of brown, billowing pants that stopped just below his knees. For some reason he looked salty, a thought Aster shook away along with the attending flourish of heat it ignited in between his thighs.

"How long have you been at this?" Aster took timid steps for the land looked like it had been shaken and rumbled. Raw earth opened to the sky.

"Few hours, I'd say." Sedge drifted away from his work until he bumped into Aster.

The contact prompted Aster to entangle himself with Sedge and his sweaty limbs, the heady aroma wafting off his body practically tugged Aster closer until his chin rested on that glistening shoulder. Aster kissed it. He pulled the moisture off with his lips.

Sedge smiled. "Your land is ready. Is your fire fruit?"

They walked hand-in-hand towards the small spit of land where the magic would happen. The history of that small pit was sharp as ever, undisturbed after all the time away. At the edge of this familiar little bowl, dug out from the earth, it was time for one more attempt. The last one.

The conical fruits sat placidly in their little grave, which seemed to be the best way to describe the pit. No tools or implements, for this process was intimate. The only implements to employ—aside from hands now carved with better understanding, both inside and out—were some words.

The Burial Rite.

Talk about intimacy: after reading the page time and time again, the incantation was engraved with a permanence that went beyond inscriptions and letters. That lullaby was no longer accursed, jagged and mutilated by a fear of death. This rite was now an anchor of creation, giving life and bounty; given in hope, not desperation or dread. So easily did the spell come to Aster's mind, like repeating the names of people seen every day—Oren, Pixee, Rustle, Rose…Sedge.

Each syllable, wrought by a caring voice, slipped away gently. They landed just as softly as finely sieved sugar even while spoken with confidence. With each pronunciation a handful of dirt went down upon the fire fruit until they were buried and their resting place concealed.

Aster ran his hand over the plot, smoothing it over. His caress was stopped by Sedge's palm. Their glances met. Their smiles mimicked one another. There was a giddy expectation in that moment as the rite played out to its conclusion. Sedge drew closer. Aster's eyes smiled along with his lips until they touched upon Sedge's.

"**B**arkley," Aster called as he strode into the town square. "Recover your crop of roots?"

"It was a scare, I'll not lie. Seems that all is set right including the spuds. How about a helping in appreciation." He hoisted a sack off the ground and presented it to Aster. "If I'm to believe the rumors, you're the one who set things right."

Aster took the offering of various roots and hoisted the gift onto his shoulder. "I was not alone in the effort, so in memory of those who didn't make it to see the sun again, we'll make something out of these that will be worthy of their memory."

Barkley offered a modest bow, one fraught with understanding that there had been sacrifices of the most genuine nature to bring the world back into order.

With that, Aster and Sedge took their leave chatting about the possible vittles to be made with such a bounty of ingredients. They wound through the market giving and taking greetings. There was a moment when an empty spot among the many vendors and patrons stood out to Aster.

"Oren's?"

Aster nodded, his lips bent into a tuft of a smile.

There would be time enough to reminisce. For now, an appointment needed keeping. Into the Hart's Den Aster went.

Sedge found a seat; their booth, he deemed it. Aster left the roots with Sedge and continued on towards the kitchen. Therein he was occupied for some time. Bits of aroma stole away into the tavern. Murmuring rolled amongst the denizens as they caught whiffs of Aster's cooking.

Soon, the chef himself appeared bearing a platter: a slab of broiled meat divulged a fanciful scent. Atop the crisp beef was a dressing, almost akin to jam, the same hue as wine. Sitting beside the meat was a scoop of crisp vegetables, vibrant in color and sprinkled with red flakes and what looked like dried garlic. From among all the fragrances wafting off the plate was a curious smell. It tickled their noses as Aster guided the food to a particular table, at which he presented the meal.

He set the platter down. "You remarked, some time ago, that my food lacked a certain kick."

Serenoa smiled, but with a bit of embarrassment.

"So, you'll be the first to taste my solution."

She took up the eating utensils provided and cut herself a small piece of the meat onto which was added a scoop of the jelly-like dressing. There was a shimmer to it. She eyed Aster.

He smiled and waited.

Into her mouth went the meat. Her chewing awoke the flavor that had been merely hinted at by the aroma. Flavors collided with her tongue, the riddle had an answer to which she winced in surprise.

Her chewing stopped. Her glance paused upon Aster.

"That's a kick," she sputtered.

Back to chewing she went, her face writ with the expression for which Aster had hoped, had imagined in every tiny moment he contemplated the fire fruit's potential.

There were calls from others to taste what Serenoa experienced and each one was indulged for hers was not the only plate that had been prepared. It was time to retreat back into the kitchen and let the willing of Lamiston introduce their senses to this new creation.

Before he left the tavern floor, Aster looked to where Sedge had retired.

That face. Those lines casting a net around a smile, full of pride and maybe even relief. There'd be time for them to talk about this moment and all the ones preceding it.

There would be time enough for the two of them to cultivate together: a life, a bond, and love; even more fire fruit.

THE END.

Acknowledgments

The author does not operate in a vacuum, and this phantastical process began with a stroll around California's state capitol building with Dr. Samia LaVirgne. She asked me to be honest with myself about my writing. Her questions spawned this entire adventure.

Dusty, Brian, and Cal endured the first ragtag version of Phantastical Tale. Their questions made the story better. Maria and Ari were the good fairies who gave me the insights to fill in said plot holes. There's no telling how far off the yellow brick road I would have been without their incisive and encouraging feedback. Dylan gave it the polish so you, dear reader, would endure fewer typographical errors.

And, of course, Mom and Dad. They may not have given me trauma to mold into whimsical and gripping tales, but they gave me a sense of stability so I could feel free to go out and dig up trauma on my own.

If you were at all curious, the Lord of the Rings soundtrack is music that accompanied my writing process. Thank you, Howard Shore.

To you gentle reader, a deep acknowledgment of the time you've invested in taking this adventure with these characters. If you found this tale engaging please consider sharing a review either on social media or whichever platform you purchased this humble book.

About the Author

It all started in 1989, with the doodles and scribbles of a second-grader, but that was merely the beginning. From that experience blossomed a love-affair with the written word and storytelling. I even endured teasing from older siblings as I read through the dictionary like it was just another novel. I've learned to spare folks the pain of my "illustrations". Fortunately, the storytelling has only improved over the years.

Here we are, decades later. A legitimate story and an improved sense of craft. I hope you enjoy the world and characters I've created.

When not writing, I'm selling socks. Yes, you read that correctly. My day job, which funds this book, is managing a family-owned sock boutique. Out of the 150 pairs I own, my favorite to wear would have to be the pair sporting a scarf-wearing giraffe.

Sacramento, California was home for most of my life. I now reside in the Great Salt Lake valley despite not loving snow although, I do respecting its place in the great circle of life.

www.ingramcontent.com/pod-product-compliance
Lightning Source LLC
Chambersburg PA
CBHW021415310726
48971CB00005B/1340